Duboce Park

Duboce Park

Stephen Medoff

To order additional copies of this book, contact:
Xlibris
844-714-8691
www.Xlibris.com
Orders@Xlibris.com
849624

DOG PARK

I've never met anyone in this world who wasn't crazy. There's no looking for sanity in this world, you'll never find it. A disconsoling thought.

Yes, we go plodding along, cheerful sometimes, sad, confused and angry. Crippled by tragedy, twisted into unraveable knots, trying to make sense of it. Shoved grudgingly along into anonymity and the unknown, or guided by a celestial belief in our specialness, blissfully skipping around uncertainty.

Life is motion and emotion. Not to be confused with Email, which I do not have. I am forced to use the telephone, which I have but do not like. Luckily, I have a machine to do the answering.

Dori Four had left a message.

She was complaining. Petty things. But she liked to find fault. It gave her pleasure.

"He's grubby." she said. "Dandruff on his eyeglasses. I was surprised he could see the movie."

She he was talking about her date from the night before. She loved to nit-pick people to death.

"And his hands! Sticky from popcorn. And no napkin!"

Get to the point, Dori!

She rambled on another five minutes, excoriating yesterday's slob.

Her name is Dori. I don't know her last name. I call her Dori Four, because she comes to the dog park behind a phalanx of four wildly yapping dachshunds.

She is a striking woman. An exotic dancer by trade, but not that keen on it, anymore. She is currently waitressing to keep her dogs in kibble.

Men forget themselves with her, which is probably why they revert to the grubby state. A smile and a crossed leg could mush up a man's brain pretty good.

That's why she was doing this job for me.

She was truth serum in a tight dress. Truth is beauty, beauty truth. Don't know if Keats meant it that way, but it sure works.

I find the truth.

I am a truth detective.

There's a lot of truth waiting to be unearthed. Truth paved over with forgetfulness, buried so deep it needs a jackhammer. Truth so tired it can barely wiggle its big Tee. Truth squeezed so dry, it crawls aimlessly in an endless desert.

Truth is now a business. A banal livelihood.

But in this time of disenlightenment, disingenuousness and just plain dissing, it'll have to do.

The "date" was Philip Roman, a bona-fide, best-selling biographer of the still-alive, rich and fatuously famous. A mercenary of muck.

No, I am not preternaturally hardboiled. But I am well-poached, simmering over a small flame of hope, worried about being flipped and so searing forever the bright, bulging eye.

Yes, there is a half-baked poet lurking in me. But there is menace in it. Others' truths are the staple of my appetite. My own are pending and unprobeable.

It started out casually, as most things do in the dog park. I was chatting with Henry the Chef, asking after the health of his dog, Titus, a Shar-Pei with bad eyes, bad skin and a flinty disposition.

Henry prepared dinners for a couple in Pacific Heights. The woman was Robin Hayward, reigning queen of the mystery novel.

"The man has a penchant for le hot dog, le beans and le beer," winced Henry.

But he assured me, with boastless pride, that he could turn beans, hot dogs and beer into a sumptuous dining experience.

He stroked the folds of skin on his dog.

"Philip Roman was over for dinner last night," Henry said, with obvious displeasure. "I think he is going to do one of his trash bios on Mrs. Hayward."

My dog, Gustav, part border collie, part spaniel, had moved to a stalking position a few feet away, intently eyeing a pigeon. Henry paused to watch him.

"It was very convivial and decorous and they were effusive in praise of my meal."

He turned back to me.

"It was a stunning performance," he added. "Despite the sleaze, the men acted like chums at an old English club, and poor Mrs. Hayward sat bejeweled and jaded."

"You'd make a fine social reporter," I said to him, laughingly impressed.

"All I want to do is serve and get out," he said, dismissively.

But I could see that he relished my remark, and turned to peer at Titus, who was rolling in something.

"Titus! Stop that! Titus come here! Here!"

He smacked his thigh hard and Titus stopped, looked up, and dutifully ignorant, went back to his rolling.

"I'll probably have to give him a bath tonight," he sighed, resigned.

"Mr. Hayward wants to hire a private detective, to find out what Roman's up to."

I pulled out my card for a lark.

It read: Beamer Todd-Truth Detective, and my phone number.

Henry took it, studied it, and nodded.

"I'll give it to him."

"It's only a joke, Henry," I smiled.

"Well, all you have to do is talk to him. You know, make casual conversation. Let him talk about himself. Be sociable."

I cringed.

"Hayward pays well."

The beam brightened.

"You could play the part," Henry insisted. "I know you can use the money. Nothing illegal.

"How much do you think?"

"Don't know. You can negotiate. Maybe a few thousand."

I steadied myself.

"Here's my card." He reached into his fanny pack, searched among the doggie bags and treats, and came out with a bent card.

"Gotta go."

He rounded up Titus after only minor stubbornness and left.

The idea was absurd. But, I have to admit, it sounded interesting. Be social? I was practically a recluse. It could be dangerous, but it seemed unlikely. All would be is a nose. Then an ear. Then a mouth. Let's face it, a well-paid snoop.

It would also be a chance to hobnob with the wealthy and well-known. To see what they were like. To satisfy that curiosity.

And I could sure use the money.

Apparently, this guy Hayward was desperate. He called me at home the next morning.

There was to be no meeting with him. If it was distasteful to him, it was okay with me. The less contact the better, as long as the check cleared.

He sounded drunk, but he was direct and emphatic:

"Get the goods on Roman!"

"The goods?" I answered.

"Get some slut to pump him. He can't hold his liquor."

"Uh huh."

"He likes 'em mean and stupid, but pretty."

"Right."

I wanted to click off, but those beautiful bucks had wings and were floating in front of my eyes.

"One time is the deal, I said, to get it over with.

"That's all you need, if you know your stuff."

"Check."

"Cash. I'll give it to Henry. 2Gs."

It was surreal. I felt I was doing a scene in an old gangster movie.

"Just do as I say and he'll pour his guts out."

As much as I wanted to live up to my end of the bargain and accommodate him, I couldn't come up with any sluts. But I did make a proposition to Dori Four, which, for a promise of five hundred bucks, she leaped at.

"Do you think I could do it?" She said with feigned naiveté, extravagantly batting her eyelashes. She could read men the way an astronomer reads a spectroscope. "What do I have to do?"

"Show up."

"Okay."

"Ask him about Albright. Hayward said to ask him about Albright.

"That's it?"

"That's it."

She was to call him at his hotel and pretend to be from the 'agency'. She was to be sultry. Mean and stupid were up to her.

We met next day in the park, her dogs on leash and barking up a storm at anyone who passed within five feet. Gustav stayed peacefully by my side. We sat on a bench with gang motifs carved into the wood.

"Well, when he wasn't groping me or nursing the wound on his hand from the fork I stuck into it, he was very talkative." She grimaced. "Childhoods amid the snowdrifts of Minnesota and teenage years in seminaries are not as interesting as the average person might think."

Good old New York sarcasm. How I miss it. No wonder I am enchanted with Dori.

"I don't know if he was rubbing his nose or picking it. Either way, it was disgusting.

Ah, the enchantment fades.

"Then the footsies started," she continued, tugging against leashes holding four eager dachshunds, straining in four different directions. It was a dexterous performance. I felt lucky to have only one dog. "He got a good shot in the shin, that moron. Are you sure this guy's a writer? He sure seemed dopey to me."

"Keep your dogs quiet!" Someone yelled from a nearby window.

"Drop dead!" Dori screamed back.

She wasn't crude, but she liked to act crude. It kept people away. No one wants to tangle with a crude woman.

"Don't you read trash, Dori?" I teased. I knew she read good books.

"Well, I did read this story about this guy named Ahab trying to trash this huge, white whale," she said with cutting nonchalance.

I laughed.

"So what about Albright?"

"Well, after sitting through a schlock movie and then wiping a ton of his crumbs off my clothes, we went to a cruddy bar where I managed to inflict a few more bruises."

"Your punishment, Dori."

"I sure am."

"Go on."

"Albright wasn't Albright, if you know what I mean. It wasn't the name of a person, but All-Bright, the name of a cleaners."

A cleaners? Laundering money?

"All-Bright was his fondest memory, when he wasn't fondling me. It was the first place he worked after he quit the seminary."

"That's it?"

"The people there were very nice to him. It was first introduction into the real world."

"Doesn't sound very sinister."

"He tried to invite himself in, but I stomped on his foot and told him to take up finger-painting."

"You're ludicrously sublime, Dori."

"I sure ain't lemonade."

I said goodbye to Dori, then to the dachshunds in turn: Thalia, Calliope, Clio and Erato. They barely acknowledged me in their tumultuous running to and fro.

Amusing creatures, I said to myself, savoring the pun. Ah, puns. The last gift of the wholesomely impecunious.

I ambled off home. No Gustav. He hadn't moved. I called to him. He stayed motionless. He was probably perturbed that I had decided to leave the park so abruptly, without consulting him.

"C'mon, Gustav," I said, waving for him to come.

He remained motionless.

"Gustav! Let's go! Let's go!" I cried out. "We'll come out again later!"

Thusly reassured, Gustav burst into a trot and caught up to me. He nuzzled my hand and I gave him a pat on the rump.

When we were back in my small studio, I set out two treats for Gustav, and checked for the blinking light on the answering machine. There was none. I called and left a message for Hayward.

An hour later Henry the Chef said over the phone that he'd bring the money with him to the park.

Extra money sure made my brain hum with ways to spend it. But banking it was the smartest thing to do. Gustav was getting on, and it would be good to have a reserve for vet bills.

If love of money is the root of all evil, let's just say I have a very strong affection for the stuff.

Feeling chipper, after persuading myself that I could spend a little of it on myself, I popped Vivaldi's bassoon concerti into the CD player and prepared a meal.

I took out a precooked Safeway BBQ chicken from the fridge, pulled it apart, and separated the white meat from the dark. Gustav looked into my eyes with grave and penetrating interest.

His tail wagged in anticipation as I spread newspaper on the floor in front of him. I put down small chunks of white meat, and he ate them ravenously. He looked back up at me.

"That's it, Gustav."

He walked away, rubbed along the futon and then lay on the floor, licking himself.

I ripped off a clump of green leaf lettuce, put it in a large, wooden salad bowl and poured Newman's Oil over it unsparingly. Then, I tore open a bag of Trader Joe's kettle chips, without salt, poured a half-glass of red cabernet into a real wine glass, arranged dark chicken meat on a plate, and settled in to read the box scores.

It was my gourmet meal.

I met Henry in the park. He passed over an envelope. I fingered the bills and put it in my pocket. There were five fifties.

"I expected more."

Henry shrugged. "That's what he gave me. I didn't look at it."

It was a bum deal.

I walked angrily back to my place, hauling the reluctant Gustav behind. Punching up Hayward's number was something I felt like doing to him.

"Who?" He answered, with his usual bludgeoning charm.

"Beamer Todd!"

"Fuck-off!"

"Hey! What happened to our deal?"

"2Gs for a freaking piece of a jigsaw puzzle? You gotta be kiddin'."

"You got what you asked for!" I countered, blowing steam.

"Do you really want to earn the 2Gs?" Hayward's growl switched to a raspy purr. A conniving purr.

Could I trust this guy?

What the heck. I had started to fancy myself a sleuth. Maybe, I was just a stooge. But it was a point with me to see things unfold to the end. The way to learn. As William Blake wrote: 'The path of extremes leads to the palace of wisdom.'

"Lay it on me," I told him, with blunt indifference.

Hayward spoke mockingly.

"I know all about you nuts and your dogs. Roman is a dog nut oo. He misses his mutts. So I told him to go down to your park and check it out. He'll be up to his ass in dog shit." He chuckled.

"Make friends with him. Be a dog buddy." He chuckled again. "You can't miss him. He wears Hawaiian shirts and white pants. A weirdo. Philip Roman."

"I know his name," I piped in. "I'll need expenses."

"Expenses?"

"You know, in case we want to pick up some mademoiselles along the Champs D'Elysee."

The silence told me the joke and the request fell flat.

"I'll wing it," I conceded.

"Do that."

This guy was as tight with a buck as he was with a polysyllable.

I phoned Dori to tell her that Hayward had only come across with $250. She called him a louse and said she'd take it. I clued her in on the new development, and told her we could wangle some more money out of this deal.

She was in a playful mood.

"Beamer, what would you do if you had a lot of money?"

"You mean thousands? Millions?"

"Gazillions!"

"Well, I'd have a gazelle ranch. To go out every day and watch graceful gazelles gazelling would be a pleasure."

"You and your jokes."

"Jokes keep the bogeyman away."

"Beamer?" She asked with a solemn concern, which in other people might be construed as bordering on tenderness. "Beamer, do you think you're doing the right thing to get involved in this?" She paused. "You know as much about being a detective," she cracked, with her usual truculence, "as I know about being an Avon Lady."

A conversation with Dori was worth a whole flock of gazillions.

"You know," I said, trying to answer her question seriously, "I'd like to travel. That's probably what most people would do. An RV, credit cards, a dog, a ..."

"A woman?" Dori interjected.

I stayed silent on that one.

"Go around the country leisurely and in comfort. You could learn a lot."

"You and your learning, Beamer," she chided. "Don't you want to have fun?"

"I have fun."

"Fun. What? Learning?"

"Learning to have fun," I retorted.

"You're a circle, Beamer."

"Better than being a square."

"You're that, too."

"I hope this geometry lesson is about over."

There was an edge in my voice.

"See you in the park, Beam.

"See you."

"And you can recognize Roman," she advised, "he's the one with the limp."

I could picture her coy smile as she hung up.

The dog park was long and sloping, bounded by statuesque Victorians on one side and auto traffic and MUNI tracks on the other.

Cypress, olive, plum and anchor trees were arrayed in front of the homes, while small chatty birds darted in and out of the two cypresses.

It was perfect for dog owners whose dogs were ball hounds. The easy throw downhill and the more vigorous trip back up after the fetching.

It was summer evening. The park was filled with frolicking canines and their watchful owners, who huddled against the incoming fog and cold.

It was a wind tunnel. To stay out for very long required insulation. Down jackets, gloves, woolen hats and boots could be part of anyone's attire. Not picture postcard San Francisco. If it was a postcard, it would have the caption: 'Winter, Spring, Summer and Fall in San Francisco.'

In the middle of the park, with dogs playing all around, was an Hawaiian shirt hugging a Newfoundland.

The dog, Mountie, placidly enjoyed the attention, shaking his large head and spraying drool ten feet in every direction. The sad-eyes dog, with its slack jaw and huge body was the current drool distance champion. When he started to shake people scattered.

Roman hung in there, taking a few globs on his shirt with good spirit.

Mountie was a mild-mannered beast, but because of his forbidding size, he was often forced to rollover on his back in pretended submission, to get other dogs to play with him.

They'd pounce on him with merciless delight, as if they really believed they had subdued him, while he played along, kicking his legs in the air in feeble defense.

I couldn't blame Roman for keeping that thick fur against his body. It was a raw night and it would take another Mountie to keep him warm.

I drifted over to him, smiling at the antics of the dogs I passed. Tail-biting, ear-chewing, dewlap-pulling and general mayhem. I called for Gustav to come. He did not budge. He had spied someone sitting on one of the benches that lined the path in front of the trees. She was eating.

He went over and sat unashamedly in front of her. He stayed stock-still. His eyes riveted on her every move. Gustav had lifted begging to an art.

He had mastered the 'Look'. An appealing innuendo that suggested he hadn't eaten in - week and was counting on the noble generosity of this wonderful person to spare him the indignity of having to pitifully howl for his supper.

The woman's insouciance was remarkable. Gustav's wide, brown, imploring eyes and dignified stare made no dent in her composure and the enjoyment of her food.

She cared not a whit for his perseverance or his uncanny ability to inflict guilt.

Was Gustav losing his touch?

When I turned back to Roman, his interest had moved to a pair of pugs simultaneously burrowing under his arms to get their butts scratched. He obliged.

How bad could this guy be? Dogs liked him and vice-versa. They were a good early warning system and seemed to have no qualms about him.

"Cute dogs," I said, as they scampered away to a more familiar butt scratcher. "Their names are Jules and Jim."

"Yes, there are several pugs in my missionary back home." He spoke with the plain mid-western speech which always impressed me with its lack of affectation.

"Missionary?" I was trying to connect the word 'missionary' to the word 'pug'.

"Yes," he said, proudly, "a ministry for pets."

"A what!?"

"A ministry for pets." He said it again. "God's creatures need spiritual nourishment."

He did not elaborate.

"Well, you know what God spelled backwards is?" I said, with jocular impiety.

He gave me a stern look.

I was barking up the wrong tree with levity. Maybe Leviticus would be more appropriate. Something about burnt offerings?

I switched to somber interest.

"Where is your ministry?"

"A small town in Wisconsin," he answered politely, "wouldn't know it. But I commune with the pets I've met." He paused, pressing his fingertips lightly against his temples. "Especially dogs. I seem to have a special rapport with dogs."

I bet you do.

"Snakes?" I ventured.

"They have not communicated with me," he said, matter-of-factly.

"They got a bad rap for meddling in human affairs," I offered.

"And they were punished for it," he intoned, creepily.

"So, what kind of work do you do?" I asked, briskly. "You know, to earn your daily bread."

"I'm a writer."

"A writer. That's great. What do you write?"

"I write about people."

"People. Hey. Plenty of those."

"Bad people," he frowned, like a displeased teacher. "I expose and admonish them."

In bestselling style, I thought. Was he putting me on?

"Could you commune with my dog?" I asked, keeping the ball rolling.

"Which one is he, or she?"

"The black one, over there. Begging. Gustav! Gustav!"

I whistled.

I am not a good whistler, but Gustav's sharp ears picked it up, and he came running towards me.

I could scream my lungs out, and he might not move, but a pathetic whistle brought him running. He was a year old when I adopted him from the pound, where he had been for many weeks. His background was unknown, but I guess he had learned to respond to a whistle from his previous owners and was inured to being yelled at. It took a long while before I could touch him on the rump, without having him flinch.

"Say hello, Gustav." I nudged him over to Roman, who went down on his haunches, smiled and greeted Gustav affectionately, with scratches behind the ears and under the chin.

Gustav was in doggie heaven.

Roman gripped his neck and pulled him close. He pressed his forehead's to Gustav's, closed his eyes, and I supposed, communed. It reminded me of Mr. Spock's mind-meld. Though I was sure Gustav's thoughts weren't that grievous.

"What's the dope?" I asked, not making any particular references.

You'd think a crowd would have gathered to watch this spectacle. Not so. Dog people know how foolishly other dog people behave with their animals. No one paid much mind.

Roman was lost in concentration. Furrows creased his brow. It didn't look good for Gustav.

"I hear music." Roman said.

Music.

Gustav was named after Gustav Mahler, whose music, when I first heard his symphonies, sounded like toilet paper unrolling. But, the more I listened, and the more I understood it, the more I liked it.

Roman was on the mark.

By golly, maybe this guy had it. Maybe, he had the touch, the magic, the power. Or, maybe he just had ringing rocks in his head.

I was getting nowhere, lento. But who cares. This detective work was fun. Although, when you've lived in New York and San Francisco most of your life, you've met Type A through Type Z, and even some who need a new alphabet.

Roman seemed harmless. I couldn't picture him doing something as mundane and gossipy as trash bios. But we all have our splits. We all have strategies to wring out the unholy sides of ourselves.

"I find Gustav very interesting, he said, coming out of his trance. "He may have been a musician in a former life."

Ha. Ha.

"I'd like Gustav to meet Gretel and Maria."

"Gretel and Maria?"

"Yes. Mrs. Hayward's Bichons. We're having a bit of a literary get-together tonight at eight, at her home. He began chattering, his Hawaiian shirt no match for the San Francisco fog. "Gretel and Maria have artistic backgrounds as well. But they do get excited and pee on the floor."

I had to stifle a guffaw.

"It would be interesting to see if they hit it off, so to speak." He rose, shivering and wrapped his arms around his chest.

"Supper?" I hopefully inquired. One does get tired traipsing through the new, enlarged Safeway. All that extra walking makes you hungrier so you end up buying more. Very crafty.

"Dinner." He corrected.

"Sorry," I said, apologizing for my faux pas.

I had never been in a mansion before. It reminded me of a museum. Huge rooms and lots of them. Lots of paintings. Lots of quiet. Lots of view. The back looked out on large, well-tended garden and a gorgeous, sweeping view of the bay.

I nibbled on my fingernails.

How could I pull it off? The great detectives were tough, but with savoir-faire. Haughty, yet assuasive. Bumbling, yet charming. I had to be conjurer. Pass myself off as someone who had good breeding, good background, good bank account, good table manners. Good luck!

I needn't have worried.

"Pass the bread!" I shouted, to the end of the twenty-foot-long table.

The bread basket came skidding down a narrow corridor between plates, candle sticks, soup tureens and crashed into my plate.

"Thank you!" I shouted.

"Don't mention it!" Mrs. Hayward shouted back.

I ducked as a muffin flew by my ear. They were raging drunk.

"Catch this, baby!" Roman announced, side-arming a kaiser roll at Robin Hayward, mistress of mystery, which she deftly batted aside with a swipe of her celery stick.

Suddenly, a young woman stepped into the dining room to restore order.

"Stop it! Stop it!" she pleaded.

She was beautiful. A knockout. Which was better than being conked into unconsciousness by a flying coconut.

"Mom! Philip! Stop!" she repeated, stridently.

But her presence only seemed to encourage the combatants. A glob of mashed potatoes plopped against her chest and slid slowly down her dress. Hearty laughter blotted out her sobs.

I sprang up and with great delicacy and a fine damask napkin, tried to wipe off the dribbling potatoes. She slapped my hand and still sobbing, fled the room, her high heels clattering staccato like on the shiny hardwood floors, then muffling away into the white thickness of the living room rug.

"A toast to your lovely daughter!" Roman sang out, raising his wine glass and swigging.

"A toast to your lovely daughter!" Mrs. Hayward echoed, sipping her wine with a gurgling sound.

I had two choices. Go after Hayward's beautiful daughter or go back to my filet mignon. The choice was simple: filet mignons do not slap back. Besides, who knows where the beauty disappeared to in this palatial funhouse. I might run into an elfin cousin flinging guacamole, or a prankster nephew's fruit salad barrage.

I stayed put and dug into my juicy, once-in-a-decade steak, protecting myself from the revelers with a jerry-rigged wall of menus. It was a flimsy fortress, but hopefully, out of sight, out of range.

I had not brought Gustav, and was prepared to make an excuse for him. But the goings on obviated an alibi. I didn't have a car, it was a two mile walk and muzzled, crowded bus trip was not fair to Gustav. So I left him home.

Neither were there Bichons. They were probably smart, and high-tailed it to the remotest regions of the house, wondering how their lunatic masters could be so blasphemously indifferent to sacred food.

So the rich are slobs like the rest of us, I smiled to myself, thinking back on the night before.

Gustav and I were on an early morning jaunt up to what I called Gopher Hill, his favorite spot. A rough crag of rock, rising like a dislocated knuckle from among the rolling hills of San Francisco, offering a panorama of the city.

Gustav did not care about the great view or the relaxed sense of isolation from the busy city. It was home to countless, unseen gophers, and he went right after them, sniffing the ground, digging frantically and then sticking his nose into the hole, his rump protruding high in the air.

While Gustav was on, what had become a fruitless gopher hunt, I remembered the conversation the night before with Henry, who had prepared the meal.

"I like my food eaten, not heaved," he said, with ironic resentment. He took his calling very seriously. I tried to soothe him.

"I thought the steak was the best I've ever eaten."

"Thanks, Beamer," he said, lightening up to a smoldering pique. "Those idiots don't appreciate good food.

I nodded and commiserated. "They have no appreciation."

"No taste at all," he said, mirthlessly.

"It's Hayward's fault. He treats everyone like property."

"What do you mean?"

"Orders people around as if they were garbage."

"You?"

"He tries. But Mrs. Hayward and Katherine ..."

"Is Katherine the one ...?"

"The crier?"

"Exactly."

"I could make good onion soup from her tears," said Henry, pensively, cooking up a chef's image. He smiled as he realized his preoccupation.

"Once a chef, always a chef."

"You will never be chefless," I said, bantering to keep him cooled down. But his anger flared up again.

"Hayward is like a petty despot. He makes everyone miserable."

"He didn't sound like a nice guy on the phone."

He was enraged. "On the phone? I swear, he hits them!"

"Who? Mrs. Hayward? Katherine?"

"Who knows. Maybe both. He's a brute."

"You ever see him do it?"

"No, I haven't seen anything."

"You can tell the police."

"The police won't do shit!" he said, infuriated.

Henry was in a dilemma. His job was at stake if he spoke out. Yet, he was suspicious of physical abuse. He had an obvious attachment to Mrs. Hayward. A very untidy situation.

"Why don't you drive me home," I suggested. "I could use a lift, and you could use some distance."

Gustav was poised with frozen attention over the gopher hole, waiting for the critter to pop his head out.

My own inner devils of reproach reared their impudent heads. In this quiet setting, with the city spread out as an innocent miniature below, I took hurried inventory of my life. I came up short.

It is a fine line to be demanding of yourself, but not be hard on yourself. The idiocies one has done cannot be changed. To try to alter the unalterable in one's mind is destructive.

The implacable demons like to lash out at me. Belligerent imps that allow an occasional truce, but never a peace. Don't disturb us, they say, these longtime residents, or we will make your life hell.

Suddenly, behind me, I heard a pitiful squeal. Gustav had snatched a gopher and had it locked in his jaws. He clamped down on it again and it stopped moving. He began to eat at its guts.

"C'mon, Gustav," I said, trying to get him to leave it. "Let's go back."

He looked up at me. He did not want to let go of his prize. He ripped at its stomach. I was not disgusted or put off, it was natural for him to hunt, kill and eat prey. His patience paid off. A few seconds of struggle and the gopher was gone, his little legs curled up and his eyes close. It may have been natural, but it was still sad.

I was back in the dog park, sitting on a bench, with Gustav lying beside me. He was alert to every movement, presumably waiting for the Great Pigeon to come bobbing by. His paws and snout were caked with dried mud, as they always were after the gopher hunt.

"Oh, what a sweet dog!" the tailored lady with the black briefcase remarked, strolling by. "Can I pet her?"

"Him. Sure."

She reached down and gently rubbed his head. His eyes flicked up, but otherwise he did not move.

"He is awfully quiet."

"He's visualizing world peace."

"Well, I hope he is doing a good job."

"Me, too," I agreed, as I closely observed the woman who passed by every morning on the way to the MUNI stop. She had attractive, long legs and a friendly smile. Her clothing and grooming were impeccable. She flashed an engagement ring in my direction.

"You're wearing eyeglasses today," I said, amicably.

She adjusted them self-consciously, but with a pleased expression that I had noticed.

"Well, I lost a contact lens," she apologized.

"I think they look fine," I said, gallantly. Tactlessly, I added: "It gives you two faces." What I meant to say, was that it gave her two looks, which might be accepted as a compliment, instead I got an accusing glance.

"I mean," I said, careful of my blundering tongue, "I find eyeglasses on women attractive. And when you take them off, there is another kind of attraction."

Her suspicion evaporated, and she smiled back at me more with her eyes than with her mouth.

"He's so cute!" she cooed, holding onto the 'so' and puckering her lips up to Gustav. He wagged his tail. She wriggled closer and planted a kiss on his snout. Gustav kissed her face.

A MUNI train rumbled by and she abruptly straightened up. She looked at her watch. "I'd better go," she said. "I hope it doesn't rain, I didn't bring an umbrella."

"It's May," I informed her. It has usually stopped raining in San Francisco by April.

"That's why they call it May. It may rain, it may fog, it may be cold. Silly."

Was I the silly or was the weather silly?

"See you later," she smiled fetchingly, and went off.

"Gee, Gustav," I said to my faithful dog, "You sure attract nice looking women. If only you could afford them."

I slumped down, wiped my eyeglasses on my undershirt, chewed on a fingernail, cracked my knuckles and yawned with open-mouthed gusto. Not things to do when women are present.

Actually, Gustav helped me feel a lot better about myself. I thought I was a slob, then I got a dog.

I watched the woman boarding the MUNI. Then I realized I was petting something.

It happened often, sitting there, my thoughts drifting off or talking with someone next to me, a small hound would find its way onto my lap. It was an automatic reaction in the park to pet something, or scratch some butt, and the dogs knew it. I was one of their favorite suckers.

Some dogs had known me so long that they'd greet me with their pushy behinds saying: 'butt first'. With all this elbow grease I've been using, I figured sooner or later I'd have a new affliction for the medical books: 'Petters Elbow.'

The dog turned out to be Big Bear, an unidentifiable breed of brown and white.

"Off!" Tall Paul shouted, shambling after her.

"It's okay, I don't mind," I assured him.

"She always seems to find you," he said, his ever present pad and pens bulging from his jacket pocket.

"You know what they say" Unlucky in love, lucky in dogs."

"I guess it all evens out."

Paul was tall and thin, with a narrow nose, slightly bent at the bridge and astute eyes. He was a tired and retired criminal attorney who became palled by his work, appalled by his clients, and had turned to writing poetry for solace. "Poetic Injustice" he called it. One of his constant themes was death, which did not draw many park people to him for pleasant chatter.

"There is a wild, weird confluence of coincidence," he recited mellifluously in my direction, then stopped, evidently stumped for the next line." I am the pallbearer of the world, galled and appalled by injustice unfair, then a blessed gift of dog, Osa, which in that most beautiful of poetic languages, Spanish, means Bear."

He began gesturing rhythmically and wildly. "Yes, there a weird **confluence ...**" I waved my hand in front of him to put the kibosh on. "I'm rehearsing," he smiled, unconcerned," reading at the Donne and Pawn. How'd you like it?"

"I like the opening, but the rest needs a better flow. Last week, you had Bear, not Osa."

"Thanks." he said, sincerely. "Yea, I thought I'd change it, so I can work some Spanish phrases in. Give it a more universal appeal.

"What are you up to?" he asked, sitting down on the other side of Gustav. Bear clambered off my lap and say down on his, the petting barely interrupted.

"Playing detective," I grinned.

"Oh?"

"You know my Truth Detective pitch. Someone actually bought it for cash." Paul was surprised but listening. "Actually, it seems to have fizzled out," I admitted.

I trusted Paul, but with the Detective Code freshly gleaned from Hammett and Chandler in my mind, I decided not to divulge client confidences. And if there was anything shady about my activities, better not put too much light on it.

"So, what do you think of the Giants?" I jostled, kiddingly. Paul was an ardent Dodger fan. The Giants were up; the Dodgers were down.

"Lucky," he responded glumly. "Just lucky."

"Bonds is the best." I pressed, with malicious merriment. "Four homers in five games."

"Give me piazza anytime," he said, insulted. "He's a right-handed hitting catcher and has a better average than Bonds, not even considering his power. He works hard behind the plate. An iron man."

The dispute rages on. The 'who's better' debate that has been a staple of baseball for well over one hundred years, continues as intensely as ever,

"We should never forget," I proposed with reverential gravity, what the great philosopher, Friedreich Nietzsche said before he was locked up in a madhouse."

"What was that?" Paul asked, keen to learn.

"He said, 'Without baseball, life would be a mistake.'"

"They probably locked him away because he went crazy rooting for a Giants team that always ended up in the cellar."

"Probably," I conjectured. "They say he saved box scores. Some of his most brilliant insights came while pondering them."

"I wouldn't doubt it."

"'Give me a stick and a ball and I shall conquer the world.'" I quoted. "Those were his final words."

"If only he could have known about the cut fastball or the backdoor slider. We might be going to NietscheLand instead of Disneyland."

"Could be ...

"Hey, Beamer!" I looked up and saw Henry coming towards me, panting.

"Beamer, I'm glad caught you here." He stopped in front of me and caught his breath. "Katherine wants to invite you to lunch. She's sorry about what happened."

"It's okay, I've forgotten it," I shrugged. "Do you know Paul?"

"Hi, Paul, I'm Henry. Paul nodded.

"Paul's a poet."

"Really?"

"Very morbid."

"Really?"

"Do you want to hear something," I said, trying to boost his audience.

"I'd love to, but I'm in a hurry." Henry said, trying to leave. "Is it 'yes' for lunch?"

"Why didn't you just call me?"

"I wanted to make sure you got the message. Katherine's been upset."

"Okay. Thanks, Henry," I said, thoughtfully. "Tell her to leave all the info on my machine and I'll be there. My social calendar is as blank as a politician's face."

"Will do."

Henry departed with a quick first step.

Breaking my code a little, I explained to Paul who Katherine was and described her.

"These beautiful women are always clustering you. What do you do to them?" said Paul, mystified.

"I think you're exaggerating," I answered, flattered, but equally mystified. "I'm old, poor, balding and a klutz." I thought a moment. "Let me rephrase that. I'm mature, financially hopeful, with a high forehead and an endearing clumsiness.

Paul looked skeptical. "Why do you underrate yourself?" he said to my profile. He had a hortatory tone. Probably the habit of years spent arguing in courtrooms. "You're a nice guy."

"I'm not so nice," I scouted, watching the pendulum of Gustav's leash swing back and forth between my knees.

"Why are you so hard on yourself?" Paul hammered at me.

"I'm not hard on myself," I rejoined.

"You know," Paul continued, in an accommodating tone, "I'm also hard on myself."

I looked over at him. He had a tight, close-mouthed smile. He laughed sourly. "I'm working at a gift shop on the Wharf, at minimum wage. I hear the word 'cute' so often I want to puke. I hear "I Left My Heart in San Francisco' played endlessly and monotonously on tiny bridges and cable cars that I want to murder the guy that composed it.

"It is impersonal. I greet and converse with people I will never see again. The employees are interchangeable and disposable. It is greed man, all greed." Paul finished his mini-screed with a grand flourishing of arms and leash.

"You don't have to convince me," I said. "You wanted to devote yourself to poetry," I shot back at him without empathy, "We all have crummy jobs to do."

"I don't want to be a successful poet," he assured himself "if that is not a contradiction in terms." He gave a snort. "I want to be a poet," his voice rose dramatically," so I can guarantee myself a life of penury." It was a semi-joke.

That's where the dogs came in.

We watched them chase each other in wide circles around the grass. It was always fun to watch them run. It cheered us up. Laughter can fix the soul and heal the hobbled hiker.

I met Katherine at one of the ubiquitous Starbucks which had begun building 'nests' in San Francisco. This one was on Geary, opposite the ACT theater, and had previously been Salmagundi, a before and after theater soup/salad/pastry restaurant, and a long time hangout for me when I lived downtown.

She was already sitting nervously at a back table when I came in. She looked at me, then looked away. I sat down opposite her.

"He's disappeared." she said, fitfully, her hands brushing her short, blond hair. Her baby blues poured into mine.

"Who's disappeared?"

She smoothed down the close fitting blue dress, buttoned to the neck. It primly accentuated her non-fiduciary assets.

"My father." She laid her hands flat on the table and stared at them. "He hasn't been home in two days."

"Well, maybe he went out-of-town." I said, off-handedly, not worrying about the jerk. "Besides," I nearly growled, "what am I supposed to do about it?"

She started to whimper, not tears, but the promise, or should I say, the threat of tears.

"Don't cry! Don't cry!" I said, hurriedly, as much out of self-defense, as out of sympathy.

"You seemed so nice," she blurted out, a millisecond from a sob. "Henry said you were so nice."

Not the nice business again.

"What do you want me to do I said, weakened, not really wanting to know.

"Find him." she said through a sniffle.

"Find him!"

"Find him. Please."

"I don't know what Henry told you, but this is not what I do for a living. I am not a professional anything."

"I know," she said, daintily dabbing at her nose with an initialed handkerchief.

"Hire a professional. Go to the police."

"My mother's famous," she answered, looking composed, her dander up. "If it is public, it will be blown all out of proportion. There would be smears and speculation."

That made sense.

"So, what about a private investigator?"

"My mother doesn't like them. She thinks they're sleazy." Katherine looked pensive. "The people in her books are regular people. The cops are bunglers and the private eyes looking for angles. I think she believes that,"

"Well, you know, I spoke to your father a few times on the phone," I said with suppressed scorn. "We had a tenuous rapport."

My euphemism eluded her.

"If you find him you could become friends."

Woman have such high hopes for the civilization of men. Socially optimistic.

"I know the bars where he likes to go." Her voice wavered, it was between a request and a plea.

"Do you want to come with me? That is, if I decide to go."

"Noh, no!" she said, drawing back.

Thanks a lot, I said to her by telepathy, thinking sneer. How did I get into this? My adventures were confined to mental pictures conjured up by authors' words and images from Jackie Chan video cassettes. Vicarious intrigues. Sure, just amble into a strange bar and ask about a Mr. Hayward, whose real name might be 'Johnny the Scar' something. Wait I've got it. I'll swagger in, patch over one eye, smoothing a barbered moustache, saying in a confidently menacing tone: "Say, any of you guys see Hayward?" implying that we had some important stuff to deal with. Sure, I could pull it off. Just like pulling off a chewed-up piece of fingernail. A snap.

"Well, Miss Katherine," I said, with polite forbearance, a grin oozing out of me. "I'm not a pickle." I'm not sure what it meant, but who could argue with a pickle?

"I don't think you're a pickle."

"We'll, I'll end up in a pickle. Don't you have any friends or relatives you can pick on? Who can help you?"

"My relatives can't stand San Francisco, and my friends will never do an errand."

"An errand!" I exploded.

"God, you're touchy!" she snapped. "My friends would never even run an errand; how can I expect them to exert themselves over this."

"Sorry." I don't know if I was sorry for the anger, or sorry that she had such lousy friends.

"Well," she smiled, with a bewitching smile that seemed strained. "You can see what a pickle I'm in."

"If I'm your last resort, you sure are."

My resolve not to get involved was strong, but my solver muscles were stronger. "Where was he when you last saw or heard from him?"

"He phoned that night you came over to say he would not make it for dinner."

"Did he say when he'd be back?"

"He said, 'later.'"

"Where was he."

"I don't know, but it was noisy. He had to shout."

"What kind of noise? People noise. Machine noise? Music?

"People and ..."

"And ..."

"Organ. That's it, and organ. It was strange, he never went to church."

"Baseball game."

"What?"

"He may have been at a baseball game; did you hear cheering?"

"Could be, a lot of yelling."

"Is he a baseball fan?"

"Yes, he often watched it on **T.V.**"

Darn. A redeeming quality.

"Did he bet on it?"

"I don't know, maybe."

I paused and thought about it.

"This may come out of left field," I said, then regretted the unintentional metaphor. I didn't want to be flippant on this subject. "Did he ever hit you?"

"Who?" she said, her eyes slitting with antagonism.

"Your father."

"No!" she recoiled.

"I don't mean to be impertinent," I said, raising my palms up in a peaceful gesture. "But Henry thought you might ...."

"Henry doesn't know what he's talking about!"

"Okay." I said, with a conciliatory smile.

"Okay!" she said, still fuming.

Beautiful women can make you do ugly things. This possibility, plus my natural caution about plunging into anything, made me an ambivalent listener.

It may be just a harmless escapade, with a bunch of crazy, or should I say, eccentric people. It is the poor who are crazy, the rich are eccentric. The best thing to do was to bow out gratefully and succinctly.

"Katherine, it's out of my ken."

"Out of your what!?" she bit back.

"My experience."

"So, why didn't you say that? Why do you have to use those stupid words?"

Her storm flew over most of the customers. Students from the acting school upstairs often came in to rehearse their lines. For all they knew, we could be doing scenes from a play.

I took the brunt of her boiling anger unflinchingly. I was a convenient target for whomever or whatever she was really angry at. At least, I hoped so.

"Ken means yes in Hebrew," I ventured obliquely.

"Who cares."

She started opening the top buttons of her dress with painstaking deliberateness. First the top button, then the second, then the third, in a kind of stiff, mesmerized ritual. She slowly spread open the separated halves. A huge welt stood out from beneath her collarbone.

"Who did that!?" I demanded.

She said nothing. She stared at me coolly and carefully buttoned up her dress.

That bastard! Why does she want to find him? Maybe, she has some payback planned.

"Give it another day or so." I suggested. It was all I could think of to mollify her.

"Okay." she relented.

She got up and walked out.

"She showed me a welt."

"A welt?" Henry sputtered.

It was noon. The siren had just gone off as it did every Tuesday at noon.

"So, what do you think?"

"She didn't tell me anything about a welt."

"Would she?"

Henry thought a moment. "No."

Titus started nipping at Gustav, trying to get him to chase. Instead, Gustav turned a rump to him and retreated under a bench to do what he does best, wait for pigeons.

"I thought she'd confide in me," Henry said with consternation.

"Are you that close to her?"

"I thought I was." He looked bewildered and distractedly twirled Titus' metal leash. I had to jump out of the way.

"Watch it! You almost hit me."

"What?"

"Be careful!" I remonstrated. "The way you're whipping that thing around you could hurt someone."

"Oh, sorry." He caught himself and shoved the leash into his jacket pocket.

"You're not whipping potatoes, you know." I said, to lighten it up. "Besides, I prefer hash browns."

"Forgive me," he said, overly contrite.

I had an idea.

"Why don't we have a pot-luck at my place. How 'bout Sunday evening. To hash things out."

"Ha." Henry reached into his fanny pack and pulled out a thickly stained appointment book. He bent back a mustardly page. "Sunday's good."

"Say, six."

"I'll bring the luck," Henry added, with unexpected giddiness. He was not a jolly sort. He had a great, protruding belly, which made me want to say, 'lose some weight'. But if I did, I'd be met with a withering stare. In a meaner moment, I had dubbed him, "Henry the Ate."

"I'll invite Dori and Paul."

"Dori and Paul?"

"The woman with the dachshunds and the guy spouting poetry with the shaggy mutt."

Henry nodded. It was easier to match the dogs with the people than vice-versa. You always spotted the dog before the person. If you saw the human outside the park, without their dog, you could pass them by without recognition.

"He came back." Katherine's hard voice sounded on the message phone the next morning, as I returned from my morning outing with Gustav. "It's okay."

End of message. Click. Services no longer wanted. Curtains closed.

The rest of the week lumbered by. I had a call from the temp agency on Thursday afternoon and began an indefinite stint filing for the phone company.

It was monotonous work, but I was left alone in a big room and could go at a leisurely pace. Unfortunately, there were no windows. By the next Friday, I had conceived a book entitled, 'Zen and the Art of Filing', which consisted of blank lettered pages.

One could meditate on the 'A', the move along to the 'B', 'C', 'D', and so on. By 'Z' one might have achieved satori, or fallen into a deep sleep from boredom.

When I wasn't at work, I was in the park, where most peoples' conversations inevitably centered around dogs. Often those animated and heated discussions, which from afar seemed to portend some terribly serious state of affairs, were invariably about dogs.

A pet dog's proclivity to eat garbage, or roll in offal. The new puppy's inestimable cuteness. Dogs' social and hierarchical relationships. The progress of obedience training. The latest strain, sprain or scratching problem.

It would make a good T.V. soap opera: 'Dog Park.' Who was sniffing who? Who had been recently been fixed and why? Why did Phoebe suddenly ignore Max and now played only with Ralston?

Paul was sprawled on the futon, his long legs and arms stretched to their limit. Dori was sitting cross-legged on a cushion on the floor, playing tug-of-war with Gustav. I was in my black leather swivel chair. Haydn's Sun Quartet played soothingly in the background.

The dishes were out. My tuna salad, Dori's green salad and Paul's double bag of tortilla chips were awaiting Henry's arrival. We each had a glass of table wine within reach. We were talking about fleas.

"I think the best way to combat them," counselled Paul, would be to put up a sign in the park reading: 'Flea Free Zone.' What do you think, Dori?"

"Then we'd only attract illiterate fleas."

"You have a point," Paul admitted. "We'd be stuck with a lower class of fleas. It would hurt the neighborhood."

"The property values would go down."

"Then the rents would go down, too." Paul encouraged. "Then we could afford to live in this city."

"Enough!" I butted in. "Enough with the fleas. Let's use this stupendous brain power on the Hayward Case."

Paul shifted in his seat. "So, you think something nefarious is going on?"

"I don't know. It's a big secret.

"These situations usually are," said Paul, somberly.

"Sounds like you're stuck on this Katherine," threw in Dori, not looking up from her tussle with Gustav.

"I barely know her," I shrugged.

"If you know her barely, I would think you know her fairly well," Paul chortled.

"An unbearably bad joke," I countered.

"Well, she's rich," he ragged.

"A typical remark of the minimum wage earner."

"What about Mrs. Hayward?" Dori chipped in, letting go and giving Gustav the victory, which he celebrated by shredding the sock. "She seems so shadowy."

"That's why I wanted you here, to get your opinions."

"Opinions, opinions," declaimed Paul, "he is courting opinions. Our brilliance and perspicacity, fair Dori, shall penetrate and resolve this mystery!"

"Gimme a break, Longfellow."

The subtle Miss Dori twisted to the sound of the outer door buzzer.

"It's Henry!" I said, happily, anticipating some exotic cuisine for the occasion.

He came through the door with a big pot of something.

"My private specialty," he exulted, "fried spaghetti!

Henry set himself up in the kitchen area to heat up the strange dish. When it was safely in several fry pans, he joined us.

"How 'bout salad?" I said, to get things stirring. "Help yourself."

We stood around munching, while the wonderful aroma of the fried spaghetti enticed our dreary taste buds. "It smells delicious," mumbled Dori through a mouthful of lettuce.

"Sure does." echoed Paul.

Henry was very pleased.

It looked like glop, but it tasted like heaven.

"It's fantastic."

"Yum. Yum."

"I'm glad you like it," Henry said, with an immense smile of satisfaction. I use ketchup."

"The French would shish-kebab you if they found out," I warned, good-naturedly.

He put a hushing finger to his lips. "Let's just keep it to ourselves, huh?"

"How could we turn in such a master chef." Paul applauded, and Henry blushed with gratitude.

"So, what's new with Katherine?" I wanted to catch him off-guard, if for any reason he was on guard.

His expression suddenly darkened. The fork fell slowly from his hand, clattering off the edge of the plate onto the dog-haired rug. He tried to bend and pick it up, but his girth got in the way. Gustav scooted over and began licking it clean before I could grab it and deposit it in the sink.

I offered Henry another fork, but he waved it away. He looked crushed.

"What is it, Henry?"

We watched him apprehensively, awaiting dire news, but he said nothing. He looked at us beseechingly.

Gustav was slyly moving in on the bowl of spaghetti Henry had lowered to the floor. I whisked it out from under his nose and put it on the counter. He sniffed the surrounding carpet in case any of it spilled over. "Sorry, Gustav," I said into his longing eyes, "but nice try."

"They fired me." Henry broke the silence. "Just like that!" His arms dropped heavily to his sides. He shook his head and contorted a smile. "I was working up a new salmon dish, when Mr. Hayward came in and told me to get out. Just like that!"

"I'm beginning to dislike this Hayward," Paul grumbled.

"Me, too," hissed Dori, who was now seated attentively in the old recliner. "He needs to wake up."

"I've spent the last few days buried under the covers." Henry confided.

"We gotta get in there!" I said, impulsively.

"Don't be rash." cautioned Paul.

I calmed down and looked steadily over at Dori.

"Noh, no!" Her hands went up ready to push away my suggestion. She had caught my drift. "Not that creep again!"

"He loves animals."

"He is an animal."

"Invite him to meet your dogs. Tell him they're spiritually depressed. He goes for that."

"You're crazier than he is."

"I'm telling you it's true. I saw him in the park. It's bizarre, but it's true."

"Well, you should know, Mr. Truth Detective," she threw in snidely. "Although, I don't think Sherlock Holmes' reputation is in any jeopardy."

"Sherlock Holmes is fictional. I'm real."

"Yeah. Real idiotic."

"Will you do it?" I asked, exasperated.

She gave me a calculating look. "What's it worth to you, Truth "Detective?"

She was getting annoying. "What's it worth to a woman who may be in trouble? A sister in distress."

"Don't hand me that 'sister' garbage," she jeered, and stared moodily out the window. A minute went by. "Okay, I'll do it. But only as a favor to you guys."

"Thanks, Dori."

"Call him now." I proposed, "maybe he's at the hotel." I leafed through the white pages and gave her the hotel number. She got through.

"Hi, Phil, it's Dori," she said, sweetly.

A pause.

"Yes. Yes. You remember. How nice."

A pause.

"Yes, I'm so glad the feeling has returned to your hand,"

A pause.

"Yes, and the swelling has gone down from your shin. I'm happy to hear that."

A longer pause.

"Yes, I wish it had been more fun, too." She stuck out her tongue to us and let it hang. "Listen, Phil. I heard you're good with dogs. Yes, from someone in the park. Listen, my dachshunds ...yes, dachshunds. I think they need some spiritual help." She looked at us with a 'can you believe what I'm saying' expression on her creamy-skinned face. "You'd like to. Great! How 'bout tomorrow evening around six, in the park?" she caught my o.k. sign. "Yes. See you then," she purred, and hung up.

"Happy!?" she scowled.

"Happy." I smiled back.

Most everyone in the park had gathered around the sight of Philip Roman doing battle with the four dachshunds. They were alternately charging forward and racing back, barking madly at Roman, who was making a dogged effort to befriend them.

Other dogs ringed the action, lending their voices to the racket. The circle widened and shrunk, as the dogs dashed ahead and then retreated, while Roman, who had now come down to their level on the ground, extended a friendly arm toward them.

Finally, he sat up panting. He extracted a handful of doggie treats from a deep pocket and held them out on his palm, with the certain hope of drawing the dachshunds near.

He had not reckoned on the rest of the aroused dogs.

There was a sudden and unstoppable rush of Labs, Rots, Goldens, Jacks and 'Basic Dogs' toward the goodie laden palm. Roman was bowled over and the treats flew out of his hand. A frantic, four-legged scramble ensued.

Dori's dachshunds had roiled the pack and Roman had gotten a come-uppence. Her face registered a smiling approval.

"Are you okay?" she asked, languidly walking over to the supine Roman.

He stared blankly up at the sky, while a friendly wire-haired fix terrier vigorously licked his face. His eyes focused on Dori.

"Yesth," he said, his answer muffled by a pink doggy tongue sloshing through his open mouth.

"Watch out he doesn't pee on you!" an urgent voice cried out, as Hercules, the grey Great Dane, lifted his leg over Roman's outstretched arm.

He jerked out of the way just in time.

"Sorry, man."

Roman sloughed it off. "It's okay. It wouldn't be the first time."

Everyone laughed in agreement.

Roman got up gingerly. If he was aggrieved, he didn't show it. He gave the Hercules a playful swat on his rump, and walked toward Dori, holding the lower right side of his back. He walked an exaggerated mask of pain considering the comical flop he took.

The Wild Bunch Dachshunds had stopped barking and were crowding around his feet, sniffing very inch of him they could. He did not notice them lifting their tiny legs.

Some of Hercules' shower had hit.

"What happened to your back?" Dori asked.

"It's okay," he replied, clenching his teeth. I twisted it once throwing a football. I might have wrenched it again. It was a flare pass. It flares up occasionally."

Dori's dense on football, there was no flicker of understanding. Just a suspicious look.

I was eager to ask her about it, but it would have to wait. She had an invite to the Haywards, courtesy of Roman, but prompted by the charming instigation of Dori Four.

But what of my buddy, Gustav? What was he doing during this melee?

As a dog of peace, he kept away from the thick of the action and merely barked from the sidelines. Whether he was exhorting his fellow canines to cool it, or adding his vibrant encouragements, I shall never know.

I do know that he suddenly disappeared.

Gustav stuck by me like Super Glue, so only one thing could make him leave: pigeons.

I looked around until I spotted a trio of them wobbling casually up the path, alongside the trash pails. From there, I drew an imaginary line to the nearest bench. Voila! Gustav was scrunched down behind it, watching.

His classic stalking form always looks good, but he is not fast. He is not stealthy. He just bursts out after them, and if the pigeons have an ounce of sense, they are well off the ground before he arrives in a barking rush.

He doesn't catch any, I tell people who want to know, but he keeps them in line and aerobically fit. I cover for the poor dog.

But he may be giving me a bad reputation.

When strolling around San Francisco without Gustav, I see flocks of pigeons flying low, and I am nagged by the scary thought that pigeons will one day gang up on me for being the owner of their canine nemesis.

It is not a pretty thought and I hopefully chalk it up to an overwrought imagination. But, sometimes I wonder, will the pigeons get their revenge.

A stack of Robin Hayward mysteries had been waiting patiently on my desk. The library had a slew of them. They were short.

Eric Hopper, the iconoclastic San Francisco longshoreman, self-educated philosopher and writer, once said that in a short book an author writes everything he or she knows, while in a long book everything he or she doesn't know.

I figured Robin Hayward knew a lot.

Her popular heroine, Diana Osgood, was a middle-aged, Professor of Psychology at a large, fictitious university in Wisconsin. This was the famous 'Campus Mystery' series, where everyone was a dolt, except the intrepidly determined, yet exquisitely feminine, Miss Osgood.

Of course, woman ate it up.

There was no pretense at deep, philosophic insight. Rather a killing, a milling, a spilling, a thrilling, a chilling, and finally, a willingness to confess.

It was done deftly, economically and with a conveniently decorative romance for Mrs. Osgood, to brace it.

None of the half-dozen books I read through dealt with abuse. None had as belligerent a character as Mr. Hayward, or a theme of vengeful children, or any salient clues that might hint at what was going on in the Hayward household.

It was usual stock motives: Jealousy, Ambition, Greed, Academic Competitiveness, Love Affairs Gone Wrong, School Politics, etc. I was disappointed.

Truth could hide behind many guises. It could be there right in front of me and I couldn't see it.

We tend to overrate our own acumen, thinking we are so discerning of others' motives, while we keep our motives cleanly concealed from others. At least, that's the way it strikes me, Beamer Todd, Truth Detective.

The trumpets did not blare as I congratulated myself on my modesty. But, I left her books with a thin thought that wiggled in my brain. Something was missing. It wiggled and wiggled.

The next day I was back filing for the phone company. I was an anachronism.

The rest of the building was tapping away on computers, while I was still pulling open file cabinets. But, the physical act of it seemed to stimulate the filing mechanism in my brain, if there is such a thing.

Ordering and arranging held a certain fascination. It was neat, like Hayward's mysteries. Rational, functional, almost dispassionate, yet her life was stormy. Was that the twist? The fact that her books seemed to have no relationship to her life as I knew it?

Ah, the facile diligence of the dilettante.

"She's daffy."

Dori was expatiating on last night at the Haywards.

"Drunk. All night," she continued, admiringly. "I never read her books, but I heard of her. Staid was what I expected. Proper, you know. But she was a riot!"

We were in Dori's tiny studio. The dachshunds were skittering around, content to play among themselves, occasionally jumping on and off the daybed we were sitting on. But it wasn't bothersome. They were really cute, affectionate creatures.

The coverlet on the daybed was a blast for the eyes. Abstract art. As if a painter had haphazardly poured globs of vividly colored paints over a canvas, and smeared them in.

The rest of the room was darkly drab. A rickety table with two poky chairs and an ancient purple and green armchair backed into the corner. The window faced the blank wall of a taller building across a narrow alley. There was rarely sunlight. But it was enlivened by her wit.

"Another food fight?"

"Food fight?"

"When I was there she and Roman had a food fight."

"Huh?" She was unable to picture it. "No, he was well-behaved. Quiet. Even pulled out a chair for me. No one had ever done that before." She drifted into her memory.

"He's smitten. Hayward was gone again?" She was in her reverie. "So, Hayward was gone again?"

"What?"

"No Hayward!"

"Off to Las Vegas."

"Mr. Elusive. And Katherine?"

"Noh, your sweetheart," she jabbed.

"She's not my sweetheart or anything. You know that."

"How do I know that?"

"I told you."

"Huh. Well, if I can't believe the T.D., who can I believe?"

"That's right!" I affirmed.

"Ha!"

"C'mon, Dori!"

The whining sharpness of my voice did not phase her. "Well," she said, her voice dropping to a conspiratorial whisper. "It's rather secret."

She looked around affectedly, as if there were an X-Ray telescope and high powered listening device trained on the room. "Well," she said, milking the moment, "Katherine was eating."

"Eating?"

"And talking."

"What was she talking about?" I insisted.

"Eating."

"Eating?"

"She was talking about eating." Her voice returned to normal. "You know the usual mind-boggling things women talk about, like calories, vegetables salads, quarks, atom smashers. You know the usual quaint stuff."

Next subject. I was surprised that Dori was not awed by the house and babbling on about it.

"A giant playpen," she wisecracked, unimpressed.

I looked around the room, especially at the milk carton used as a foot rest. "You sure live elegantly, Dori. I bet those Haywards envy you." It was cruel, but I was trying to draw more than a yawn from her.

"So, you think I should be drooling over that mansion, heh?" she said, resentfully. "Not me, buster." She hoisted herself up on the daybed and threw out her chest defiantly.

"You got more buster than me," I quipped.

Her look was one of incredulous disgust.

"You always ruin things with your crackpot jokes, she said, bitterly. "Why don't you like me?"

"I do like you," I said, appeasing her. "I was just teasing."

"Do you really like me?" she softened.

"Sure I like you."

"I think you're one of the nicest people I know," she said, shyly.

"I'm not so nice," I pleaded, "but I think you're one of the nicest people I know."

"Do you?" She curled up and wrapped her arms around herself. She let out the faintest beginning of a blubber.

"**Yes.**" I assured her, with all the tenderness a 'nice' person could muster. "I think you're an exceptional person." I caressed her cheek and felt a teardrop rollover my hand.

It became a full-fledged blubber. I held her awhile, stroking her back, not saying anything. The dogs were whimpering. "It's okay girls," I told them. They settled down a bit, trusting me.

Dori fell asleep on my shoulder. I eased her down on the bed and tip-toed to the door. The dachshunds leaped up and nestled against her.

The door locked behind me. She was left in good hands. Or, should I say, paws.

I decided to walk straight downtown. Get the juices flowing. Check out the current culture. Be part of the crowd.

Powell and Market, the cable car turnaround.

The crippled unwashed beggars brushing against the spic and span tourists.

The stentorian proselytizers pleading for repentance.

The bullying shaved heads, muscling contemptuously through alarmed crowds.

The well-dressed and the ragged, the blind balloon maker and the all-seeing cop.

The innocent-eared kid listening to the lashing imprecations of bereavement.

The jiggling, hip-swinging, jewelry-clinking, gaudily dressed woman/man parading lasciviously and smiling temptingly at a group of gawking teenagers.

The delicate and the dissolute, the destitute and the delivered, the Congregation of Soul.

The relentless, scab-ridden old woman, with her sing-song request for food money, with the monstrous insinuation that she could be someone's grandmother.

Up to Union Square Park, where the armless, legless, electronic playing wonder uses his stumps to bang out hearty, happy, rousing tunes. His case chock full of bills, not only because he was handicapped and pitied, but because he was good and enjoying it.

Up to California and Powell, where the cable cars intersect and the great hotels loom like lords on top of Nob Hill.

There is a kinship of sorts between those on the bottom and those on top. The poor dreamed of being rich and the rich dreaded being poor. Real change came from the pressure of the outside in, to bulge the middle.

The maelstrom of life's miseries spares no one. No one is immune.

The material dominates our lives, as it must. But, it's the wiggle of curiosity, the tickle of compassion, the inkling of transcendence, the tingle of remorse, that sparks us.

In the end we admire the gentle over the gargantuan.

As we must.

I was heading into the park with Gustav after my trip downtown, when Philip Roman came out of the passenger side of a tinted-windowed Mercedes, blockbuster model.

"Hello," I called out, approaching him.

He stopped, turned around, and recognized me.

"Hello," he responded with a quick wave. "I'm looking for Dori."

"I'm just coming here myself."

As we were conversing, Gustav began barking at a pigeon on the branch of a tree next to the car. His claws scraped down along the fender as he hopped around trying to climb up to the pigeon.

The driver door opened. "I'll kill that son-of-a-bitch if he scratches my car!" I glared at the pocked marked face of a white-haired, stocky, bruiser of a man. It hit me! Hayward!

I leashed Gustav and pulled him into the park. I was locked in a fog of rage. I moved along on habit, my body coiled and tightened, craving movement, words I could hardly hear spewed from my mouth. People edged away from me, Gustav was crying and jumping against my leg in protest. I finally latched onto Paul who was standing right in my path.

"Whoa!" he broke in, "take it down a notch."

"Hey, Paul," I grunted, "that guy wanted to kill Gustav."

He glowered at the Mercedes. "Yeah, I saw."

"I'm shaking."

"Yeah, I know."

"I mean ...." my voice trailed off.

He squeezed my shoulder. "Hey, it's all right. Forget it. It happens."

"That was Hayward!" I said, compressing my anger.

"What?"

"Hayward. The guy who fired Henry."

Paul's long head nodded. He watched the Mercedes as it wheeled a U-Turn and roared up the street. "When I was growing up," Paul began, "there was a gang that terrorized the neighborhood. Big, husky guys who could beat you up with impunity, but," he joked, "mostly used their fists. They weren't dealing drugs. The cops didn't bother with them. They got their kicks roughing you up and demanding money.

"I was skinny and didn't have any allies, so I was an easy target. On my way back from school, it was a contest to make it home without a confrontation." He swallowed and blew out some air. "I didn't know how to deal with these guys. My father was dead, my mother was anxious and gave me mixed messages. I shouldn't let myself get pushed around, but I should be careful not to get hurt. So, I felt fragile and afraid, with this terrible anger inside me."

"What did you do?"

"Nothing. I lived with it." He looked down at the ground, as if seeing images of the past preserved in the concrete. "I retreated to the library, where it was safe and to learn things, to use my brain, you know, to outflank these guys."

"Is that why you went into law?"

He nodded. "Exactly. It's the standard plot. Boy humiliated. Boy earns power. Boy takes revenge."

"Did you?"

"No, never did," he said, regretfully. "By the time I knew enough to bring the law to bear, they were gone, or model citizens." He laughed ironically. "I guess what I mean, is that you never forget that helplessness as a kid. Like this Hayward. I know you wanted to do something. Hit him, scream at him, curse him out. But, when you're actually faced with a big, mean guy like that, unless you're real stupid or a martial arts champ, you'll get hurt. Anyway, that didn't warrant a fight. I mean, he did have a gripe."

"I suppose."

"You did the right thing. You walked away." He smiled and raised his fist and shook it in front of me. "You're right to be angry. Your dog. But drop it now. Don't blow it up." He smiled again. "You meet jerks every day, if you come out of your house. It's part of living Just say, well, I've met my jerk for the day and now I can meet some good people. I'm sorry, I'm rambling on."

"No. No. I appreciate it. Thanks. I feel better. It's important to get perspective."

"Okay!" he cheered.

"I'll just walk it off."

"Good idea." encouraged Paul.

I had not gone ten yards when I thought about ramming Hayward's face through the windshield of his precious car.

Gustav and I walked up through the park to the children's' fenced-in playground, me still seething, Gustav peering in for pigeons.

Before the fence was put up, he could chase the pigeons at will. Now, he was stuck outside, while the pigeons safely and leisurely searched for crumbs, ignoring him.

He still stalked them, staring intimidatingly through the fence. Sometimes, I egged him on, telling him they were saying bad things about his mother, but he hardly needed a spur.

He would stand rigidly, or race back and forth along the fence barking fearfully, letting them know he was a dog and they were pigeons and the fence was just a prop. The pigeons eventually got nervous and flew off. His persistence had paid off in triumph.

His shenanigans always lightened my load.

We stopped and sat on a backless bench by the basketball court. A spirited game of three on three was going on and I watched with nostalgia. I missed playing. Some of my happiest times were spent on the schoolyard basketball courts. The friendly rivalry, the team play, the camaraderie, and there was no cheating in the schoolyard.

I surveyed the park and the East Bay in the distance.

Hayward's threat had taken me by surprise. I had been stunned into inaction. I had been having a friendly chat with Roman, and then Boom! someone wanted to kill my dog. My emotions went through a wrenching shift of gears, from pleasant to angry, and this anger took off on the speedway, drawing fuel from old, unfinished encounters. The past always has a way of creeping or exploding into the present, and waits in ambush in the future.

"Isn't love the most amazing thing in the world?" I heard from behind me. I swerved and there was Charles and his yellow Lab, Guinevere. "Love's the most amazing thing in the world!" he said again, ecstatically.

"I guess so," I answered idly, still smarting from the unlovely Hayward.

"The birds are singing! The bees are buzzing! It's in the air! Can't you feel it!?" His arms pumped into whatever was in the air. I call him Good Time Charles. He was young, so he could be forgiven his rhapsody.

Guinevere was putting the moves on Gustav, licking his face with great enthusiasm. Gustav couldn't care less and discouragingly twisted his head away from her advances.

She jumped back into play posture. Her paws flat and extended, her chin to the ground, her eyes intent on Gustav, her tail waving madly. Her body arched up so that her butt was the highest point. He looked at her without interest.

She sprang forward and nipped at him, trying to get him going. He growled. She settled back into her play stance, eager. Gustav ignored her. Then, she spotted another Lab dashing toward her and she bounded off in its direction, a happy dog, for a happy person.

Gustav had his eye on a bee. He leaped and spun after it, in a frenzied chase.

"He really loves those bees," Charles laughed.

"That's where he gets his B Vitamins," I dead-panned.

Charles' buoyancy damped a bit. "No kidding?" he said, interested.

"Yes."

Charles' high eyebrows rose even higher in perplexed sunniness. "Where does he get his C Vitamins?"

"Dogs produce their own C."

"I see."

"How's your job?" He worked as a dishwasher.

"Great!" he exclaimed.

"Doesn't it get tedious."

"It's illuminating! he said, radiantly.

Now I was baffled. "Illuminating?"

"Yes. Each dish has been sent to me by God. It is holy work."

"Would you do it for nothing?"

"No way, Jose! he beamed, tugging on his small goatee, which was prematurely greying. The beard, along with long, straight hair and burning dark eyes, gave his face a faintly, saintly look.

On the other hand, he wore faded jeans, torn at the knees, Air Jordan's, a white sweatshirt with the letters CCCP in red and a New York Yankees baseball cap.

A saint packaged for the millennium.

Charles was a park denizen before he had the brazen young Guinevere. He used to come with a dignified old English Setter named Winston, who was very fond of beer. He preferred Budweiser.

He liked to lick the tops of cans, and there was always someone to give him a surreptitious snort or two. He held his beer well and the only stagger came as a result of his failing back legs.

He died last year and the loss was so painful to Charles he swore he'd never go through it again.

Six months ago he saw Guinevere at Animal Care and Control, where he volunteered, and he was hooked and adopted her. Most of his resurgent, happy state of mind came from this joyful, adoring creature.

Before he dish washed, he picked up rent money as a street performer doing impersonations of famous people, alive, dead, long dead and fictional.

Hamlet in the booth for the Super Bowl: 'To punt or not to punt.' Julius Caesar tossing off his recipe for salad as he expired: 'Et tu can enjoy a fine salad.' Lincoln's Gettysburg address, which turned out to be a rooming house, two blocks south of the battlefield. Karl and Groucho Marx swapping bawdy songs about the lumpen-proletariat. Moses parting his hair.

He decided to quit when he got punched in the nose for his zaniness: Jesus Christ as a New York cabbie, sporting a lop-sided yalmuke and kvetching about his lousy tips in a Brooklyn accent: 'I give good tips, I should get good tips.'

When he wasn't scrubbing plates he was working up new material, trying to break in at the comedy clubs, making the rounds of open mikes.

"Actually," he effused, "I have a girlfriend." He scuffed his Air Jordan's sacrilegiously along the ground. "Well, she's not exactly a girlfriend," he elucidated, less dazzled. "She's a girl who is a friend. But, who knows!"

"Good for you."

"She's beautiful," he declared, with the blissful, lunatic gaze of the love-struck. "She washes dishes too."

"Exciting."

"Yeah. We talk all the time when we're working together. She's from Argentina. Her English is very good. She wants to teach."

"Sounds good."

"Yeah. Never thought I'd get so impassioned over dirty dish water."

"God can really dish it out." I observed. "I suppose you guys will be spooning soon."

"Did you ever think of becoming a comedian?" Charles asked, making awful taking noises.

"No." I said, uplifted, never thinking anyone would go for these corny jokes.

Charles came back with professional finality: "Don't."

Ouch! The truth hurts.

I was itchy to move. Charles took off after his dog and I took a long stroll with Gustav up to Pacific Heights. I was drawn back to the Hayward's mansion, and with it in view, I could do some on the spot cogitating.

It was true what Dori had said. Mrs. Hayward was the enigma. She drank excessively, yet she had to be disciplined to crank out her mysteries. If her writing revealed anything of herself, it was too coded for me to grasp. Maybe, she wrote under a pseudonym in a different genre, like Romance. An author's first novels tend to be the most autobiographical. It was worth a shot to check the library.

The dilemma was how to meet her for a cozy tete-a-tete. She was not someone you 'accidently' bumped into on the street or shared a table with at a coffee shop. I needed some trickery. A decoy. A pretense. A charade. Who? Who had such a mind?"

"Who Gustav?" He tilted his head in trade mark dog fashion. "Who? Who? Who? He perked up his ears. "I know I sound just like an owl." Not that Gustav had ever seen an owl.

"An owl. An owl." I repeated, absentmindedly. "Yes! Yes! the horned rimmed glasses, the computer game brain. Could be, Gustav, could be." He wagged his tail, glad to be contributing to this brainstorm.

I was thinking of the park's computer wizardess and chess prodigy, the thirteen year old, Armbruster Jones. Her fame spread by classmates and friends who traveled through the park, and computer adults who had compared notes with her.

"How come your name is Armbruster?" I once asked her.

"I don't know," she answered.

"Is it after some relative?"

"I don't know," she answered.

"It's an odd name."

"I know," she answered.

The wizardess was not a conversational marvel.

It might seem silly to be thinking of enlisting the innocent mind of a thirteen-year-old in this duplicity. But then, I wasn't putting her on the payroll.

The idea had popped into my head after deliberate percolation, so there was a good reason for it, or maybe not. It was worth a try. Maybe, the girl in Armbruster could reach the girl in Robin Hayward.

I would pose the problem to her one morning, when she was out walking the family dog, Angel, the phlegmatic Rottweiler, before she went to school.

Angel looked like a killer, but he would keel over at Armbruster's command. She could be pretty bossy.

The library yielded nothing. Then I ran into Dori.

"You're crazy!" she lambasted me, when I explained my plan. "She's a child!"

"I thought," I said, suddenly feeling ridiculous, "that she could come up with some clever scheme. She invents those ingenious computer games."

Dori shook her head.

"It was an idea," I said, bowing to her judgement.

"Listen, lame-brain, why don't you just write to her."

"To Robin Hayward?"

"Sure. Why do you have to be so Byzantine?"

Why didn't I see this simple solution? That's why we need other people, to remind us how dumb we are.

"It's all a game to you, isn't it?" she said, contentiously.

"No, it isn't." I squirmed, biting on a thumbnail.

"What a gross habit!" she scolded.

"What's up, Dori?" she was more pesky than usual.

"Nothing's up!" she sagged a little.

"Bad day at the restaurant?"

"Always a bad day at the restaurant. A bunch of squawkin', gawkin' rudies!"

"You and Paul could be the disgruntled employees of the month."

"Well, Ill tell ya. I'd rather be sailing." Fatigue rimmed her eyes.

Switching tracks, I asked her what I could say to Robin Hayward in a letter. What would appeal to her as a woman?

"Tell her you're thinking of marrying Katherine."

"Be serious."

"I am. Don't tell me you never thought of it." she needled.

I thought of it.

"A man thinks of that."

"Then it's true." She didn't say it outrageously.

"Only in a general sense."

"Then make something up. That's what you wanted to do in the first place. I don't care." She suddenly sang: "I'm beat and I wanna soak my feet."

She soft-shoed away, and then yelled back: "Pretend you're the Mayor!"

I had to admit, this detective pose was wearing thin. I had as much detective in me, as the sun had ice. Even truth was vague.

The Haywards were insulated. Katherine's bruise, Hayward's hostility, even Robin Hayward's drinking sprees could be pretenses.

It crossed my mind that they could be playing a game. A morbid entertainment concocted to hoodwink someone or amuse themselves.

I bristled at the possibility.

How did it start? Hayward hiring me to find some obscure detail from Roman he then thought worthless. Then offering me more money, or the rest of it, to discover who knows what? And me naively accepting.

Katherine had a welt. Robin Hayward drank and her husband was a scoundrel. Roman was strange. Big deal.

As Dori said: Who cares?

Katherine was in the hospital.

She left a message asking me to come see her. It was night. I'd have to wait until tomorrow.

I berated myself for turning callous. If I had done something, even if it meant looking the fool, this wouldn't have happened.

I couldn't sleep. I played the message over and over, hoping to gauge from her voice how badly she was hurt. She sounded weak. But the fact that she was conscious and able to make the call was good news.

The message was short. It was hard to tell anything more.

I imagined scenes of her being beaten by Hayward, helpless and unprotected. It was an image that enraged me and had me pacing and cursing until my downstairs neighbor banged up from the sound of my heavy tread.

The blame was mine. It was in my lap and I walked away. Poor kid, I thought, as my feelings shifted from remorse, to concern, to pity for her.

A picture of a swollen, bandaged face developed in my disjointed mind.

I dozed off at four. After a glass of wine and distracting myself, mechanically doing one crossword puzzle after another. I took a series of long, slow deep breaths and drifted into sleep. Katherine was safe for the moment and there was nothing I could do to alter what had happened.

I hardly felt I had slept when I awoke at eight. I called in sick and took Gustav out for the morning walk.

I exchanged casual waves with the morning people spread around the park, their dogs happy to be out and dashing around, releasing all that pent-up, overnight energy. The owners always looked like statuary, as the dogs scrambled around them.

As visiting hours approached, my agitation increased. Gustav, my mobile biofeedback unit, also became more agitated. I sat down on the bench to read the news, but it wasn't important. I petted Gustav, to calm him and myself.

I was sticking to routine.

We took our usual ramble around the neighborhood and came back for breakfast. I doled out the dry, healthful dog food for him, poured out cereal for myself, glanced through the sports section, made coffee and drank it trying to concentrate on the daily puzzle. Time crept by.

I shaved, showered and dressed in nice clothes and after telling Gustav I'd be back later, went out the door. There was plenty of time to kill. I walked to St. Elizabeth's in the Avenues. An hour's stroll.

I got there early, thumbed through magazines, went to the drinking fountain several times, then took a walk around the grounds. Finally, I asked for Katherine Hayward at the desk. A friendly woman, wearing a volunteer's outfit, checked the roster, and told me the ward she was in.

I got off the elevator at the sixth floor and located the ward. It was locked. I pressed the intercom and a crackly voice said: "Yes?" I told the voice my name, that I was expected by Katherine. "Just a minute," the voice said.

Five minutes later, the door opened, and I was led into a large, bright "Day Room". I looked around at the shuffling, mumbling, crying, hyper-agitated and stone-still patients. It was a Psychiatric Ward.

The nurse ushered me to the far side of the room and left. Katherine was seated quietly by the window, in a pale, blue bathrobe.

"Katherine?" I said softly, stepping towards her.

She turned with weary slowness, looking at me with a doe-eyed reticence that barely acknowledged my presence. Her mind seemed to have jettisoned all burdensome thoughts.

"Just a show for the nurse," she winked, as I pulled up a chair.

"What!? You're not sick!?" I was confused and angry.

"Well, I was sick," she admitted, "but I'm better now."

"I spent the whole night worrying about you." I said, peeved, "thinking something terrible had happened."

"I'm sorry."

"Then, when I realized you were here, I thought you tried suicide." I paused, looking at her wrists. "You didn't try suicide, did you?"

"No."

"Now, I talk to you, and you act perfectly fine."

"Sorry," she repeated, guiltily, "but I had to get away from my house.

"But a hospital?"

"My shrink arranged it. I was flippin' out. Suicide. Homicide. It was toss-up. The way my stepfather treated my mother."

"Your stepfather!?"

"Yes, stepfather," she said, "and his threats against Philip and Philip's threats to him. And his temper." She shivered, as if a sudden, cold wind hit her. "There was danger in every room." She stared out the window. "I had to get out. Either they were drunk and screaming at each other, or just drunk."

I listened unmoved.

"To be honest, Katherine," I confessed to the back of her head, "after dealing with you and your family and friends for weeks, it's a muddle to me. I've even thought it might be a game."

She turned around abruptly and looked me square in the eye.

"How'd you know?" she said.

"What do you mean?"

"How'd you know it was a game?"

Her eyes were on mine. They were sincere. Or were they?

"Katherine, am I a dupe?"

"Yes!" she crowed sardonically. "We were all in on it. We all sat around the table one night, skimming through the phonebook and decided that Beamer Todd was an interesting name and let's have some fun with him. Jesus, Beamer!" she spat, "you should be in here, not me!"

I was not convinced.

"Where'd you get that welt?" I demanded again. "Level with me, or I'll assume you're play-acting and leave."

My ultimatum surprised her. She began fiddling with her bathrobe button, twisting it back and forth until it loosened and hung down on its threads.

"He hit me." she said quietly, not raising her head.

"Who? Your stepfather?"

She nodded.

"Why didn't you tell me before?"

"I couldn't, I was scared," she said, meekly.

"Okay," I consoled her, holding her hand and watching the tears flow.

I left the hospital, promising to return tomorrow evening. At the bus stop, I laughed to myself that I needed to carry a box of Kleenex with me from now on. It was a flippant though, but it satisfied my grim mood.

My thoughts rushed back to Hayward, my hatred rekindled. There was no doubt now.

I've had violent thoughts, but like most people, never act on them. There was, luckily, always a restraint. The conflict wound down, the cross word and the threatening gesture petered out.

I fantasized being Marlowe or Spade and cornering Hayward in a dim alley, telling him what a louse he was, and when he went for his gun, putting a bullet through his rotten heart. Or to slug him so savagely, he would be forever afraid of his own shadow, and slink off into oblivion.

But the real Hayward was a proper thug. Ensconced, untouchable inside a columned mansion.

The next morning, I crossed the park to pat Angel and talk to Armbruster.

"I got a puzzle for you Armbruster."

"Okay."

"Say you want to get someone out of a comfortable, formidable castle, but they don't want to come out."

"Blow it up," she said, off-handedly.

"Nothing destructive."

"Hostage?"

"Nothing that illegal," I added, "you want to make friends with the person, not have'em call the cops."

"Trick' em."

"How?"

"Wires."

"Wires?"

"You know. Computer. T.V. Telephone."

"Maybe no computer."

"Telephone."

Armbruster let me down. Not very inventive to use the phone. Mrs. Hayward could just hang up.

"Record an important person talking on T.V." Armbruster said. "Splice words together so it sounds like they're speaking to the person in the castle."

"Hm. Like the Mayor?"

"Sure."

"Not bad, Armbruster."

"Thanks," she said, yanking on Angel, and dragging him home.

It was a pleasure doing business with such a wholesomely devious mind. But her idea needed a little refinement. A recording could not anticipate Mrs. Hayward's responses or questions. I needed a real, live Mayor.

The mundane intrudes.

"Off to work we go" the Seven Dwarfs sang so animatedly. Work is always more fun when you're a cartoon character in a cell. But, then, I should be more cheerful, for I was in a cell, too. For eight hours a day. Amid a steel grey array of metal cabinets, getting cabinet fever.

It drained my spirit, but was not taxing enough to keep me from mulling on the Haywards. I slammed my way through the day.

What is the sound of one filing cabinet drawer slamming, when one's brain has already gone dead? I was no longer captured by Zen, I was more like the prisoner of Zen-Duh. If only Charles were here to catch my act, he would change his tune. He could do a great Zombie.

Eureka!

Two disparate thoughts had collided and lit up my dimming brain. Charles as Mayor. A natural. A challenge to his talent. He couldn't resist. He could play the Mayor on the phone.

I hope he had the ham to imitate a Jewish Mayor.

I apologized to Gustav for taking him out so briefly, just a quick turn around the block. When I came back from my visit to the hospital, I told him, we'd spend some time in the park.

He didn't like being shunted aside for some female, but he took it like the manly dog he is. Besides, what could he do about it?

After a bit of last-ditch face licking, to make me change my mind, he four-legged it acceptingly behind the futon to await, my hoped for, speedy return.

Katherine was in a wheelchair, clowning around as if she were in the Indy 500. She made revving noised as she zipped around her howling fellow patients. Hilariously howling, I should say.

The staff was smiling indulgently.

The prevailing tension had briefly given way to fun. A crescendo of cheers accompanied Katherine as she zig-zagged around the room, and then lapsed into silence, when she stopped. The patients drew back into their own worlds, the spaces between them immense.

"Well, I see you're having a good time," I smiled down at her face, flushed and panting from exertion.

"Whew." she gasped, "I'm out of shape."

I didn't say anything.

She got up out of the wheelchair and leaned back limply on the sofa. "I didn't think wheeling could be such hard work." Her breath settled to a slight wheeze.

"It roused the patients," I complimented her.

"Things are awfully dull here."

"What's your mother's number?" I interjected as painlessly as I could.

"My mother's ...number?" she stumbled.

"Yes, her telephone number."

She gave it to me.

"You want to know why?" I asked.

There was a glint of interest in her eyes, but it dimmed.

"No," she said, "not now."

"How long are you going to be here?"

"I don't know, no place to go," she said, rubbing the hem of her bathrobe.

"Don't you have any money?"

"Not my own. I'm on allowance," she laughed, self-mockingly.

"Can't you ask your mother?"

"Don't want to," she answered, with girlish stubbornness.

"What a pickle, heh?"

"What a pickle," she agreed, giggling.

"How'd you like to be Mayor for a day?" I inveigled Charles. "You'd be good at it."

True to my word, Gustav and I were out in the park. It wasn't cold. By park standards, it was a balmy evening. A trace of wind. Many regulars were still out.

Charles smiled broadly and stared myopically, an excellent mugging. He spoke with the bluff familiarity of Mayor Abraham: "Let me be blunt, my fellow citizens. As my beloved Bubby would say:

'Don't hide from the bad.'"

"Well done," I congratulated Charles, "it sounds just like him."

"Thanks, he's not too hard."

I outlined my plan to him, giving him an opportunity to help a lovely damsel in distress. Putting it in those terms made it hard to refuse, but he also wanted to see if he could pull it off. Professional vanity.

We made arrangements for tomorrow evening.

When I got home, I phoned Paul, and he agreed to come by, mainly, he said, to make sure neither of us ended up in jail.

It was a restless day at work. I did my mindless filing and worked out a script for Charles. We'd spend some time going over it before making the call.

There was the possibility that Robin Hayward would not be home, or not answer the phone, and we would get an answering machine. I called Katherine at the hospital, and with a background din of a blaring T.V. and a screaming patient, she told me her mother rarely went out at night, if at all.

She did like people over and wouldn't answer the phone if there were guests. But otherwise, she would pick up the phone before the machine clicked in. On weeknights, like tonight, she watched old movies in her bedroom. That was the number I had.

It sounded promising and nerve-wracking at the same time. I was plunging into something I knew nothing about, and it behooved me to take it a step at a time.

The outcome of each step was unpredictable. Being raw in these matters, I didn't know how people would react to what I was throwing at them, or what unseen consequences were waiting for me.

All I felt I was trying to do, in this roundabout way, was to gain the confidence of Robin Hayward, or at least start swimming downstream, past the rapids of confusion.

We ate cheese, munched chips and drank ale, to relax and fortify ourselves.

"What if she knows the Mayor well enough to know it's not him?" questioned Paul.

"Hang up." I said. I looked over at Charles. "If anytime you think she's wise, hang up. Don't dally."

"She's liable to call the police," said Paul.

"She shuns publicity," I corrected. "Remember."

"Right."

"She'll think it was someone playing a joke on her, or at worse, a crank."

"With her number?"

"Which she can change."

"What if she's drunk?" suggested Charles.

"What if she's out cold?" Paul egged on.

"What if she's not a she?"

I cut into their badinage.

"Didn't you hear the bell?"

"What bell?" they asked in unison, listening for it.

"The school bell," I explained. "High School is over."

"Mr. Principal! Mr. Principal!" Charles cried, waving his hand desperately over his head. "Can I go the bathroom?"

"Okay. Okay." I got the hint. "But listen," I added, trying not to sound severe. "This is serious and I know you know it is. It may work. It may not work. Let's give it a shot."

"Okay."

"You ready, Charles?"

"Ready!" he saluted smartly.

"Now remember to throw in all the personal stuff, especially the dog names."

"Gotcha!"

Charles took a deep breath and pushed the phone buttons. He cleared his throat. He hummed. He drummed his fingers on the table. His free hand went palm up. 'nothin', it meant. He tapped his foot. "No answer." he said, disappointed, "maybe she ..." he stopped short and made a circle of his thumb and forefinger and aimed it at us.

"Yes. Hello, Mrs. Hayward." He said brightly into the phone, struggling to get into the Mayor's voice. He coughed and rasped, as if to show an incipient cold. Very clever. "Yes. Hello, Mrs. Hayward." His voice was straightening out. Yes. Do you recognize my voice?"

A pause.

"No. No. He's dead, and I'm no angel," he bantered. "What if I said my Bubby reads all your books."

A pause.

"Yes. It's me. Or I think it's me. It could be fa, sol, la, ti or do," he laughed.

A pause.

"Yes, I used to be a standup comedian, many years ago, now you know why I quit."

A pause.

"Why thank you, that's very kind." Charles basked in the compliment. "How's your family? Your daughter, Katherine and your husband?"

A long pause.

"She is? I'm so sorry to hear that. The rest will do her good." Charles looked sad and took another deep breath. "The reason I called you, Mrs. Hayward, is to see if you would do a big favor to the city and to me, and of course to Bubby."

A pause.

"Yes, I know you don't do much traveling. But it will. ...he Hello? Hello?

A pause.

"Yes. Hello." He clamped his hand over the mouthpiece and turned to us. "She dropped the phone." He spoke into the phone again. "By the way, how are your Bichons, Gretel and Maria?"

A pause.

"How do I know? Ah, a political secret. As Bubby said to me, when I asked her how old she was, 'secrets are meant to be secrets.' Charles made another O.K. sign with his fingers and gave us an emphatic wink. "Yes, I love dogs too. That's what my call is all about."

A pause.

"Yes, dogs are wonderful."

A pause.

"And very loving, yes. Let me get to the point," he interrupted, with a noiseless sigh. "Some of your fans are staging a dog show in one of local parks in honor of 'Pooch', your wonderful dog in the college mysteries." He stopped a moment to listen. "They asked me to ask you if you would be their judge?"

A pause.

"No, it's not ridiculous." Sweat was collecting on Charles' face I opened the window wider, to cool down the room. "You have devoted readers. No, you can't refuse. Would you rather do it or get a stern lecture from Bubby about donating yourself for the public good?

A brief pause.

"So would I." Charles closed his eyes, he was fatiguing. "When? Next Saturday. Noon. Descartes Park."

A brief pause.

"Yes, I'll try to stop by if my schedule permits, but no promises. Yes, you too, Mrs. Hayward, and thanks."

Charles put the phone in its cradle and kept his hand on it, as if to make sure it stayed down.

"Great job!" I said.

"I entirely concur."

Charles looked at Paul and me with indecision. "I just thought of something. What if she decides to call the Mayor?"

"We're out of luck."

"How did she act? Did she sound drunk?" Paul asked. "Maybe, she won't even remember."

"She seemed very flattered. She swallowed the whole spiel."

"Did she sound drunk?" Paul pressed.

"I couldn't tell. She wasn't slurry." Charles curled his lips. "You know that old joke: 'I didn't know she drank until I saw her sober.'"

"Do you think we should make refresher call?" I asked.

"A confirmation call, you mean?" said Charles.

"Yes."

"What do you think, Paul?"

"Let's just leave it." he said, relieved that the cops weren't at this moment breaking down the door.

"Okay! That's that!"

"Now, we set up a dog show."

"Sounds fun," Paul said, cutely.

Setting up a dog show turned out to be easier than I thought. A stack of flyers, an emcee (Charles), and dog treats as prizes. Categories would be simple: Biggest, Smartest, Dumbest, Most Obedient and Best Trick. I handed out and tacked up flyers and it was done.

The Braves were in town for three televised games, so there was a sweet diversion from the insidious inroads the Hayward family problems were making into my life. Ice Cream, Beer and a Ballgame were just the ticket. Baseball was my meditation.

Three innings of bliss were shattered by the insistent ringing of the phone. The machine did the work. The message came, someone listened, then hung up.

My experience told me that calculated guesses as to who was calling and why would be wrong. So I shut down that part of my brain to watch the art of pitching as demonstrated by Greg Maddox. The man who could paint corners the way Rembrandt painted faces, and got paid a lot more.

The poor Giants' bats were feeble against him, but then, so were every other team's hitters he pitched against.

I scooped another bowl of ice cream, mocha almond fudge, glugged Sierra Nevada Pale Ale, and tried to ignore the commercials. But, no remote, no mercy.

The phone rang again. This time I was more interested. The message ran. The caller hung up. Now, I could probably rule out a wrong number.

I turned down the ringer to mute and watched three more scoreless innings. It was a tense and engrossing game. But I did occasionally glance from screen to telephone to catch a flashing light. There was none.

Who was I worried about? Dori? Katherine? Hayward out for me? It's amazing how your imagination can get fired up over a mystery. The invention of doom is automatic. Why I didn't think it was something good, I don't know, but I didn't.

A person wouldn't leave a message because it was fixed and recallable, if he or she had something to hide. Or if he or she wasn't in a fixed spot to be called back. Or, they just didn't like talking to machines. So, it didn't seem urgent.

It was the ninth inning, a beautiful one to nothing game. Maddox went out for a pinch hitter in the top of the ninth, and now a rookie lefty was coming in to face Bonds with Mueller on first and two out.

Why a rookie in this critical situation? The only thing I could think of was that since the Braves had such an enormous lead in their division, they could afford to give the Rook a chance to pitch in a pressure situation and test his mettle. Although Maddox might not be too happy if he blew it.

I heard the message phone engage, as the lefty narrowly missed the outside corner with two sweeping curves. Bonds barely checked his swings. The next pitch, if he didn't want a runner in scoring position, would have to be on the plate. I was tempted to pick up the phone.

The green light went on. The message was recorded. The caller hung up.

The light blinked tantalizingly, while Bonds wagged his bat at the upcoming pitch. It was high and inside. Bonds laid off, but the umpire called it a strike. Bonds stepped out with a look of innocent disbelief on his face. The fans erupted with boos.

He stepped back in, composed and steady. He was set for the outside pitch again. He drove it into the hole vacated by the shortstop with the shift on. It was nifty piece of hitting. It was not a heroic home run, but it put the tying run on second. A single would tie the game.

The lefty stayed in, even with Kent coming up. The rookie had shown some cool by not trying to blow the fastball by Bonds, which would have been fatal.

Kent kept the suspense going by hitting a screaming liner past the third baseman that hooked foul by two feet. Then, on a two and two count, he blooped a ball into short center. The second baseman and the centerfielder converged, but it looked like it might drop in. At the last moment the centerfielder dove and plucked it out of the grass. The ump's arm flew up with the out sign and the game was over.

The fans, who were crazily cheering a minute before, were now dejectedly filing out. The Braves celebrated joyously on the field, pounding the back of the rookie, and the Giants disappeared through the dugout.

Tomorrow was really another day in baseball. The Giants could outslug the Braves 14-13 and there would be elation for them.

The ice cream was polished off, the last of the beer raised to the lips and savored. A fraction of time contemplated.

It was Philip Roman. He wanted to talk to me, Dori told him I was someone he could trust. He begged my pardon and said he would be in the park next evening to meet me, if I didn't mind. I didn't.

I put on Bach's Goldberg Variations and sat quietly. Gustav came over and looked up at me, eager for attention. I slowly stroked his head and back, sleepily pondering the vicissitudes of baseball and life.

To file B, or not to file B, that is the ultimate question of the tormented filer. Or maybe, to defile B, which is probably illegal in most states.

My brain had turned to mush, in what I called, with tortured levity, my 'Mushroom.'

Gustav and I drifted into the park around six. I spied Philip Roman sitting in the grass, off to the side, away from the dogs. He seemed bulkier.

As I got closer, I could see he was wearing a sweatshirt under the flowered Hawaiian shirt. He also wore a dark woolen cap. If his eyes appeared glazed and his demeanor remote, at least he remembered to stay warm.

We exchanged perfunctory greetings, he patted Gustav, who sat down between us, and with a pained voice, he told me Katherine was not his child. He had been deceived.

"I know we promised to keep it a secret, because I had cold feet and abandoned her when she told me she was pregnant." He tore at a blade of grass. "This is the first time I've seen her in ten years," he said, ruefully. "Now that I look at her, I don't see any resemblance. Do you?"

I didn't. He was slight, dark complexioned, with close-set eyes. She was curved and blonde, with wide-spaced blue eyes.

"Not on the surface."

"Hayward thinks I'm doing a Bio about her, but it's really a pretext to spend time together. She says she's forgiven me for vanishing." His expression changed from moping despair to alert concentration.

"Hayward's jealous, or afraid I'm going to write something mean-spirited. He's either protective of her, or protective of her book sales."

Roman caught his breath. He sized it up well. He was not the dumbbell the Pet Ministry compulsion may him appear to be.

"Why did she do it? Why did she lead me on?" He looked at the past, but it was if he could only see a void. "I just found out two days ago.", he said, with a shudder of disbelief. "For twenty years I thought she was my daughter, and out of the **blue** ..."

"Maybe she is."

"What?"

"Maybe she is your daughter."

"I dunno," he said, already distancing himself from the possibility. "She said it and I believe her." He was adamant. "Did she want to spite me? I thought of it, but that's not her way. She's more convoluted than that. This grand deception could be just like her."

"How'd Hayward get into the picture?"

"It must have been the same time, ten years ago. She met him on a cruise. Katherine was in summer camp. Here I was thinking she was my daughter, all the time she was **really ....**"

He was slipping back into self-pity. I tried to buck him up: "You don't know."

He wiped his eyes and came back to my question. "He evidently swept her off her feet, if that is possible. They married a month later."

"It must have been pretty confusing for Katherine." He nodded heavily. "Did he know who she was?"

"Who?"

"Did Hayward know she was successful and wealthy writer?"

"Don't know." He looked at me quizzically. "Do you think he was after a rich woman?"

I shrugged, as if to mean, 'Why not?'

"But he's been with her for ten years. He didn't bilk her and run off."

He had a point.

Paul came by. Big Bear jumped into my lap and Gustav rose up in protest and tried to displace her. I lifted Big Bear to the side, apologized, and made room for Gustav.

"What's up, guys?" Paul was chipper. It must be a boon day for him.

"Alright," I said, while Roman eyes him warily.

"Got trouble?" he asked, watching Roman tear up a clump of grass.

Roman searched my face for a sign of Paul's reliability. I nodded. Roman filled him in, eager to unburden himself.

"Sure is a tangle," Paul said, and pressed him on some legal niceties. It appeared Roman was alone at sea in a very big ocean.

Roman threw down some more torn grass, propped himself up with a miserable sigh, and walked off with a sad-eyed, 'thanks.'

"Too bad," Paul sympathized. "It must be quite a blow."

"I bet."

"Got something to show you." He pulled a folded newspaper from his back pocket. "Did you see this?" He pointed to an article and handed it to me.

The heading was: 'Mayor To Host Literary Gathering.' It read: 'The Mayor's Office sent out two dozen invitations yesterday to the city's literary luminaries for a dinner at the renovated City Hall, Saturday, May 21 at 8PM.

"The Mayor, who is a voracious reader and a strong advocate of the arts, intends this event to kick off his Read More Program.

'Among the invitees are Luis Sanchez, Poet of the Mission, William Jones, Historical Novelist, and Robin Hayward, Mystery Writer Extraordinaire.

'As usual with the Mayor's events, anyone with $10 to plunk down, may stand in line at City Hall for tickets.

'As Bubby, the Mayor's yiddish grandmother said: 'To Read is to Open the Doors of the Mind.'

"Oops." I said.

"Let's hope she was drunk and forgot the whole dog show thing."

"Let's."

"Should we cancel?"

"Yes. If she shows up, we'll tell her it was a hoax."

"She's not going to show up now," Paul maintained.

"As the Mayor said at his swearing in: 'Tread softly and carry a big shtick.' His favorite president was Teddy Roosevelt, you know."

"I know."

"And did you know that the Teddy Bear was named after him?"

"Yes, I did know that."

"And did you know that a twelve-inch replica of the Golden Gate Bridge has gone up fifty cents?"

"No, I didn't know that."

"Aha!"

"You're just trying to be saucy," I said to Dori as she chucked me under my five o'clock shadow.

She peered at me. "You look like a sad-eyed hound."

"Just thinking."

"Jeez," she suddenly blew on her fingers, "don't you ever shave? I have rope burn."

"I shaved this morning."

"What time zone?"

"Ha."

"You know you've got some grey sprouting," she observed, minutely inspecting my face.

"I know."

"It doesn't make you look distinguished," she decided, "it makes you look old."

"Thanks."

She gave me a light punch on the arm. "Just teasing, Beamer babe. Don't get so uptight."

"Who? Me? Uptight?"

She backed up and sat herself down, yoga style.

"Where are the dogs?"

"Home."

"They must make a hell of a racket. Must drive your neighbors batty."

"They're quiet at home. It's only when they see all the other dogs that they go ballistic." She changed her tone. "Why are you disconsolate?"

"I'm not disconsolate. Just thinking." I brought her up-to-date on the newspaper article. "We're canceling the show."

"Oh, don't do that!" Dori pleaded.

"Why? Were you going to enter?"

"It sounded like fun and I was going to enter all four dogs," she said, determinedly.

"What category?"

"Most obnoxious. Why don't you have that one?"

"You'd be a shoo-in. It wouldn't be fair to the other contestants. Maybe, next time."

"Oh, please."

"You know, we were only doing this to lure Robin Hayward here. "Now," I reminded her, "there is a conflict."

"You're still trying to get her? She laughed with a rich appreciation of ineptitude. "What muttonheads! What amateurs!"

"Thanks for the vote of confidence."

"I'll do it. She knows me, I think."

"What will you do?" I asked, feeling like a failure.

"I'll think of something," she said, confidently. "Something not so ridiculous."

She popped up like a happy piece of toast and trotted off, waving backwardly with her hand.

"Well, Gustav," I turned to my steadfast dog, who still looked up to me, "shall we take a walk around the block?"

With these magic words, Gustav was up and wagging his tail. I leashed him at the edge of the park and we crossed the street back to where the humans ruled.

As we walked and stopped and walked and stopped, while Gustav sniffed and peed and sniffed and peed, we passed the usual street denizens and familiar workers flooding home from their jobs.

It was the very ordinariness and everydayness of life, I realized, that must be appreciated and relished. To be like Gustav, when every time is the first time.

I sat through a 9-3 drubbing of the Giants by the Braves. The Giants kept threatening to come back, but were stymied in three straight innings by double play ground balls. Atlanta's pitching was just too good.

I sometimes did with baseball what I often did with football. Turn the sound off and put on some classical music, usually Mozart or Bach. When the commercials came on, I'd shut my eyes and listen restfully to the music.

I could get by without most of the commentary, since so much statistical, game score and situational information was flashed on the screen.

Before hitting the sack, I read some chapters of P.G. Woodehouse's Jeeves stories, which were wildly funny in the droll English way, and gave me some good belly laughs.

I lay in bed, staring out the window at the several stars and planets that could still be seen despite the city lights. With my eyeglasses off, every distant light became two blurry ones, like an impressionistic rendering. A soft haloing effect enhanced the whole image, and it was quite beautiful.

Occasionally, a plane would move across the sky, its lights fuzzy and glowing, like a giant spaceship trekking to a distant galaxy.

I didn't think of work, that would be non-thinking.

I started a conversation with myself that I had fruitlessly pursued before. What was going on with the Haywards and Roman? If there was something going on.

My brain is not the classically deductive one, which leaves one in awe of its brilliance. It is a pleasure to follow Sherlock Holmes and Nero Wolfe with their cogently assimilating minds, neatly dissecting the events, and nabbing the culprit without breaking a sweat.

Real life is sloppy.

Each time I washed my hands of them and went back to my uncomplicated life, something would happen to compel me to sink back into the morass.

I secretly hoped Dori would fail, too.

I wanted to keep my feet planted on the rough concrete of my own neighborhood. The machinations of the rich should stay among the rich. My worries were more vital: would my money last the month?

Now that I was working as a file clerk, it put into perspective my notions of being a detective. It was a laughable fantasy. A brief fling at the exotic life at least satisfied one of my curiosities: the rich were as nutty as everyone else.

I awoke the next morning with no magical solutions, just another plodding day ahead. I did by ablutions and brought Gustav to the park. He did his duty and then battled a blackbird who kept dive-bombing him. The nestlings were chirping away in the trees and to their parents he was the enemy.

The sky was grey. It was foggy, windy and chilly. A beautiful San Francisco morning. To me, weather meant movement: wind, rain, snow, fog. The static warmth that polluted the air and set people's hearts aflutter, belonged down south.

Gertrude, the white German Shepherd, rushed up to me, and dropped her ball at my feet. She looked from the ball to me and then waited rigidly alert until I threw the slimy thing.

She dashed after it and snatched it from the air on the first bounce. She went in search of another thrower.

I had learned something watching a dog chase a ball.

An experienced ball chaser will run faster than the moving ball, overtake it, and wait for the ball to come her, rather than lunging after it and have it keep bouncing out of reach.

Once, my hat flew off in a gust of wind and I started running after it. It was a futile chase. Each time I bent to reach for it, it blew further away. I remembered the dog. I raced ahead of the hat and waited victoriously as it came to me.

It never occurred to me that I could learn from a dog. It made me realize there were other attributes we admired that we should not be embarrassed to emulate: perseverance, not holding a grudge, living in the moment, uninhibited goofiness, oneness, many qualities we tend to overlook as only doglike. It reminds us that we too are animals, maybe with bigger, broader brains, but still, animals.

Three or four dogs were initiating Rachel, a small, torpedo-like Staffordshire mix to the park. She loved being chased, and would stir up all the dogs with her energy when she came to play. In park parlance, she was called a dogalyst.

Rachel, and her owners, Pete and Mary, had recently moved from L.A. and were still trying to acclimate themselves to the sometimes cold, gloomy days. For the dog it was heaven. No hot sun to sap her, fewer bugs to chew her up and lots of regular playmates.

For dog owners all the weather forecast they needed was: Good Dog Weather or Bad Dog Weather, it would certainly simplify the job for meteorologists.

What people didn't like to see in the park was what was happening near the benches. A man was berating his Boxer for not coming fast enough when he called him. The dog was still a puppy and cowed and slunk slowly to where the owner was sitting. He hit the dog across its muzzle, while the dog looked up uncomprehendingly, not knowing what it had done wrong.

It wasn't sure-fire, but you can form an opinion about a person by the way he treats his dog, or the way he responds to Gustav. Owning a dog is like a crash course in human nature.

The meanness, the misunderstandings of a dog's motives, the paralyzing fear that turns into vicious kicking, the need to control, the need to show one's toughness through a dog, the savage teasing, all expose people.

Mary went over to the man with the Boxer. I couldn't hear what she said, but the man began spraying her with curses, grabbed his dog by the collar and tried to sic the dog on her.

The dog lay flat, refusing to move. We went towards them and the man seeing us, yanked the dog to its feet, and still hurling slurs, left the park, dragging the unwilling dog.

A man with a cell phone called Animal Care and Control and gave them the location and a description.

People probably reveal themselves more truthfully with dogs than with God. You may think you can hide from God, but you know you can't hide from your dog.

When I got home, I called the agency and told them I would no longer be coming in for the filing job. They accepted it. I had done it for weeks and had reached my limit. It was an easy job to fill, so there was no problem. I was to call early in the morning if I wanted to check on a new assignment. I thanked them.

My rent was paid for this month, and with my forthcoming check for the next month, too. The sudden, brief freedom was exhilarating. I had a week or two before the gnawing worry of running out of money hit me.

I put on the CD of Duke Ellington's exuberant performance at Newport and danced around the room to the crescendoing rhythms. Gustav picked up on the mood and wagged his tail and wriggled his body in accompaniment. He looked up at me with bright, anticipating eyes.

"The Big Park?" I said to him, which meant, Golden Gate, his most favorite. Gophers galore and a passel of pigeons.

We walked through the Panhandle, with Gustav sniffing and clawing at the ground every fifty feet and stalking the pigeons by hiding under the benches. It was a slow trip.

Golden Gate was a beautiful, open, man-made park which made you feel you were out of the city. We walked to the Band Shell Plaza, where the band gave a free concert every Sunday, year 'round. Where the DeYoung Art Museum and the Academy of Sciences framed a wide space that included benches, a fountain and flocks of pigeons Gustav could spend the rest of his life hassling.

We passed by the Japanese Gardens up to Stowe Lake, my favorite spot. It was really too small to be called a lake. You could walk around it in a brisk fifteen minutes. But it had ducks and geese and pedal boats and an island in the middle with a waterfall. There was a section where it felt like a forest, lush with trees and grasses. It was simple pleasure to sit on a bench, facing the still water and soak up the tranquility.

Since I grew up in Brooklyn, I was not big on nature. We had never been formally introduced. To me wild animals were pigeons and alley cats. Grass was the stuff that stuck between the blocks of concrete.

I don't think it awakened anything primordial in me, but I felt serene watching the ducks drifting by, the sinuously rippling water, the swaying loftiness of the trees, the deep, rich, blanketing greenness of it all.

I contemplated a billion years of Earth in a fraction of a second, before restlessness got its usual hold on me and had me walking.

We walked around the lake to get a head-on view of the waterfall. While Gustav watched the ducks, I watched the rushing, falling, musical water.

Wouldn't you know it?

Dori Four and Mrs. Hayward were coming towards me from the other direction, two Bichons capering ahead. Gustav ran forward, recognizing Dori. She nuzzled him and turned to smile at me, jerking her head to show she had bagged a Hayward.

Mrs. Hayward was wearing a wide-brimmed yellow sun bonnet which concealed her eyes. She began throwing pieces of bread to the quarreling ducks and swooping, bullying seagulls. She didn't recognize me, or at least there was no acknowledgement. After all, she was bombed the last time I saw her.

"Hey, Beamer!" Dori greeted me, and Mrs. Hayward turned to look. She stared for a moment, then went back to feeding the birds. "How's it going? Whatcha doing here?" Dori was surprised, but glad to see me.

"A little excursion with Gustav."

"Not workin'?"

"I quit."

Dori showed the barest disappointment, but then waved me closer. "Say hello to Mrs. Hayward," she whispered.

Mrs. Hayward was smiling at her Bichons, who were trying to cajole Gustav the birder, to play with them.

"You remember Beamer Todd," she spoke to Mrs. Hayward's profile.

"I'm pleased to meet you again," she said formally.

"Beamer's a friend from the dog park."

"Noh, really," she said, politely, not remembering that I had dined at her house, and tossing a handful of crumbs into the water.

"I'm happy to see you, again," I told her, with forced graciousness. "I've read some of your books." I didn't say 'scanned', that would be tactless. They are well-done."

"Thank you," she said with modesty. I guess she knew they were not literary gems.

"I saw Katherine in the hospital." I didn't sit it out of callousness, or to probe, but because I didn't know what else to say.

"How is she?"

"They call her the Chairwoman of the Ward."

"How humorous."

"I was telling Robin about the dog show," Dori chimed in, the dummy, "she can't come, she has a hairdressing appointment. Don't you?"

"Yes, I do," she smiled, "please accept my apologies."

I gave Dori a sharp look. "It's O.K."

"She said maybe another time."

Dori, you're a fink. "Sure."

They turned their attention to the dogs, who were quietly playing, Gustav and Greta and Maria were enjoying each other's company.

I didn't want to hang around and be teased again by Dori over the dog show. I called to Gustav. "We're going to the Band Shell," I informed them, trying to corral Gustav.

"What! Already?" said Dori.

"Yes. Time to go." I began walking away, expecting my loyal dog to follow. He was in no hurry. He was getting smothered in pets by Dori and looked at me as if to say, 'Why can't you do that?' He definitely liked women. They seemed to have a touch that men lacked, less rough in the rubbing department and more thorough in the love department.

It was rare to have a woman whack him on the rump the way I did. He had it good and wasn't about to disengage.

"C'mon, Gustav," I called, half-heartedly.

He yawned.

"Thanks, Dori."

She got the message and gave Gustav a gentle push in my direction. He pranced over happily and then remembering where he was, he continued his pigeon patrol.

Going back was a slower trip. Partly, it was because Gustav was tired. He was ten. Partly, it was because he knew we were heading out of the park and was reluctant to leave. He called on all his Beamer manipulating skills to let him stay. Stopping short. Laying down. The 'please can I stay stare', the 'I'm so tired crumple.'

When we finally meandered our way home, it was mid-afternoon. There were no messages. There usually weren't. It was a good time to take a snooze. Gustav went behind the futon and fell asleep instantly. I put on a Mozart piano concerto and drifted off.

I woke with a start, sweating. The music was off. Gustav was barking at the door. Was it morning? The disorientation from the nap had me guessing.

The barking stopped and Gustav came trotting up alongside me and sat down looking very pleased with himself. He evidently had done a good job keeping the kids from running through the hall.

It was almost five and I called Dori, anxious to hear about her time with Mrs. Hayward. She answered the phone and I could hear a yapping commotion in the background.

"So, what's new?" I asked hopefully.

"She's morose."

"How did you get her to go with you?"

"Simple. I just reminded her that we had made plans for a walk."

"So you were taking advantage of a drunk," I joked.

"It's not funny, Beamer," she admonished me, "I think she really is an alcoholic."

"You said she was morose?"

"Yes. She barely spoke. So if you want some true confession, you'll have to wait,"

"Did she say anything revealing?" I asked, confounded.

"She mumbled something about her husband's gambling, but I didn't press her."

"Anything else?"

"You know, the usual rich girl things. Clothes. Maids. Paris.

"I thought you fired your maid."

Dori ignored me. "She's a nice person. I feel sorry for her."

"So, you're friends?"

"Sort of."

The park that evening was sparsely populated. A chill wind was blowing strongly and if dogs and owners came, it was for a short stay. I was dressed warmly and braved it. Gustav liked being out-of-doors. After all, he was stuck inside most of the day, without a view of the street. I had no back yard and my estate was only in my imagination.

Tall Paul was seated on a bench, feverishly working on his notebook. Big Bear was wrestling silently with a Chocolate Lab named Lucy in front of his feet. He was in shirt sleeves, oblivious to dogs and weather. I asked him how the poetry readings were going.

"Not bad. Not bad," he said, scribbling down a last thought. He looked up. "It's so hard to tell. Most of the others who show up are poets and they're usually absorbed in their own work."

He sounded unappreciated.

"There's respect, but no fiery interest," he declared.

"So, what did you expect?" I clued him in. "For them to hoist you on their shoulders and carry you around the room?" Poets can be a suffocatingly snobby bunch.

"I thought at least they should have given me a torch," he said comically, realizing his bloating self-expansion.

It must be tough to admit being a poet. It doesn't have the cachet of a real profession. Yet, its practitioners are shamelessly self-important, convinced they are illuminating the dull, clouded minds of the rabble. And, the more you are not listened to, the duller the nonreaders become.

"So, what are you writing about?"

"Revolution!" he boomed.

"Revolution?" I said caustically. "The only revolutions still talked about in this city are the ones comparing revs in luxury sports cars. We are in a world of things, not ideas. Wood and metal, not flesh. The big green, not the wild blue. The only God is the one in gardener."

"Whew! You should be a poet."

"No way! Besides it's more pontification than poetry."

"You'd make a fine pontiff."

"You mean Pontiffany."

"He does sparkle, doesn't he?"

"I'd sure like to ride in the Popemobile. I understand the dashboard lights stay on even when you get to Heaven."

"Well, I'm freezing." Paul was hugging himself in a non-poetic way. He jogged off, with Big Bear leading the way.

I whiled away the short evening listening to Brahms Trios and doing crossword puzzles. I tried to read, but nothing held my attention.

I stretched out and listened to a couple of old-time radio shows on the radio. The first was Burns and Allen. By the middle of the second, The Shadow, with Orson Welles as the first voice of the Shadow, I was asleep.

A low rapping woke me. It came from outside my door. Gustav was not in a frenzy of barking, as he usually is when someone even brushes the door. The light was still on. The clock was at 12:05.

There's an old joke I tell when I haven't slept well. I tell people a woman was banging on my door all night. Finally, I had to get up and let her out.

Tonight, there was a woman trying to get in.

The peephole distorted face of Katherine Hayward peered anxiously back at me. I opened the door and she rushed by, perching herself on the edge of the lounger.

"He's after me!" she gasped, and fussed inside her purse. "Look!" She gestured at me to come over and look at the paper she was holding. I tried to act composed, and walked slowly over to her.

"Here!" She pushed the shaking paper into my hand. It read: '50,000 is what I need, or else you bleed.' I must lead a sheltered life, because I'd never seen a message like this before.

"He means it!" Katherine grabbed the paper from my hand and stuffed it back into her purse.

"Who?" I asked, my stomach churning, as if I didn't have an idea. I was still trying to digest the sudden intrusion and the threatening letter.

"Who!? she barked. "Who do you think? My stepfather!" Visions of the bruiser froze my brain for a moment. A disastrous sense that he was trailing her and ready to pound on my door, made me very uneasy.

"Did you see him lately?" I asked, trying to mask my own apprehension and at the same time, allay it.

"It came in the mail," she squeaked.

"Listen. Listen. Listen." My voice attempted to sound pacifying. "No one's after you here. Try to relax. You're safe. How 'bout some cheese and beer? It'll do you good. Take some deep breaths."

It worked. She flopped back into the lounger. "Thanks," she said, a smile trying to break through.

"Take off your coat. Put your feet up." I tried to sound jolly and infect her with my jolliness.

She looked critically around my studio. I was not a conscientious cleaner. "You need a housekeeper," she informed me. Although it was information that didn't seem congruent or even appreciated, at least her thoughts were off the letter for a while. You never know when your slobbiness may be a benefit.

Her panic had subsided. She nibbled on cheese and sipped beer, while appraising my taste in paintings, books, furniture, drapes and wall color. I nibbled on my fingernails.

"You can stay here tonight," I suggested. "Unless you want to take a cab back to Pacific Heights."

"No. I told you already. They're ruthless."

"Okay."

"I'll sleep in the chair."

"You can have the bed," I offered, "I'll take the chair. It flattens out."

"No. I'm smaller. It'll be cozy."

"Well, I'll just sit up awhile, while you fall asleep." I could see the beer had made her sleepy. I gave her a blanket. "Not to worry."

She gave me a shy smile and went into the bathroom. "Do you have any pajamas!?" I did have an extra pair and slipped through the door. She showered and came out looking fresh despite her ordeal. She snuggled into the chair. I put the cover over her. Quite the domestic scene.

"Music helps you relax. Do you like classical?"

"Sure." she chirped.

"Anything special?"

"You choose."

I bent to my CD rack to pick out something. Mendelssohn, Sweet music. When I turned back she was sleeping. She looked comfortable curled up in the lounger. She trusted me and accepted my protection. I hoped I merited it.

Mendelssohn's piano music played quietly while I readied myself for sleep. The old aphorism that some had greatness thrust upon them lodged in my head. I remembered hearing it as a kid and interpreted it as 'Grape-Nuts' thrust upon them. It seemed strange to think about it now, but it was a very palatable image.

When you're used to living alone, and you wake up hearing someone puttering around in the kitchen cove, you think of ghosts.

A pan clanged down on a metal burner. Plates and silverware clattered on the countertop. "Rise and Shine!"

I rose.

"Eggs?" a cheery voice called out.

I felt my head. I was coming out of a dream where I was being battered over it by the arm from a one-armed bandit. It made a pinging sound.

Katherine was poised over the stove. I nodded. She deftly broke and dropped two eggs into the fry pan. They sizzled. The aroma of butter and eggs wafted around me and my nightmarish dream was blotted out.

Gustav who spent the night by Katherine's chair, and who is usually next to me when I wake up, to give me an encouraging lick and get his first strokes of the morning, was in his usual place near the stove when something was cooking. It was odd to reach down the side of my bed and feel nothing.

I should have known. The source of his food had changed to Katherine, and I was temporarily dispensed with.

I am not grumpy in the morning, but neither am I hopping to get going. I lay there collecting my thoughts, which felt as scattered as a bunch of dead leaves on a windy day, and just as useless.

Thinking about things, which meant Katherine, vis-a-vis her unloving stepfather, did not produce any well-knitted ideas on what to do except to keep her safe. On the other hand, I was still plagued by the thought that this was a hoax or a sick game.

It was probably because I had never seen anything actually happen. The note was typewritten, was retrieved and was now out of sight. That Katherine was in the hospital and might be suffering from paranoia. That Hayward was a bastard and nothing more. That Mrs. Hayward was your run of the ginmill alcoholic. Your typically dysfunctional rich American family.

The welt was the only unexplainable. Self-inflicted? An accident? Who knows.

Sadly, my beat-up nature has come to be suspicious of other peoples' motives. Like many people who have been burned through misplaced trust, I do not find myself plunging in with the same easy spirit of innocuous delight and palpitating enthusiasm.

To have a lovely woman happily preparing breakfast for me, while perhaps in mortal danger, if not for me, seemed a bit, well, fishy.

On the other hand, it is at times, not a good idea to look a gift-fish in the gills. And if it was a role I was playing, then I should play it to the hilt. I'll go along, pretending it's all true.

"Coffee?" she wanted to know after I scarfed up the meager breakfast of fried eggs.

"I'm going to make some toast first."

"Noh, I'll do it!" she insisted and delicately dropped two slices in the toaster.

She was lively this morning. She must have reached some conclusion last night or early this morning and was about to let me have it.

"Let's not get married."

"What?"

"I was thinking about it last night and I don't think it would be a good idea."

I was flattered, but does it count when your flattered by a lunatic?

She continued as if I were a prop in her delusion. "I thought if we got married, for show you know, then my stepfather couldn't bother me anymore. But, she pursed her mouth thoughtfully, and pressed the heel of her hand to her forehead, "I'd have to split the money with you, or," she turned to me expectantly, "we could sign a prenuptial agreement."

Boy, am I glad I quit my job, otherwise, I'd be riding to work on MUNI and miss this whole thing. I guess when you're rich you do have certain options other people don't have. Beauty, brains and money, a potent combination to derail any man from right thinking. But, fortunately, or, unfortunately, I was Beamer Todd, Truth Detective and had to say:

"What!?"

"Noh, well," she said, buttering the toast, "it was a thought."

"You could at least let me shave before you make a marriage proposal."

She dropped the plate in front of me. Her brain was busy clicking away, working on some other hair-raising scheme, if I had the hair.

"Give that computer between your ears a rest. No more hare-brained ideas." I tried to straighten her out. "But, you do have beautiful hair and a luxurious brain."

"And a heart," she whimpered.

"Yes," I solaced her. "And a heart."

"By the way," it occurred to me, "when did you get discharged from the hospital?"

"I left."

"What do you mean?"

"I had a day pass. I didn't come back," she said stiffly.

"Don't you think you should tell them where you are? They're probably worried and looking for you."

"I will," she said, unconcerned.

I wasn't convinced. I took a stab at the letter. "Do you have the envelope from the letter you showed me? Maybe there was something to show where it came from."

"I know where it came from. Besides, I tossed it."

I pushed on.

"Is there anything familiar in the letter? The kind of paper? Idiosyncrasies in the typewriter?"

"Don't you believe me?" she hissed. "It's from him!"

"To be truthful," I admitted, I don't know. **I ....**"

She slapped me on the face, snatched up her purse, slung it over her shoulder and slammed the door on her way out.

Whoosh!

Big mouths generate big winds. The only thing that felt smart right now was my jaw. I dashed after her.

She hadn't gone far. She was sitting on the front steps bawling. I sat down next to her and put my arm around her shoulder. She shrugged it off.

"I'm sorry," I said.

She started wheezing violently, fighting to breathe. She dug into her purse and took out an inhaler. She held it between her lips and gave herself a puff. She waited a minute and repeated it. She returned it to her purse, gasping for air, but less desperately.

"Are you okay?" I asked, touching her shoulder.

She was bent forward, seemingly exhausted, then straightened and took in a huge gulp of air, as if to test and refill herself. The sudden attack swept away her anger, she realized how vulnerable she was.

"I think I'll go back to the hospital," she said quietly.

"Good idea," I seconded, "you'll be safe there. I'll call a cab." I raced upstairs, called a cab, and raced back down, hoping she didn't take off.

She hadn't moved.

She was struggling again, her chest heaving, straining to get enough air. She tried to speak, but could barely string together more than two words.

"Thanks ...Beam .... I ...."

"Don't mention it," I interrupted, "the cab'll be here soon. Try to relax."

"I am ...it's a little ... better."

The cab rolled up. Quick service. I helped her in, told the driver the hospital and waved after her as the cab sped away.

I went back to get Gustav and we headed to the park. Charles was flagging me down.

I walked over to him as Guinevere spotted Gustav and went haywire, licking him relentlessly over the snout in greeting. Gustav was not so gregarious, fending her off, trying to let her know that a simple 'woof' would do. Never was love so strenuously fought against. Gustav chewed on her dewlap until she gave up, for now. Next time, they would go through it all again.

"Some guy was looking for you," Charles advised. "A mean-looking dude."

I described Hayward.

"Yep. To a tee."

I felt a little sweat trickle down under my arm. Was it that hot? "When was he here?"

"You just missed him."

"What'd he say?"

"Asked me if I knew a Detective Beamer." Charles squinted at me. "A detective?"

"No, but he thinks I am."

"He'd said he'd be back."

Why couldn't the guy just call me. Was he delivering some money? Ha! Did he know about me and Katherine?

"Did he'd say when he'd be back?"

"Nope."

Great. "How good are you at doing FBI?" I asked Charles, "Off-duty." He looked interested. A game fellow. "If this guy comes back with murder in his eyes, when he sees me, will you step in as an agent out with his dog?"

"I will try to avert an unnecessary tragedy." Charles put on a stern, official face. "I will speak the lingo."

"Thanks."

"Always glad to be of service," he said, with tight-lipped ceremony.

What Hayward was doing there at 8AM, I don't know. Was he on an all-night gambling binge? Was he following Katherine? He just didn't seem like an early riser, a man of the soil, a commoner with the dawn.

But, then, I could be mistaken.

Maybe, his crude features belied a delicate, poetic, feminine soul, his rough manner concealed a foppish gentility.

Or, maybe not.

The news was a thorn in my side the rest of the day. Whether walking to the library to pick up some videos, to browse through bookstores' remainders, or taking Gustav to Mission Dolores Park, I felt a jab each time a Mercedes slowed down, or someone lingered behind me, or I heard a voice bellow.

As the day wore on, I was less edgy and concluded that nothing dire was going to happen. If Hayward had any malicious intent, he wouldn't go public. The more I thought about it, the lighter my step became. I looked forward to seeing him, preferably in public place.

I decided to throw some sand in his face by calling him and arranging a meeting in the park. It would spare me the unexpected collision, and let me choose the turf. I hoped a lifetime of learning from **T.V.** and movie detectives, would not be in vain.

Joking aside, I was on slippery ground. But when I think of the filing in my future, the present danger was irresistible. Senses are more acute. Pretense is dropped. Instinct kicks in. Powers are heightened.

When I was down and out, there was immediacy to life. A desperate immediacy, unfortunately. When food and shelter are paramount, morality slides, you feel more animal-like and lose the connection to other people.

Desire is pitched. Emotion boils. Senses are keenest. Then some bucks come along and you are a dull, satisfied human again, whose main interest is to get duller and more satisfied.

So, to keep the old wires zapping, some danger and risk is not a bad thing. Especially, when it is not an inanimate object, but a spontaneously thinking, reacting, unpredictable and combative human being.

I phoned Hayward. I was steeled for a rough exchange. Instead, a feathery female voice answered.

"Hello, who's this?"

"Who's this!?"

"I asked first," she lilted.

"Beamer Todd."

"Beamer Todd. That's a funny name."

"Is Mr. Hayward home?"

"Malcolm?" she said, drifting away. "No, he's not here."

"Will he be back?"

"Yes he will." She sang back, unhelpfully.

"When?" I sang back.

"Don't know," she trilled. "He's in the bathroom."

It would make a lousy operetta. Besides, I didn't have a great singing voice and it was a tiresome way to hold a conversation.

"Can I leave a message?"

"Sure can."

"Tell him I called. Beamer Todd."

"Okay."

"Who are you by the way? A singer? You have a lovely voice." Flattery is a wonderful grease.

"I did sing once," she dropped her flightiness and her voice aged ten years. "Maybe you remember me? Jan Paris?"

"No," I said, kindly.

"Oh well," there was long, rehearsed sigh. Then a reprise. "Malcolm's going to get me started again. He knows a lot of big wheels in Las Vegas."

"Really?"

"Yea. It's like a dream. Living in a gorgeous mansion, singing in Vegas."

I bet it is.

"I'm his protégé," she said proudly, rounding out the cliché. "Wait, here he comes." Her voice tailed off. "It's for you, honey." The phone went dead. A quick smooch?

"Who's this?"

"It's Beamer Todd," I said brusquely, "I'm still waiting for my pay."

"You see Katherine?" His tone was mild, almost friendly. Must be to impress Jan Paris.

"I did."

"I love that girl. How's she doing?" His oily solicitude made me queasy.

"She has a big welt on her chest. Inflicted."

No response.

"She said you belted her."

Nothing.

"Well, tell Katherine," he cooed, if vultures could coo, "tell Katherine that we'll make it all better."

I was possessed. "Why don't you come to the park again and we can talk about it."

"Just a minute, please." He was full of pleasantries. "We'll be in Vegas."

"When will you be back?"

"That is confidential, my friend."

I could picture him winking to his protégé-honey and she lapping it up.

"Gotta go, sport."

He hung up.

Closer and farther away, the contradiction in life.

At least I learned one thing. Hayward was not offended by the charge that he hit Katherine. But then, he might not broach the subject with Jan Paris hovering around.

My impression was that he knew. He wasn't outraged as a parent should be when their child makes such a devastating accusation. He wasn't even resentful of my intimation. Nor, was there even a small, throat-clutching sound of surprise.

His sudden turn from felonious lout to coiled unguent was almost fiendish. A clever man.

Theories can collapse from the barrage of their own thoughts. I obeyed my feelings and put the Hayward business in abeyance. Let it settle into the old brain and let the unfettered subconscious do its work, if it had any stake in this.

I thought you couldn't get any lower or more boring than filing. You can. Stacking.

A pile of pre-slit envelopes. Take out the contents. Put the checks in one pile and the invoices in another. That's it. Pretty exciting. It's a good thing I could count to two, or my employability would be nil.

I sat with six others around a big table and we dug into the constantly replenishing supply of remittance envelopes. The others were all younger than me, barely adults, with fantasy lives still intact, and able to do the work while thinking of tonight, tomorrow or an extravagant future.

Or, they could pass the time talking to each other about myriad interests, still keen on ideas, dates, current movies and T.V.

To me, it was a drudgery. I actually thought about what I was doing. It was depressing. I should be out there tearing up the world, fighting hunger or poverty or dictatorships or meanness.

"Sir?" One of the kids addressed me with a friendly smile. "Whatcha doin' here?"

Who could admit it.

I gambled. "Secret Agent. Looking for aliens."

"Illegals?"

"Outer Space," I said with no-nonsense authority. They have infiltrated San Francisco, pretending to be office workers."

The kids glanced at each other with shrew looks of agreement that this guy was wacko. But I kept the fiction going, anything to break up the monotony.

"They can change shapes so they can pass off easily as human," I instructed. "It is almost impossible to detect them." I was trying to leave a hint of plausibility. "We in the government don't think they mean any harm. At least, not yet." We were all busy stacking at not looking at one another. "We think they are just observers."

"Great story." I heard someone speak up from the other end of the table. It was a guy with a white shirt, tie and slick crewcut.

"Cool," said a gum chewing high school girl across from me. "Do these aliens, you know, go to school?"

"Of course," I replied, with certitude, polishing my official image.

"How do they change shapes?"

"Atoms rearrangement."

"So they can change back at any time?"

"If they want."

"Gross."

"Naturally, they don't do it public," I made clear to her. "They do it at home or in the bathroom, probably in the stalls. So it's always a good idea to knock before you push in the door."

I looked around with a still severe expression to see if anyone was buying even an inkling of my extemporaneous science fiction. There were smiles, furrows and annoyance.

"After a while, their atoms begin to lose their cohesion and disintegrate. That's what we're trying to catch. It's a painstaking and laborious process to try to be there when this happens.

"We've tracked, with our new, sophisticated satellites, bodies of rambling atoms to the agency you all work for. We think the alien glue which holds these people together is losing its grip, maybe from the warming of the Earth."

I confronted them. "Did you all know each other before coming here?" I asked with sudden bluntness.

They looked at each other with the merest flicker of mistrust. How easy to get caught up in a tall tale? It was like being in summer camp all over again. Except, I was on the other side.

I remember the counselors telling us poor, quaking camper's gruesome stories of vengeful man-monsters lurking around the camp preying on its campers.

I wished I had the grisly imagination of those guys. But my interest was in science fiction, not horror. And I was doing it out of boredom, not sadism.

The storyline was over. I redoubled my efforts with the envelopes while occasionally peering disconcertingly at one of my co-workers. Imagination could spin out strange plots. I left it up to them.

"Do you have I.D.?" the guy in the tie asked, smugly unconvinced, hoping to trap me.

I stacked a few more envelopes before answering him.

"I don't carry Government I.D." I gave him a puzzled look to show him he was way out of his depth. "If they capture me, I am concealing nothing. It would be foolish. I communicate with the satellite and the Agency with my unique voice patterns.

He didn't buy it, yet, there was no rebuttal.

Finally, we went out to lunch.

I always paper bag it. I bought a container of milk in the lobby of my building, and then strolled around a block or two until I found a small grassy area to relax and eat. Peanut butter and strawberry jam. The best.

Pigeons surrounded me. I threw them pieces of bread. If I get up to heaven, and pigeons are in charge, it might come in handy. They should know, that despite my dog, I did feed them.

Everyone was back in their same places when I sat down before a mountain of envelopes. I hoped I would make it through the afternoon.

I picked out one of the talkative guys who had a slight blemish on his left cheek. I hadn't noticed it before.

"Did you have that blemish before?" I asked him.

He broke off his conversation and fingered the barely discernible mark.

"A little acne," he guessed, embarrassed.

"I see."

Everyone tried not to stare at the blotch.

"I was on the phone to Washington during lunch and I've got the latest dope on the alien transformation."

They listened intently. This was my capper installment.

"It seems," I started grimly, "that when the human form wears off, they don't return to their hideous alien bodies." I let the suspense sink in. "No. You know what they turn into!?!I I watched the almost rapt, almost worried faces.

"What?"

"Pigeons!"

I got up and left.

It wasn't smart to leave the temp agency in the lurch. They had always been fair with me. But you can't always do the right thing. You can't always be smart.

Stacking made me feel stupid.

I walked swiftly around downtown, trying to reinvigorate my senses. It's amazing how dumbing a few hours of boring, repetitious work can be. I could not envision doing it for a whole week. Parts of me would probably drop off from atrophy. The only part of me it actually stimulated was the desire to flee.

Work options were narrow.

My resume the last few years was sketchy. Cashier. Sporting Goods Salesman. Health Food Store Pusher of Vitamin C, and sprinkled in between, various temp office jobs. Not a glittering past or a promising future.

But, with the sanguine thought of another agency to sign up with, I felt a brief liberation.

It was good not to be stuck inside an office, but to be breezingly strolling the rolling, colorful streets of San Francisco. Exploring with no destination and no time clock, except for Gustav, whose image reminded me that he was alone longer than usual. I cut short my peregrinations and headed home.

The tail was going full blast when I came in. It is always nice to be welcomed as if your homecoming was the greatest thing on Earth.

I gave Gustav some return rubs, as his tail flip-flopped, back and forth, without a stop. It made me wonder if that tail muscle ever got tired. Dogs seemed to be able to get that tail going at full speed no matter what the circumstances.

It was good to be back with Gustav and something interesting to think about again.

It was also time to take him out. He had been cooped up and part of the tail wagging was anticipation of going to the park.

It was less crowded than usual. The regular late afternoon group hadn't arrived yet. There was more a balance between dog people, sunbathers, children, readers, eaters and hangers-out.

A girl and guy tossed a baseball around, and a hound followed the ball ceaselessly, from one to the other, hoping for the miscue, at which point they'd have to hopelessly trail after him to recover the ball, while he carried it around teasingly. It was a good show.

Gustav and I sat back on the grass, me petting him, and him contently watching for anything flying or waddling by. It didn't seem to be a bad life being a dog in this park. A dog's life as they say. Dogs here probably get petted more in one day than some people in their whole lives.

It is not widely known, but the original Bible is hidden away. The one that we've come to use is a fraud. Our Bible tells us that God created men and woman. What this fake Bible doesn't tell us, what it leaves out from the original, is that God created men and women to pet dogs.

Checked the mailbox on the way in. Assorted mail. Magazine offer. Bill for cable T.V. Coupon packet and a letter from Robin Hayward.

She was thanking me for a homemade cassette of silly dog songs I'd made up, which I gave to Dori, to give to her. Never pass up a connection.

I'd forgotten about it.

Not only was there a warm thanks, but an invitation to play the songs for her friends at their monthly Bichon get-together every fourth Sunday at noon in Pacific Heights Park. They called it the, fluffy fourth.'

All I had to do was tune up the dusty guitar and rememorize the songs.

Enclosed was an R.S.V.P. card and a stamped, addressed envelope. It was hard to refuse. It would be a social, not a detection call.

It is the surprises in life that keep us going. To map out one's life, is to eliminate the detours. It is the detours that lengthen life.

It sparked me. Then, getting over the tribute to my powers of silliness, I figured it was a good chance, after all, to learn more about the Hayward clan, particularly Mrs. Hayward. To subtly inquire without being a boor. A true test of my Brooklyn background, where subtly meant saying on the subways, 'excuse me, you idiot,' instead of just 'you idiot.'

It keyed me up. Hobnobbing with the rich, pitching my songs and being a bit of a spy. I wondered if they served food? Was it catered? Spare ribs?

"Want to go to the park, Gustav?" The rhetorical question of the century.

Dori Four wasn't at the park that evening, so I phoned her when I came in.

"Hi, Dori!" I said bountifully when she answered.

"Hey, Beamer." She sounded down.

"What's up?"

"Not much."

"Guess what? I got an invitation from Robin Hayward."

"No kidding?" She perked up. Then felt slighted. "Hey, how come I didn't get one?"

"It's about the dog songs you gave to her for me."

"Yea, I remember. She liked them?"

"She wants me to sing them for her Bichon Club!" I enthused.

"Good for you, Beamer," she said, her voice dragging on the ground.

"Wanna come?"

"I don't know. I may be working. When is it?"

"This Sunday."

"Working," she said flatly.

"Well, I'm going to do a little snooping," I said, conspiratorially, "maybe her friends could crack open a window or two."

"I wanna go!" Dori cried.

"Can you get off work?"

"I'll try."

"Good."

I hoped she could make it. She loved intrigue and a stage was set. Besides, she could get into the gossipy cliques that were closed and anathema to me. Even by New York standards, I thought it was rude. However, I was not averse to listening.

We all have something prudish in our natures, as well as something flamboyant. It evens out down the line.

Since I wasn't engaged in work, involved with a Hayward or a Roman, the days whizzed by, with hardly a bump in the routine. Paul was working the evening shift at the gift shop and Charles had landed a job as a 'Joking Waiter' at a new 'concept' comedy club near Union Square. Dori was putting in extra time to get Sunday off.

There was usually someone to strike up a conversation with in the park. There were many people I had known for years, so it had a casual atmosphere. It was a relaxing, even restful place, weather permitting, like a cocooned valley. A Valley of the Dogs.

On Saturday evening when the park had the fewest dog people, I noticed an attractive woman sitting alone at the end of one of the benches. She held a tiny Yorkshire Terrier on her lap. She looked Japanese. Both she and the Yorkie seemed overwhelmed by the dog park melee.

"It's just rough play," I reassured her, and sat down at the other end of the bench. "They don't hurt each other."

She turned and smiled politely. She reached into her Pooh Bear backpack and withdrew a chunky Japanese-English Dictionary.

"Rough ...Play ..." she repeated, with an adorable accent. She expertly found the words. "Ah," she said, with a big smile. Then she said something in Japanese. "Ah, I understand. Rough. Play. It's okay." She beamed.

I nodded, returning her wide grin.

She had smooth skin, innocent eyes and a petite, curvaceous form. Like a doll.

"No hurt," I assured her.

Back to the dictionary.

"Ah, not hurt. It is good." She laughed. "Please forgive," she apologized. "Just visit. English not good."

"It's okay," I mimed with my hands. "Better than my Japanese," I added, mostly to myself.

She nodded, but not sure.

"Your dog?" I asked.

"No. My friend." She petted the rascally squirming thing.

"Name?"

She stared at me for a minute. Then it clicked in.

"Ah, name." She understood and pointed to the dog. "Bessie," she pronounced eagerly.

"Bessie?" I expected some exotic Japanese name.

Bessie gave me a savage nip as I put my hand over to meet her.

"Not ...friendly," she said, unnecessarily, as I passed a wary look to Bessie and examined my finger. It was not bleeding, but I sucked on it all the same. It did sting.

"Probably nervous," I said, forgivingly, shaking my hand.

Out came the book.

"Ah, nervous. Yes. Nervous. Me, too. Nervous," she confided, "so many words to learn."

It seemed a gigantic task to learn English from Japanese, but she was willing to endure the difficulty. I'd hate to think of myself in Japan, in her position. She had guts.

"I **want** ..." she paused, concentrating, "to learn English." She finished with a winsome smile and a graceful flourish of hand.

"Good for you."

"You are nice. You do not ..." She was stumped. A quick trip through the book. "You do not laugh at me."

I did smile.

Contrary to my ideas about young Japanese women, at least the students I've seen in groups, she was very direct. No demure giggling and hands covering the mouth. To be here by herself, made her an independent sort.

"Your dog name?" She gently stroked Gustav, who was now sitting next to her.

"Gustav."

"Gustav?"

Rather than see the book again, I simply said, "Yes."

She pointed at herself. "Komako," she said, and smiled profusely.

I mimicked her. "Beamer." I waited for her to ask me to explain it and to hear how it sounded in her charming accent.

She said nothing, but showed a lot of white teeth.

"I must go. Meet my friend." She stood up and formally offered her hand. I lightly shook its softness.

She zipped up her Pooh Bear back pack, slid her arms through the straps, arranged it comfortably, picked up Bessie and cradled her in the crook of her arm.

"I come tomorrow," she said.

"Me, too." I answered, drawing a pleased smile.

She went off, with short, almost soundless steps, as if she were wearing slippers. She didn't turn around, but put Bessie on the ground, attached her leash and walked out of the park, occasionally quickening her pace to keep up with Bessie's rushing little legs.

We exchanged only the most basic words, yet I sensed a deeper conversation going on. As if there was no language barrier, as if we knew and understood each other. Or, I could be mistaken.

I had a habit or a propensity to weave silken romances from soggy noodles. Still, my heart gave a little thump, and I felt an enraptured desire, though Gustav's tongue was not my first choice.

He was licking my face and making little cries, to get my attention back to him. His put his front paws on my chest and then pressed down with the full weight of his body. That usually got me out of whatever reverie I was in.

"Okay, Gustav," I surrendered, grabbing his paws and lifting him off me. "Oof. Let's walk."

His tail was going a mile-a-minute and his mouth was open in a dog smile, a winning dog. I thought dogs were supposed to obey you and not vice-versa. But I had a lot to learn. When they capture your heart, you're just jelly.

We went up on the grass and sat down. Gustav made himself comfortable sitting between my legs and watching down the hill, while I rubbed his back. His all-time favorite set-up.

There wasn't much going on, it was grey and chilly and the few people out before had left. But it was nice to see the wind going through the trees, ruffling the leaves and bending the slighter limbs, like a bushy-haired conductor swinging a graceful baton to Strauss waltzes.

Robin Hayward's blast was not catered, nor was there any food at all. A disappointment.

There must have been more than twenty bichons gamboling in the grass, chasing each other through the trees and shrubs and wrestling with ferocious delight.

It was a cozy atmosphere. They were cute, irrepressible and friendly dogs, and they were all white. With all the playing and running, it was like watching a snowball fight with real, live snowballs. These were dogs with a lot of moxie.

If Mrs. Hayward knew me, it was because I was the only one carrying a guitar case. Gustav was home, pining or sleeping or barking at any stranger who came by the door, and Dori would be here after she finished preening.

I spied mostly women in this uncult-like gathering, though the stray man was equal to the women in doting attention to the dogs. Mrs. Hayward spotted me and tried to introduce me to her two dogs who were reluctant to leave their playmates. I told her it was okay; I wasn't insulted by their poor manners.

I was standing around, awaiting my cue, when Dori showed up. She was breathless, as if she had rushed not to miss anything.

"Nothing's happening. Just a lot of hanging around," I told her.

"Looks like our park," she said, discouraged, "I thought it would be fancier."

"No posh here," I observed, "no nosh either," I added, in case Dori was hoping for fish eggs and champagne. "I told everyone the Duchess of Bichon was coming. So why don't you introduce yourself."

Dori punched me in the arm.

"Are you mad because you lost your tiara?" I joshed, and flinched, but her fist loosened.

"Okay. Okay. I'll get in duchess with the girls," she said, putting on a yenta face. "I'll do your dirty work."

"You can't miss," I said, appraisingly.

She was wearing a dress for the occasion. Also, a touch of makeup and some tasteful jewelry. She was stunning in a dog park way, and easily outshone the other women, who were in sweats or shorts or wore fastidiously subdued church clothes.

Dori was easily welcomed into their number and I sort of drifted around the knots of conversation, especially bobbing up where Robin Hayward was.

She was sober in the truest sense of the word. Taciturn and expressionless. Perhaps, a drink would liven her up, but this was not the place. I wondered if the others, who were courting her attention, knew of her vice.

"What's your next book going to be about?" A hefty woman, clutching a large, bottled water, asked her with affectionate interest. "How about race?"

Mrs. Hayward considered it. "I may," she replied with a genial smile.

"I know," A tall, thin, stooped octogenarian wedged in and said with a piercing voice, "forced retirement revenge." He twisted his mouth into a diabolical grin.

Mrs. Hayward nodded approvingly.

"What about abuse?"

"What?" She turned sharply, and gave me a purposeful look.

"You know," I responded airily, "it's very topical."

"Thank you for your suggestion, Mr. Todd," she said with aplomb, and the barest quiver in her voice. She stood rigidly, and in deference to her celebrity, the rest of the group resumed conversations among themselves.

"I'm glad you liked the songs," I said, jovially, approaching her.

She stiffened even more. "They're very clever," she said. Her eyes shifted away from me. She knew, I knew.

"Can I help you in any way?" I asked, sympathetically.

"Help me?" she said to the ground.

"With your husband."

She looked at me with a fierce resolve. "I don't know what you're talking about," she insisted, politely. "I do not discuss family matters. Besides," she suddenly brightened up, "this day is for our dog family," and swept her arm across the dog scene.

She did not reject my offer out-of-hand, so maybe I had made some progress, some chip in the fortress wall. But she avoided me for the next hour and did not ask me to play any songs.

I didn't have the audacity to ask for everyone's attention and then launch into my opener about fetching dogs. I bet they would have enjoyed it. However, there were a lot of distractions to contend with: barking dogs, gusts of wind, screaming kids, peoples' eyes glued to their dogs and the fact that we were outside and my voice could not project to such a scattered assembly. So, with the unopened guitar case and the protesting Dori in tow, I left.

We were heading for the bus stop.

"Why did you drag me off like that?" Dori groused.

"I didn't drag you off. I asked if you were ready to go."

"Right. You kept twitching your head toward the street like some crazy marionette."

"I wasn't twitching. I was gesturing."

"I never heard of anyone gesturing with their neck."

This was not an argument I was going to win.

"You enjoyed it?"

"These people are filled with horror stories," she said gleefully.

"Anything on Hayward?"

"The speculation is rampant," she said, as if she were chewing on something juicy.

"What?"

"You name it. Incest. Drugs. Mistresses. Bankruptcy. Blackmail. Attempted Murder."

"Holy cow!?"

"A plague of opinions."

"Anyone see anything or hear anything?"

"You know how everybody exaggerates when remarks get passed on. I was trying to pull the reckless balloons back down to earth." She looked sturdy. "Mrs. Parker, the one with the plastic face, said she saw a shoving match when husband and wife went from the car to the front door." Dori dismissed it, as one who has been shoved around kiddingly and one who has been shoved around in anger. "It sounded like it was just a spat, or maybe a jiving squabble couples have."

"Or, maybe not."

"I guess. She couldn't hear anything."

"Anything else?"

"Let's stop in for some coffee, big spender. I want to sit down. I'm always on my feet."

"I'm sorry."

"No apology. Just buy me a calorie-laden, chocolate-filled, scrumptiously delicious mother of all pastries." She looked at me and winked. "My reward."

We sat in an Upper Fillmore bistro, Dori joyfully devouring a giant, flaky, creamy thing, flecked with slivered almonds. I had one, too. We sipped twelve ounce French Roasts and Dori dished the dirt. If anyone overheard, they'd probably think we were rehashing a soap opera.

"Well, she said, leaning forward, after wiping her hands on a paper napkin. "They had to shut up and change the subject every time she came by." She swept a crumb off her dress. "Why does she even come? She must know they talk about her."

"I guess she's used to it." As if I knew.

"If it was me," she whispered loudly, knotting her nose, "I'd kick them all in their sucked out butts!"

"An artist with words," I lauded, trying to block out the image.

"I feel like a heel." she said glumly.

"At least you're a high heel." I immediately regretted it. She liked Mrs. Hayward. "Remember, we're trying to help," I consoled her.

"She hardly spoke to me."

"She hardly spoke to anyone." She thought about it and seemed reconciled.

"What about Malcolm?"

"Malcolm?"

"Mr. Hayward," I smiled. "Anything specifically about him?"

"When I slipped him into the conversation he got a mixed reception." Dori was concentrating, looking past me. "One lady thought he was thoroughly charming and nearly swooned at the mention of him, but another suspected he was a beast under the glamour and would gladly feel safer if he were gone. The rest scarcely knew him."

"And Katherine?"

"She's on holiday."

"Is that a euphemism?"

"No. They believe she's traveling in Europe."

"The bigger the house, the more you can hide," I suggested to her.

"Tell me about it," she agreed. "My neighbors can tell what program I watched the night before and I don't play it loud. I hear them humming the songs I sing in the shower!"

It was quiet.

We listened to the snatches of babble from around the other tables. Very animated, urgent talk, almost deafening in its upness.

"So, what do you think, Dori?" I was stalled for ideas.

"I think I can. I think I can. I think I can." She started choo-chooing, "I think I can eat another pastry."

"Another one!" I was amazed at her sweet tooth.

"Okay, a half. We can share."

Did I detect a flirtatious smile? When a woman says share, my hackles go up and a fire alarm goes off. The last time a woman and I decided to share, the only thing we ended up sharing was a disaster.

The second pastry, this one with chocolate filling, stood dauntingly between us. We stared at the nut pieces arranged in a happy face. It was too much. We were cloyed by the sweetness.

Dori cut it and transferred the halves to our separate plates. She picked hers up and nibbled at it, while I rearranged the nuts to make a frown.

"Don't play with your food!" Dori nagged, embarrassed by my whimsical restaurant manners.

"Oops. Sorry, Sarge."

She looked at me darkly.

The vaunted Truth Detective did have chinks in his Golden Rules. He was deviously trying to skewer a woman's interest, if, in his ridiculously swelled notion of himself, there was one.

I turned the plate around and it was smiling again.

"The frown is on your side now," I said, meaning nothing.

"Your plate, your frown," she replied, laconically. "Let's go."

We walked silently together to the bus stop. We waited silently together for the bus. She let me sit silently next to her on the ride home. When we descended silently from the bus, she gave me a farewell sneer and headed to her place. I pretended to drag myself home.

At least Gustav was not teed off at me, and after shedding my going out costume, I put on my dog park duds and became the mild-mannered dog park guy.

Halfway into the park, I saw Komako sitting in the same spot she was sitting in yesterday. Gustav veered off to do dog things while I went straight to Komako and Bessie, who was grrring in my direction.

"I forgot to say 'Sayonara' yesterday." I smiled, dredging up one of my two Japanese words.

"Ah, you know Japanese," she said with confidence. She was speaking English better than she did yesterday.

"No way." I raised my hands, palms out. "That's it."

"You are ...modest." She formed the words haltingly.

"Just honest."

The book was out.

"Honest?"

"Yes, honest."

She riffled the pages. "Ah ...honest!" She smiled with discovery. "I too am honest."

"Wonderful," I complimented her. "It is difficult ..." she tilted her head, "...hard," she smiled and nodded, "...to be honest."

"Yes." She nodded her head rapidly, catching my point. "You like Japanese food?" she asked me in smooth English.

The one time I went to a Japanese restaurant with friends, I was impressed by the artistry but not by the portions. I have the ungourmet preference of quantity over quality.

I held up one finger. "I eat Japanese food once," I enunciated slowly.

"What did you eat?"

I didn't remember, except there were a lot of colors. "Vegetables?"

"You like sushi?" she encouraged.

"No." No hesitation here.

She seemed crestfallen.

"Not like raw fish," I explained, coming as close to the truth as I could without making her cry.

"I make rice, vegetables, teriyaki steak," she determined, happily.

"Great!"

"You come, my room, tomorrow." She handed me a card with the address typed out. It was downtown.

"Thank you. My pleasure. What time?"

"Ah, time." She unzipped a small pocket in her Pooh Bear pack and took out a ball point. She wrote '7' on the card.

"Okay." I bowed, not knowing why. She never bowed. "You don't ..." I made a bowing motion.

"Not here," she laughed, "Japan only."

"I see."

"I go." She picked up Bessie and stood. "See you tomorrow." She smiled and walked out the same way she did yesterday.

"Bye. See you tomorrow."

It all happened so fast. Was it a Japanese custom to invite strangers to dinner? It didn't matter. It was set. My irresistibility quotient had shot up 1000% She was a very attractive woman. Maybe, she had lost her contacts.

The building was on the outskirts of the Tenderloin, situated between the seedier lower altitude and the posher residences of Nob Hill. Uphill was rich, downhill was poor.

I buzzed the apartment number, got a long buzz in return and pushed in the outer door.

The lobby was small and stuffy, with a faded brown rug and a long, barren table along the mailboxes. There were no chairs and the outside light penetrated only to the elevator, which was manual.

I pressed the button and heard it clunk into action. It sluggishly creaked down and thumped to a stop. It sounded alive. I hoped it had been fed today. I held the heavy outside door open with my back, while I mightily slid the steel gate halfway open so I could slip in. The gate banged closed from its own weight. It was an outspoken contraption.

It lumbered up to the third floor and bounced to a stop. I precariously held both the gate and the door as I spilled out into the hall.

If I thought I was in the Twilight Zone, the long, dark hallway confirmed it. It was quiet and creepy. How did Komako get into a place like this? Cheaply, I supposed.

I walked slowly down the eerie hall, clutching my contributory bottle of wine as a weapon, hearing the faintest murmuring of voices and an occasional squeal of music, as if a radio dial was being spun.

I knocked on 324.

"Komako?" I said softly, my face pressed to the wooden door, trying to hear.

Nothing.

"Komako?" I raised my voice and rapped a little harder. I heard steps move to the door. Not short steps like Komako's but striding and heavy.

The door opened. I stepped in. No komako. I moved further in. The door closed solidly behind me.

"Hello, sport."

I whirled around. Hayward stood blocking the door. A big smile creased his face. I had a very trapped feeling.

"Hey, brought some wine. Let's open it."

He walked toward me in a casually menacing way and snatched the bottle from my limp arm. He deposited it on the coffee table with a jolt, went into the kitchen and came out with two glasses and a corkscrew.

He popped the cork with a practiced movement and handed me a full glass.

"What do they say? Let it breathe?" He held the glass up the light and twirled it. "The color of blood," he laughed, morbidly.

I set my glass on the coffee table. "Where's Komako?"

"At home." Hayward said, idly, taking an appreciative sip of the wine. "Good wine."

"You mean she went back to Japan?"

His laugh was like a cackle. I could sure crack this guy up.

"She lives in San Francisco," he grinned at me.

"She's American?"

"Of course. A good actress don't you think?"

I felt like a fool. A worried fool.

"A pretty girl is the best bait," he said coldly and sipped more wine. "Have some wine?"

I walked to the door.

"Where you going? he asked, ominously.

I kept walking.

The wine glass flew by my head and smashed against the door. I covered my face against the flying pieces of glass. Hayward was on top of me.

"Why can't you keep your nose out of my family's business?" His ham fist plowed into my stomach and I doubled up, gasping for air. I saw a blurry Hayward watching my throes. I collapsed to the floor and lay for a while regaining my breath.

Hayward gave me a swift kick to the head. Then to my ribs. Then to my head, then back to my ribs. I crumpled up in a ball. I said nothing.

"Like I said." He was pathologically calm. "Please keep your nose out of my family's business, if you want to keep it." He laughed contemptuously and left.

I was a lump of pain. Dizzy and nauseous. And angry. I had no chance. Whatever part of me I touched, it hurt. I tried to move around, testing here and there. I didn't think anything was broken, except my ego. I crawled to the sofa and lifted myself up into it.

I touched the side of my head. It was swollen. My ribs ached with every breath. The wine was the nearest medicine. I drank half a glass and settled back.

I was surprised I had my wits about me, that I wasn't sprawled unconscious on the floor. Maybe, Hayward took it easy on me. It was only, according to him, an introduction.

The bruiser only bruised, this time.

Gustav licked my wounds, as I lay immobile on the futon.

I had left the Komako rendezvous with a swelled head, splitting sides and a breathlessness that had little to do with amore.

People probably thought I was drunk, as I tended to reel around disoriented until I seated myself on the bus and tried to cover the lump on my head with a hand, as if I had a headache, which I did.

I stroked Gustav's back, which made me feel better. Better to be with someone who wants to heal you, than one who wants to put his heel through you.

My thoughts were tumultuous. Angry, vengeful, foolish, murderous and shook-up. I had gotten into scrapes before, but nothing that could not be resolved by an interceder or a lot of yelling and screaming and posturing and maybe some wildly thrown punches that never land.

I've been threatened, but never took it seriously. If someone means to do something he'll do it, not say it. Hayward proved my point, unfortunately. No threat, just action.

It was still light when Gustav and I took our turn through the park. Paul was throwing a ball for Bear. I told him what had happened.

"That bastard!" he scowled, and flung the ball with extra emphasis. "I guess you're okay, if you can make it out here."

It was an accurate, if not touching assessment of my awkward mobility.

"Witnesses?" he stabbed.

I shook my head wearily.

"Anybody hear anything?"

I shrugged. How did I know.

"If I had a good law practice, I'd have investigators running around the joint."

He looked dejected.

"Did you see anyone? Did anyone see you?"

"No."

He looked defeated.

"No one?"

"No one."

He picked up the squishy ball and hurled it as far as he could. Bear skidded after it.

"Your word against his," he said, matter-of-factly. "Unless he left his fingerprints on your intestines or an imprint of a signet ring on your forehead."

"How 'bout a shoe sole in the temple?"

"I'd say," Paul seized my daze, "that religion was kicking in."

"You're becoming quite the symbolic poet."

"I bet all you can hear are cymbals."

He was right. A band of percussionists were rehearsing on and off in my head.

"How are all the scurrying tourists?" I asked, trying to mute the band.

"Still scurrying. But why? he speculated. "Why do they want to hurry around so much? They're on vacation. You'd think they'd want to take it easy. Go to some quiet, peaceful place and relax."

"Not everyone is as lazy as you."

"I remember when I was a kid and we visited New York in the summer. The newspapers would report that there were a million people at the beach." He made a disbelieving face. "There were pictures of the beach from the sky. But you couldn't see any sand because it was completely covered with bodies. Why go to the beach when there are already a million people there?"

"People like to be with people," was the only answer I could come up with. "Stop digging, Gustav!"

I could imagine Einstein out with his dog in the park, his mind wandering over the Universe, on the verge of the formula for the Unified Field Theory he had been working for decades. He just about had it. The tiniest, most elusive, the most critical fragment was about to formulate in his mind. He was just about to grasp it, when: "Stop digging, Shotsi!" and the discovery drifted away, never to be recovered.

I must be in shock still, I thought, having all these weird thoughts. My body was numb, but my mind was kinetic. Or, maybe, I was just coming back to normal.

"Paul, why would he get so violent with me doing some harmless poking around?"

"Obviously, it wasn't harmless."

"I don't know. I wasn't nosing around in his affairs." I felt both naive and dismayed. "I don't even know what they are."

"Maybe, you shouldn't know," he said, dissuasively.

"What could it be?' I said, mostly to myself. "Must be something with losing money. Maybe gambling."

"Why would he provoke someone against him? Paul pondered. Unless, he'd done it before."

"Is it some secret thing or does his family know?"

"Don't know," Paul conceded, and threw a high arcing pop-up that Bear circled and almost caught on the fly. "Nice try, girl," he praised. He turned to me. "If I can help in any way, let me know."

"Thanks, Paul, I appreciate it."

Gustav grabbed the ball and was playing keep away. The more Paul lunged for it or tried to wrest it from Gustav's jaws, the more intimidating was his growl. It was Gustav's game.

After ten minutes of fruitless chase, with Gustav having his fun, I told Paul to ignore him. If no one went after him, he'd eventually lose interest and drop the ball. Paul turned his back and walked away, and after a few minutes, Gustav looking disappointed, dropped it and walked over to me.

I held his collar while Paul retrieved the ball. Bear would make sure from now on, to be more careful where she placed it, before taking off on the run to await the toss.

"The only thing I can do now is lay siege to his house," I quipped, with grandiose illogic."

"Sure, cut off their supply of cable."

"Katherine's gone from the hospital."

"Again?"

"This time she was discharged home."

"When?"

"A few days ago," I said, distractedly, "I wonder if she's there?"

"Call."

"What if I get ...?"

"Don't they have their own phones in that huge house?"

"I suppose."

"Listen," Paul advised. "Cool it for a while. Get better." He gave me a sage smile. "I bet you'll think of something."

"Thanks," I said, with gratitude and relief. I needed to be off my high horse for a while. I was calloused in all the wrong places.

If I was hounded by feeling of self-doubt, I tried not to let it show.

I returned to the park the next morning, after a mostly sleepless, aspiriny night, still castigating myself for being a dupe.

During the long, wrenching night, I had a minor revelation. Maybe, I was trying to complicate things. Making an ugly mountain out of an ugly molehill.

Maybe, Hayward was not more than he seemed. No gangster. No killer. But a simple bully. Throwing his weight around against weaker women, and intimidating through violence or the threat of violence, protected by his position and his money. In short, a coward.

He was canny. He was on the hill. He was untouchable. Unless? My battered brain cells began revolving around the germ of an idea. My first duty, though, after bringing Gustav in, was to phone Katherine.

I rooted in my desk drawer, through the scraps of paper with odd bits of information I tossed in there. No luck. I called information. No luck. The hospital couldn't give it out. I wrote a short letter, put it directly in the post box, and hoped she'd receive it tomorrow.

Then I went to buy a pair of shoes.

When I came back, Gustav was ready for another trip out. It seemed I spent half my life on the other end of a leash. If World War III suddenly hit and devastated the entire city, you could be sure that the next morning people would be out walking their dogs.

Why bother? Why butt in? Certainly there was recourse beyond me. Why continue on this very bumpy road?

I lay on the futon, staring out the window at a blank, blue sky, listening to the pensive cello suites of Bach. Gustav lay on the floor, his legs churning, chasing pigeons in his sleep.

One rarely gets a chance to resolve something from the past. I had one. It would be a belated retribution of wrongs. It would appease the gnawing quest for absolution. The perception of my youthful weakness, though out of my control, has haunted me.

My motives were not entirely vengeful. Heroic myths intrude into the most mundane lives. The yearning to obliterate the dark, go for the good, to ascend to the Godlike, to struggle against evil, to illuminate the world, and to suffer because of it.

The everyday is bogged down in ambiguities. The philosophical and the farcical, the intent and the deed, the righteous hypocrite and the honest faker, the winner and the loser, success and failure. The list goes on.

Is thought a prelude to action? Actions have reverberations, but lie along the same road. And like every road stamped out the wilderness, it is free to cover itself, and make the going back impossible.

It is a leap ahead. Action makes change. And while we may think we are acting, we are reacting, or going through motions that appear to be movement, but are really formalized calisthenics.

We are bound in a circle. Actions widen the circle. When we think of a beginning and an end we think of a line. From there to there.

No matter how far we go, we come back to the same place. A ruthless axiom. A cloud drifted by.

Gustav was licking my hand, it was time to get up and walk the dog.

Walking the dog is a yo-yo trick. Yo-Yo Ma is playing the Bach Suites on cello. Funny how the down-to-earth mixes with the ethereal.

As we went out into the mixed-up world, conflicting thoughts ran through my head. Unfortunately, not all thoughts are smooth sneaker thoughts, some thoughts have cleats.

The next day Katherine phoned.

She was not distraught. She sounded calm and unafraid. She told me not to worry, she was doing fine and everything was straightened out with her stepfather.

It was a bizarre twist. It resurrected my suspicion that she was never on the up and up.

It was upside down now. Maybe Hayward, though a jerk, was protective of his stepdaughter and was aware of her fantasies. You could turn the knob a quarter of an inch and have a completely different picture.

If she was sick, maybe she was back on her medicine. It seemed to fit together neatly for the first time. It helped explain Mrs. Hayward's drinking binges and her desire to push Roman away to keep him from becoming a target. It would make more understandable Malcolm Hayward's other life in Las Vegas.

But why resort to intimidation when an explanation would do? Maybe, I was an outsider and not privy to such consideration. Still, it was a pretty extreme way of getting his point across. I guess he didn't like me.

"So, what do you think, Dori?" I said over the phone, nervously working my teeth over an almost bleeding thumbnail.

"I dunno. I don't care. I'm sick," she groaned.

"You sound clogged up."

"I am," she grumbled, "some idiot was sneezing allover me."

"At the restaurant?"

"Sure at the restaurant. Where do you think?"

"So," I tried to solicit her opinion, "do you think it all boils down to Katherine having fantasies?"

"She must, if she likes you."

"Be serious," I urged.

"Yeah, could be," was her reluctant answer.

"What's bugging you?" I asked, mistakenly.

"What's bugging me!?" she lashed out. "I'm sick. Can't work. Can't make money. God, what a lunkhead you are."

Dori was right. I was feeling very stupid.

"If you need a few dollars let me know."

"Thanks, Beamer," she said, calming down. "I didn't mean to be bitchy. But jeez, you know, money."

"I know."

Dori was quiet.

"Get plenty of sleep. Drink lots of water," I said in my most doctorly manner." If you treat it early, you can knock it out in a day or two.

Hopefully.

"I'll take it easy."

"Good."

Gustav and I took our evening trip to the park.

I saw a familiar, short figure going from dog person to dog person, handing out leaflets. He spotted me and came over in a great hurry, very excited. He pushed a leaflet into my hand.

Spiritual Guidance for Pets
Reverend Roman - Advisor
A Roman Cat-O-Lick Church
No Dogma

Market nr. Dolores

"Clever, don't you think?" Roman looked pleased with his creation. You've flipped, is what I thought. "Very clever."

"I've rented a storefront." His eyes lit up. "Gonna have a pulpit and everything."

"Religious symbols?" I dared to ask.

"I'm thinking of making a new one just for pets."

"What? Crossed paws?" I joked, irreverently.

"Crossed paws?" He considered it, scratching his chin stubble. "Hmm. Not bad." He crossed his forearms on front of him and studied the composition. "Yes, maybe." He held his arms further away and focused on them. "One cat, one dog, symbolizing their true friendship, and perhaps, resting on a bird's outstretched wings, symbolizing being lifted to heaven." He looked at me with moist eyes. "I think you've got something there."

"You know," I said, changing the subject, "here's someone who might be willing to give a guest sermon."

Good Time Charles had just come into the park.

"Hey, Charles." I called out, but got Guinevere's ears first. They shot up and turned in my direction. She spied Gustav and made a beeline. "Sorry, Gustav, I forgot."

Guinevere was over him like a pack of kids over Ronald McDonald. Only Gustav did not have a painted-on smile, but very working growls and teeth. He was like the old Timex watch: Takes a licking and keeps on getting ticked-off. Unfortunately, he was not spittle proof.

Charles loped over, pulled the love-crazed Guinevere off him and aimed her in another direction. She shot off toward a rolling pile of dogs.

I introduced him to Roman who gave him a leaflet.

"I told Philip you might like to do some preaching."

"The wages of sin should not be tax exempt," Charles began, in his best evangelical voice, "we should not taxidermy animals but prepare them for heaven!"

"Amen," said Roman.

"I sat unto you, my fellow Americans, do we want these poor, innocent creatures to fall into the hands of the ungodly? No indeed!"

"Great, Charles." I jumped in.

Roman shook his head in astonishment. "That was moving, my friend. You have the gift."

"Thank you, kindly gentlemen." Charles put his hand over his heart. "As Billy Graham has often said to me while we sat at dinner together: 'Please pass the salt.'"

Charles strode off, theoretically, his eyes raised to heaven. It was a spirited performance.

"Wow," Roman said, "that guy would make a great Pope."

"Yes, he can really throw the Papal Bull. But, he's not Catholic."

"I mean a Pope in my Church."

I shut-up.

"I'm abandoning my writing career," Roman declared firmly. "I've got money. I want to concentrate on my Pet Ministry." A disgusted look crossed his face. "The book writing was sordid. I made tons of money, but I have tons of guilt. This is my true calling, not just a sidelight."

"Good for you," I commended, "Dori told me you were in a seminary."

He gave me a sidewise glance, as if it were a taboo subject or a sore spot. "At the time," he said, relaxing his features, "I thought it was my calling. But human beings were just too sinful and wicked and I despaired of ever accomplishing anything. I was sickened looking into their filthy hearts." Gustav went over to him and got petted. "That's when I hit upon the idea to write exposes. Use the Word to ferret out the sins of prominent people, so the rest would not exalt them, but see them for what they really were, amoral sinners. A kind of well-paying shortcut to paradise, was the way I saw it."

"But you heard the Call of the wild."

"You could put it that way."

"Did you know Katherine was sick?"

"No." He was surprised. "What's wrong?"

"From what I can gather, she suffers from fantasies or delusions. Confuses reality and imagination."

Roman was silent, turning in on his own memories and understandings. I didn't pursue it. He looked remorseful and hurt. I hadn't meant to catch him unawares, just give him the dope. After all, there was a chance he was her father. It seemed whatever passion he might have had for his family was now going to the dogs and cats and birds and other winged and finny things. I felt for the guy, He was a decent sort. I hoped it worked out.

"Animals are so pure," he trumpeted, as if to free himself from the complicated human heart. "They are God's good creatures." He reached down and gave Gustav a light squeeze on the snout. Gustav licked his hand.

"We all have our demons."

I don't know if that helped or hurt. I wasn't trying to buttress Roman's belief in human sinfulness. We tend to see the world through our own experience. The colors we use may not be the same colors others use. We mix different palettes. I can't imagine the Master Painter using a soiled brush and tainted colors.

"Well, Gustav and I have some pigeons to check out," I said, taking my leave. I clapped Roman on the shoulder. "Good luck with the Pet Ministry."

"Thanks."

"when will it open?"

"Soon." He brightened up. "Soon."

The fog galumphed in on big dog's feet.

The cold energizes them. They chased each other in wild, wide swathes around the delighted audience of nimble people. It was a moment when everything did seem to be pure. The purifying sweep of the fog and the pure pleasure of following the dogs around and around in an endless, joyful circle.

The next day I slipped a note through the letter drop of the soon to be converted storefront. I was asking Roman to hire me to distribute leaflets downtown, where people were the thickest. It seemed a harmless, even helpful enterprise for pet owners. It was almost as if he were getting to the sins of the people through their animals.

The plate glass windows needed a good scrubbing, but I could see folding chairs unfolded and arranged in rows, with a wide aisle between.

On the walls were a gallery of primitive dog and cat paintings, and in the far right corner, a large, standing bird cage, minus the bird.

There was a raised platform in front, with a small lopsided desk, director's chair and a portable chalkboard, recently erased. Behind, on the far wall, was a thinly sketched mural, waiting to be filled in with color, whose motif I could not see, but could guess at.

I scanned the facade of the store for any lettering or signs to indicate what the neighborhood would be getting. There were none.

On one side of the store was a musty used-book shop and on the other a vacancy.

Through the smeared reflection of the window, I saw a shape coming up behind me. It peered over my shoulder into the store. I turned and did a double-take.

"Katherine!"

"Hi, Beamer," she smiled, giving me a soft poke in the side. "What are you doing here?"

"Trying to get a job."

She tried to open the door. It was locked.

"Mom told me Philip was opening a store. It's exciting. What's in there?"

"Not much."

She was avidly interested. "She said it had something to do with animals. I love animals."

"It's a church."

"A church?"

"A church for animals."

"How cool!" She squinted into the window. "What are those awful paintings on the wall?"

"I guess he's decorating."

She grimaced. "He must have raided the local kindergarten."

I shrugged. I didn't think they were that bad. Kind of impressionistic or abstract. The colors were nice.

"I can do better ones for him," she said with confidence.

"You paint?"

"Took some courses," she said proudly, if modestly.

"So, you have talent."

"Mother thinks so."

"What do you paint?"

"Mostly drawings. Watercolors out my window. The garden. The Bay. Portraits from photos. Did the bichons. It's just for fun."

"Can I treat you to coffee?" I asked, picking anxiously at a fingernail. She was sizing up the store's location. "What?"

"Coffee?"

"Just had some."

"You look very elegant."

"Thank you," she answered smiling, taking the compliment in stride.

She did look good. After the dishevelment of last week, she was now perfectly groomed, with fresh cut hair, and a sleeveless, short-skirted summer dress, showing off her sleek legs. Her fragrant essence filled my nostrils and set my inner nose hairs aquiver.

Her expression now was of someone looking outward, looking at the world. Not like I had seen her before, when her mind was engulfed by the tidal waves of her own fear and despair.

"I'm glad you're feeling better."

"Thanks. It was hell. I can hardly remember half of it. Like a dream." She paused, closed her eyes tightly. "Or rather, a nightmare. Still get headaches, though."

"Considering what you went through, there's bound to be some carryover."

She looked at me admiringly.

"That's what the Doc said. You're smart, Beamer."

I knew I wasn't. But why admit it.

"Well, you know, things just don't stop on a dime."

"That's true." She thought about it briefly. "Let's get coffee sometime," she proposed.

"Sure."

She swung around and her skirt made a swirl. "I'm going shopping!"

I couldn't compete with shopping, so I just had to wait my turn. To be honest, though, I didn't expect her offer to come to anything. It was a whim of the moment and nothing to get excited about, at least in reality. I stared wistfully at her departing figure.

I remember someone being offended when I told her I felt pity for her. She had bouts of self-pity, so her interpretation was different than my intention.

As I watched Katherine leave, I already felt a nostalgia mixed with pity mixed with affection mixed with eroticism. I guess, I shouldn't have stopped with pity. When I said pity, I meant love, but pity is what came out.

Fifty years in prison or one day in Paradise.

You'd have a bounty of time to read, think, meditate. But you'd be locked up. One day would go by in a flash, but you'd know complete freedom.

It was a question I posed to myself, out-of-the blue, as I walked back home, dodging oncoming pedestrians, my thoughts wandering off into nowhere.

I called Dori to see how she was.

"Miserable," she snuffled.

"You sound better," I coaxed.

She was convulsed by a hacking cough.

"Rest."

"Thank you, Mayo Clinic."

She could still ripple the smoothest conversations.

"I went to Roman's Church."

"You went to a Roman Catholic Church?" She perked up. "To pray? For me? How sweet."

How did she infer that? I made a quick, silent prayer.

"I did pray for you, but not there." I held my breath. "Phillip Roman is opening a church for pets."

"A what?"

"A Pet Ministry. Remember?"

"Oh, yeah. Yeah," she scoffed.

"You can have your dogs blessed."

She sneezed three times.

"Bless you. Bless you. Bless you." I rattled **it** off. "A triple. I award you third base."

"Your humor totally eludes me, Beamer." She was pointedly formal. "I'm tired. Goodbye."

Gustav was flat on his belly, one paw under his chin.

"Well, Gustav, another faux pas." His eyes shifted sideways and watched me with tentative curiosity. "Or, as you dogs say, 'faux paw.'"

Roman was grateful for my willingness to work for him. He gave me exclusive handing out rights and double the usual hourly wage. I encouraged him to have FREE printed on top, in large letters, on the next batch of leaflets. It would be a cinch to pass them out.

I spent the next two weeks in various downtown locations hawking the free services of the Pet Ministry. People with dogs started showing up. No cats. No birds. They would have to be served with home visits. That was added to the leaflets.

Roman stood behind the wooden pulpit, which had crossed paws inlaid on a field of wing, and surveyed the dozen attendees. He had just finished his sermon. Sweat shone on his forehead. His hands were clasped together and he had a blissful expression on his face.

"Come up and be blessed," he offered, and the motley crew formed an irregular line to drink from a gilt edged water bowl and receive a Milk Bone wafer.

The paintings on the wall had changed. Bichons were in the center, flanked by Lassie Collies and horses. They were a technical improvement on the originals, but less lavish with color and imagination.

The mural was complete. Not surprisingly, it was adorable with playfully posed puppies and kittens, watched over by several dogs of indeterminate breeds, who were in turn watched over by a discreetly painted likeness of Philip Roman. At least there were no foals.

The next service would be in an hour. I chatted briefly with Roman.

He went into the back room and brought out more treaters, a refilled bowl of water and a box of newly printed leaflets. I decided to get the rush hour crowd emerging from the MUNI stations on their way home. In their hurry, they were apt to grab anything thrust in front of them to avoid slowing down. That was my theory.

For the first time, I saw a bird in the cage. A parrot. Roman explained that John, a dog parker I knew, had donated the parrot to the Church. He already had 38 parrots and macaws in a room in his flat.

Basil, the parrot installed in the cage, enjoyed the flurry of activity. However, he had picked up the expression, 'bad dog' from John, who had kept him in the living room, and who regularly disciplined his own rowdy dogs. So, any dog in the Church who passed too near Basil was greeted by, 'bad dog' in a condescending squawk.

I left the Church, walked the seven blocks home, took Gustav out for a last trip around the block, then settled in with a book.

At 9:30 the phone rang. It was Roman. He was furiously upset.

"Malcolm's here! It's mayhem! Come over!"

"Okay! Be right over!"

I quickly changed shoes and ran to the Church. I could hear barking dogs a block away. I pulled open the door.

Dogs were straining at the leash to get to Hayward, who was standing in the middle of a few overturned chairs. His hand on Katherine's wrist, trying to haul her away.

Katherine was holding onto Roman, who was slowly losing ground. She had a look of panic on her face.

"Let go of her!" I shouted, enraged. He stopped short and looked at me. He released her and came at me. His hands shot out to my neck. I took a step back, ducked to the side, held my ground, concentrated, and gave him a short, swift, vicious kick to the kneecap with my metal-tipped shoes. I heard a dull crack.

Hayward let out a stunned cry and his leg buckled. I felt an intense rush of adrenalin and was going to go for the other knee when Roman pulled me off. I watched the writhing agony of Hayward with a sweet mixture of vindication and relief.

"Help me get him to the car," Katherine ordered Roman, as she felt in her stepfather's pockets for the keys.

Roman let go of me and I sat down.

They each got under one of his shoulders and dragged him to the door. Katherine turned and glanced at me accusingly, and my long-awaited victory melted in confusion.

I watched them, agape, but not in the religious sense, as they went out into the night.

It was like an episode out of a long, distant past, though it happened only an hour ago.

I sat on the edge of the bed, petting Gustav, calmer after striding up several steep hills at break-neck pace and getting the pounding call from my heart to slow down.

I sat with Gustav, trying to get the violent spasms of my body under control, digging my fingers unknowingly into his fur until he yelped.

"I'm sorry, Gustav." I stroked him gently over the same spot. He looked up at me forgivingly.

The pangs of guilt sharpened as the violent feelings subsided. Did lover do it? I was defending myself. No qualms.

I called Paul but he was out. Dori had the late, late shift. I put the headphones on and listened to the late Beethoven Quartets, the most profound music I knew. Deep feelings had surfaced and they needed something to latch onto, to join to, to be part of the common experience, not isolated, not inhuman.

The phone remained silent the rest of the night. I slithered into a sleep filled with grotesque, murderous creatures bent on destroying me. I awoke with a start and it was morning. Sleep had provided no sanctuary, yielded no secrets.

I was jittery all morning, fumbling with everything in my hands. Was I worried about retaliation or just trying to integrate the brutal action.

One thing was certain. Gustav had to go out.

Once outside the ruminative thoughts vanished. There was open space for them to reach out to and other people to focus on. The reassurance and perspective of the everyday world was welcome.

The main thing right now was to have contact with someone. No Charles. No Dori. No Paul in sight. But Henry the Chef was back, from wherever he had been. I hailed him.

"Ah, monsieur," he doffed a beret, "how are you?"

"Okay, Henry. Where you been?"

"Nowhere but home," he answered, despondently.

"Where's Titus?"

"In zee dumps." He let out a sigh. "I think he has the malaise, the ennui."

"Why are you talking all this French stuff?"

"Oh," he returned to his Texas roots, "been brushing up on my French cooking."

I thought Titus might be a good candidate for the Pet Ministry, but held off. "You remember Hayward?" His expression turned sour. "I had a fight with him."

Henry looked at me in wonderment, hanging on the next revelation. "I won."

A slow, appreciative smile curled his lips. I don't know if the French were big on relish, but he certainly was.

"I think I cracked his kneecap."

"Wow," was all he could say. I'm sure he had fantasized doing the same thing.

"Did he ever have, you know, dangerous looking friends up for dinner, when you were his chef?"" I asked, just checking.

Henry rubbed one hand over the other as he thought back.

"No." He looked at me positively. "I don't think he had any friends."

"At least, none you knew."

"Yes."

"So, you've been holed up. Don't you bring Titus here anymore?"

"I do," he answered with a sunken voice, "but usually late at night."

"No wonder Titus is depressed, he misses his doggie buddies."

"You think?"

"Sure. Why else would he get so suddenly down?"

"From me?"

"Some. But he needs that outdoor play. Rough-housing with other dogs."

Henry chewed on it. Flipped it over. Scrambled it around in his brain. He finally put a crust on the idea.

"I'll bring him out this evening."

"Good." I felt good. I wasn't turning into some insane killing machine. I had a sensible conversation and I was giving sound advice.

"So, you beat up Hayward."

Henry looked at me with astonishment. I could produce not one bulging muscle.

"He beat me up first, but," I hastily added, "it was a trap."

"Why'd he want to beat you up in the first place?"

"He thought I was bothering Katherine."

I waited for him to say something enlightening, but he just looked down and shook his head in bewilderment.

I clued him in. "She's sick. She needs medicine. All that abuse stuff was a fiction she invented."

"If you say so."

This was not something I was going to pursue. I put a cap on the conversation by telling Henry I would see him this evening and moseyed up the hill. I sat cross-legged while Gustav searched the terrain for pigeons.

The All-Star Game was on tonight and I intended to have the pleasure of watching it.

I was in a strong baseball mood. I had just sent away for a Babe Ruth pocket knife from the Franklin Mint, treating myself out of my last paycheck from Roman.

After an earlier than usual evening trip to the park for Gustav, I settled in with ice cream, beer and popcorn at the ready. Gustav was intently working on a 'bon' bone and my bare feet dangled coolly over the plain chair I used as a footstool.

I have always rooted for the National League. My first allegiance was to the Brooklyn Dodgers, which made me an inveterate Yankee hater. To this day, one of life's small pleasures is to see the Yankees lose.

Thanks to baseball, I knew real love and hate early in life. The elation of triumph and the lowness of defeat. My first, and probably most everlasting ambition was to be a baseball player. I never got farther than stickball. But I'd fall asleep at night cracking a grand slam in the bottom of the ninth.

This year's All-Star Game was played in a stadium designed strictly for baseball, with beautiful green grass, and stands filled with brightly dressed, cheering fans.

I enjoyed every inning of it.

It was week since the incident at the Pet Ministry. Nothing had happened.

I spent early mornings and evening holding up leaflets, with FREE prominent, to be snatched on the move by rushing workers. In between, I did my errands, went on walks with Gustav, played my guitar and read.

Each night I anticipated a phone call. None came. When I stopped expecting it, it would probably come. How can you expect the unexpected? By trying not to think about it, I was constantly thinking about it.

Then something broke in to take my mind off it completely.

My place was robbed.

Someone had shimmied down from the roof on a flimsy drainpipe and had come in through my open window. My portable T.V., radio, jazz CDs, $50 in bills on my desk, had all disappeared out the front door, which was unlocked when I came in.

Even before I opened the door, I sensed something was wrong, and I was right. It was not much of a take for the thief, who had been desperate enough to risk a three story fall from a broken down building that obviously held no riches.

I would never have expected anyone to come through the window. I left it wide open when I went out, to keep the place well-ventilated. It didn't occur to me that it would also be a wide open invitation to steal. And nobody saw anything.

The things were replaceable, but the sense of invulnerability was not. I had settled one anger and now another one against the thief rose up.

An intrusion into my domain. A violation of the basic human pact. I felt the strongest walls could crumble at a touch, there was no safe place.

I had laughed descendingly at Gustav when he chased a cat from under a car only to have it escape by slinking through a fence. He then went back to the same car to look under it for other cats, as if they all massed there.

But I laughed no more.

For the next few days, my attention was often trained on that window, waiting for another robber to come crashing through. It was irrational, but I still did it.

What was even odder, was an obsession to check and recheck the lock on my front door, even though I knew that the robber didn't come in that way.

I don't know if the Hayward assault had triggered this sudden paranoia, or the break-in itself was jangling my nerves, but I was suddenly fearing for my back, when I had never feared for it before.

I finally got hold of Paul. A tumbling torrent of words ran through the wires.

"Hey, take it easy." His voice was calm. "You had no choice."

I was still baffled by my own rashness, and still needed justification for it. And certainly, I needed an ally.

"I never hit people," I protested.

"You must have a long fuse."

"It's one thing to hit someone," I continued to argue ridiculously, "but to deliberately try to maim them!"

"He really set you off, didn't he?" Paul hit on it. "But you did act in self-defense, there were witnesses, I wouldn't worry about the law."

"I'm not worried about the law." I paused to regroup. "To exacerbate everything, mu place was broken into."

"Paul gave a short, throaty laugh. "Well, at least they didn't steal your vocabulary." He blew out some air. "What'd they take?"

I itemized it for him.

"Got the T.V., huh. Beamer, the ultimate sports junkie, without a T.V." He laughed again. "That's really bad news." I heard some tapping sounds. "I've got an extra one. Never use it. It's old, but it works. It's yours if you want it."

"I didn't hesitate. "Thanks. You're a pal."

"It's no problem. Be in the park tomorrow evening and we'll cart it over in my truck." His voice drifted away. "It's an old devil."

"That's okay. Thanks."

I didn't tell him I was worried about Hayward, but I think he knew.

The fear gradually wore off, partly from the passage of time and partly from the realization that Hayward was probably supported by crutches and wasn't about to do anything to anybody.

This last thought sat well, for in the topsy-turvy saga of the Haywards, Katherine was safer, if she had any reason not to feel safe.

I quit handing out leaflets for the Church and was searching for new work. Roman persuaded me to stick around. He needed someone to accompany him when he made house calls. He made me a generous offer, and it sounded interesting. Who knew what fascinating creatures would subscribe to Roman's outlandish Church.

Right off the bat, we were knocking on the door of a gloomy, musty Victorian in Hayes Valley. A huge woman dressed in black with a large gold cross dangling from her neck, opened the door.

"Enter!" she said gruffly.

She held the door and we trudged in. She closed the door heavily behind us and snapped shut the locks. We stood stock-still until she led us into a lamplight, old world living room. Massive, dark furniture and heavy, brocaded drapes.

"Sit down!" she demanded, and we did.

She was middle-aged, with greying blond hair pulled back tightly from a round, fleshy face. Very teutonic.

"Drinks?" she inquired, with cordial correctness, and pointed to fruit juice bottles in a tub of ice.

"Thanks," I said, and made a move for the juice. Her palm came up to stop me. She reached in, lifted out an orange bottle, twisted it open and handed it to me.

"You?" she asked Roman. He nodded and soon had a red one. "Poopsie!" she called out.

Something stirred from under the tasseled cover of the sofa. "Poopsie!" A tiny dog crawled warily out. It looked like a furry chihuahua. She reached down and snatched the intimidated beast to her full bosom and held it there.

Roman finally spoke.

"You requested an audience?" She stared him down. "I mean, you asked to see me?"

"My Poopsie has been very nervous lately."

I wonder why?

"Yes, I see," Roman observed, "he's shaking."

"I think he needs the fear of God in him."

"Has he been bad?"

"He pees." Poopsie was trying strenuously to break out of her locked embrace. "Yes!" she boomed, "people eat too much meat. They are dying of heart attacks." She pounded her free hand into the coffee table, rattling the ice cubes. "It is bad!" she fumed. "They are clogging up the arteries. It is bad!"

"Shall I pray for Poopsie?" asked Roman, weakly.

"They are dying the streets from clogged arteries!" She dropped Poopsie to the floor and he skittered out of the room. I wished him good luck.

"When we get back to the Church we shall offer a prayer for Poopsie," Roman said, and to my great relief, rose to go.

"Yes!"

"Nice talking to you," I said, not reaching out a hand.

"Yes!"

She sat frozen, her eyes like slow searchlights on our faces. We moved backwards to the door, furiously undid the locks and elbowed each other to be the first outside.

"Where to next?" I smiled.

He took out an appointment book from his inside jacket pocket, the one emblazoned with a crossed paws crest, and flipped the pages.

"Fish." he said, unflappably.

The client lived in a three floor walkup in the Tenderloin. A frail man in his seventies, wearing a bathrobe and slippers answered the door. His teeth were out.

"I forgot all about you coming, Reverend," he mouthed, and threw up his hands. "Glory be, I'm getting more and more forgetful."

"You have a fish?" For a Reverend, Roman had very little formality.

"Yes, Reverend." The man's hands went flying up again. He shuffled over to the other side of the room, where a small aquarium tank shared a table with a large-print Bible.

"Goldilocks?" he whispered endearingly. "We have visitors."

We peered into the murky water of the tank.

"I don't see her," Roman frowned.

"She's in there somewhere." The old man tapped the tank with the backs of his fingers. There was a slight movement under the tiny Japanese bridge.

"There she comes!" he exulted.

The goldfish drifted listlessly upwards. Its gills were working overtime.

"She's been under the weather lately." He tapped the tank again and shook his head with concern. "I pray for her every night."

"Change the water," came the Oracle from the Pet Ministry.

"Lost my glasses. Put 'em down an' can't find 'em again."

"Change the water and get Goldilocks a friend."

"But I'm her friend."

"A fish friend." Roman plunked down a twenty. "Make sure they have enough food."

"I will. I will." He shook our hands fervently in gratitude. "You are very kind, sir." He almost lapsed into tears.

"Call again if you need help."

"Thank you. Thank you."

We walked back down the stairs. I had a good feeling towards Roman. Generosity was an admirable trait. I wish I could afford it.

We settled into Roman's luxurious car and he started the engine.

"Where next?" I asked.

"One more stop. Pacific Heights."

He shifted uncomfortably in his seat and gunned the powerful motor.

"Hold on!" My allusion to our rocky association with Hayward not missed. Roman was biting his lip.

We stopped three blocks from the Hayward Mansion. After circling the block twice and not finding a space, Roman parked in front of a fire hydrant and had the audacity to put a placard in his front window with the crossed paws symbol and the word 'CLERGY' in bold type beneath.

The condo building was a modern, glistening, glass-faced, faceless monstrosity with curved patios jutting out, two to a floor.

The elevator soundlessly glided up to the twelfth floor and stopped without a hitch. The carpeted hallway had a door at one end and a door at the other end. We went left.

A petite, uniformed maid answered the door and led us onto a spotlessly white carpet, through a short foyer, with copies of Degas ballerinas on the walls, and into a sunken living room, smartly decorated with sleek, blonde Scandinavian furniture and glass top tables. I counted seven cats in various positions of repose occupying the sofas and chairs, their steady eyes watched with a distant and drowsy interest.

"Please sit down," said the young maid, with a friendly drawl. "Mrs. Brosnan will be right out."

I looked for a spot that would not encroach on the cats. But to sit anywhere was to disturb them. I approached a padded arm chair. A black cat with intense yellow eyes rested on its haunches on the arm. As I came nearer, it slowly raised up and arched its back defensively.

"Nice kitty," I crooned, and tried to sidle into the chair without giving offense. The cat hissed and swiped at me. I sat on the other arm, out of reach.

In the meantime, Roman had one cat rubbing up against his leg, another nuzzling his neck and a third, a Siamese, indolently walking towards him.

They ignored me completely. They seemed to know who had experience with cats and who didn't.

We don't want to waste our time on amateurs, they seemed to say, give us a veteran. One who knows proper obeisance. Not some heavy-handed, rough-houser who doesn't appreciate our exalted position in the scheme of things.

Since I am allergic to these guys, and they to me, we've had little experience with one another. Like pigeons, the cat grapevine probably has my number, remembering the small cruelties I inflicted on their number during my insensitive toddler years.

Mrs. Brosnan made a grand, ballerina's entrance into the room, smiling a big smile.

"My sweethearts," she purred, spreading her arms to encompass the whole room, which I suppose included Roman and me. She jounced towards us and we both stood up. She extended her hand and we extended ours. Instead of a soft lady-like handshake, we got slaps across our palms.

"Give me five!" she frisked, with pristine good humor.

She had a just washed head of freefalling dark hair, an exquisite figure wrapped in jeans and a white sweater. She had animated, restless eyes. She could be anywhere in her thirties.

"So, how are my babies?" She went over and gave each attentive cat a gentle tweak on the nose. She sat down and we sat down.

"You have beautiful cats," Roman complimented,

"Yes, they are gorgeous." She smiled adoringly at her feline family. She told us the name of each cat. "Say hello," she encouraged them. The cats looked vacantly back at her. "Oh, well, guess this is a silence day."

She meowed at them and a very good imitation it was. One jumped on her lap, another perched on her shoulder and a third ensconced itself against her thigh. Lucky cat.

"It says in your letter," Roman held an open letter, "that you were curious about my Ministry. I hope ...."

"I should have said 'fascinated,'" she broke in. "I've always wondered if animals have souls."

"Of course they have!" Roman answered with righteous conviction.

"How do you know?" she asked politely.

"People have souls, why not animals," he answered, not expecting to be contradicted.

Maybe, she was thinking what I was thinking. How do we know people have souls?

"Can animals go to hell?" she asked, innocently.

"Then the people in hell wouldn't suffer," Roman countered, with his unique vision of suffering.

Well, maybe animals have their own hell. But, if there were no people there, it wouldn't be hell, I thought cynically.

"And you?" she said jovially, handing me a glass of wine and pouring one for herself. Roman declined. "Are you his bodyguard?"

"His translator," I said, with a straight face. "I speak reptile, walrus and elephant."

Roman gave me a look of scorching rebuke.

"A wit-ness," she joked.

"For conversions," Roman quickly emphasized.

"You convert animals?" she asked, intrigued.

"Many."

"How do you know they've been converted?"

"They tell me."

She looked at him peculiarly. "They tell you?"

"By their expressions."

"Oh," she said, relieved.

"Yes, I know when they've accepted salvation." He hung his head piously.

Mrs. Brosnan tilted her head and twirled her hair around her fingers, smiling at me. When Roman lifted his head, she turned away and stroked one of her cats.

"I don't need your services this minute," she advised Roman, "But I hope you can pay me another visit and we can discuss this at more length."

"I have a full schedule for two months," he declared.

"No sooner?" she said, disappointed. "How 'bout your witness here?"

"I'd come, but I'm not an acolyte." I could see that he did not trust me with his theology. "I could bring his writings, though." He looked more interested. "Maybe, some of your friends would like to join the Church?"

The prospect of a potentially wealthy and influential elite in his congregation, boosted his confidence in me.

"Please feel free, Mr. Todd, to bring any material to Mrs. Brosnan at any time."

I was disconcerted by Roman's frosty silence on the ride back.

He lucked-out not having a ticket planted on his windshield or having his car towed away, and had done a good deed, for which he was rightly praised.

Did my goofy humor disparage his Church?

He said nothing. Just stared fixedly at the road, ignoring me. His grip on the steering wheel could not have been tighter. Finally, he spoke, a drop of acid on his tongue.

"Croak. Croak."

"I'm sorry, it just slipped out."

"Hiss. Hiss."

"Rattle. Rattle," I contributed.

His tone was conciliatory. "Listen, Beamer. During the Lord's business please don't be facetious."

"Okay."

His fingers relaxed and he leaned back restfully in his custom, contoured leather seat.

"She's a looker," he said.

"Who? Mrs. Brosnan?"

"The maid!" he said, surprised there could be a doubt.

"She's attractive," I agreed.

Now I became silent. I thought of Mrs. Brosnan and smiled. It wasn't the staggering force of hurricane love that hit me, but a sweet zephyr.

Roman dropped me at my door and sped off. I brought Gustav out for a walk around the neighborhood.

I thought of him among all those cats. Maybe, he would be a King to them, and they would lick him and preen him until he was delirious with attention. He would settle among them spoiled forever.

On the other hand, they might tear him to shreds. He did not have a way with cats. He charged them. Though he was becoming more circumspect. The last one he rushed, turned, held its ground, while Gustav skidded to a stop in front of it, too close. He got a bloody claw cut near the eye.

I had to admit I was nervous around a beautiful woman. A representation of perfection. But beauty is really the combination of the inside and the outside. It is a wholeness, not a part. Or should I say, not apart, it belongs. You expect beauty to be good.

The philosophical notion of evil. Does evil belong? Or is it just an aberration of the good?

I like to think that evil does not belong in this world. There is no definitive argument to make for it, except to rely on one's deepest human feelings and to have a dog.

For Gustav, this trip was not an amble, as it was for me, but a reconnaissance. He was extremely busy poking his potent sniffer into everything and peeing on it. Where did this enormous supply come from? Nature seemed very generous when it came to male dog bladders.

Some nights, it's just hard to get to sleep. Especially weekends, when there is nothing on the social agenda, and you can hear partying all around you. It made me realize how desperately I needed female companionship.

I wish I was more of a fling artist, a bar tripper, a good-timer, where I could take things more lightly. But I seemed to be cursed with a serious bent. I was even appalled by light ice cream and lite beer.

Mrs. Brosnan appealed to me. She seemed to be a woman of taste, and from my experience, light anything had no taste.

Sometimes, it helps to write out your thoughts until they crystalize and give you a bearing. I tried, but my thoughts were too tangential, touching all over the place, caroming off each other, like billiard balls gone amok.

Emotions need a place to rest. Gustav had done it for a while, but my feelings were broadening again. Even at this stage of my life, I was still moving up the evolutionary ladder.

My first years in San Francisco I stayed in cheap hotels and my main relationships were with the cockroaches that infested the place. Then when I moved from downtown, the birds outside my window became regular company. After the insects and the avians came the canines and my long-term commitment to Gustav. The next rung up had to be human.

I suppose I could make friends with a porpoise, but it would be very impractical and a chimpanzee would be illegal, so unless I skip a rung and get scooped off the Earth by an alien spacecraft, or put my foot constantly in my mouth, it's bound to land on a female toe.

With this sense of propitiousness lightening my heavy thoughts, I looked forward to seeing Mrs. Brosnan again as soon as I could arrange it. Call her tomorrow, I told myself, invite myself over, in a 'professional' capacity, of course, and see what develops.

"If it wasn't for you, Gustav, I wouldn't be where I was." He looked at me. There was a devotion in his eyes that seemed impossible to deserve.

Marge, the maid, told me Mrs. Brosnan was out of town for a few days, visiting her sister in L.A. I said I'd call back and to let her know I had phoned. I left my name and number.

I put the phone down, deflated. I had been puffing myself up for this moment and I felt the air whoosh out of me as it does out of a kid's balloon.

I filled myself up again with a promising evening of house visits for the Pet Ministry. Roman did them twice a week. The rest he reserved for Church Services.

The day passed slowly, as it always does when you want it to go faster. Finally, I said goodbye to Gustav and headed to the Church to team up with Roman for our excursion into PetLand.

Our first couple had a menagerie of small reptiles, took umbrage that their darlings were maligned as slimy and stupid and worst of all, connected through the snake with man's downfall from Eden. Quite a burden.

"It wasn't their fault!" The man, in his forties, stout and rumpled said, cuddling a small black snake, presumably harmless. "Some idiot picked on them in the Bible and they suffer for it."

This posed a dilemma for Roman.

He became squeamish when asked to bless Max, who had been presented to him and was now coiling around his arm.

"He's cute, don't you think?" said the wife, a woman taller than any of us, with a giant lizard mounted on her head.

I don't know if she was referring to the snake, or to the iguana. If it came down to a beauty contest, I'd have to go with the snake. To Roman, it might be a toss-up.

Roman said some words over the snake in Latin, which seemed to stop Max in his tracks. I wondered if the old snake memories of being tied to sin were evoked hearing this classical, liturgic tongue. Did he think he was going to be hacked to pieces?

Roman was sodden with sweat. He had blessed two more snakes, both bigger than Max, the iguana, a gila monster, and after donning some heavy gloves, some restless scorpions. The tanks were crammed with green, unmoving things, and the room was hot.

Why did some people have a penchant for soft, furry pets like bunnies and dogs and cats and others a penchant for scaly, repulsively regarded reptiles?

I was waiting for someone with an ant farm, who would have each ant individually identified and ask Roman to bless each of them by name, as they sat on his palm. If he unexpectedly gave in to an urge to applaud himself and his mission, he could instantly wipe out his newest saved parishioners.

We washed up thoroughly before leaving. The couple thanked him and bowed to kiss his crossed paws ring, which he would not permit.

"Not until we are recognized by the Mother Church," he said with deference. "Well, as one Swiss cheese said to the other Swiss cheese: 'Stay holey.'"

With that we went out the door.

Roman was a corker. He was proud of his joke, of his attempt to blend humor into his very serious calling.

"Like that?" he turned to me and asked on the way out to the Avenues. "I made it up."

I doubted it. But then who am I to discourage a good laugh. They leave out the funny stuff in the Bible. Where Jonah tickled the inside of the whale's stomach, and thus was allowed to set up housekeeping, or that one of Noah's sons had to clean up after the animals, and was so unclean, his name was Ham.

So I was glad Roman was punching it up.

"Very witty," I told him.

"You may not believe this," he confided, "but I was considered a cutup at the Seminary."

"Really?"

What we need is a Messiah with a good sense of humor. They are always so dour and weighty. Roman had his strictness, but he also had his lighthearted moments. My vote would be Roman for Animal Messiah.

Rats.

We visited a little girl with her rats, Phoebe and Smalley. Her parents were devout church goers and would never let her take the rats to church.

Once, they told us, she snuck them into church in her jacket pockets, and the strange, moving bulges caused people to stare, and when she took them out, one slipped out of her hand, and headed straight for the Altar.

The congregation skeddadled when a rumor quickly spread that it was an omen of a new Biblical plague, or at least that it was a rodent.

The priest, who had been a slick fielding shortstop in high school, snared the darting rat and handed it wriggling back to the girl. It was forever barred from the church.

"So, how are you?" Roman asked the girl, who was seven or eight.

"Fine," the girl said, watching the rats run over her cupped hands.

"They are very cute." He smiled.

"Phoebe and Smalley," she said, holding them to eye height for him to see.

"Hello, Phoebe and Smalley." He touched their little heads.

"No!" she said abruptly, "that's Phoebe and that's Smalley!"

"I'm sorry," he said, appeasingly. The girl looked a bit snotty. "What's your name?"

"Teresa," she answered, with a bit of haughtiness.

Bit by bit, Roman was biting his tongue.

"Do you want me to bless them?" he offered, in a sugary voice.

"Why?"

"So they'll go to Heaven," he assured her.

"Rat heaven or people heaven?" she asked.

"Rat heaven," Roman answered, evenly.

"Won't they get beat up by other rats?" she said defiantly.

"There are no bad rats in Heaven."

"Why can't they go to people Heaven?"

"People Heaven is right next door to Rat Heaven," he said smoothly, "You can visit them."

"Can I take my hamster along?"

I could see that Roman had wandered into arcane religious territory. He did the smart thing. He pulled out.

"Well, Teresa. Do you like magic?"

"Yes," she said, eagerly.

"I'm going to say some magic words over your rats and they will live happily ever after. Will you like that?"

"Yes," she said, brightly.

Roman spoke his Latin. The girl listened and watched transfixed by his words and his movements. The rats seemed mesmerized.

"What did one mouse say to the other mouse?"

"What!?" she asked, expectantly.

"My Swiss cheese is holier than your Swiss cheese!" he said and laughed.

Teresa stuck out her tongue and made a sound like an outboard motor.

We left through the front door, saying goodbye to her nonplussed parents.

"One more?"

Roman nodded, with an expression that said the show must go on. The next theater was a housing project.

A group of young men moved languorously to the car, critically eyeing this monument to European engineering. We opened the doors and got out. The men blocked our path.

"Whatcha doin' here?" the closest one asked, coming face to face with Roman and looking at me at an angle.

"Clergy," he answered, unruffled.

"Clergy!?" The young man laughed with a snort. "In that car?" the rest of the group looked balefully at us.

"I'm here to see Mrs. Wright," Roman said forcefully. "She has parakeets."

They snickered. "Parakeets?"

Someone yelled out belligerently. "She paying you!?"

"There is no charge for a blessing."

"You gonna bless the birds?"

The remark caused another wave of laughter to invigorate the group. Then another.

"Maybe it's the Birdman of Alcatraz!"

"Yeah. And the other one is the Birdbrain of Alcatraz!'

Roman was unfazed.

"Take me to Mrs. Wright!" he demanded and whipped out a pocket Bible from inside his jacket. He pointed it at them. "Am I going to have to use this!?" he threatened.

"An itty bitty Bible?" the main man sneered. "A Bible book never hurt no one!"

"God's word carries a sting!" Roman waved the book threateningly. "Those who disobey shall be thrown through the portals of Hell, never to be seen again. In eternal damnation, spitting up the fires of unrepentance, howling at the pain of unforgiveness, forever in the crushing arms of Satan!"

They looked on stunned, trying to make sense of us.

"This man's crazy," said the leader, "don't want to fool with no crazy man. Do your stuff, Reverend. Take care of those damned birds!" He laughed cheerfully and laughter echoed behind him.

They parted and let us go past into the crumbling building. Roman gave me a wink as he rang Mrs. Wright's bell.

"Nothing like the fear of God," he smiled, clicking his tongue for his performance. He scared me. It's true that nobody wants to mess with a loony man. Especially, one invoking the Devil.

The elevator did not *come*. We walked up five flights and after negotiating a passage pitted with recently pried up floor tiles, knocked on Mrs. Wright's door.

"One second. One second. I'm comin'. I'm comin.'"

A minute later the thin door opened and a smiling older woman, wiping her hands on her apron, invited us in.

The room was surprisingly bare.

"Been robbed," she said, still smiling. "Took most everything not nailed down. Was at my daughter's place overnight."

"We're very sorry," Roman consoled.

"It's alright."

"It doesn't look alright." I said.

"You know, I'm not dumb," she said, looking around her. "Put all the valuables in a trunk in the closet. Locked it and the closet. Left some easy pickings so they can be satisfied. Didn't think they'd cart away my big old T.V. Gonna miss my soaps."

She led us into another smaller room where there were half a dozen birds in a large cage.

"When you live in a place with so much crime, you ain't immune." Her eyes were sharp with intelligence and hardship. "But you got to be crafty." It would take a lot of smarts to deal with implacable thieves.

The bird saw us and launched into some high-pitched chirping.
"Your birds are safe."

"If they touched my birds, they'd have to face thunder. And they know it!" Veins stood out on her wide forehead. "They're all shook up from all the commotion those robbers probably made. When I called you they were calm, now they're shaky little birds."

We moved slowly closer to their cage. The birds went silent and huddled at the back. Mrs. Wright looked from birds to Reverend apprehensively.

"Are you a churchgoer Mrs. Wright?"

"Every Sunday."

"I suggest you read the good book to these birds."

She considered it. And approved.

"Sounds like a fine idea," she smiled, "I should have thought of that."

"That's why the Pet Ministry's here."

Roman chanted some Latin at the terrified birds, which seemed to intensify their terror. Then he whistled a happy tune and they didn't seem so afraid. They didn't sing back, but they were more interested in the whistling than in the fear. Score one for Roman.

Mrs. Wright asked us to stay for tea. On the condition that it would be brief, because he had so many animals to attend to, Roman agreed.

"It's fine work you do, Reverend."

"Thank you," he answered, sipping Red Zinger.

"Ever go to the Zoo?" she said, with a delighted look on her face. "I take my grandchildren there when I can. They just love to see all those animals."

"I do pets."

"Yes. I guess those Lions and Elephants would take a heap of praying for."

"Piles," I added.

"And you, Sir, what do you do?"

Not much, I wanted to say.

"I'm a witness for conversions."

I almost said 'conversations.' There was definitely a needle in me ready to puncture the most serious conversations with a prick of levity. That's what made it tough working for Reverend Roman.

On the other hand, witnessing animal conversions was something that would look good on my resume.

Back to the first hand, working with Roman forced me to try to treat serious concerns seriously. My approach had always been truth with a large dash of humor. Roman worked in the other direction, begrudging the humor.

He was restive.

"Must go," he said, rising from his chair and nearly toppling the tea in his lap. He took a Church card from his pocket, wrote a few lines on the back and handed it to Mrs. Wright. "Give this to the T.V. store down the block from me. They'll deliver a new one."

She held the card, read it over and put her hands over his. He squirmed out and backed to the door. I followed him out with a wave to the teary Mrs. Wright.

Mrs. Brosnan opened the door herself.

"Got your message," I said, dry-mouthed. "Here I am."

"And so you are. Come in."

She led the way into the living room, or should I say, cat room. She was almost catlike herself. She wore black leotards and a Mickey Mouse sweatshirt. Her long hair glistened. Her movements were buoyant.

"Beer?"

"Sure."

She came back with two Heinekens and two beer glasses. I poured.

"Are you a dancer?" I asked, after we each had taken a swallow of the cool brew.

"Was. Ballet." She leaned back lackadaisically.

"Wow!" I was impressed.

"I was in the San Francisco Ballet Corps."

"Professional?"

I don't know why I was so excited. It was dancing. Something I rarely watched or did. But I thought of ballet as the epitome of dance, a high art, or a high-brow art associated with the wealthy and the beautiful.

"I quit," she said, acridly.

"How come?"

"Politics. So much back stabbing and jealousy."

It did not seem right that all that gracefulness and fluid energy could turn so ignoble.

"Wasn't it hard on your feet?"

"You can end up crippled. I'm glad I got out of it when I did."

"Why do they dance on their toes?"

She shrugged and smiled a bitter smile, full of disgust and disillusionment. So much for my romantic view of ballet.

"Now what do you do?"

"Collect alimony," she said, gloomily. "Why do you ask so many questions?"

What could I say? It's a Truth Detective's prerogative.

"You're very interesting." That enlivened her. "And pretty." It slipped out.

She moved closer to me on the catless sofa, realizing a little of her power over me. She brushed her hand against my arm as she settled into a more cat-like position, her legs tucked under her, dawdling the beer glass on her lap.

"How'd you get involved with the Pet Church?"

I told her the history, leaving out the dark side of the Haywards.

"So, it's a job," she said, perceptively.

"Yes. But better than filing. I've met some interesting people."

"Me? she asked, leadingly.

"Of course. The most interesting."

She kissed me lightly on the cheek. "Thanks," she said.

Do a good deed and good deeds come back to you.

"And pretty." she bowed her head with a slight blush.

Well, not every time.

The cats were taking all this in. What were they thinking? Even God could not guess. If they were thinking. Maybe, they just turned their motors off, but kept their inscrutable expressions on hold.

"Why do you have so many cats?"

"Why not? They need homes and I've got one."

No dispute there.

"No dogs?"

"No dogs," she said indifferently.

"You should come to the dog park where I hang out with my dog. It's fun to watch the dogs running around and playing.

"Maybe I will."

"I had a strong desire to caress her abundant hair. But she was just out of reach and it would be an awkward stretch. I didn't want to look awkward. I wondered how she would respond to a sudden, bold gesture, when we were ostensibly investigating the immortal souls of cats.

"Did you know," she enthused, "that cats were revered in Ancient Egypt?"

"Yes, I did. And did you know they were also beetle fans?"

She gave me a sly glance, "I think they took it to heart," she argued.

"I agree."

A striped cat with the end of its tail missing, leaped into my lap and made itself comfortable.

"Tony likes you."

I stroked him and he purred contentedly. A nice cat.

"I had a kitten once," I began, "adopted her from the SPCA. Spent the whole night reassuring her and getting her to trust me. Finally, she relaxed and played with me, convinced this was going to be her new home."

"How nice."

"But during the night, I had trouble breathing, and realized it was caused by the kitten. I took her back the next day. It was awful having to stuff her back in the carry box. The people at the SPCA gave me dirty looks. But there was nothing else I could do."

"Oh, how terrible."

"I did feel terrible. Guilty."

"Are you having trouble here?"

"So far, so good."

"I'm glad you're okay," she said.

She was a good woman. The problem was she was rich, or at least well-off. My esteem suffered from being broke a lot. Actually, I wasn't in poverty. By Governmental calculations I was sub-sub poverty, which gave me a perverse distinction among my peers and former school chums.

My confidence was not peaking. It was off the snow line, way down in base camp, while Mrs. Brosnan was the heights.

"You're very pretty," I said, as romantically as my dry mouth would allow, and touched her shoulder.

"You said that already." Her shoulder, including the rest of her body, slid out of range.

"You have luscious red lips, hair that shines like ...like ..."

"Keep going."

"...like ...diamonds ...eyes ..."

"Hair doesn't shine like diamonds," she frowned.

"Aren't there any black diamonds?" I said, obtusely.

"Not that I know of. What about my eyes?"

"What color are your eyes?"

"Brown," she said tersely.

"Your eyes are as brown ...as brown ...as brown as the brownest brown."

"Don Juan you're not," she marveled, and edged over to me. Another cat jumped into the small space between us. "Oh, I see you're jealous, Gauguin." She fondled it. "And maybe, you have a right to be. He is a man with a poetic tongue no female can resist." She gave Gauguin a jab in the rear and he dived off the sofa with a plaintive yowl.

"So where were you?"

"Eyes," I said uncomfortably.

"You said my lips were luscious." She closed her eyes and offered up her lips. Fourteen cat eyes zeroed in on me. I held her cheeks gently between my hands and kissed her softly. She withdrew.

"You have sweet lips," I said, meaning it.

"Luscious." She was very pleased with herself. She hopped off the sofa. "Ice cream?" she asked, one bare foot rubbing the other. I nodded cheerfully. "Rocky Road?" I nodded again.

She skipped into the kitchen, banged some doors and drawers and was back in a flash with two piled to the brim bowls of ice cream.

"You're fast."

"When it comes to ice cream, I'm unstoppable," she garbled, wiping chocolate from her mouth.

"You know what Nietzsche said?"

She rummaged through her memory. "A German philosopher. The Superman Theory. Right?"

"Right."

"What did he say?"

"He said, 'Without ice cream life would be a mistake.'"

"He did? Did they have ice cream back then?" She watched my reaction as she spooned ice cream into her mouth. "You're acting very wily." She stared at me with half-closed eyes. "He never said that!"

"Well, he did say," I owned up, that 'Without music life would be a mistake.' Isn't ice cream music for the taste buds. I'm just extrapolating."

"I'd advise you never to extrapolate indoors."

It occurred to me that I didn't know her first name.

"Margery," she said limply. "I hate it."

"Why do you hate it?"

"It's so ...so old fashioned."

"I like old fashioned names."

"Do you really?"

"Yes," I said, sincerely.

"What's your first name?"

"Beamer."

"Beamer?" She had the odd look on her face that everyone has when they first hear it. "What kind of name is that?"

"It's a nickname."

"How'd you get it?" She stopped laughing to attend to the chocolate that had spurted from her mouth onto Mickey's head. She ran back into the kitchen to wash it off.

"So?" She was back, poised for the tale.

"I used to smile a lot."

She sat and waited. "That's it?"

"That's it."

She was obviously disappointed. "You don't smile much anymore?"

"Not as much as I used to."

"Why don't you call yourself Low-Beamer?"

She had a wicked wit, and a laugh to go with it.

"Now I can use it to beam in on the truth,' I confided, and showed her my card.

"Beamer Todd, Truth Detective," she read aloud. "Very impressive.

"Keep it." What else could I say?

"Thanks." She placed it on the nearest glass table, face up.

I hung there, wondering if she'd rip off another shot in my direction. It was embarrassing to hand her that card. I'd rather have it read, M.D. or Attorney-at-Law or even Musician.

"Well, Beamer, I think we had a shining time together."

It sounded like an invitation to leave. It was.

"I've got to take Mona Lisa to the Vet."

"Anything serious?"

"Hope not," she said with a thin smile.

"Shall I call you?"

"Please do." She offered a hug and I hugged, feeling her ribs and small breast against me. Her back-bone and shoulders seemed fragile, but her tongue was full of bite.

"Go and ferret out the truth, Detective Beamer!" She shoved me out the door, saluted and closed it. The door opened a few inches and her eyes peered through the narrow space.

"Good luck."

I bounded down the stairs, too fidgety to wait for the elevator. It was a long time since I felt so elated, with energy to burn.

Amid the elegant mansions and swanky condos, the sun was shining bright. I jogged out the door, running effortlessly for three short blocks, until I was winded and slowed to a brisk walk. I didn't notice the cane tapping by me, until I stopped at the corner and waited for the cars to pass. I winced as it poked into my ribs.

I turned and looked into the malevolent eyes of Hayward. I pushed the stick aside until it returned to the ground. I noticed a bulge under the right pants leg, where the knee was.

"I owe you one."

Hayward pointed the cane at my chest and I slapped it down. The spell from my time with Margery was broken by the rising anger at Hayward.

"We're even."

He shook his head slowly, side to side, and grinned maliciously.

"I owe you one."

He twisted away, his right leg stiff and unable to take his weight. He was a slow healer.

I crossed the street, almost bumped by a passing car, cursing to myself. People must have thought I was nuts. They gave me looks that were patronizing and sympathetic, straddling some invisible line of etiquette for the crazy.

In San Francisco, people can take their craziness outside. In most other places it must be confided in homes with a sane and polished persona presented to the outside world.

Here that dividing line is smudged.

Who knows if it is not better to withdraw into the happier fantasies of one's own mind. We can create our own best Universes, where truth is not so muddled and we are not considered lesser paradigms of psychological perfection.

With growth comes grotesqueness. The sharp pin punctures the bubble of childhood.

I chewed anxiously on my thumbnail as I sat in the park with Gustav that evening.

Dori and Paul were entering at the same time. Their paths must have connected on the way. The dachshunds were off leash and making a ruckus as usual, announcing their presence so the other dogs would clear the way and let them pass without a fuss. Big Bear was straggling behind, keeping out of their way.

Dori and Paul were bantering and passed without noticing me and Gustav.

"Hey!" I called out. They both turned, caught my hurt expression, and in one voice said: "Hey, Beamer!"

That made me feel better.

They had a quick conference and decided to veer off their intended course and sit on the grass beside me.

"What's up?" I socialized.

"The moon," Dori intoned, with a creepy waver of voice. "It's full." Her eyes opened to their widest and she made a sudden, scarifying lunge at me.

"Sure does bring out the crazies," I suggested to Paul, indicating Dori.

"Sure does."

Dori came out of her seizure. "You think this is crazy?" Imagine what it's like on Jupiter. They have sixteen moons. They must really go bonkers."

"How come," I questioned thoughtfully, "people only get loony when it's a full moon? What if it's a seven-eighths moon? Aren't they seven-eighths crazy?"

"Are you all right?" Paul asked in mock concern.

"Well, I did run into Hayward."

"What happened?"

"He's gonna get me."

"Get you?" Dori piped in. "Get you?"

"That's the gist."

"I thought it was over."

"Me, too," I lamented.

We were silent. Gustav who had been stalking a pigeon for the last ten minutes, finally gave chase, and it flew up and away, circled and alit ten feet from where it was in the first place. Gustav chased it again. This time it circled twice and alit twenty feet away. Gustav stalked.

"If this keeps up, you'll have no fingernails left." She caught me gnawing a pinky.

"I know." I pulled the finger away from my mouth and studied the nub of a nail.

"Ease up," said Paul, "grudges don't usually come to fruition."

"Besides," I leaned to Paul's judgement, "he can't move very well." I felt better. "So, how are you guys doing?"

Dori's expression was easy to read. Still saddled by her job. Paul was dolefully watching Dori. Her pain was his. I felt a twinge of jealousy. But why shouldn't I be glad that a good guy like Paul was interested in her. He could give her the attention and support she craved. Or to put it succinctly, love.

While Paul was mooning over Dori, and she was contemplating the moons of Jupiter, Henry the Chef with his dog, Titus, in tow, were heading toward us.

He told Titus to sit, which he did, and undid the leash. He then said, 'okay' and Titus dashed into the fray of playing dogs, Gustav almost getting bowled over as Titus streaked by.

"Hey, Henry," I welcomed him, as he tried to sit cross-legged next to me. He gave up and sat sideways.

"Still too fat," he complained, tapping his blooming belly.

"Rotund," I suggested.

"Fat is fat is fat," he said, mercilessly, but truthfully. "So, you put Hayward on crutches?" His expression was saturnine.

"How'd you know he was on crutches?"

"I have my sources," he hinted, and watched Titus barely outmaneuver a lumbering Newfoundland.

"Well, now he has a cane," I said, reawakening my worry. "And threatened to get back at me."

"That jerk!"

Henry was still seething about being fired, especially in such a humiliating way, and was certain that Hayward was beating up on Katherine and Mrs. Hayward.

"I have to admit, I'm a little jumpy, expecting a bullet to whiz by my head." I laughed a nervous laugh. Henry's face was turning colors, but not like the perishable beauty of a rainbow. "I'm sorry, Henry, just being melodramatic, watched too many bad movies."

"I wouldn't put it passed him!" He said, his face so scrunched up in anger, the words squeezed through a barricade.

"Still doing the French cooking?"

"Yes. Thinking of going to Paris."

"That'd be great!"

"Gotta clear up some loose ends first." He became locked into his own thoughts and didn't notice Titus pawing him.

"When would be you be going, Henry?"

"Soon."

"Titus?"

"Upstairs neighbor adores him."

"Guess I'll take a stroll," I announced, to nobody's interest. "C'mon, Gustav."

We ambled over to Roman's Church, for the exercise, and to peek in and enjoy the festivities. Both Katherine and Mrs. Hayward were there with the Bichons, who were waiting to be blessed.

I sat with Gustav in one of the back pews (no more dinky chairs), and listened to Reverend Roman.

"We must not forget, friends, that animals are but blotters for our sins!"

"Amen!"

"They are the tracing paper of our writings in the book of life!"

"Amen!"

Roman must be running out of material, or else he's giving a special audience to stationers.

"We must always remember that we and our pets are stapled together for life, that there is a bond between us, as long as we both shall live! Amen!"

"Amen!" the Church people roared and dogs barked. They charged up front to congratulate and be close to him. I moved up too, but stayed on the periphery, Gustav didn't like being surrounded by so many energized dogs.

Roman plowed through the outstretched hand and backslaps. "Robin and Katherine, how are you?"

The Bichons came over and sniffed at my trouser legs, then discovering Gustav, gave him a double sniffing, which he obligingly stood for.

Katherine came over to me and said quietly, "Kill him!" I closed my eyes to ward her off. "Kill him!" she repeated, in the same low, steady tone. I opened my eyes and looked at her. She was sick again. She read my expression.

"No, I'm not sick. I'm sick of it. So's Mom."

I had nothing to say.

"He'll kill you," she insisted, "I know he will."

I felt very heavy, like I was under siege from an unknown, black force.

"What about your Mother?" I finally said, "How's she doing?"

"She's always so quiet. She goes into her room and drinks. Drinks and types. She never drank when she wrote before."

Her Mother and Roman were moving towards us.

"Shh," Katherine whispered.

"Good to see you, Katherine, and you too, Beamer. Glad you could make. Did you like my sermon?"

"I only caught the end of it. But it was interesting."

"So, you missed the part about the fountain pen of goodness," he smiled.

"I'm afraid I did."

"Why don't you accompany Katherine home, Beamer? Mrs. Hayward and I are going to have a late dinner."

"I can drive home myself," Katherine assured him, and took the leashes of the Bichons. "Goodnight." She gave me a harsh look and headed for the door.

Back home.

Put on some lush Brahms, poured a beer, played with Gustav and settled in to ponder my role as designated hit-man. Though I would much prefer being the designated hitter for the Oakland Athletics.

It was a muddle.

I wondered if, in a world with no penalties, I could do it. Were the moral constraints too strong?

It is easy to make hypothetical decisions. What would I do if? But then only reason is involved. In real situations, your heart is thumping and pumping and your emotions take over. It is hard to plan your emotions.

I dismissed the what-ifs.

Katherine had patently ambivalent feelings toward her stepfather. 'Hurt him!' one minute, then 'Why did you hurt him!' the next. She was a swinger, but not the ravishing kind.

Besides, I've never killed before, excluding thousands of flies, mosquitos, cockroaches and billions of microbes. But that goes with the territory.

It is said of a person, 'Oh, he'd never hurt a fly.' Yes, he'd wipe out half the population of a country, but a fly? 'No, he'd never hurt a fly.'

Cast myself as a professional killer. Get away with murder. How would I do it? Stealthily. If anything happened to Hayward, I would be a suspect. If I had no alibi? It was getting sticky.

My tyro's brain was stubbornly trying to make sense of it all. Katherine's 'Kill him! 'made me think I was someone's handy tool.

But if not me, who?

Katherine, who seemed as stable as a two legged table? Mrs. Hayward, who knew the many ways of murder? Maybe, she was plotting with Roman right now over sushi. Raw fish. Raw emotions. Then there was the embittered Henry, whom Katherine held sway over.

It was a sour pickle.

I reined in my rampant imagination with another beer and filled my gurgling stomach with cheddar. My body fell into a satiated snooze.

I woke once, to empty the beer, then went to bed.

The dismal thoughts were swept away by the sunlight streaming through my window. But I needed a human light to dispel the gloomy preoccupation with murder. I decided to phone Margery and invite her to a restaurant that would fit my meager budget.

She agreed to lunch, but wanted a picnic in Pacific Heights Park. I demurred. She wheedled. I agreed.

I debated whether to take Gustav. We already had a whirl around the neighborhood, even spending some time in Mission Dolores Park, which was five stars for pigeons.

It was a long jaunt up to Pacific Heights on a warm day and the heat would sap him. It would also be a nuisance keeping him out of the picnic food. He was not a finicky eater. If it had atoms, he'd eat it.

It's rare to see someone, when you have the urge to see them. Margery was open, without pretense, someone who didn't need to sustain the image of a busy, sought after woman, deflecting passes right and left, turning down countless dinner invitations and scheduling romance. Or maybe, she was desperate and lonely.

We sat on an enormous Golden Gate Bridge blanket and dined on cold cuts and potato salad, courtesy of Margery.

She wore a loose jogging outfit, covered by a light blue windbreaker without a logo. Her cascade of hair was held back by a red ribbon.

We made the usual small talk about the unpredictability, yet the blessings of the San Francisco weather, her cats, her growing up on a farm in Vermont, escaping the frigid winters, her interest in herbs, and her volunteer career at the SPCA.

Finally, I gave her a brief rundown of my predicament.

"They live so close!"

"You can almost see the house from here." I swung a thumb over my right shoulder. She strained to look past me.

"Which one?"

"If you could see it, the one with the columns."

"Oh, I know that house." She was impressed. "I always wondered who lived there."

"Now you know."

"Why don't you go over and talk to him?" she said, like we had a tiff, and could be buddies again.

"Talk to him?"

"Or, Mrs. Hayward. Maybe she could patch things up."

The objective view is always simplified. Without involvement one sees an easy resolution, if only the disputants are reasonable.

My bones are in jeopardy and she's playing social worker.

"I think it's past that stage."

She took my word for it.

"So, what are you going to do?" she looked hard into my eyes, appreciating the possible danger.

"Don't know."

"Do you think he's serious?"

"Don't know."

It's tough to act on the premise of 'don't know,' waiting for something to happen, which might not happen.

"Then don't worry about it," she said jauntily, with a naughty tilt of the head.

I didn't say anything, but made myself another thick sandwich, slavering on the mustard, which made Margery shake her head in comic disbelief.

"A mustard man!" she declared.

"And a ketchup man," I said proudly. "Condiments for the Connoisseur."

"You?" she laughed.

I knew my taste in food was pedestrian, but she didn't have to rub it in.

Suddenly, I felt someone looming behind me. Margery's eyes lifted warily. I jumped to my feet, stepped back and confronted the stranger.

It was a tall young man with a curious stare and an unfolded map. "Sorry to bother you," he said unsteadily, "but which way to the Park?" He sounded British.

"Golden Gate?" I asked, looking him over suspiciously.

"Yes."

I showed him on the map.

"Much obliged." He quickly went on his way.

"That was nerve-wracking," Margery spoke, surprised at her alarm.

"I see what you mean."

"And it was completely harmless." I turned and standing up I could see the top of the Hayward's Mansion. "What a dumb place to sit!" Margery stood up and put her hands on her hips. She glared at me.

"You didn't know." I tried to mollify her. Too late. It is never wise to question a woman's judgement, especially when it comes to aborted trysts.

We went back to her place.

Once inside, I made a friendly, casual move towards her. She stepped away, infuriated, telling me not to expect any 'romance.'

I settled in one of the armchairs and sought the comfort of the Siamese with the blue eyes, who sprang into my lap.

"You're a beauty," I said to it, stroking its back and listening to its thick purr. "What's this cat's name?"

"Cy."

"For Cy Young, the immortal baseball pitcher, who won more games, 511, than anyone else.

"Cy, for cyclone."

"Too bad."

"What?"

"To bed with you, Cyclone," I said loudly, as he fell asleep across my legs.

Margery warmed up after a testy silence. We drank wine and spent a cozy hour with warm bodies pressed together. There were tender words and brief, arousing clinches. They would have to be saved for another day.

"Myron to the Vet today," she said, pulling away from me.

"You have a cat for everyday of the week," I said, mildly annoyed.

"That's right!" she said, perkily, trying to spot Myron among the many suddenly sprinting for cover. They knew. "C'mon, Myron," she cajoled.

Poor Myron was stoically sitting behind a bookcase. She reached in and grabbed him by the nape and lifted him to her chest. He snuggled in, making the best of it.

"Could you hand me the carrier in the hall closet?"

I did, and with great delicacy and expertness, she had Myron in it with little protest.

I walked her to her car.

"Can I drop you off?" she asked.

"I'm going the other way."

"See you." The Honda sprang forward. I watched it disappear over the hill and walked home.

The phone was ringing, when I opened the door. I answered it and petted the welcoming Gustav.

"Hello?"

"I killed him."

"Katherine?"

"I killed him!" she repeated, panicky and resolute at the same time. "He was slapping Mother around and I hit him over the head with a blender. He's dead!"

My first reaction was shock. Then disbelief. The relief. Then worry.

"Are you all right, Katherine?"

"She's okay, Mr. Todd." Mrs. Hayward's controlled voice was on the phone now. "Katharine didn't kill him."

Who did? I thought.

"Mr. Hayward and I were having a disagreement, Katherine misconstrued it and hit Malcolm." There was total silence at the other end. "He lost his balance and fell backwards, hitting his head on the marble floor. He lost consciousness for a few minutes. Katherine ran out of the room, thinking he was dead."

There was a pause.

"I took him to the hospital for X-Rays. He has a concussion."

I didn't know if I was pleased or disappointed. Pleased for Katherine's sake that he wasn't dead, but disappointed he was still alive.

"Did you tell Katherine?" I asked her.

"I did." she answered, her modulated speech tinged with resentment. Baffled.

For a fleeting moment I thought of calling the Police, but I didn't want to get officially embroiled. The Haywards would probably ingenuously smooth it over, anyhow, as a family squabble, their emotionally oversensitive daughter overreacting, and the Police genuflecting on the way out.

"Can I speak to Katherine?" I asked, civilly.

"She's gone to bed."

"Please ask her to call me when she feels better."

She hung up.

Gustav watched me move over for the treat canister. I dropped two on the floor and he lay down to leisurely eat them. It was the closest he ever came to savoring anything. Usually, it was gulp and gone.

"So, Gustav, what do you think?" He looked at me but said nothing. "Tinkering with chance, evermore," I recited nonsensically, "I am hopelessly enamored, yet waiting for a tap, tap, tap at my door."

I went to sleep plagued by the Haywards, or the Haywires, as I now came to think of them.

By morning I was out of it. The Haywires were on their own. The fuse was lit and burning. An explosion was sure to come. Stay away, I told myself. Don't return calls. Don't answer doors late at night.

Buoyed by a fresh outlook, I sauntered over to where Dori was sitting downcast, toying with the grass. Paul's pursuit of her had fizzled.

"He's a nice guy," she said, turning to watch her mischievous dachshunds patrolling the area. "But there's no chemistry." She reeled in Chloe, who was digging up a clod. "But we're still friends."

"That's good."

"So, what's by you?"

I told her Malcolm was out of commission, without my help, and that I was glad it was over. What happened is a big mystery. But that's their secret, their affair.

"So," I declared brightly, "I can move on to something else." I pulled out my Truth Detective card, symbolically tore it into pieces and deposited it in the nearest trash can with a flick of the wrist.

"No more crazy detective stuff."

"No," confirmed Dori. "It isn't you. You were a big flop."

I think she was glad that I was out of it, but the path between her heart and her mouth was very steep.

"Thanks for your candor."

"Speaking of candor, how do pick up a dime?"

"What?"

"Your fingernails. You haven't any. When you get change on a counter, how do you pick up the dimes?"

"I brush the coins into my palm."

"What if a dime drops to the floor?"

"It's a pain, but I use another coin to tip it."

"What if you have no other coins? Do you just leave it? Ask someone to pick it up for you?"

"Stop, Dori!"

"Just curious."

She lay back lazily and watched the fast moving clouds. The stalwart dachshunds immediately surrounded her.

"New job?" I dared ask.

"How'd you know?" She glanced over. "Not so neurotic, heh?" Cashier. It's boring, pays less, but at least I don't have to serve dodos."

It was nice to be back at home base.

I watched Dori study the shapes of the clouds. She had a vivid imagination. She was good at spotting aliens and Godzilla-like creatures and the occasional cow.

She was attractive and feminine even with her tawny hair cut short in the current style. She preferred to keep her femininity buried beneath the roughness. It only peeked out now and then.

"I have to find a job again," I told her, dreading it.

"I thought you were working for Philip?"

"Don't want to bump into the Haywards."

"Ah, don't sweat it. You liked it. Do you want to file again?"

She was right. The idea of filing again made sweat pop out on my forehead and my toes go numb.

She unwrapped a stick of gum and pushed it into her mouth. She started a furious chew and was soon snapping away. If my fingernail chewing bothered her, her gum chewing bothered me. It had started to become more annoying.

But, being a gentleman, and not wanting to be the object of her sometimes unlady-like wrath, I put the discussion off for another time. At least, she didn't draw out the gum string-like and do tricks with it.

I wanted to bite a nail in retaliation, but suppressed the urge.

"Is Paul still at the gift shop?" I asked instead.

"He was fired," Dori said dryly.

"What? Why?"

"He was chanting his poems to customers."

"He's really into it, isn't he?"

"Sure is." She smacked her gum loudly.

"What's he gonna do for money?"

"Unemployment."

It couldn't be very much, but it would cover his rent. You could always scrounge around for food.

"Now he can concentrate on his poetry."

"Suppose."

What was it with gum and thinking? One cancels out the other.

The noisy gum chewing bugged me, but it was funny to watch the dachshund's heads swivel as one, to stare at Dori when she cracked her gum, trying to figure out where the sound was coming from. When they turned around, she cracked it again and they swiveled again, still mystified.

At times, the park could be called an amusement park.

The expressions on the dachshunds' faces, on dogs' faces were pure feelings, no fakery. It was like the silent films where the intensity of the expression had to take the place of the words.

It is one of the reasons we like animals so much. Their language is in their body and their face. But if dogs did talk, what would they say. If they did talk, they'd probably speak doggerel.

Dori heaved her shoulders and sat up. "You gonna see Charles tomorrow night?"

Charles was eking out a career in comedy clubs. Since he worked all day, we rarely saw him around.

"He's at the Line-Up."

"You going?"

"Paul and I might you."

"Maybe," I hedged.

When I got back to the studio, I poured out some dry dog food for Gustav, which even the cockroaches snubbed. He would eat it. But knowing it was not high on the taste chart, I supplemented it with more delectable chicken and tuna, rice and vegetables, anything I ate was on the top of the list to him.

He paused over the kibble, looking at me hopefully, to see if he could do better. He understood when I told him. "That's it, Gustav," and he began to crunch away.

I phoned Margery, and after a short, trying conversation about her cats' digestive, ear and arthritic woes, she agreed to meet me at the Line-Up.

Feeling energetic with possibility, I strode over to the Pet Ministry.

It was clean-up day, and a bedraggled trio of street people were manning mop and broom. Roman waved to me from behind his newly installed, mahogany desk

"These guys were camping outside my door, so I hired them to keep it clean. Good for me, good for them." Civic pride swelled in his voice. If he had lapels he would be pushing them outward with his thumbs.

"Anything for me?"

"Come back this evening, Beamer. There may be an overflow."

"How come?"

"Lassie's Birthday!" He mugged a groan. "I know. I know it sounds silly. But the kids love it, and it brings in the adults, too. The mailing is out."

Homage to Lassie, the paragon of dogdom, still spanning the generations.

"Are the Haywards coming?"

"Mrs. Hayward and her Bichons, maybe," he said, simply.

The scraping 'whisk, whisk,' went by us. "Good job, Gus." The gaunt, clear-eyed, rumpled broom pusher, lifted his tool to Roman in tribute and pushed on.

"They promised me they would pool their money to find a place to live," he said, optimistically.

Roman was right.

Adults and kids and dogs crowded in to occupy all the pews. I brought out folding chairs to accommodate the overflow.

As each person came in I handed them a frosted cupcake with a dog silhouette in chocolate sprinkles, a small candle and a couple of dog treats. When my supply was exhausted, I took a break outside in the cool air.

Soon, I could hear snatches of Roman's sermon exhorting dogs and people to be more like the virtuous Lassie. Then, in a touching moment, with the store lights off and the flashbulbs popping, candles were lit and a swaying, barking 'Happy Birthday to Lassie' was sung.

A cheer preceded the laying on of paws, a minute of silence, during which people and their animals communed. Mrs. Hayward did not show up.

A huge birthday cake, with a portrait of Lassie in pink icing came rolling out from the back room. People applauded. Dogs sniffed and drooled.

Roman and I sliced and dished out sizable portions and indicated where soda and juices were available in the commercial sized fridge.

The screen was lowered for a classic Lassie film. I ushered some people over to meet Roman, who was becoming a somewhat saintly figure to the older and poorer regulars. A view he did not discourage. Unfortunately, Saint Philip was probably already taken.

The night ended with owners and their kids and their dogs trickling out with smiles on their faces, love in their hearts and dog biscuits in their pockets.

Roman dug into his pocket and peeled off a few twenties, handed them to me, slapped me on the back and euphorically walked me halfway down the block.

When I got in, Gustav gave me a going over. I was scented head to toe with strange dog smells. He didn't give me his usual unrestrained greeting. He was glad to see me, but a little standoffish, either irked that I didn't take him or jealous that I was in the company of so many unknown canines. He didn't say.

Charles was a newcomer, a rookie in comedy and was scheduled to be first up at the Line-Up. He did not need to hit a home run with the audience tonight, the important thing was to get to first base. He still wanted to knock one out of the park.

I waited as long as I could outside, but Margery didn't show. Reluctantly, I went in. I didn't want to miss Charles, but I didn't want to miss Margery. Then I figured she'd come in to look for me, if she came later.

I wouldn't be hard to find.

The Line-Up, which was furnished with mismatched chairs and tables straight from Goodwill, was half empty. The small beer, soda and sandwich bar was unattended and the microphone was just being set up. It was ten minutes to show time.

A flashily dressed Emcee appeared onstage and after shooing the help away, adjusted the mike and tested it for loudness. The audience shrieked along with the amps and clapped their hands to their ears.

"Sorry," said the Emcee, patting down his fluffed out, iridescent blue shirt. "Hot stuff," he laughed. Las Vegas transplanted.

A buxom young lass opened the bar and the men flocked over. I was amongst the pushing, disorderly bunch, not to stare at the décolletage, but to buy beer for my tablemates and me. Right.

"I wanted stout," Dori whined.

"They didn't have stout," I answered, aggravated.

"This is good ale," Paul said placating her, which, being with her a lot, and liking her a lot, he probably did a lot.

"It's only okay," insisted Dori.

"C'mon," I said, "stop bickering. Charles is coming on."

"I'm not bickering!"

"Okay." I put my hands up in surrender.

"Ladies and Gentlemen, and I use that term loosely," the Emcee squared off, "my name is Mel Rose and I welcome you to the Line-Up, San Francisco's up and coming comedy club, with the best up and coming young comedians.

"without further ado, put your hands together for Charles Rogers and his distinctive brand of comedy!"

There was friendly applause.

Mel Rose, already sweating, greeted Charles with a handshake and a 'go get 'em.'

"Yo, Charles!" We yelled and clapped heartily.

Desultory noise came from around the room. The barperson was inadvertently banging bottles of beer together, new patrons, though trying to be quiet, were not made of marshmallow and collided with furniture and each other.

Charles didn't notice all this. He looked nervous, clasping the mike in both hands and forcing a smile into the crowd. He spotted us, made a natural smile, coughed to clear his throat and began his routine.

"Hi, I'm Charles and I'm from Iowa."

He got a quick laugh.

"You know," he said, appraising the microphone, "this microphone reminds me of a girl I once took out on a blind date. She wasn't skinny, she was silver."

He got some chuckles.

"Halfway through the evening I began to suspect she was a robot." He paused. "I asked her what her religion was. She said she was planning to be converted to quarters."

All the tables laughed out loud.

"She had a very strong identification with old cans." A pause.

"She was programmed to have an anxiety attack every two hours."

Pause. "Her father was a 1932 nickel. She told me about her love affairs. An electric fan. A brief fling with a turnstile."

Laughter.

"She had been engaged to a vending machine, but she broke it off when it refused to give her correct change."

A big laugh.

"She had been jilted by a computer dating service computer."

Charles stopped to reap the laughter.

"I was a sickly kid," he said, looking sad. "My family was very protective. They didn't tell the Earth was moving until I was nineteen."

Glasses were clinking, and there was -a sudden, uproarious laugh, independent of the punch line.

"I had asthma as a kid. I wanted to go to camp but I was allergic to nature." Charles sensed he wasn't funny. "My family finally sent me to a special camp. We used to camp out in tents." Pause. "Oxygen tents."

Our table was rooting him on, but interest was fading from the others.

"We had lessons in mouth to mouth resuscitation three times a day. Even now, when I kiss a girl, I hyperventilate her."

Good for a laugh.

"Our softball field had only two basses, no one ever made it past first."

The Emcee was poking his head out from the side.

"We used to have movies every Friday night," he rasped. "Not really movies. Slide shows. In the old war movies, pilots and gunners were trained to identify silhouettes of enemy planes and ships. We were trained to automatically identify the shapes and colors of pills."

Mel Rose was moving in on him.

"We had a nature hut. All the animals were covered in SaranWrap."

"Thank you, Charles Rogers," said the Emcee, deftly reclaiming the microphone and easing Charles off the stage with a bid to the audience for appreciation. "Let's hear it, folks, this man is clever." We applauded with gusto, the rest was perfunctory. "Don't take any wooden nickels, Charlie!"

After Charles joined us and I congratulated him and praised the first part of his routine, I excused myself and walked outside to the nearest phone booth and called Margery. After three rings she answered.

"It's Beamer."

"Oh, Beamer, I'm sorry. I forgot." She sounded genuinely apologetic, but it didn't salve my irritation. It was pointless to ask why, it surely had to do with cats.

"My 'ex' called me. We made plans for dinner."

"Have a good time," I said, fighting to keep the sarcasm from my voice.

"Thanks," she said. "How'd it go?"

"Swell."

"That's good," she said meekly, suspecting the anger beneath the candy coating. "Well," she added with ingratiating cheerfulness, "see you around."

"See you," I said and hung up.

I didn't go back to the club, but walked the downtown streets for a while, peering into lit and darkened storefronts, and then took a long walk home.

BY the time Gustav and I were walking around the block the anger had dissipated.

It was none of my business if she wanted to see her 'ex', a half-word that sounded like some unknown commodity people once had, which they no longer have. A word devoid of emotional content, but signifying a past hope, and a culturally pronounced former commitment.

I didn't want to say that I could never count on people, but rather that I could always depend on Gustav, and I hoped, vice-versa. Coming back to him softened the blows.

No matter my condition, financial or mental, my state, inept or insensitive, my voice, yelling or yodeling, my case infirmed or my ideas inane, I was always I to him.

Back inside I put treats down for him, played tug the sock as long as my energy would hold out, and took out my new Babe Ruth pocketknife from its soft leather case, to admire it.

I received it this afternoon in the mail, an expensive treat to myself that helped offset getting clobbered by Hayward.

It was a hefty piece, with a figurine of the Babe in his home run swing, astride a large autographed silver baseball stuck onto the wood handle. A big number three on a baseball diamond was affixed to golden metal at the base. The three-inch blade was stainless steel. It was a beauty.

The only problem was that I barely had fingernails to fit into the groove in the blade and pull it open. I did it, but it took a while and sometimes I had to resort to using a dime.

But I wasn't planning to carry it around with me, although I did want to show it to Paul, who could appreciate the utilitarian homage.

When I brought it out the next evening to show it off, Henry wasn't impressed. He was not a baseball fan and did not revere the Ruthian legend.

"Show me a Julia Child's pocket knife and maybe then I'll get excited," he said.

I canvassed the park, but there were surprisingly few baseball fans. Some of the women meant to humor me as they admiringly handled the knife and tried to be enthusiastic for two things they didn't really wholeheartedly embrace: Baseball and Knives.

Gustav was slowly drawing closer to the remains of a barbecue at the upper end of the park. The celebrants had done a good job of cleaning up, but smells stayed and there were bound to be some leftover bones.

The place had been picked clean.

We walked through a narrow stretch of grass between the Rec Building and the MUNI tunnel on our way to a neighborhood coffeehouse where Paul might be hanging out.

I was keeping my eye on Gustav as he foraged for the remains of bones, when I heard something to my side. Gustav, who was off leash, barked sharply and lunged to the left, taking the blow of a baseball bat against his side. It was Hayward. The bat raised up again and came at my head. I put my arm up instinctively to deflect it. Gustav jumped at him and pushed him off stride. Hayward limped badly, but he had enough balance to swing back at the snarling Gustav and swat at him, grazing his head. Gustav fell, stunned.

I had a chance to pullout my knife.

The bat swooshed by my face as I jumped backwards, almost tripping over a sprinkler head. I tried to open the knife but I couldn't. My nails were too bitten down to get a quick, firm hold in the groove and pullout the blade.

Hayward was grunting with exertion, poking the bat tauntingly at my chest. There was a crazy look in his eyes. I dug into my pocket for a coin. Nothing. I never took money to the park in the evening.

The next swing glanced off my shoulder and I fell to the grass. I tried again to pull the knife open, using my teeth. No good. The bat came down as I rolled over, just missing my head. I scrambled backwards, as Hayward came inexorably on, driving me against the building wall. He waggled the bat over his head.

I kept my eyes on him as I bent down, feeling wildly through the grass for something thin and strong to use to open the knife. Nothing but bits of crumbling wood. I rolled over and felt a jab in my thigh. My key! I frantically dug into the wadded up plastic bags filling my back pocket, pulled out the key and fumbling, opened the blade.

I got it open just in time to parry the next blow, but the strength of the swing almost knocked the knife out of my hand. I was up on my feet, as Hayward went sprawling from the effort. He got up, dragging his leg. Instead of trying to back up, I charged, preventing him from winding up for the long swing. I went past him slashing, but only nicked his bat.

I circled around, never forgetting I was still dealing with a powerful man. I forced him to turn and swipe at me and I again slashed at his hand, but was way short. The bat caught me solidly in the side. The breath went out of me and knife flew out of my hand.

He hobbled towards me, a glazed, demonic look in his eyes. I crouched, watching him and inched toward the knife. He smiled widely. "Fuck you!" I said. It erased his smile, and enraged him just enough to take a wild lunge at me. I dove for the knife as the bat skimmed over my head. I picked it up and got a good grip. He was tiring and so was I. I hoped I could be quicker.

His movements were now ponderous, and he began to rely on the bat as a cane to keep his balance. He must still have effects of concussion. He had to weaken.

Steady and calm, I told myself, as I stood mockingly before him, an easy target, inviting him to hit me. With the pain and the exertion his wits must be slowed by now. I hoped. Without thinking he raised the bat high over his head, like an executioner poised for the head chop.

The instant the bat moved forward, I swerved to the left and slashed at his right arm as the bat crashed into the ground. This time a thick line of blood appeared. He didn't drop the bat, but his right hand loosened. Blood dripped to the ground.

He looked at me, looked at his arm, as if it was not his. He dropped the bat and reached into his jacket pocket.

There was a sudden noise.

I turned and saw a mob of dogs and people coming from one direction and two burly cops rushing towards us from the other. I dropped the knife and braced myself against the wall, exhausted. The cops tackled Hayward and wrestled him to the ground.

The dog people swarmed in with their dogs.

"He's hurt," someone was kneeling next to Gustav, who was gamely trying to get up. I went over, bent down, gave him an affectionate pet and told him to take it easy.

"I'll take him to the Vet," someone else volunteered.

"Thanks."

"Wait! I'll bring my car!"

Henry was next to me. "I saw him driving around, looking into the park. He must have seen you. He stopped where he was and came out with a bat. I called the police on my cell phone. It didn't look kosher."

"Thanks a lot. I didn't hear sirens. I guess I was too busy."

"They were here in a shot, pardon the expression. They knew about Hayward, were looking for him. Mrs. Hayward had alerted them earlier. He went berserk and stormed out of house waving what she thought might be a gun. She thought he might head here."

"Maybe his brains got rattled by the concussion," I tried to sound reasonable, but I was shaking allover.

"You were lucky."

"Not Gustav."

There were more people around, buzzing with 'what happened.'

I stayed with Gustav as the cops put Hayward in the patrol car, after doing some first aid to his arm and getting my name address and phone number.

It felt like a storm had hit without warning, ripping everything apart, yet sparing everyone in its path except a lone, brave dog, who may be saved my neck, sacrificing his.

We brought Gustav to an emergency vet clinic and everyone telling me not to worry about the cost. Gustav kept on watching me. An ineffable trust in his dulled eyes that I would take care of him.

Gustav was not okay.

But he would get better. Dogs have incredibly hard heads.

I once watched one dog chase another around the park. One zipped full speed between benches less than two feet apart. The other miscalculated, and went 'thunk!' head first into the heavy wood.

Instead of dropping like a sack of potatoes, he wobbled around for half a minute and resumed the chase as if nothing had happened.

Gustav and I were back out in the park.

He still had the bruise on his hip and was limping around, but recovering. The soreness probably wasn't as bad as the frustration of seeing pigeons walk defiantly in front of him, knowing he was temporarily on the disabled list.

There was nothing in the paper about the incident.

Mrs. Hayward sent me a generous check and hoped someday to invite me to hear my dog songs. There was no mention of Malcolm. Enclosed was a thank you note from Katherine, without mentioning what she was thanking me for.

I never heard from the Police.

With Gustav on the mend, the old park routine was safely satisfying. Paul with his poetry and Bear, and his tourist tirades, now that he had a job at another gift shop, Charles with his dishpan hands comedy and the impetuous Guinevere, and Dori Four with her dachshunds and acerbic tongue.

One day, she gave me a sweet smile as we sat side by side on the grass, watching our dogs play.

"I could go for you, Beamer," she said, "If you didn't bite your nails."

THE ACTOR

A pounding on my door set Blondie madly barking and me jumping out of bed. I slipped into my slippers on the cold floor, turned on the lamp and rushed down the hall shouting at Blondie to be quiet before the neighbors formed a posse.

I looked through the peephole and slowly opened the door. Roman swept in and planted his behind on my messed up futon-bed. He seemed to be in shock. His hands covered his face. He sat there unmoving, making pathetic, whimpering sounds. I was angry he blasted me from sleep until I heard his story.

"Someone stole Molly!" He finally bellowed.

Roman, with round, pious face was an ex-seminary student and tell-all celebrity biography writer. Now he was a self-proclaimed Pet Minister for the spiritual needs of animals, mainly dogs, in the Church he established at Market and Dolores Streets.

Blondie went over to him and licked his nervous hands. He began stroking her. It calmed him a bit. He hung down his head and blew out a long breath.

"What happened?" I asked anxiously, as I pulled a sweater over my chilling body.

He lifted his head and looked directly at me for the first time.

"Molly was a new rescue and I was taking her out for a walk around the block at eleven," he said evenly, "Then," his hands clenched and his voice stammering, "This guy comes running out of a car, grabs the leash, pulls Molly away and runs back to the car." He held out his hands in helpless dismay. "Beamer, it happened so fast."

I was trying to get the picture. "Right. You never expected it. Don't blame yourself.

"I threw some coins at the car."

"You were pretty close then."

"I ran after it"

"Did you get a license?"

"I was too busy screaming at it." he said, turning his head away in embarrassment. The rest of him sagged.

"What else could you do?" I consoled him.

"It was a big car. Dark color," he remembered suddenly, snapping alert. "It was all a blur." He sank back, realizing that description was a wild stab in the dark.

"Do you think it was deliberate?"

"I know who did it!" he grimaced."

"Who?"

Charles Forrest,: he accused. "I exposed his infidelities and he vowed to get me."

"The actor?"

"Yes."

"To steal a dog?"

"He's a low life," Roman said, with unChristian like malice.

Would a well-known actor stoop to snatch a dog, even if he played evil guys on the screen?

"I know where he lives."

"Where?"

"The other side of Buena Vista Park," Roman smirked and pointed yonder. "He's an actor you know," he added obsessively, with a short sniff of his nose, as if a bad odor had suddenly permeated the room. "He likes to act the bad guy in real life," he insinuated. "He has goons to protect him."

"From what?"

"Probably from his own misconduct," he continues snidely.

Roman was on a roll. Was it true? It seems I've been saying a lot of things with a question mark at the end.

"Would you check his house for Molly?" he suddenly brokered. I'll pay you."

"I'd been a clumsy accidental sleuth awhile back and wasn't very good at it, but I could use the money and Roman had plenty of it. Discreet snooping to turn up a stolen dog would be a good deed.

"These goons you mentioned," I brought up delicately. There had to be at least two people in the pirate car. "Do they hang around?"

"Don't know," Roman replied, distracted by writing a check.

"It could be dangerous," I reconsidered.

"Find a way to get inside."

Right!

He handed the check to me. Zeros did add up to something: Persuasion.

"I spare no expense for animals," he declared nobly.

"It would barely cover hospital expenses in this city," I joked, mordantly.

"Bring Dori," he said in a business tone. "She's got the charm and the looks to get in."

The scheming side of Roman made sense.

Roman went out as abruptly as he came in.

I managed to get a few hours of sleep and woke with the Sun and Blondie's paw resting on my arm. Time to go to the Park.

The early morning crowd was mingling and Blondie quickly went over and collected her several treats. We then took our regular stroll around the area so Blondie could make sure that everything was intact, sniff for discarded scraps of food and watch for any door openings where she could get in and nose around.

Neighbors were generally tolerant of her visits, though they sometimes had to shoo her out when she didn't heed my calls. She particularly liked going up the stairs. I would explain to them that she was Real Estate agent in a former life and couldn't shake the urge for reconnaissance of all the neighborhood houses.

We returned to the dog area and Blondie sat on the grass nuzzling a bit of found bagel and defying other dogs to come near her. She liked to tease other dogs with her prize. But the dogs were thinning out as people had to go to work.

One guy still hanging around with his old Basset was Moe. Like me, Moe was a passionate baseball fan and when he was around, he drove a long-distance truck, we'd discuss baseball.

He was a middle-aged guy, with hair popping out where clothes did not cover, slightly rotund, easy going and not a snappy dresser. Overalls, Squashed hats, battered boots and face that says: "Hiya." Of course, his love of baseball was tempered by being a life-long Cubs' fan.

This morning we commiserated on both our teams having a lousy season. Although, the Giants had managed to win a World Series in the last hundred years.

He spoke in that melancholy, Cubs' fan way, with that flimsy strand of hope for the future," he said bravely. "Let the new kids develop together, not saddled with a loser mentality."

"Sounds good," I snickered to myself, "Wrigley Field is a great park." "Yes, he reminisced forlornly, "I get there a couple times a year."

Since I was flush with money and feeling kind of frisky, I couldn't resist: "Did you ever think of when the World will end?" I asked him seriously.

He looked quizzical, as if, 'where did that come from?' and suspiciously, knowing I sometimes made jokes.

"No seriously," I assured him.

"When the Sun dies," he said obviously, "Or when we get hit by a meteor or blow ourselves up."

"None of those," I said with confidence. "I know when the World will end."

"When?" he ventured, half-heartedly.

"When the Cubs win the World Series."

He thought about that for a few seconds and said: "At least Cub fans will get a chance to party," he said happily.

"The World will end right after the last out, so the fans won't have the chance to celebrate." Gosh, I'm mean.

"Oh," he muttered, "Too bad."

You can't take a Cub fan down. They are already there.

We parted laughing about the bungling antics of our respective teams and wished good luck for the next season.

Roman was right about Dori. She has the nerve the looks and the feisty charm. Plus, a fondness for Drama and a yen to fondle cash. We would be closer, but she had the unshakeable idea that bitten fingernails are "gross." I think she is too obsessed with the meticulous car of her nails. We have reached an impasse: I'm trying to let my fingernails grow.

I was hoping to meet Dori in the Park. She usually showed up at eight with her querulous quartet of Dachshunds and I waited. I hoped to find her in a good or at least a talkative mood.

She had been less than her sardonic, critical self since she began her new job selling flowers from a stall in the Ferry Building. She had a bloom about her. She had worked as a stripper and many years as waitress in a number of dumps. She could turn morose, carrying her jobs and her leering and grabbing customers around with her.

She had perked up since she had been surrounded by the beautiful colors and scents and the lively, gregarious atmosphere of the Market. Her quips were brighter and her eyes shinier.

I got impatient and phoned her. The phone rang and rang and I was about to disconnect when she answered,

"Hey, Beamer," she chirped.

"Hi, Dori, got a proposition for you.

"Right to the point," she asked, "No sweet talk, no asking about my Nobel Prize or why the sky is blue?"

'Why is the sky blue?"

"Because Michelangelo ran out of red paint." She laughed. "Isn't that what you told me once?"

"I don't remember."

"What's the scoop?"

I was still not used to the sunny side of Dori. I kept waiting for an Eclipse. "I'll treat you to a meal and tell you then."

"Wow," she teased, "The suspense. And you are treating."

"Okay." It was all I could say.

Dori and I agreed to meet at my favorite inexpensive Chinese restaurant the next day.

Now it was off to work. It made me think that if we really liked it, we would say "ON" to work. IN my case it didn't matter.

I worked for a giant company called SGARBL. Now only was it unpronounceable, the letters were impossible to decode. Nobody I met who worked there knew what the letters stood for, there were many humorous, unflattering guesses, but the answer was in the Clouds.

The company sold everything: Rifles, Diapers, Candy, Lawnmowers, Lots of plastic stuff, Clothing. Myriad things. Which would be a good name for it.

My job was handling complaints that showed up on my computer. Mostly, I used the standard company policy statement to direct and assuage endless streams of customer dissatisfaction.

People could be mean, meek, enraged, outraged, nasty, friendly. All of human nature showed up on my screen. But, I had the prerogative of answering a complaint personally, as long as I stuck with a fair set of guidelines.

An example: I got a complaint from a mother who had bought a Superman costume and her kid and a friend had a water fight. The costume had shrunk so fast and tight, she had to cut it off with scissors. It was defective product. I assured her the munificence of the company would reimburse her.

That settled that.

The next day, the same mother told me there was psychological fallout for the kid. It turned out the costume was not impervious to a pair of shears and he denounced Superman.

I wrote back: "when you pack the shreds of the Superman costume in a box to be sent back, be comforted in knowing that Superman was from an alien planet and came here not by choice. Tell your son not to be mad at Superman, but to feel sorry for him. He can't be President, but you can."

That was the highpoint of my working day.

There are persistent gripers: The man who found flaws in the simplest item. Offended by a single dancing fish, on a roll of paper towels, because it was slightly off-kilter and gave the man a headache each time he tore of a towel to wipe a spot or something and had to face that rebellious fish. People can be irritated by the minutest discrepancy.

I told him to close his eyes.

Dori and I sat opposite each other in the restaurant. It was not tourist place and ambiance was not a priority. There was no heat. Sides of beef and pork hung leisurely near the front window. Crackling music poured out of the radio in the kitchen. The tables and chairs were basic wood. The waiters did not smile.

One waiter appeared. He had taken my order a few times before with charmless efficiency. I always ordered Pork Fried Rice. It was cheap, tasty and was a generous portion. When I ate out I did not want to see plate.

My name for this guy was Curt Brusque and he quietly appeared. He had a bony frame and sullen expression. The nub of a pencil was poise over a folded pad.

"Order?" he barked at Dori.

She looked at him coldly, which he ignored.

"Pork Fried Rice," I said. "Dori?"

She chose some complicated vegetable concoction. He scribbled on the crowded pad.

Off he went.

Dori was aghast. "I would have been fired in two minutes."

"It's family," I smiled.

"Right," she sneered.

I filled her in on the events with Molly. She jutted her head toward me and said nothing. Then she leaned back and her features contorted in disgust.

The food came and we dined. I outlined my plan to discover Molly while she was on an eggroll. She couldn't speak, but her eyes were full of eloquent amusement.

"It's terrible what happened," she said, "but there must be a legal way to handle this"

"Roman doesn't want any publicity and I'm sure the Police are not going to jump at it." She seemed to understand the predicament. "It's not a rescue, it's a scouting mission and it's a paying gig."

Her tongue was working to loosen a speck between her teeth.

"I'll bring my guitar." I continued, "You pretend he is your idol. Charm him, no fuss."

She looked at me and laughed. "Are you kidding?"

"Tell you what," I said, after sipping some tea and rearranging a napkin. "Tell you what," I said airily. "With my half of the money, I'll take you out to a fancy restaurant, where the waiters bow obsequiously and the food only takes up one-third of the plate and we sweat from the heat."

"Some deal," she answered dryly, scooping up the last of her rice.

"Is that a yes?"

She toyed with some grains that slopped over her plate. "It's a maybe."

"Aaargh!" I thought, but not being a pirate, I could not compel with a sword or sharp word. But in a Green Society, I could offer this"

"Money!"

"What?!" She was startled out of a daydream.

"Money," I distilled, "Is what is left over. Money is what helps us rise over the crappier parts of life."

She looked thoughtful, her lips pursing. She relented. "True."

"It's an adventure," I said soaringly, trying to invent a romantic portrait of the Actor. "Maybe he'll sweep you off your feet, put you in the Movies. Take you to Paris and Rome and meet all the Stars." I know it's a big con, but there was a flicker of temptation in her eyes.

"He's such a scary looking guy," she demurred, demurely.

"It's an act, I'm sure he's a sweet person in real life."

She spent a long minute on interior calculations. "OK," she said blushingly, with tugging resistance.

Our waiter clattered two plates in front of us. Fortune cookies.

Mine read: "Kelp me, I'm a prisoner in a health food store."

Dori's "George Washington had Ivory teeth, but they named a Bridge after him."

Our mostly combined opinion of these messages was that a comedian was Shanghaied into working for the Restaurant and was rebelling with subversive humor.

We left the restaurant. We left a decent tip for our waiter. He played his part very well. Dori and split up. She went to her Aerobics by the Bay studio and I went to visit Roman at his Church.

I arrived at the tell-end of his sermon. The themes didn't vary. He was at his stentorian best recriminating the sinful people who abused and neglected the poor animals. I had no quarrel with it, nor did the patrons and their pets in the pews, some with tears in their eyes.

When he finished, his patrons formed a line to have their pets blessed by Roman and given a free, full bag of dog goodies and food. There were some hugging lots of "Thank you Reverend," which clearly touched Roman.

When the crowd left, I went over to him. Sweat glistened on his pale face and his round eyes were enraptured. I broke his spell.

"Anything new about Molly?"

The rapture shut down and a shadow took its place.

"Nothing," he said disheartened.

"A ransom note?"

"No. Nothing."

"Have you considered other possibilities beside the Actor?" The Actor thing was starting be a stretch for me.

"No," he stammered. He seemed to be trying to mobilize his thoughts but they were jammed up in self-reproach. A man consumed with fighting sin, must also be consumed with fighting guilt.

"Don't blame yourself," I warned. "You'll end up crazy."

"I can't help it."

I tried to give him a jolt: "Where's Dori's money? She's angry and might back out if you don't come across."

"No. No. No," he said apologetically, "I'll write the check."

He pulled out his checkbook and wrote with a steady hand. When it comes to money, one's foggy thoughts clear up in hurry.

The issue of money reminded me that in San Francisco's wild and soaring housing market, my building could be the next one coveted, corralled, carved up and converted.

I could be casted out into the bewildering streets with only my instincts to guide me and meager finances to house me. I quickly pushed the screaming thought down the list of things to worry about.

I took the check from Roman. "Is there anything more I should know about this guy before Dori and I barge in?"

Roman thought. "Sometimes he gets his movie life confused with his real life."

Great. "You mean he's a real gangster?"

"Mostly for show," Roman contributed.

I blew out a sharp breath. "Geez. So he might have goons around? Just for show, of course."

Roman shrugged his shoulders. Then he stiffened and said: "I think Molly may be undergoing a spiritual collapse." All logic is swept away. He claims to have telepathic lines to dogs. He looked vacuously in my direction, as if he didn't realize what he was saying. Was he crazy? Was this whole caper in his imagination?

I swallowed my disbelief. Impecunious me.

Roman stood before me like someone I hadn't known. He was still short, with a round, monkish face, sparse, straw like hair, pellucid blue eyes and a doughy body.

But he was different. All his features seemed be misplaced and not belong together. Funny, how a few words out of someone's mouth can alter their appearance.

Well, I wasn't going to hang around and see what the next Roman would look like. I had shopping to do.

I bought the get-ups Dori and I were going to wear when we visited the Actor: An oversized street map of SF, two Alcatraz sweatshirts, medium and small, two SF caps, cheap cameras with long straps, to hang around our necks. I planned to take a walk with Blondie across from his house the night before, to make sure there were lights on and it was occupied.

Back in the Park with Blondie, I ran into Charles and his dog Guinevere. I hadn't seen the Comedian for months.

"Hey, good to see you," I said with a handshake, then patting his dog, who gave me a lick in the face in return. "Where have you been? Working in a bakery?"

"Now that you mention it. No," he said in his usual friendly way.

I told him about the messages inside the fortune cookies.

"Clever."

"Dori and I thought you might be working there."

"Not that fortunate."

"Still handing out punishment," I lightly jabbed.

"Always."

He was not the same buoyant fellow, bursting with enthusiasm and good will I last saw.

He confirmed it. "Trying my luck in LA," He said gloomily.

"Not good?"

"Tough," he sighed, head drooping.

"Sorry," I commiserated, "I know what it's like."

"I bombed so many times, the Clubs were building underground shelters."

"You're exaggerating," I said, annoyed, "You're too self-deprecating."

"Self-deprecation is my best quality," he shot back.

"Where are you staying?"

"Got a closet in a flat."

"A closet?"

"It's a big closet." He spread his arms wide, mockingly. "It's a place to sleep, some privacy, kitchen privileges, bathroom, cheap as it can be now."

I knew how to perk him up.

"Got any new material?

"Glad you asked," he sparked. He straightened up, rubbing his fingertips together. "Working on some new stuff. Some relevancy. Tossed the old, Still sketchy. Different approach.

"Okay," I boomed in, "Make me laugh," I encouraged, "Or think."

"I'm founding a new Party," he said in a theatrical, somber tone, "To address and relieve serious problems in the World." He made a pretense of scanning an imaginary audience. "I call it the Donner Party."

"He set his jaw firmly and continued: "we can solve the population problem. The hunger problem, organ donation problem ...to name a few."

"Is this what I think it is," I interjected.

He heard me but addresses open space. "Yes, we eat each other. Nobody will want to be fat. Less food will be consumed or wasted. And, the first thousand people who give me a million dollars will be exempt. And I, as head of the Party, will also be exempt.

"What about me?"

He looked me over. "You're too skinny." he decided. Not a prime candidate, but you'll do in an emergency. He gave me a more examining look. "As I friend, I recommend that you stay skinny."

He snapped out of his character. "The I ask for questions and give some zippy answers."

"It's not funny," I clued him in.

"It's practical," he struck back, "And there's truth in it."

"It'll make people squirm."

"It's Black Humor."

"You're half right."

"It's a fit for SF," he declaimed. "Here's a chance for people to sacrifice themselves for the good humanity. Think of the new cookbooks that will be written. A time to come forward and donate yourself. The clarion call of the Party will be: "Be Food!"

"You're kidding?"

"You think?" He said with a blank face.

"Maybe if you weave in some comedy," I suggested. "It's more appalling than appealing."

"Thais good," he'd laughed, "Maybe I can include some zany characters?"

A thought occurred to me. "What about vegetarians?"

"Hmm," he hummed, and mulled it over for half a minute. "Vegetarians can eat only vegetarians," he said authoritively, sweeping his arms toward the Buena Vista Hills.

"It's getting funnier."

He was long-limbed. When he punctuated his comments or observations with gestures, it made them more comical.

"Do you think Roman's bit crazy? I asked, tentatively.

"He's not your average Joe," his words squeezing out of the side of his mouth like an uncouth gangster.

"I know that," I said impatiently, trying to ignore his obsessive routines. I'm surrounded by crazy people or eccentrics. What's the Difference? Money! Which is why I'm obligated to be part of make-believe and delusion.

"He is in an interesting space," The Comedian said dreamily.

"You're no help."

He stood there in a thrift shop get-up of dark jeans, black jacket and white shirt A trickle of beard spotted his chin, and his gray tinged black hair was parted severely down the middle. His eyes were intense and jittery as if were searching for new material. He looked like the benevolent Rasputin.

He tried to be helpful. "I did sell door-to-door once, cold-canvas."

"Any advice?"

"Make sure your zipper is up," he sniggered.

I stared at him.

"Sorry, but it's true," He said, crossing his heart. "I couldn't get into house the whole evening." He stared into empty palms. "Later I realized my zipper was down." I tried not to stare at his zipper. "I must have looked pretty pathetic with my simpering smile and lowered zipper. He couldn't resist: "I had a lack of zip for the job.

While we were talking, dogs were zipping by, chasing each other in mad ellipses. The dog area was rutted from so much activity. It was amazing how the dogs navigated the holes without injuring their legs,

The days were shorter. Stepping through the Park was more treacherous in the dark. Yet, they had no problems. Humans, however. We're not so well guided. But we developed a sixth sense for the Mess.

Charles followed Guinevere as she went off to explore the Park. I was ready to leash Blondie and head home when I heard arching voice of the General.

"Hello, my pal Beamer!" he called out.

I turned around and there he was, moving with a stately step and holding a knobbed cane that never touched the ground. He had a conman's smile and a mustache twisted devilishly at each end, which he never touched and seemed frozen in place.

He always wore a long, tan duster that reminded me of Cowboys on the Trail and a fedora rakishly tipped to the side. It accented long eyebrows that rose up sharply, as if they were trying to escape from his face. He looked diabolical and harmless at the same time, not to mention comical.

"How are you?" he enunciated, not showing any fangs. His smile favored you. His accent was a mixture of Transylvania and Brooklyn.

"I'm OK," I parried.

"Very well, very well," he oozed out the syllables. "Did some good business today."

It was useless to ask what his business was. He never revealed it. He favored mystery.

But it was all a charade. He told me, 'confidentially, of course,' that he was Four-Star General in the U.S. Air Force and the duster concealed his various medals and ribbons

Since he needed to be in uniform, he felt he would be very conspicuous parading around the Park. People would think he was loony. But he loved to bring his old phlegmatic Rottweiler Hans to the Park and mix with all the dogs and people.

However, he shared his 'confidences' to anyone he thought could keep his secret. It included him flying fighter jets back and forth around the Country; Which explained his haphazard appearances in the Park. He looked fifty, so he must be in superb health.

The Count liked to regale Park people with his adventures, true or false, flapping his arms, twisting his body, as if were recreating mythical Aerial dog-fights of the Past. Himself as Hero. He was indulged everyone got a kick at his masterful storytelling, as if it really happened. I suspect that all his gyrations and self-centered behavior was really to Lannie.

Lannie was twenty years younger than him, a foot shorter, red-haired, freckled, full of good will and bad advice. She had a Cocker Spaniel named Russell and was studying to be a nurse after years at short-term jobs to finance her wanderlust. She was intimate with so many cultures that she sometimes got them mixed up.

She had a lot of interesting stories about her travels. Eager to see the wild world since she was a kid. Daring to go to risky places. Was it for adventure?

"Well, partly," she explained once. "I didn't want to put myself in danger, but I wanted to see up close how other people lived and the places they lived in." She hesitated. "To look for Truth, in capital letters."

"The Truth?" A vague concept I've been toying with for years

"Yes," she answered, gravely.

"Did you find it?" I boldly inquired.

"Pieces," she declared, with a gleam in her eyes, which quickly faded to soft diffidence. "At first I thought it was like a jigsaw puzzle and to connect the different shaped pieces together would form a whole. The whole picture.

"Like connecting the dots," I said impressed.

"Not exactly," she demurred with a smile. "Not like making Constellations out of the Stars."

"True."

"Who knows," she said sadly, if there is such a thing as "Truth."

"What about God?" I tossed in.

She moved her head slowly, side to side, as if it were a metronome. Measuring. A thinking quirk.

"I've thought of that," she said, her eyes drifting. "God is faith. I want tangible and not scraps."

"I admired her mighty ambition. Many people think of God as love in action."

"I'd like to try to pin it down a little more," she answered, respectfully. "Something solid. Something I can poke in the stomach, and get a little yelp."

"Good luck." I meant it sincerely. But as a pair of Docs in conversation once said: 'The invisible far outweighs the visible.'

If the Universe is a great Campfire of Truth around which we all could be gathered and warmed, and toast marshmallows, the world would be a cozy place. And if the Universe were made of marshmallows it would be a lot quieter, but stickier and harder to get around and we would be posed with different problems.

"So," I said to her serious face, with a hint of joshing. "You've been looking for Truth everywhere."

"That's right." She looked me square in the eye. "What's your idea?" She squished her lips together like a little kid. It wasn't a challenge. She was genuinely curious.

"I have none."

"You have nothing!"

"Nothing."

"You're not empty headed," she frowned, with irking disappointment.

"My idea is nothing."

"What!?"

"What's left when everything is gone?"

She gazed at me strangely, then finally said: "I suppose, nothing."

"Exactly."

"You're crazy," she said, with sympathy and confusion.

"Like everyone else," I retorted calmly.

"The Truth is what we are left with."

"What?"

"That's what I think." I amended it. At the moment.

"She let out a sigh of relief. "I'm glad that's over."

"Do you agree?"

"I'm stumped," she admitted. "I'll think about it. About Nothing."

"Thinking about nothing takes up a lot of space in the brain," I joked.

"You do seem to have a lot of empty space in your brain," she half-joked back.

We never talked about Nothing again.

She was standing in front of me, looking steadily into my eyes. They said: "That's enough. My turn. Let's go." I deferred to my dog. I said goodbye to Lannie in accordance with Blonde's wishes. And with all-time number one Doggy song: "Please Release Me, Take Me Home". I leashed her and made the short walk home with only ten or so sniff-stops along the way.

I was chomping on thick chips, watching the Warriors. Blondie was sprawled out on the floor sleeping, when it hit me. Tonight was the night to check the Actor's house for lights. How could I forget poor Molly of the fantasy version of her.

Within an hour Blondie and I were back. I left a message for Dori to get ready. She had two weekdays off a week. We'd meet in the Park and change into our awed tourist costumes. Dori would pretend she was an adored fan. Her looks should get her an invitation to come inside, with me, her brother meekly tagging along as an appendage. How she would know where he lived was a big gap in our planning. We hoped to be resourceful. We didn't look suspicious. We looked silly and naive.

We met at the Park next morning. We put on our sweatshirts and our caps, slung cameras around our necks, ruffled our maps and headed up Haight to Buena Vista Park.

The street along the far side of the Park had some grand houses. The Actor's house was squeezed between two of them. It was old and dignified. The front door was burnished wood with a shiny, brass knocker. All-white painted wood was pristine, and a small, plump tree with thin limbs outstretched, stood guard on a mostly smooth-cut green lawn.

The two long windows on each side of the door had matching red pleated drapes, as did the three upstairs windows. Everything seemed clean, simple and despite its relatively smaller size, imposing. Did it also describe the occupant? The place was not very gangsterish outside.

I knocked firmly. There was no sound for almost a minute. Finally, the edges of a drape on the right side separated from the window. Part of a face peered out. We passed muster. The door unclicked and the door opened halfway.

A bald-domed head, followed by a husky body in a bathrobe appeared and sleepily scrutinized our faces, outfits and what we were carrying and maybe any bulges we might have under our clothes. He looked satisfied and naturally, his attention lingered on Dori, who was offering a quaintly suggestive smile with a slight lift of helpless shoulders.

"Yes." Was it a question or was it an answer?

"Sorry to bother you," winced Dori, gripping her knee. "I twisted my knee on the sidewalk and I'd like to borrow some ice."

He looked into her pained, beseeching beautiful eyes. "It hurts," she whimpered softly.

Poor guy.

"Sure," he said without blinking. "Come in." He opened the door wide. Me, he ignored. I was an ornament on the lawn.

Dori limped into the entrance hall. I crooked my arm for her and steadied her until we arrived at the Big Sofa in the main room. She dropped down into the comfortable cushions and I sat next to her. The man introduced himself as John and went to get some ice.

The room was dark, the drapes closed. It was barely furnished. A lounger. A large, expensive desk. Small chairs sprinkled around. The floor was shiny. Not very lived in. But lots of room for a dog to be scampering around in. No dogs jumped into our laps, nor did we hear any barking for the Guests.

John came back with ice wrapped in a cloth. Dori thanked him and applied it gingerly to her knee and yelped that it was cold

"Of course it's cold, it's ice!" John laughed and snorted.

Dori laughed with him. "You know," she said, studying his face. "You resemble that movie star, you know, the who plays all those gangsters."

She's good.

"I'm a cousin, I think," he said proudly... "but you're the first person that ever connected us."

"No kidding."

"You look like him," I snuck in.

"Well, you had some genes together," Dori convinced him.

"Yes," he conceded, and went back to being proud.

We introduced ourselves to John. We told him we were sightseers from the Midwest. We did not elaborate and John did not ask. He seemed like a very proper man.

"Some coffee?" he offered.

"Sounds good," we said in unison.

"Be back." he left.

I whispered to Dori: "When he comes back, talk with him and I'll poke around looking for sleeping dogs." She nodded and started picking through the scattered magazine on the coffee table.

We heard a kettle whistle. In a minute he was back, holding out two cups. He first recognized that I was in the room. "It's instant," he apologized to Dori. I took both cups and handed one to Dori. "Not at all, thanks." I asked for the bathroom. He pointed the way.

I sipped some coffee and then ambled out of the room, tapped on a narrow door, probably a closet, snooped into a Den with a monster TV and DVDs scattered around the floor A family-sized couch faced the TV.

The bathroom was opposite a glass partition, that faced a small back garden. I had a morbid thought and followed it into the garden looking for upturned dirt. The garden was an overgrown tangle of nameless plants and high grass. No fresh signs of digging. A relief.

I went into the Bathroom, splashed my face with cold water, flushed the toilet, came out and approached a staircase. I tip-toed up some steps and coughed heavily a few times. Nothing.

In the living room, John was sitting next to Dori. They were wrapped in conversation. My stomach caved in a bit, but it was probably reacting to the plate of chocolate donuts sitting temptingly on a Gun magazine.

I caught Dori's attention with an indelicate scratching of head.

"Could I have a refill?" she asked John.

John popped up, took her cup and saucer and left.

I moved closer to her. "There's no Molly down here. Maybe, upstairs." She considered this. Then her s eyes twinkled.

John was back in a flash. He placed the coffee delicately in front of Dori and looked intently into her eyes.

"You know," she said to him., "My knee feels so much better, that I feel like singing a song."

She was just being silly

"I'd like to hear it," John said, enthusiastically.

"Okay, hope I don't wake up the neighbors," she laughed. She cleared her throat dramatically. "In Dublin's fair city where girls are so pretty, I first set my eyes on sweet MOLLY Malone, as she wheeled her wheelbarrow through streets broad and narrow, singing cockles and mussels, alive, alive, O. MOLLY, MOLLY, MOLLY Malone." She bowed triumphant.

John clapped like an idiot. I chuckled. It was a brainstorm. But no yapping, barking, arfing, crying came in reply.

"Is your cousin around," I paused to ask John. "I'd like to get his autograph."

"He's making a film." he answered tersely, distracted by Dori putting on her coat. "I'm just house-sitting," he grouched.

"Well, Brother, Dori said sprightly, "Let's hobble out of here and see the City."

John looked dejected. I didn't feel sorry for him.

At the door, we both thanked him and Dori gave him a loose hug. I shook his hand lightly. Dori and I exited, comparing the fairy tale facade to the gloomy inside.

We started walking back to the Park.

"What were you and John talking about so avidly? I mentioned, breaking a two block silence.

She looked at me with her deep eyes, "Are you jealous?" she teased.

"Of course not," I said stiffly, "Just curious."

"Well, he works at the DMV."

"With those hands!?" John's hands were bestial. Long, curved fingers like a fork. We pretended not to notice, but he had trouble carrying the coffees. His hands were a freakish deformity that ha kids and adults staring at him his whole life. "DMV!"

"Not glamorous, but steady."

"With those hands?"

"Oh, you're magnifying it", she scolded. "I'm sure he can be very dexterous."

"Okay," I conceded. Maybe, I was exaggerating. "By the way, do you know what they call some who can suck two sugar cubes at the same time?"

She gave me a dark look. "Not another one of your stupid jokes? Steadying herself to feel the punishment," she said grudgingly: "OK, what?"

"Ambidextrous!"

All I got was her profile. We parted at the Park.

When to the Church later that day to deliver news to Roman The services were over. He bent over, comforting a grungy mutt someone just down deposited in his lap.

He stood up when he saw me coming over and couldn't miss my expression. Telling him that our undercover operation uncovered nothing was painful.

"Nothing!?" He spat out in disgust, leaving the little dog to wander away.

"Nothing," I swore.

His chin dropped to his chest, ruffled rubbed his cheek, tightly shut one eye and made a growling sound.

"Maybe, he took Molly with him?"

"Thanks," He said quietly, after looking up and seeing my pity and remembering what I had done.

"His cousin was there," I said to rally him, "That's how we got in."

"A cousin?"

"That's what he said. He had weird hands."

Roman was pensive, but said nothing.

"I tried to find out where the Actor was filming, but he was smitten with Dori and ignored me." I grinned to lighten the mood. As a make-believe detective I couldn't insist."

Roman was barely listening to me. He was very agitated. Something was going off in his head. "That maniac!" he fumed. "He's no cousin!. The Hands!" He clenched his fists on pounded on the nearest pew. It scared the new dog.

"What? What?" Digging up dirt he's met some unsavory characters.

Roman sat down and drew a deep breath.

"What's wrong?'

"That guy's a hoodlum."

"John? He seemed like a nice guy."

"John," Roman sneered. "He's called 'Fingers.'"

I had to stifle a laugh. "I'm sure people call him 'Fingers.' Or the 'Man with The Long Fingers.' How could they not?"

"He strangles people!"

"You're nuts!" This was getting out of hand, pardon the pun. "Where did this come from?"

"Roman calmed down. "From a colleague."

"And who is this colleague?" I pressed, furious.

"He's a crime writer. An impeccable source."

"He had his eyes on Dori."

"Roman said nothing and turned his attention to a small puddle a pup had made. He picked up the cute pup, gave him a few strokes and handed him to me. He sat on my lap, accepting some pets and bounded to the floor and off somewhere. It eased the tension.

It was a good time to go and digest or indigest this explosive news I hoped to be dud. Roman was sharp despite his lunative proclivities, so

I always gave weight to what he. He had more experience in the sordid life, and with accurate sources. Dori cannot get near "John."

Back at work Monday morning, after taking Blondie on a few tours of the Park. I scanned my delivered Chronicle while eating a nutritious breakfast. Squeezed into a MUNI train for the ride downtown.

Commerce does not stop. Commerce comes with ads and with ads come promises. With promises comes disillusion, and with disillusion comes complaints and with complaints come compliant me.

The co-worker who occupied the cubicle next to mine was a silent fellow. In the months I had worked alongside him. The most acknowledgement was robot-like nods.

He had a nameplate on his desk: Robert Willard, in gold-tinged letters and an infinity sign inside a circle, personal crest. Let me, he had few personal items showing, no knick-knacks, just essential work stuff.

He sat erect at work. He sometimes hunkered close to it, his fingers a flurry blur over the keyboard. The commendations he tacked up, attesting to the outstanding employee the Company thought he was. He showed if off despite his taciturn nature. He felt appreciated.

Does really being good at something make us feel different? Robert was machine-like at work. Was he a wild carouser in his private life? Peoples' interiors are a mystery. What a brimming world of thought and feelings go on in our heads. Never stopping. An endless tale of wonder and horror, with no plot, that is, until the end.

I popped up over the partition and gave him a thumbs-up. He met it with his usual distrusting gaze. We both went back to work.

Most of the stuff coming in was cut and dried. I sent the regular Company response, which made me pretty much an automaton. I looked forward to some bizarre complaint that I could get my creative juices into. Some poor, hapless soul struggling with a malevolent product that was slowly sapping their brain power, turning them into enraged beasts, vowing to burn down the Company's ten thousand stores. Rah!

It wasn't that catastrophic.

A man couldn't get out of his alligator, hand-stitched cowboy boots he bought at one of the Company's upscale stores. He felt glued in. Did someone leave some adhesive material in there? he asked.

He's been clomping around the neighborhood all evening, trying to find a friend who could successfully pull them off. No dice. The boots were stuck fast to his bare feet. He was mad.

It was nighttime. With a residue of humor, he said that he'd like to die with his boots on, but he didn't want to go asleep with them on. At least they didn't have spurs.

He got testy. Did some put Gorilla glue in them as prank? Was it malicious? He wasn't a guy who resorted to lawyers, but had them and use them if this situation wasn't rectified in a hurry.

I thought of some options I kept to myself. One possibility was to join a cattle drive. Another to wait out the glue. Stand next to a red-hot furnace to melt the glue.

The only quick fix I could think of was to cut them off. But that would be sacrilegious to some folks. It will probably end up litigious. I dropped it and sent him a standard form. He can stomp his way to Court.

I have to call this one: 'Too sticky to handle.'

Later that day, I got something I could my nose into.

A man bought a hand-held battery radio. His complaint was that when he went to bed and listened to his favorite talk show, the Devil would break in and begin enumerating his sins. Was somebody fooling him? Then how did the voice know about the toy car he stole from the 5 and 10 store when he was only nine.

I informed him that I knew no one in the Company who had telepathic powers and that he was crazy (I deleted the last part before sending) and the Deil was only broadcasting on that frequency.

Maybe, the radio was reading his mind. I doubted it. But, then, technology was making quantum leaps, so maybe, you accidentally got some futuristic innovative demonstration model that turned up on the

Company's pile. Was he crazy or just ahead of his time. He should feel special.

That seemed to console him. The best thing to do about the Devil is to ignore him. He gets his kicks from scaring people.

As I was packing up to go home, I saw Robert in his cubicle doing the same. I had the urge to ask him if he also had these strange complaints and how did he handle them. Did he just forward everything on with the standard forms, or did he give his helpful and healthy perspective on things.

If he was more receptive I would have a clue, but, watching him hurrying, fumbling with his books, hat and coat, to get away before bumping into anyone, the question was hanging around the office, twiddling its letters.

I was ensconced in my Lounger, munching on chips, sipping beer, watching Sunday Night Football. When there was the always ominous screech of my smartphone.

I hesitated, then dragged myself over to where it was implacably beckoning and lifted it slowly to my ear. Did I have premonition? It was Dori and she was angry.

"I came back from work and there was note under my door!": 'Your Dogs Are Next.' I could hear her teeth grinding.

Stunned, I said dully, "Who left it?"

"How should I know!?"

"Maybe, it's a stupid joke?" I said stupidly.

"It's your fault! You got me involved with this!"

Jesus! "It doesn't make sense?"

"It doesn't have to make sense, it's a threat!"

It can't be connected. A serial dog-napper running around the neighborhood?

"Did you mention Molly to the people in your building?" I tried to get her reasoning. "Do you think someone has a grudge against you and wants to scare you?"

It was quiet at the other end.

"I was doing my laundry, in the laundry room yesterday," she said, forcing herself to be calm, "And I did mention it in conversation with other women there."

"It hit the rumor mill."

"Do you think someone doesn't? like me?"

"Or your dogs."

"Makes me nervous."

"Any ideas?"

"I'll think about it."

"Hold on to that note."

"Sorry I got mad at you," she said quietly

"It's Okay. I think your neighbors should know about it. You Have four fearless protectives beside you and another a block away. See you in the Park.

A woman jealous of her? A man feeling rejected? I'm sure she'll come up with some candidates. She hasn't mention any troubles. Has something been brewing? Why would anyone strike now with a sneaky and anonymous note?

Is someone angry with her dogs? Four dogs barking in unison makes disturbing racket. People have been known to get violent from incessant barking, even than from jackhammers or screaming car alarms.

A few have complained about the dogs and she has tried to settle them down. But a noisy parade in the hall or running feet can set them off. They are nervous, protective creature and minor things can set them off. At least they are better at night.

I grabbed the leash, which excited Blondie to a frenzy of tail wagging, and licking. We took off for Golden Gate Park and more greenery. Many it would make my brain move a little faster.

I wanted to shed my Junior Detective badge. I was saddled with it. Things are invisible. Who took Molly? Where is she? Who's threatening Dori's dogs and in turn, Dori? Straw men in the wind. I'm assuming they are men. I don't want any new angles.

It's not like everything is on my shoulders. Roman has plenty of resources and Dori can take care of herself. But there is intrigue in all this. A puzzle to solve. Even a chance to do good. But, I do have to own up to the original instigator: Cash.

Blondie is a notorious food hound. A 'Stomach On Legs.' A sobriquet the SPCA would agree with when I adopted her. She was skinnier then. Now, she is not, but still vigorous, especially when it comes to skateboards.

She has no scruples about lolling innocently about a picnic or a sleeping homeless person, waiting to dart in and snag any edible that is loose. She is quick and shameless.

I remember stopping by a homeless man sitting on the sidewalk downtown. He was begging with a smile on his face. Not pushy, polite, not ragged or sickly looking. We got to talking.

He did okay, he said. "I watched the pigeons and learned from them." He didn't go into details.

As we walked through the Panhandle on our way to Golden Gate Park. Blondie was already stalking the covered gopher holed that dotted the park. She could over a spot motionless and suddenly dig manically and end up with her snout in the hole. But, no how fast she dug, she was never fast enough to snag the elusively wary, short-sighted gopher.

I had a clue why she was obsessed with gophers. When I first adopted her, and I was giving her wings off leash, I encouraged her to: "Go for it!" She took me literally.

In our neighbor, she had captured a gopher when it was suddenly exposed after a City Gardener had been working on a small plot in a corner garden and left a gaping hole in the ground. The gopher peeked out and in an instant spotted the poor varmint and a flash had it in her mouth.

It was done for. Blondie started walking home with it. I tried to pry it out of her mouth. She realized it and decided to eat it right there. It was small and Blondie crunched her way through it, every part of it, until there was no more.

There was nothing politically correct about it. Canine vs Gopher is Nature's way of reminding us that most species Dine Out.

Autumn showed up. New scents in the air. Leaves tingling to fall, the air crispier and the primal unease of darkness creeping in.

There were always new people to the Park. They were quickly frustrated when their recall failed. They yelled and yelled. No dog. They have yet to realize that sound travels more slowly in the Dog Park.

It takes longer to reach where the dog is, and by the time sound gets there, the dog has moved. The acoustics are unique. You have entered a Twilight Zone where the dog has the upper paw.

I sat down on a bench and Blondie sprawled in her usual place behind it. She kept watch, alert to any sudden trouble in her Queenly realm. A local Catholic Priest who occasionally comes to the Park with his two small dogs, called her 'Mother Superior' of the Park. She broke up fights, protected small dogs, knocked off humping dogs and allowed no "hanky-panky."

As we moved through the edge of the Park, on our way home, Blondie and I passed another group of homeless. These were kids. They left home for adventure, or by necessity, drifting through, smoking, trading stories, hanging together with the easy camaraderie of the young.

We were back in Duboce Park. Clumps of gray clouds cozied and a nippy wind jiffed in as dogs romped with abandon: Tumbling, racing, leaping and twisting their amazing bodies, invigorated by the cold.

Then in a startled moment, I saw Molly across the Park. The dog exactly matched the description Roman gave me. The gentleman at the other end of the leash was a newcomer. Bearded, with a baseball cap pulled low over forehead. He wore a stylish red jogging suit.

I needed a closer look.

I got up. Blondie got up. We ambled with carefree intent, meandering and mingling until we paused next to the fence where the guy was standing.

"Cute dog," I said his profile, reaching down to pet a.k.a. Molly. He looked at me. He looked at Blondie. Said nothing. No expression. His eyes gave him away. It was definitely him.

The eyes on a screen that could make innocents blanch, posed no threat amongst the dogs. But they still carried a real or pretended menace.

"What's your dog's name," I asked, in the language of one dog owner to another, while at the same time feeling around Molly's collar for a name tag or a license. Nothing.

"Molly," He gave me a crafty look.

"Is she a rescue?" I probed with a phony smile.

"Nope."

He jerked Molly toward the sidewalk and walked away. Either Molly had a twin or this guy had a lot of brass. Was he taunting Roman? The withering stare he gave me as he turned and exited the Dog Park was not convincing. Maybe he was just a jerk. Maybe.

We walked back to the same bench. Dori was there, half sitting, half bending with her riotous crew of dogs surrounding her legs. They barked their perfunctory warnings or greetings to me and Blondie and then began nipping playfully with each other.

"I'm so suspicious of everyone," she looked up at me, questioning her stubborin fear. It surprised her.

"A kook. A coward."

"People in the building never saw me acting so weird." She nervously twisted the leashes she was holding into a jumble. "Conversations are the usual mundane stuff."

"So, no perpetrators?"

"Not yet." She scrunched her face at me. "Just fancy words."

"I didn't mean to be facetious, "I laughed at her expression and before this conversation escalated I told her about meeting the Actor and believing the dog was the original Molly."

"Wow! What was he like?"

"Icy."

"Like the Movies," She said, Hollywoodized, her intelligent eyes now vacuous in blank surrender to her fantasies. He worries on hold, her fears aborted, etc. Hollywood was the etcetera of our dreams.

"What do you think, Dori?"

"You're sure it's the same Molly?" You've never seen her.

"I'm not positive," I answered, tendentiously.

"Maybe, she's his dog."

She wasn't hearing me.

"Quite a coincidence," I said edgily. "Considering she and he have never been to the Park before."

"So?" She cooed.

"So. I'll tell Roman and let him deal with it."

"Okay. I gotta go."

She miraculously separated the mass of leashes, attached her dogs and shooed them in front of her. They charged forward, Dori, leaping behind, shouting: "Stop at the corner!!"

I called her when she got home. She said she found a note, signed by a bunch of her neighbors; "We've got your back!"

We've all left the theater still in a trance from the film we saw, only to quickly wake up on a dirty sidewalk and to the noisy traffic. In my opinion movies should only be showed in the middle of the ocean in a luxurious cabin-cruiser with all the fixings.

Opinions are filled with onions, layers peeling away to the nub of a person. Or opinions can contain a pin to jab with, and a poison to debase.

I hurried over to Roman's Church to unload the news and deparate myself from the consequences.

He was sitting in a front pew nodding off, his incipient double chin bobbing on the Cross around his neck. The Cross was not traditional. It was furry and I imagine, itchy.

"Roman?" I broke in.

His eyes opened warily. His head swiveled and seemed to get stuck.

"I found Molly."

He shook his head to wake up fully. His cheeks wobbled and came to a stop in a moist grin. "You found her!" he gushed.

"I think so," I said cautiously, knowing when I told him how, he would not be so upbeat.

I told him, and ducked.

"That rat!" he exploded, clenching his fists and shaking them towards Buena Vista Park. "That rotten rat!" Then he remembered Molly. "Is she okay?"

"She seemed fine."

The few people who were in the Church with their dogs, barely turned around. They were used to hearing Roman's bursts of moral outrage and expected nothing less. He spoke he them. But no solemn amens or furied applause were forthcoming for his private jeremiads.

He went over to his desk, reached into the bottom draw and with back turned to me pulled something out and stuffed it into the inside pocket of his jacket. He held his left forearm across the pocket and tried to conceal its shape.

Maybe, it was a wad of bills? He hoped to ransom Molly. A gun? In his Church? He went into his rooms in the back. I waited fifteen minutes. He didn't come out and I left. I threaded my way through the ripple of people and dogs moving down the aisle to seat themselves for the next Service. Roman must be preparing for it.

I drifted out into the street, planning to miss Roman's next sermon. It was bound to be more blistering than ever; after what he had just learned. My ears and brain needed a rest from this capricious caper.

Blondie was excited to see me when I came home. She expected to be taken out immediately. I had other plans. After assuring her, to her satisfaction, would happen, I slid a CD of the Late Quartets of Beethoven into the Walkman, clapped on the headphones and elongated myself on the sofa.

To me, these Quartets were the most profound music, almost on another plane. For the time I listened, the surface world vanished and I was drawn into something deeper and purer.

I luxuriated in this evanescent realm. The world was knocking. A long snout was tapping urgently against my leg. Flesh and blood needs to walk.

It was peak evening times at the Dog Park and the usual assortment of characters and dogs gathered in small bunches. People conversed and dogs dispersed, ranging proprietarily among the blakes of grass, noses keen for newsy smells, eyes seeking playmates, ears listening for the crackle of bags holding treats. Blurry legs cranking out pent up energy and the flurry of dogs mixing it up in friendly combat.

I sat on a bench with Blondie behind it, placidly observing the action. When Charles and Guinevere came bobbing by. He stopped, jogging in place, while she lunged towards Blondie. Blondie, seeing that Guinevere was leashed, looked at her and then lost interest.

Guinevere had no luck befriending Gustav, my last dog, who thought her too wild and impetuous. Now, she was striking out with Blondie, who was about to give her treasured spot or invite any dog in. Guinevere was still a youngster, which meant aggravation for older dogs.

"What's up?" panted Charles, with a luminous smile on his face.

"Not my bank account," I countered. "And please stop bouncing. It's tiring me out"

He stopped. "Sorry." His smile notched down to an offended pucker, which stretched into a toothy grin, which backed up into a darkened brow. And ended its travels into the original bon homie.

His dopiness over, he spoke. "I know the guy who put the jokes into the fortune cookies. Only, it wasn't a guy, it was a girl."

"A start-up like you?"

"She's starting."

"Under your wing?'

He flapped his arms idiotically. "Arms are made for hugging and lugging and bugging people by sending them crazy letters on Email and tugging on dogs that don't want to go home, and piloting airplanes, except when they're on automatic pilot."

"I thought the jokes were funny," I elocuted.

"She got fired."

"Why did they hire her in the first place."

He tipped an imaginary cap. "She's Chinese."

Guinevere was restlessly and methodically winding her leash around Charles' legs. The conversation stopped as he slowly unwound himself.

"I'd better get going," he waved, shortening the leash and pulling Guinevere close to his side.

He stopped short after a few hurried steps and snapped his fingers. "I forgot."

He pulled his newly minted cards. Simple. Business like. Serious colors. He wanted me to have his phone number and asked me to leave mine and know when his next gig was.

I watched him jog off, Guinevere slowing down to keep pace.

Conversations with Charles were like diving into a sea of soap; There was something cleansing about the experience, but it would also make your eyes smart.

Blondie came out from her spot and sat in front of me. She intended to get petting attention after my brief interlude with Charles and Guinevere. Charles had been my focus for a while and she needed to regain her rightful, top place in the hierarchy of those I paid attention to. Her big, round golden eyes were steady and solemnly aimed at mine. She was stately in posture, befitting her claim as Queen of the Park;

I rubbed the top of her head and she moved in closer, no longer looking at me, but savoring the pleasure of her primacy. I had little idea what she was thinking, but was an august moment in my mythical imagination.

When Blondie was felt satisfied and resumed her vigil behind the bench. I pulled out the book I was carrying and skimmed through paintings and photographs depicting the early American history I like to read about.

Fire Engines suddenly shrieked and dogs, including Blondie began to howl. I looked to enjoy the dog chorus and not twenty feet away from me was the Actor and his strenuously howling little Molly. And he was howling along.

Before I left Roman, we had agreed that if I saw the Actor in Park again, I was to call him immediately. Which I did.

Within fifteen minutes a puffing, chubby figure was churning through the grass, looking wildly about, then settling on me, and coming over.

"Where is he!?" he wheezed, straining to see across the Park. He had hurried out without his distance eyeglasses.

I directed him to the water fountain, where dogs had lower the lowest bowl. He walked angrily towards it. He got the crowds' attention. At the fountain he dropped to his knees and hugged Molly, while the Actor looked on in consternation.

"What did you do to her beautiful fur?" Roman moaned, smoothing Molly back.

"Nothing," the Actor replied, testily. "Aren't you the guy that wrote nasty stuff about me?"

"Why did you take my dog!?" He held on tight to Molly.

"She' not your dog," he warned, taking firmer hold of the leash, as if Roman was going to spirit her away.

The crowd that stood by was baffled by the encounter. They stayed quiet.

Roman was in a quandary; He didn't want to let go of Molly. She was nervous and wriggling to break free. He finally released her and stood up. He summoned a hard, quasi-menacing stare. "Where did you get her?"

"None of your business."

Roman was stymied. He was not going to intimidate the guy, despite standing on his tip-toes to look the Actor in the neck. But the sentiment of the crowd swung in his direction.

I thought, maybe they were both right. Whoever stole the dog, if she was stolen, sold her to the Actor and he had no idea he was getting a hot dog. Or, they were two Molly's from the same little. Or, a bunch of Molly's had fallen from the sky when no one was looking.

The Actor strode out of the Park with Roman shouting 'Thief' after him, and don't worry, Molly will be back in the Church where she belongs. It wasn't so much a threat as a Holy cry. The Actor had upset God's plan and he was in trouble. The crowd was rooting for God. I was rooting for a glass of beer.

I tried to console Roman. He said he had another plan. I went home with Blondie and poured out a refreshing glass of ale. I pondered nothing but the lifting effects of the brew. The world was too heavy outside, falling on too many shoulders that bent under the load. It became evident the next day, when responding to a complaint.

A wishful thinking man had sent away for a Magician's Kit, featuring a white tipped magic wand. It came with a booklet of tongue-twisting incantations that when spoken, waving the wand would do magical things.

He chose one with a lot of exs and zees and proceeded the wave his wand at his wife who had just ended their conversation and was entering the bedroom. Ten minutes later, he went into the bedroom and she wasn't there. She had vanished and there was a recent pile of dust on the floor. He searched the other rooms and the garage, but she was gone.

I suggested that she was playing a trick on him to cure him of his obsession with the Magician's Kit. He didn't believe me. The Kit had promised to make things disappear and it worked. The magic wand was not defective. It was not a legitimate complaint.

He brought a new angle to the discussion.

The power of the wand was connected to an Alien civilization, which was beaming her to another planet in the Galaxy.

"Of course," I told him, that solves one problem, at least we have an idea of where she might be, but there are billions of Planets in the Galaxy to search."

"Do you sell anything like that?" He asked, sounding a little guilty.

"A Galaxy/Planet GPS?"

"Do you?"

"You have to check with the Warehouse," I told him frankly, unable to direct him to any specialty houses.

"Thanks for your help."

"Sure."

I have to admit, getting loony complaint brightens my day. If it wasn't for the looniness that squirts into this world, it would be a far more parched Earth. However, ninety-eight percent of the ones I see are cut and dried dull, easily cleared and forwarded the action of a refund or an exchange or a polite No.

Lunchtime had me claiming a spot on the grass in nearby minipark, bucking the wind. I unfurled, from my American flag plastic wrap, a thick tuna salad with cheese, melted on toast. It had been nested in aluminum foil, but didn't stay warm.

Despite biting into a cold, wind-chilled sandwich, I couldn't resist watching the woman, quashigly close to me and sitting on a NT Times, pouring coffee from a thermos. Then, she reached into a handbag with a strange Orange and Purple Flag. She pulled out two sealed bags, with a large succulent turkey in each one. Voila!

After dismissing the idea of an exchange, I was curious about the Flag. I had never seen those colors on a flag before. Also, she was attractive and in a position to talk to me after gobbling her lunch and washing it down with more coffee.

"You must be very hungry?" I ventured, trying not to sound like I was talking to a denizen of the Street.

She turned to me with a smile. "I was." She wasn't fluttering anything. Her eyes stayed still watching my face. She was pretty, and my old, shy clumsiness was taking over.

"What country is that flag from," I asked, pointing with my sandwich as a dollop of tuna fish fell into my lap.

She quickly pulled a wad of tissues from her bag and handing them to me.

"Thank you." I watch her retreating hand, wiped off the fish and held up the tissue. "Now it can go back in the can," I smiled.

She nodded. "In the garbage can. It's a joke."

"Yes. I got it."

I was expecting a groan. This was a surprise.

"It's not a Country flag," she explained with pride.

"What is it?"

"It's for fun."

"For fun?"

"Usually, I make up a Country to go with it."

"For fun."

"I create my own Country." Laughter sprung happily over her deception. "Life is so serious. We need some silliness."

"That's how I feel." I said, shaken.

I studied her. She wore jeans, sandals and no socks. All clean. A yellow sweatshirt and blonde hair in a ponytail. Her eyes were greenish and she needed no make-up.

The wind suddenly upped the ante with a cold gust and drove some people out of the small park.

"I hope the people in your Country are warmer than we are"

"My Country maketh good sweaters," she declared, and pulled one out of her bag. It was Orange. Next came a Purple scarf which she swept royally around her neck and shoulders.

"Are you a Princess in your land?" I indulged her.

"You are embroidering," she chided, with a sharp wink. "Princess Grandiosa,"

Did she think she was a Princess? Or was she just goofy. Don't make a move you'll regret, I thought to myself.

"I have to go back to work." I said in a rush, pushing myself hastily up from the grass. "I hope it's not as cold here tomorrow."

"I'm gonna have some socks on," she smiled, rubbing her naked feet. "My Country is known for sock making".

"Bye." She gave me a muted wave, if there is such a thing.

A woman had bought a full-length "Talking Mirror," which you could program to speak to you when you stood in front of it and looked at yourself. She asked it to sat to her: "You Are Beautiful," which it did every day for several weeks.

Then, one day, out of the blue, while she was preening herself for a dinner date, she asked the Mirror: "Am I beautiful"? The Mirror responded: "You Are Too Fat."

Naturally, she was flabbergasted and indignant.

She posed the question and the Mirror said: "You Are Beautiful." She was relieved, felt jolly again and was happily off to her date.

A few days later, feeling giddy over compliments she received from a new boyfriend, she asked the Mirror: "Am I the most beautiful girl in the room?" The Mirror answered: "You Are The Only Girl In The Room."

Mirrors can be sarcastic image wise, but it is rare to find one that does it vocally. The thought it nasty and was fed up with its insinuating attitude. She brought it back to the store for a replacement, without specifying the details of her complaint. It didn't fit the decor of her bedroom. She wanted another color.

Her new mirror responded politely and positively to all the questions she put to it. This lasted a month. On alternate days, the Mirror was telling her how fat she was and pointing out some local spas she could enroll in and shed that extra poundage.

On reflection, it was the wrong thing to say. It was the final shattering moment for the Mirror. Or as it might be called: 'The Mirror of Truth'

I did not know the girth of the woman, nor wanted to ask, but I had my suspicion and tried to ease her pain by explaining that in these new computerized contraptions often got their molecules twisted around and things came out in the wrong way: Hadn't she heard of GPS systems sending people to State Prisons, when they only wanted to go to State Parks. Or trying to cross a bridge had vanished.

I suggested she should shine up one of large fry pans and use it for a mirror. It would correctly distort an image of herself.

With that insult, I quit my job.

My decision was firm—for a few hours.

When I got home, checked the mail, checked a bill or two, thought of rent, I realized I was going back to work tomorrow.

There would be a backlash for my insult. I don't doubt the woman in a justified huff, turned me in. I expected a reprimand. There still stood a feeble hope, that my last advice was confusing enough to mystify her. Did it carry too much weight?

There was a message on my commuter, informing me that a customer had complained about an 'Outrageous Tatic' she endured. It was a violation of the Company's Rules and Credo, and future like acts will be unforgiven, etc.

I let it ride. Made no apology or defense. Stay quiet. Just pass thing through. Sit innocently at my desk with the Company Credo emblazoned on my eyeballs, whatever I was. It was in Ancient Greek.

There were some tempting moments to reach out creatively. I closed my mind and sent the standard apologies and compensation forms. I had nothing against the Company. No sign they were cheating or taking advantage of people. Every tenth commercial on TV was selling their products and people embraced them as old friends. I wasn't in the business of sabotage, at least consciously. This was an Empire, after all. A dent here and there wasn't going to rock. And dents can be easel fixed.

So, I was still a slug, counterfeit employee. But, a slug with a paycheck. And, as I slugged it out, spiritually, over my new minimalist work ethic, there was the bright promise of tomorrow's lunch with the intriguing woman who invented countries.

What about Molly?

Walking back home from downtown after work. I remembered that I had forgotten about her. Roman war still in a storm, convinced the Actor's alleged Molly was his Molly; though he wasn't absolutely sure and had no proof.

DogPark people thought the Actor was an egotistical nitwit and a thief to boot. Which fit his Movie persona. Roman's supporters saw him as a Goodhearted, generous dog lover. But his high fervor would put them off.

Things might have simmered down if the Actor hadn't shown up one afternoon with "Fingers." It's as if he expected, or intended some rough stuff and brought along a bodyguard.

I was at work at the time but learned that Actor and 'Fingers' made deliberate, spooking turns around the Park, as if daring anyone to accost them or bring up the subject of Molly.

Of course, Molly led the way, excitedly jumping to other dogs but was yanked back and finally led out of the Park when the demonstration ended.

Since Molly's true guardian was still in debate, no one had reason to confront the Actor. Plus, the unexpected arrival of a belligerent, scarying looking guy, with freakishly enormous hands, whose leather wardrobe featured an equally scary knife in sheath, attached to a studded belt at the hip.

This description I got form Linda, Great Dane lover, was "freaked-out." But, however dismayed she was by 'Fingers,' she took the time to be impressed by his accouterment. "Like something you'd see in the Movies."

She was studying to work in the Fashion Industry. She seemed doubly struck by his sheath. "Is that a designer sheath?" She wondered.

"Is there such a thing?"

"What about the knife?"

"I'm sure it was sharp."

Sharp.

I excused myself from Linda's lethal wit and effusive fashion scrutiny when I suddenly spied Roman A as the group of people surrounded and dwarfed him, started peeling off. When I got to him he was standing silently, head bowed and running a leash through his fingers like a Rosary.

His dejection supposed that something had pulverized his Faith. His mournful eyes looked weakly up at me.

"I lied," he said.

"You lied?"

"I never really saw Molly in a good light."

"It was night."

"It was an emergency," he remembered. "Took the dog from her at the door of the Church. It was wrapped in a small blanket. She lady left and I immediately put her down and walked to see how she was doing. That's when the car pulled up."

"Quite a coincidence."

"She was a nice lady." he assured me, throwing off the connection between the giving and the taking away.

His expression dampened. He looked miserable at the thought he was hood-winked. "For what?"

I couldn't answer him. "So you're not sure. All this chasing after the Actor is a mistake?"

"I have my doubts," he mumbled.

He was so adamant and now in retreat. "Did he cow you?"

"Cow me?"

"Intimidate you. You were so sure."

He considered the situation. "He has the dog. I have no proof."

"And I doubt the woman who gave you Molly is still hanging around the Church."

He looked defeated.

"It sure looks like a set-up and a payback," I said defiantly. "The Actor is a worthy culprit."

"You believe?"

"Who else?"

His spirits rose. "Who else would stoop to this, the big rat!"

"Molly's counting on you," I sallied.

Blondie and I headed home. I looked back at Roman. He was chatting with Linda and almost eye to eye with her male Great Dane named Prince. His hand was over his heart.

Back in my Lounger. I was thinking ahead my lunch in the minipark. Would she be there? Her name was Tamara. It had a Shakespearean poetic sound: "Tamara and Tamara and Tamara," as if Shakespeare was born in Brooklyn.

Would I blunder? I could feel my other self slipping through the cracks. The dark, destructive self, that with one whack could crumple a heart. I shook my own hands to make friends of the two sides of me.

Next morning. Blondie and I took our customary long walk around the neighborhood before work. The air was an awakening chill and a high, gray dome of fog cocooned the Park.

We walked through the depleted trees their splayed limbs, with pencil sketched fingers were eerily silhouetted against the gray. The sun, patiently waiting for the fog to burn off, seemed like a distant memory beneath our pale shroud.

But neither fog nor rain nor gloom could keep the pent-up morning energy of the dogs from bursting through the sullen haze, providing their own sunshine to brighten the humans' workday.

Blondie joined the dogplay, contributing her own vital energy to the ribbony ranks of canine tradition: Dogs chasing dogs. It was good she was getting tired.

"You know," The General called over, walking towards me, "When fighter planes used to maneuver and shoot at each other it's called a 'Dog Fight'.

"They're not really fighting."

"I know," he smiled. "But the planed would chase each other's tails." The General always wore his long duster coat when he infrequently came to the Park. He claimed it covered his Four-Star uniform so it wouldn't be conspicuous. One of the guys. I was always waiting for him to slip-up; to be too hot and unbutton his coat. By the flaw in that hope was that it rarely got that hot in SF.

The General stood stiffly and scanned the Park. His dog, a stout, black-furred creature, stood reverently and obedient at his side, not sporting any decorations.

"Nowadays," The General explained, "The pilots shoot without even seeing each other, except as a blip on a screen." He looked back at me. "In this kind of conflict, a woman can be an effective fighter as well as a man, or even better."

He noticed my respectful air and my attention. He patted the left side of his chest, where his heart was and his medals might be. I thought I heard a rustle of metal. It could have been the wind blowing tins cans around. The wind was strong today.

"Did you engage in any 'Dog Fights', I wondered.

"Yes." He became pensive and rubbed his jawline, slowly with his left hand. A bit of pajama slipped out his sleeve cuff. "It's not something I like to talk about."

"I understand," I said, appropriately

He sniffled a few times, dropped his head to his chest, as if he were recollecting an enemy plane going down in flames before his guns. His eyes, which held a hint of tears, belied his age. They were sky blue and very clear. Pilot's eyes? In any case, he was intelligent and certainly inventive in some areas. I asked him what he thought of the Molly situation.

"Yes, I've heard about it," he said crisply. "Do you believe the Actor is a thief and the man Roman if afraid to pursue him?"

"I believe that."

He assumed a military bearing. "Something has to be done then?"

"As a man who has been to war, I thought you might have some suggestions."

"Yes," he said jovially, "Call in the Marines."

Not so helpful.

But he has a point. In this case, the Marines would be more helpful than the Air Force. I see scenario of a Marine platoon, weapons drawn, rushing into the Park, scattering the dogs and the people Zeroing in on the Actor and 'Fingers', hauling them away, freeing the prisoner Molly and handing her to Roman while the Dog People cheered.

Yes, it could be a TV movie, with the Actor, as an act of contrition, playing himself.

I could not mock the mock General by snapping a smart salute, but I wished him a nice day, leashed Blondie, petted his dog and prepared to go to work.

I tried to avoid Blondie's "Why are to leaving me alone look," as I crafted and bagged my peanut butter and orange marmalade sandwich, and washed off a Red Delicious apple for dessert.

By the time I boarded the MUNI, the crowds had thinned. There's no need to forcibly wedge oneself into the mass of bodies, as earlier riders must do. I won't always get a seat but my limbs will be working when I get off.

Work piles up overnight. I sift through it, separating form stuff from what is interesting enough for a personal touch. My vouch to be diplomatic and tactful has evaporated. The urge to needle or irreverently placate complainers is strained. I need to throw some gut funny punches without a referee in the ring. I am desperate but my job hangs in the balance. I will try to be kind, helpful and a little whimsical.

A customer from Washington state purchased a recliner. It worked correctly for a few months and he was happy with it. But it developed an odd problem.

When it was in the Lounge position and he pressed the side handle to set it upright, it flung him to the floor. It didn't always do that, but he couldn't predict when it would happen. It sorta spoiled his enjoyment and was afraid of getting hurt.

Why didn't he return it or get a replacement? He said it was the exact style and color he wanted. It was the last one and he got it at a discount. He couldn't understand why it was ejecting him. He dealt with it by laying some thick area rugs to buffer his flaw. His kids thought it was fun.

My recommendation: Seat Belt.

I looked over at another Box in the room. The one occupied by my silent neighbor. Actually, he did speak to me once, when I first arrived and asked him if he lived in SF or commuted. Just a friendly question to open the door. His laconic answer was covered in frost. "I don't have to tell you where I live." Other than sneezes of coughs, I heard nothing more from him.

He tacked up his commendations from the Company on a wall where everyone could see them. He was not oblivious to what passing workers thought of him. But it must take a lot of energy to maintain the tension needed to insulate himself. When I stood up, I could see him pitched forward in his chair, practically nuzzling the computer screen, risking a crease in his trousers.

He didn't dress casually like the rest of us behind the scenes workers, but showed up in tir and white shirt and a suit jacket folded over his arm. Of course, he wore wire-rimmed eyeglasses, which he religiously wiped clean and a haircut whose hairs would not move in a hurricane. He made the rest of us look pathetically indifferent to our jobs and our work ethic.

But he was a complete mystery. All I had to go on was what he presented of himself. What went on inside him and away from the Office. Did meticulous neatness outside cover up a chaotic mess inside?

When I go into someone' house or apartment for the first time and there is not even a magazine askew on a coffee table or pillows are perfectly placed on the sofa, I feel uncomfortable. Where's the stuff? I feel better when I spot some disarray. There is life here. No pretentions. No shame over a little sloppiness, which is the natural state of humanity on this planet. And I bet, when we get around to landing on some distant world, and the first gal or guy steps off the rocket ship and trips over some Alien kid's Tonka-like toy, we'll discover that a proclivity for having stuff all over the place is universal habit.

I scanned a hundred complaints before I found one worthy of a deeper look. A man in Arizona was disturbed by an Aquarium he bought from a local Company store, it came with a variety of the usual tropical fish and he was delighted with it.

He was mostly house-bound, so a dog was out of the question and he was allergic to cats and didn't want a constant chatter of birds. Fish were moving life and easy to take care of. They satisfied his desire for company and were interesting to watch.

The problem, he recently discovered, was that were plotting against him. Theyed me face to face with him through the glass, their mouths opening and closing, invariably hatching nefarious plans, staring at him with malice in their eyes.

They were beautiful to look at, especially the Golden ones, which he assumed to be the leader of the Cabal/. They knew people underestimate their intelligence, so their actions were no surprise to him. He was an avid fisherman once and wondered if they got the word.

I asked him. What could they do? They were in the water. How could they harm him? He believed they communicated with another species: An alliance with air-breathers, who would do the dirty work.

Rather than explain to him that he was crazy and jeopardize my job I advised him to have somebody come by to reason with the fish or buy another group of fish or if he really felt himself in danger, dump them in the toilet.

After sending the message, I thought: Fishy! Was this a fish tale. Was somebody pulling my fin? Just another bizarre life? Let it ride. It brought color to my otherwise drab employment.

Lunchtime finally came, and with it, thumping. Would she be in the minipark today? I took the crowded elevator down to the street, nodding distractingly at people I've talked with in the Lunchroom. I was jettisoned from the parted doors into the Lobby and then into the street to breathe in fresh, but mildly polluted air. I hurried to the minipark, trying to beat the hurrying mob and caught a break. There still a patch of virgin grass and quickly sat down, heedless of stains. I spread my newspaper and lunch out beside me, claiming a spot for my friend.

The park filled rapidly. Fifteen minutes went by and there was no sign of her. I bleakly munched my sandwich with the small solace that we had no appointment and with the stupid idea nothing was sometimes better than something. Something I probably heard on TV.

My misery was assuaged by a good-looking woman peering hard in my direction, as if she had forgotten her eyeglasses. She was ritzy. Not one to sit among us working minions, but one to walk breezily by us, with silky apparel flowing colorfully after her.

She swerved gracefully and regally into the park heading right towards me. I did a quick scan, left and right. People were busy eating and reading and talking, no one was paying attention to her. She finally reached me and introduced herself: Princess Grandiosa," announced formally, "We met yesterday."

I was stunned. I rose to my feet with the ungainliness of a man whose mind was sorting out his body. "I didn't recognize you! Please, sit down," I offered with an un-squelched stammer.

She looked regally at me through layers of folds. "Princesses don't pop down on pedestrian grass."

"And proper Princesses don't elide," I tweaked.

"Besides," she bent her head, losing the hauter, "I don't want to crease my outfit."

"You sure fooled me."

She smiled slyly. "I like to surprise people."

"Do you often assume different personas?

"It depends on the Country."

"So," I tempted her, "If you pretended to be someone from a very poor Country, would you come to me in Rags?"

"Basic Black Rags, with a flower in my hair."

Nothing like a quaint sense of humor to make you like a person.

Her ponytail from yesterday was now a sweep of blond hair down to her shoulders, adding her allure. She wasn't tall enough to be a model, I guessed. But it did not distract the imagination from creating a picture of her sarong or smiling from the ubiquitous covers of fashion magazines. Like one jumped off the cover and landed, human-like, in front of me. Hmm. Maybe she wasn't lean enough.

The face on a magazine doesn't change, but the Princess' quirky faces, though not so glossy, were endearing.

"She seemed more arrayed than dressed up." Swathes of fabric were draped around her body, like she was living in some benevolent monarchy of yore. It's like she had two outfits to choose from and wore both.

She watched me appraise her costume.

"It's the dress of my country."

"Only in the mountains," she perked.

It occurred to me. "Are you in the Theater?"

"I am," she answered brightly, as if she was waiting for me to ask.

"You have access to a lot of costumes."

"I do."

"Actress?"

"How did you guess?" She teased.

"Either that or you're mad."

"My favorite roll, of course, is Lady MacBeth," she said, her tone wore serious. "But are too many words to get out in one breath. I have asthma. Asthmatics shouldn't play Shakespeare."

"I'm sorry."

She laughed it off: "It's Okay. It would just be funny to pull out an inhaler and take a few puffs during a duel."

"It's good you can make fun of it."

"Well, acting is a tough business," she stated darkly and then mugged with a forefinger under her nose, "ya gotta lighten the mood sometimes, buddy." She pulled an invisible cigar out of her mouth and blew some smoke into the trafficked air.

We stood together awkwardly. I couldn't offer a seat and didn't have time for a walk.

'I'm on my way to perform in a novice one-act play,' she explained solemnly, then said merrily: "But I stopped by to say hello. It's fun talking with you."

"Same here," I returned, trying not to sound dejected.

"What's your name?"

"Beamer."

"Really? Isn't that the name of a car?"

"And yours?"

"Arcadia."

"Isn't that the name of a National Park?"

"It is?"

"I think so." I think we've squandered all our wit here. "By the way, are you going to have a Cast Party after the show?"

"I don't know," she thought idly. She gathered her many drooping garments around her and was ready for an exit.

"Well, still, Break a Leg!"

"Thanks," she said vacantly, not catching the Joke, sagging slightly under her misaligned wardrobe. Not everything was in the right place and she was in a hurry to go. Some of her clothing ballooned from the wind. She sailed off, almost tripping over a renegade scarf, swept bulkily into the train of pedestrians chugging down the street until she vanished around a corner.

Can you avoid a void? Perplexing. There's a blank space where there was a charming solidity.

I sped through the complaints that afternoon, answering them with official aplomb, sending them through to their relevant departments, all in correct, dry, unbroken bureaucratese, making my contribution to the vitiation of the English Language.

It was raining hard when I left the building. Heavy drops splattered on the pavement. A peevish wind knocked off hats. Hoods and collars came up. Folded umbrellas opened.

Faces screwed up in a hunching battle against nature's bad timing. It is well-known that standing in the rain for too long can make a person deranged.

Rather than be squished inside a packed MUNI train, I hoofed it home, arriving strangely elated but sopping wet. I braved insanity and felt the vigor of nature. Blondie greeted me wet or not, effusively, her tail wagging at maximum speed, eager to out. It was her time. Tempest or not.

I quickly changed into rain gear, attached her collar and leash and with Blondie in the lead, zipped down the stairs into the very wet afternoon, she, blinking against the falling water that will soon be soaking her fur. Did she notice or care? No way. She was off in a romp.

The only shelters in the Park were a few leafy trees bunched in front of a building. But they were sieves against the pelting rain. Blondie plowed forward, checking her favorite spots.

The wind swept through with its usual insolence. In SF, wind had a personality. It was storming. It was cold, wet and dreary. Earnest umbrellas were whipped around backwards.

To Blondie it was outside. I trudged behind, trying to give her as much outside time as possible. A storm means limited time out side later. I knew, eventually, she would turn her head, with pleading eyes, want to go in. How much rain that would take, I did not know. So, mostly waterproofed, I waded after her.

There is a primal joy in the rain, an elemental connection. We are made of the stuff. It made me work out a poem as Blondie and I walked the blocks in the softening rain. "Rivulets of water rolling down the street, shining in the streetlamps, breaking 'round my feet. Me and my dog walking in the evening rain. Getting soaked in the beautiful business of rain.'

We went in for the evening, getting Blondie mostly dry with towels and paper towels. No elegance needed. She was happy to be moisturized and happily savored a broken up Granola Bar. She earned a good treat after taking me out in the rain.

She ensconced on the sofa-futon on an open sheet I laid out for her. I turned on the TV, turned up the heat, got down to my boxer shorts, had some Vanilla and Honey Yogurt and readied the Veggie/Corn Chips.

I put a handful of kibble in Blondie's bowl. I didn't give her kibble as her main meal. I thought of it as prison food for dogs.

I had settled on the futon next to Blondie, still munching my chips, watching Law and Order when the phone rang. Darn! I checked to see who was calling. It was Dori. Funny she had fled my mind since Arcadia took it over Dori never called to say hello.

"Hey, Dori, what's up?"

"Did you hear about Roman!?"

"No," I groaned. "What?"

"He got himself beat-up."

"No."

"Not no!" she corrected angrily, twisting the words like a piece of spaghetti. "He tried to sneak into the Actor's house to abduct Molly. He was climbing through a window. Molly started barking, and they, probably 'Fingers', socked him a few times escorted him across the Street to Buena Vista and dumped him there." She was boiling. "He has a fractured jaw and his right eye is shut closed!"

"Geez! Where is he?"

"Back at the Church after a visit to the Emergency room."

Why doesn't this shock me? I thought. I have to admire his chutzpah. At least he wasn't murdered. "It's ironic," I said derisively, "That the Molly he was trying to rescue was the Molly that gave him away."

"Irrelevant!" she snapped. "They could have shot him!"

"Legally," I impressed on her. He was an intruder. "Fingers' is allergic to Cops" Some reassurance.

"Well, go over and see him."

"I will.".

"Before he does something rasher."

"What? To eat too much pork?"

"You know Beamer, your humor sometimes gives me an upset stomach." Probably casting an icy glance at the cellphone that I would feel at the other end.

"Sorry, I couldn't resist."

"Resist."

Goodbye Dori.

"So, Blondie," I said to my faithful dog never rebuked me for running amok. "Shall we pay a visit to the gallant, but not too bright, misnamed Roman. She wagged her tail in consent, in recognition of what a good person I really was. And we were off.

The Church on Market, off Dolores. The high outside windows, usually brightly lit, were dark. The door was always opened in the evening, but when I tried to turn the doorknob, in the shape of a dog's tail, it wouldn't budge. I rang the bell, which triggered of happily barking dogs and waited and waited. Apprehension kicked in and started to bang on the heavy door and callout: "Roman! Roman!" Passersby gave me questioning looks. But I kept going. I was pounding on the door, making a tremendous racket, furious for Roman for not answering, hurting my knuckles. Blondie started howling at a Fire Engine going by. Her howling must have done it. The door unlatched.

Poking through the sliver of opened door was the worried face of Roman. Gauzed, bandaged and swollen. One eye gave a little flutter, trying to open all the way

"Oh....it's.... you... Beamer." These sputtering sounds squeezed painfully from closed teeth.

"Just me and my dog buddy."

He opened the door wider to greet and be slobbered over by Blondie'

"You...know...what....happened?"

"I do."

The door opened wider so he could scan the street behind me.

"Checking on you." I had become the model of succinctness, after my outburst at the closed door.

"Thanks., Beamer... I'm o.k."

I would disagree. But, then, hr God on his side and that gave him sustenance.

"Hard ....to...give...Sermons...now." he smiled crookedly. "Write... them...pass. Them...out."

"Good idea."

His eyes betrayed his new calling. His eyes flitted everywhere, all over me, up high, around the street, he must have felt betrayed. He had been battered and humiliated, doing what he considered God's work. What he did was stupid on Earth but praiseful in Heaven. He dealt with ornery people, on his own.

He was tottering right now. But I bet that in a week or two his zeal will blast out of its slumber and his jaw will be a muscular sin-fighter, healing the World,

He left me a weak but generous smile as he slowly closed the door.

"Any problems, call me." I wasn't worried he wouldn't. He had Dori looking after him. Good girl.

Blondie and I walked back to the Park, past the Safeway filling up with After workers, up Church, a busy pedestrian and MUNI street, where various young homeless rested, congregated and cadged money and food, then down Duboce, along the MUNI line going from the Ballpark to the Beach, with a crowded island of waiting passengers, and into the open Park where the wind picked up speed and the temperature dropped.

Unleashed Blondie took off on her preliminary sniffing rounds, while I ambled through the confabbing klatch of kindred dog people and squatted to greet the many small dogs who nudged up to say hello or check for treats. The sharp yip-yips, the deep woof-woofs and the strident bark-barks were the rock and roll music of the Park.

The dogs were joined in locomotion with mothers and babies and toddlers in All-Terrain baby carriages, tykes rolling down the hill on scooters and foot-driven wooden bikes and the oblivious teenage skateboarder, running a gauntlet of aggravated dogs.

I drifted around the buzzing, excited conversations, listening. There was no talk of Roman's near fatal escapade. Roman had clammed up. I said nothing.

Blondie found me and we took a desultory stroll around the blocks, indulging her choice her streets to go up and down, which were usually ones she had found street fare. She as quick lunging at a Pizza crust on the edge of the sidewalk as a New York bleacher boo-bird lunging and yelling at the garbage on the field.

As we walked, I phoned Dori. She was at home. I invited myself over to talk about Roman and without a phalanx of demurrals she often raised, to keep her sacrosanct place private. She hushed her dogs and welcomed me. She gave Blondie a chew-bone to keep her busy and her four beasts willingly accepted my pets.

It wasn't the shabby space it used to be. The crappy furniture I once saw was even over for trash, or had crumbled into dust on its own. The nostalgic sofa-bed with bright, new coverings was still the nesting spot for her four, now reposing dogs.

The chairs were now plusher and colorful drapes replaced mottled, yellowing window shades. A large mirror on the wall reflected a smiling array of blooming flowers, resting on top of a nearly full bookcase.

Dori had been through bad times, which she kept to herself, but were etched into her features if you looked hard enough or caught certain expressions. They were softening lately, becoming more delicate, less defined. In SF vernacular she was "In a more comfortable space."

She was delighted in her job and a coterie who liked and courted her. Even Roman confided his humiliation to her before he went into seclusion.

"He called me," she said, sitting down with her dogs, while on sat on the nearest cushioned chair. She spoke with the same surprise she must have felt when Roman called and described his disaster "I didn't even know he had my number."

"He can be very resourceful."

"It was a shock." She reflected: "What a dummy."

"Amen."

"Did you go with him to the emergency room?"

"He had already been." She made a disgusted face.

"He picked himself up from the sidewalk, called a Cab and got to a Hospital."

"He came here?"

"He did," she said terse "He was a mess." She rubbed her nearest dog. "The dogs went crazy."

"They are not used to visitors," I said academically.

"Nope."

"Maybe you didn't appreciate being chosen, but he rusted you and you should feel good for helping him."

She granted that, but said with a choppy laugh: "He whispered," she said, "Maybe so my dogs wouldn't hear, but was probably his busted jaw" "No publicity." Like I was going to run out in the street like a Towncrier and shout the news!" She shook her head and made a sour sound. "What an idiot?"

"You helped him."

"I didn't really do anything. He rushed in, told me his story and rushed out again."

"It had to be harrowing for him. He had to find a gentle soul."

"I'd rather be yelling at him than comforting him." She looked at me with astonishment. "You think I'm a gentle soul?"

"Absolutely."

She was mulling this over.

"Nice bookcase," I said, going over to it and surveying a true wooden structure holding a raft of books that used be in piles against the wall.

"Street sale," she smiled proudly, "It's good, sturdy wood."

"Nice to see them organized."

"They were never haphazard," she told me pointedly, making her case against having a disorderly house. She craved order in her life after a disjointed past, which she tried to keep hidden but which sneaked out in revealing observations and anecdotes of fictitious people.

She watched me look through her books.

"You're transported," she said dreamily, into other times, immersed in other peoples' lives, especially when your own life feels barren." Her unfocused eyes leveled with mine, "You disappear into another world, It's magic!"

"An escape?"

"No," her voice sure, "It's finding riches."

I was finding out that her language was more decorous. Not that it was ever nasty, but she did have a tendency to carp, like a fish struggling on a hook. She was more sensible about biting at the bait.

"Your vocabulary has really built up."

"You know what they say," she tossed off, "Use a word three times and it's yours."

"I've heard that."

"And when you plow through Thomas Hardy and Jane Austen, you keep a Dictionary nearby."

"Sounds like you've been saving up this conversation to impress people," I threw in, good-humoredly.

"A bit," she confessed, picking up a book.

"Do you talk pedantic to your customers?"

"Do you mean do I speak to my customers that way?" she rebuffed me, "Only the literate ones," She added snootily. "Actually, conversations with customers are more pedestrian."

"Enough!" I cried.

"Am I being too pedantic?"

"Do you know what Thomas Hardy said at mealtime?"

"No, what?" she shined her eyes on me, avid to know something special about one of her favorite authors.

"He used to say: "Would you kindly uplift that shaker of salt and place it where I may have easier access to it."

"Did he really say that?"

"When he was dressed formally." She looked at me eagerly. "When he came to the table all grubby and smelling of unwashed clothes and body."

"Gimme the salt, Dunderhead!"

"You are ridiculous."

"The lesson is, pedantry favors formal clothes or something."

"Can we end the silliness?"

"Absolutely," I agreed. "Shall we have casual or formal silence?"

"My dogs will eat you!"

"If I'm good enough for your dogs you must think highly of me."

"Not at the moment."

What more fun could I have than talking or speaking with Dori?"

On the more serious side.

"Have you gotten any more threats?"

"No, I haven't," she said, her words hardened. "Why?"

"Just asking."

"If I did, I'd let you know," Her voice was softer.

"Good."

"I would have said something," she repeated, distractedly plucking at a loose thread in her jeans. "But," she continued, head down, tugging purposely at the same slippery thread. "I heard," she paused, ripping the thread out, "Second hand, that a woman on the top floor got a strange note."

"What did it say?"

"I don't know. It's all gossip."

"Well, keep alert," I cautioned.

"If someone stood at my door when I was home, my dogs would go ballistic." She grimaced at the unknown person on the other side of the door. "I'd snatch the door open and spot the freak who was running away!"

"It was good to know that her plunge into Literature had not dulled her feisty edge. She went over to her dogs and gave each a tummy rub. As if she was a Queen, dubbing them as Knights."

The dog laid there, showing their bellies. I quipped: "Are your dogs auditioning for Playdog magazine."

I got the stony look I expected. But I couldn't resist. To me a harmless joke.

To Dori or Roman: Crossing the line.

The name Roman brought back what I came over here for. I apologized for the joke, with as little articulation as possible. She accepted and the stone chipped away and her beautiful face had a beam of satisfaction. "It was funny."

For a few minutes we were silent, as we listened to the MUNI train grinding through the intersection. The trains passed below her windows. The commanding blast of its air-horn warned vehicles and walkers she was coming through. She stopped at the boarding island where waiting riders lifted themselves from the Art Project array of bronzed chairs embedded into the sidewalk, hopped aboard. The train then rumbled ahead up the hill, causing a bit of shake in a house or two.

"Do you think Roman will try again?"

"His face tells him 'no' but I bet his bumbling brain is conjuring up something just as stupid."

"I don't trust him either."

"Who knows if he's already hatched a plot?"

"Yes."

"What should we do!"

We muse on this topic as a screaming match between two guys broke out into the street, right below the window. Luckily we were three stories up, so the crashing of bottles and the hurling of curses had some distance to travel. The MUNI waiters moved back from the combatants, who seemed to be relishing the commotion they were causing. There was a hazard as if in getting too close, but there was also benign familiarity with the event, as if were a planned amusement and shock for the onlookers. I'm surprised they didn't go around with a donations hat. Visitors might contribute.

"Does the noise bother you?" I put it to Dori. "People practically living on the street, the constant MUNI vibrations and screeching."

"When I'm more uptight," she admitted, blandly, "Street people get to me MUNI is a fixture, you accept it and get used to it. You feel it." She thought about a little more and said with more animation. "But, when it's really too much, I out on Organ music."

"Organ music?"

"Nothing gets through Organ music," she grinned, "It is thicket of heavy, screaming notes. It can make people crazy." She was almost dancing. "A Bach toccata played with volume can make people fall down in confession or drive them to flee." She grinned with wicked intent.

"Hmm," I put in my two cents. "The ultimate musical weapon. Just the word 'Toccata' would make them nervous."

"Yes."

"Never realized Bach was so a force for good."

"Didn't he write for God?"

"Yes, he did. He also built Organs."

"Wow!"

"People often think of Classical music as abstract, but it can also have its practical, down to-earth applications."

"It supplicates without mercy."

"Maybe?" I suggested, "We can talk to Roman about putting a baby organ in the Church. It may distract him from his Molly monomania."

"We could try," Dori surprisingly agreed.

"Does it bother your dogs?"

"They can always hide in the bathroom."

"There's an expression," I said, bathing the dogs with a smile, that 'All Dogs Go To Heaven.' They should feel right at home."

"There are harps in heaven," she corrected me.

"That's right. "I've never heard of an Organ in Heaven." Can't see those ethereal angels pounding away on a mighty, booming Organ.

"Maybe Bach was better off writing for the Harp."

She stood up and went to a small table piled with leashes. The dogs scrambled, like Pilots ready to do battle. They submitted to the leashes which had been mangled together. Dori had twisted and pulled and fumble and unraveled until they were finally separated.

"If I didn't have Company, I'd be cursing up a very unlady-like storm."

"Not knowing what to say, I said something. "I too imprecate when I'm alone with animate and inanimate objects I cannot tame."

"Does it deserve formality," she chided, "The whole point is to let it out."

"I'm just waiting for you." I said "Watching on her haunches, trying to hook each dog to the tight leash while they shuffled and jostled and whapped each other with their tails, while trying to be the first out the door."

She completed the job adroitly and out of breath. She gave me a nod to open the door, while she maneuvered her frenzied bunch out and down the hall. Blondie was eager to catch the hard-charging Daschunds, so we zipped down the hall, made it to the waiting elevator and stuffed ourselves in.

Dori was so busy reining in her restless dogs, she didn't notice the strange guy squeezed in the corner. He was around thirty, skinny with blonde hair pouring out of a 49er wool cap. His arms were a mess of small, mostly connected blue tattoos. A bony arm protruded from an incongruous short-sleeved sweatshirt with HARVARD emblazoned on it in paint smeared letters. He fiendishly grunting at the dogs, while swaying on bare feet.

"Did this motley figure have it in him to slip a threatening note to Dori?"

Dori and her busting out dogs ignored him. Blondie gave him a specious go-over, but nothing bad clicked.

The elevator hit the first floor with a soft bounce. The Dori family bolted out. I followed with a happy Blondie by my side. The 'obvious suspect' was on his way back up without pressing any buttons.

"Dori?" I said urgently, "Didn't you see that guy?"

She nodded. She was wrangling with the excited dogs. She didn't say anything until we were at the Park, dogs off leash and she got her breath back.

"Didn't he disturb you?" I pressed, staring at her profile as she kept an eye on her scampering crew. Blondie had ventured off looking for treats.

"He loves my dogs," she replied with cool disinterest.

"He acts as it he might be...what?..." groping for the word..."Unstable?"

"Probably so."

"It must be the intangible I'm missing" I thought. If I had to picture a culprit, he would look like this guy. "What's his name?"

"I don't know."

"Are you working your way down to one syllable?"

"Yep."

Finally, she relented and turned towards me. "Are you going to end every question with a question mark?"

"At least I omitted the exclamation points," I said declaratively.

"That Heaven for that," she mused, cuttingly.

"Okay, I'll drop it. It's just easy to be suspicious when you haven't a clue."

"True."

"It sort of gives me a melancholy feeling not to be able to pin anything down."

"You do have sad eyes," she said with a mixture of warm and empiricism.

I thought: "There's a lot to be sad about" But I didn't say it.

We peeked off in different directions, me, to locate Blondie she to reassemble her brats.

Back home, with thoughts of being on a reasonably priced pre owned and simply furnished Yacht, gently bobbing on a litter free Ocean, I floated through the evening.

Watered and kibbled dog bowls

Microwaved popcorn

Seized a cheerful moment

Waded through self-recriminations

Surfed the Web

Sailed through a couple of crossword puzzles.

Listened to La Mer by DeBussy
Swam a few chapters with Moby Divk
Drifted to sleep.
Navigated a kaleidoscope of dreams.

I slump to work.
The usual non-greeting from my co-worker, adds to my lassitude.
He grinds away, devoted to his work. An artist of compulsion.
I could commiserate with the first complaint of the day.

A fellow from L.A. bought a library shelf load of self-help books, from a Company bookstore. Despite the claims that it would boost his self-confidence, enhance his self-image, improve his love life, etc., he still felt 'droopy' and 'socially dysfunctional.'

He felt mislead by the all the promises, and felt 'taken.' for Five Hundred dollars. He was motivated, however, to incinerate all the books. He wanted his money back.

I explained to him that since he was dissatisfied, he could have brought the books back to store within ninety days, with a receipt, he would have gotten a refund. But all he had now he said were "Ashes."

He was adamant. He argued that it wasn't the books themselves, but the ideas they presented that were "Phony." He paid "Good Money" under "False Pretenses", should be excused his "Wrath" in "Burning Garbage" so others wouldn't be taken in. He was providing a "Public Service" and was entitled to be compensated, at least, for "Mental Cruelty."

Not only had his life not changed as promised, but it worsened his depression by "Raising his expectations." and then dashing them with "False Hopes."

Did he pay with a credit card?
No. He paid hard cash.
Then there is no personal record of this transaction?
I suppose.
Five Hundred Dollars is substantial. How could I ask the Company to authorize a refund with no proof of purchase, I continued in my best business-eze.

I'm too depressed to lie.

Is this for real, I thought.

Do you have a street address?

No. A Post Office box.

Not sounding kosher. I suggest you contact Company Headquarters (gave him the information) and explain your situation.

Screw you! I hope you swallow a bucket of worms!

Yes! Start the day off with something disgusting and get it over with.

The rest of the day passed slowly, but routinely, with no detectable scam artists or people with strange predilections toward Company products. But it was only a matter of time before something showed up. The world didn't suddenly become greedless and sane.

It is said, "this and that" is a necessary evil in the world. Without evil think of all the jobs combatting it would be lost. The economy could be wrecked. Lots of people trying to be good would be rebuffed by other people trying to be good. Too much good could squeeze out evil.

Money, the love of which is the root of all evil, would be supplanted. The entertainment industry would collapse. Video games would disappear. Dope would describe people. Your imagination can fill in the rest, Thank God for Evil.

My imagination shifted onto something more concrete: Lunchtime in the Park with Arcadia.

She was sitting in the grass, talking animatedly to a man sitting next to her. My stomach felt a twinge of fire.

"Hi, Beaner," she said, exuberantly, "I want you to meet my Director, Walter."

He stood up agilely from a squat and shook my hand. I liked him right away. I cooled. He dressed casually in baggy blue jeans and a loose, white wool sweater, an outfit that belied the seriousness of purpose that set his features.

"Glad to meet you," he said earnestly, with the small, sympathetic smile of some who has managed to balance the weathered weariness of existence with the occasional rejuvenescent joy.

"Glad to meet you," I responded, looking at a furrowed face. Whether it was from worry or calamity, I could not say.

"Won't you join us?"

"Thanks." I sat on the other side of Arcadia, pulled out my scrumptious PBJ sandwich and chewed away, listening to Arcadia reading from a script on her lap.

The cheerful goofiness I knew suddenly became the broken, troubled voice of a wronged, petulant woman. Low bursts of anger chilled the surrounding air. A different woman emerged.

Walter looked intently up at the blank sky as she recited, as if he were picturing the performance on a distant stage. Arcadia, at times, turned his profile while speaking. It may have struck some Lunchers that this emotional scene was real. Some women tossed angry loos at Walter.

Arcadia read through the lines until Walter gave her a curt nod, which she acknowledged as approval and clapped her hands together in childlike glee. The change in her face was so abrupt I had to look at her twice.

Her excitement brought a full smile from Walter, exposing a full mouth of white teeth, which off-set his face-worn appearance. He came across as a man of striking contrasts. His hair was going but his beard was coming. His body relaxed, his eyes direct.

"You're working on a play?"

"We are learning lines?" Walter answered.

"Better here than in that stuffy theater basement," Arcadia added.

"Well," joked, "If you've got some long winded speeches it makes sense to practice them in the wind."

They looked at me impassively. An outsiders joke not invited in.

I turned to Arcadia. "You were very convincing," I retreated to praise.

"I've been working on it," she said comfortably. "I feel the woman now. Her gaze returned to Walter, who was thumbing through a larger script. She returned to me. "Walter can be very taciturn. A minimalist." She pursed her lips in thought. "Gives actors lots of leeway. We have fun."

She smiled at me. "We are all beginners, you know." It was an actress moment and I fell for it. "It's fun pretending to be someone else, even if it looks so serious."

"I can see that."

"A murderess!" She stabbed a finger into my gut. "See how easy it is?"

"Can you do it?"

"I've never played a murderess."

"I've heard that an actress can murder their lines."

"Some lines deserve to die," she countered, sharply. "Although if I were a Director...." She peered over at Walter, who offered an obliging smile."

"Is your play about murder?"

"Not yet," she laughed.

I was not acquainted with the theater world.

"What's it about," I asked, intrigued, since I now knew someone in it.

"It's about tempestuous relationships," she teased. "Not much of a plot, but a lot of emoting. Fun for the actors." She her lower her lower teeth and frowned. "It takes place on a subway platform in Brooklyn. People have to shout over the trains."

"An express station?"

"Funny. A lack of communication due to the ambient imposition of Civilization, or something."

"What are people trying to communicate?"

"They are trying to compile a shopping list for the stuff they need to buy at the Supermarket." She was talking a little louder. There is a disagreement over frozen or bin Vegetables and the choice of Fruit," She lower her voice in conclusion. "It shows a passion for Fruit can bring out the worst in us."

"You've got your Director laughing out loud."

"I'm just repeating his nonsense."

"You sure befuddled me," I admitted. "I hope it might be turning into a Musical. I have a satirical song on the NY Subways." The roar of a Jet blocked out my words.

I had chomped to the core of my apple. My face beckoned. "Time to go back to work," I said, ruefully. I reached my full height reluctantly and trudged off, with "Ciaos," fading behind me.

When I returned to my cubicle I found a bundle on my desk. It wasn't a smooth-sided box. It was a neatly corded package. It was bumpy and heavily covered with tape bearing the Company Logo: Two giant hands clutching a small, solitary Earth.

I stripped off the tape, unfolded layers of coarse paper until I reached an envelope with my name on it. Inside, was card with bouncy colored letters saying: "GOODBYE" and a puny severance check. I turned to my workmate, who gave me a curt smile and returned to his computer. Did he place it there?

The long months with the Company dropped from my memory like a bad movie as left the building and sniffed the air. No twinge of regret, no crank of anger. The World was fresh again.

I molted. Shed used-up skin. I snaked deftly through the walking crowds and the thick traffic, anonymous as a Bird.

Back in the Park with Blondie, I basked in my jostled freedom before the specter of Unemployment put its sticky mitts on me.

Lannie, The General's girlfriend and World Traveling Truth seeker, was sitting on a bench. I sat down next to her, by smiling invitation, while Blondie was free to sniff around.

"What's up?" I asked brightly.

"Not my bank account," she answered with a crooked smile.

"Me too."

"It's repulsive."

"You've been away."

She seemed surprised I noticed. "Alaska," she tossed off.

"Sounds exciting."

"It's frigid."

"Where 'Truth' has solidness," I quipped, hoping to through her frosty outlook.

"Everything is true in the cold," she said sentiently as a Bernese Mountain dog kicked up the ground behind us, showering us with bits of dirt. Lannie's dog, who was sitting between us, shook it off, and we got another round of grit. Lannie pushed her dog off the bench, hunched and brushed her reddish coat. Then she leaned back and peered up into the sky.

The clouds overheard raced by as if they were late for an appointment. Lannie watched them and her voice tuned wistful. "The clouds make me feel that we are in a hurry to go nowhere." She looked at a quizzical expression, "It's trite, I know," she reflected," but my thoughts get lackadaisical.

"You think." I complimented her, trying to assuage her gloominess. "When you really see things, you see the awful and the beautiful and they kinda take turns."

"You're sounding a little dreary yourself," she laughed.

"It made you laugh," I pointed out. "When drunks are philosophical, they can be comical. But when sober people are philosophical, they can be dreary."

"You're a 'Trickster' I think," she said lightly, with a show of knitted brow.

"I'm vintage."

"You're not that old."

"Well, at least the Earth and I don't share the same Birthday."

"Silly."

We sat back and watched the doggy antics, tots chasing soap bubbles, friends chatting news, the usual cold wind, not as cold, the newly mowed lawn exposing avoidable ruts, kids rolling by on scooters, parades of baby strollers. A happy scene.

"Sometimes I think the need to travel and find the big 'T' is running away from myself." I listened. I always felt there was something wrong with me," she continued, dismally.

"No." she disclaimed. "They were wrapped up in their own selves, their own problems, and didn't pay attention to me." She gave me a disdainful smile. "I think it was because I was not pure white."

I let that sink in.

"They made me feel I was not their equal."

I stepped in. "There was something wrong with them, not you."

She laughed. "I never looked at it that way."

"You look okay to me," I presumed. "It took gumption to do what you did. A Lot of spirit. Besides, travel is broadening."

"So," she speculated, "What I feel is what other people feel?"

"You bet."

"That's discouraging," she smiled wonderingly."

"The Human Dilemma." Also," I put forth, "The search for truth can be misleading" I ventured, based on limited resources and dubious experience. "My gut feeling is that truth is what we are left with."

"Huh." She thought about it, and gave me a wink. "Then it's all about what you ate for breakfast."

I commenced her. "A very convincing Philosophical point."

She folded her hands in her lap and sat quietly.

As if to add to the prior illuminations. The Comedian sat down silently next to me. He was dogless. Which reminded me of a fellow who lived facing the Park, whose name was Douglas, but he had a dog. Go figure.

"I awaited a cascade of jokes. I made a startling discovery," he said grandly, his hands reaching up to enfold the air. "Oh, no, what's brewing in that fertile brain. "I'm sick," he said gravely, his arms dropping with a soft, dramatic thud to his thighs, his head bent forward.

I'm preparing myself. "Sick?"

"I found out I have a gluten allergy."

"Really?"

"Yes." He looked at me stoically. "My stomach was hurting and I didn't know why."

"I'm sorry."

"No more wheat, barley or rye."

"Geez."

"I hope that doesn't include making wry jokes."

"You're kidding?"

"No it's true."

"That eliminates a lot of good stuff."

"But it led me to study up on it," He announced. "I talked to experts, I dove into Chemistry and Physics, I learned to do Lab work, I...."

"All in the last two months," I interrupted

"I learn fast," He retorted, impatiently, "and miraculously I discovered a new element: Glutonium."

"Right."

"It was always there, it just needed to be Unearthed!"

'Good for you."

"I thought you'd be flabbergasted." He hung his head in disappointment,

"And I thought you lived on planet Earth."

"A terrible thing to say to a future Nobel Prize Winner, though I don't have the scientific credentials."

"The money's good."

"Gluton is everywhere in the Universe," he claimed excitedly, "It could be what makes up the Dark Matter in the Universe which Scientists cannot explain."

"That's amazing."

"Not only that," he exclaimed, "Its structure is a long string."

"How interesting."

He was moving. "It boosts the idea of the String Theory. That the core of all matter are vibrating strings!"

"It's music to my ears."

Lannie stirred from her contemplation. She was delighted with the surreal dialog. "You guys make a good comedy team."

"He's the Comedian, I'm just the foil."

"Well, it was funny."

"Nobody takes me seriously," Charles glowered at Lannie.

"I see," she said with a sheared smile.

"It's true!" He burst out.

"Ignore him."

"I've always been interested in the truth," she said candidly to Charles. "Are you convinced this is true?"

"There is no one to contradict me."

She nodded.

"Don't tell me you believe him?" I sputtered.

"Why not?" She asked, innocently.

Well, I didn't want to crowd into their delusion, so I let it drop. But I was annoyed over Charles' prank that was sucking in a woman who had a tottering need to join him. But, I knew the guy, he was having his ridiculous fun. She'd recognize his mad play soon. Then again, there were myriad fantasies to be spun and woven into a delectable truth.

Lannie was fiddling with her hair, absently curling long strands around her ringed fingers, deliberately avoiding Charles' moon-struck eyes.

"I have to pick up my dog from the Groome," Charles announced, switching his eyes back, seemingly, to the actual world. "Good to meet you Lannie." He gave us a final jaunting, persuasive look that could have meant anything and quickly walked down the path to Steiner.

"Don't try to interpret him," I said, to a confused Lannie. "How's the General?"

"Fine," she answered vaguely. The strange Comedian still absorbing her attention. Then looking back at me, she added firmly, "I count on the General."

"That's good," I said obliquely.

"Being with him is like having a warm blanket of words thrown you, mostly outrageous."

"Yes, I know."

"Sometimes it smothered."

"But it feels good," I prompted.

"You know," she said, parenthetically, the truth can be suffocating because there's no way out."

"You feel trapped?"

"No, No. No." She objected, "If you claim to know the truth you're stuck." She blew out some air. "Your mind shrinks, your world is diminished."

"Interesting!" I nodded, appreciating her idea. "Is there a plus side?"

"You feel superior."

"Wouldn't you feel more humble?"

"Maybe, if you really know," She snubbed, "But I don't believe anyone knows."

"Okay. Does the General have any real military background?"

She smiled. "Aside from his playacting you mean?"

"He seems to know a lot."

"He reads books."

"He's intelligent."

"Yes," she allowed, "When he's not trying to be important."

"I encapsulated the Roman, Actor, Molly standoff."

"Complicated," she reckoned, "I've heard talk about it."

"I'm sure Molly belongs to Roman. But I'm stumped how to get her back to him without more mayhem. It's already proved dangerous for Roman."

Lannie brushed some fallen tree debris from her lap. "Why doesn't he buy her?"

"Too much bad feeling."

"An intermediary?"

"A good solution. But it's more a case of revenge."

It hangs in the air.

I started a job at a Sportshop.

Blondie and I had taken a long walk around the Embarcadero, ending up browsing shops at Fisherman's Wharf. I spotted a help wanted sign on a shop selling MLB, NBA and NFL merchandise.

The owner was there. The opening was in the Baseball Dept. I demonstrated an impressive knowledge of Baseball, yesterday and today. Experience working with live customers, working, when I first arrived in SF, in a Health food store downtown.

The owner, a get to the point guy in his forties was a dog lover and Blondie kissed up to him. He offered me the job.

"What luck!"

If we get what we need proved true in this need. Fortunately, everything doesn't depend solely on a little red wagon, when you are broke. It depends on Little Red Wagon with a lot of Green inside.

We walked back to Park buoyant, but tired. The elation would wear off; it was a Job. But the moment was propitious. I would be quasi-prosperous again.

We settled on a bench. Blondie sprawled out behind on the well-traveled grass. I relaxed, setting a languid gaze on the wrangling, wrestling, jumping, yapping, begging, chasing, sniffing carefree confusion of dogs at play: Small skittering under benches, dogs nibbling daintily on grass blades, Big dogs promenading regally with a favorite toy locking in their mouth, daring any dog or human to extract it, dogs acrobatically snatching windblown Frisbees out of the air with dogged finesse, dogs rolling on worms to mask their scent, creating the canine perfume eau d'worm and choruses from dogs of all sizes howling along with the Fire Engines sirens and they pass the Park.

The singular pleasure of watching this carnival of rascally dogs was broken by the swaggering presence of the Actor. He was walking with a jittering Molly on leash down the path along the dog area. Around his left arm he held a gorgeous short-skirted redhead.

He smiled innocently at the volley of hisses sent his way. Confirming him. Stony faces also sent their message. He let go a few of his famous movie smirks for free. He was relishing the role he was playing.

As he passed by me, he whispered something in the woman's ear. She made a chirping laugh which seemed to undermine his swagger. They exited the Park with the Woman walking Molly.

Now that my financial worries eased, by a new, possibly likable job, my attention, was drawn back to Roman, whom I hadn't seen or heard from in a long while, considering his condition, though I knew that Dori was in contact and keeping tabs on him.

Blondie and I walked over to his Church, rang the bell, rapped on the door. A few minutes later, the eyehole slid open and then closed. I waited for the door to open but didn't. I walked away, called Dori for the latest news. She was in a hurry and told me to meet her in the Park.

"Hi, Beamer," she greeted me warmly. I let Blondie off the leash to roam and sat down next to Dori. Her dogs had fanned out, but always stayed within sight of her. The Park was teeming with dogs and the Wind was taking a siesta.

"Roman wouldn't open the door for me."

"He's not doing well.' Her expression was somber.

"You've seen him?"

"He lets me in. But it takes a lot of pleading."

I tried to picture being alone for weeks in that cavernous building. Dori was anxiously fiddling with her leashes. She was tired. Her face was contorted, as if forcing out a thought,

"He's gone crazy."

"Crazy?"

"He rambles on about God and Dogs and Sinfulness."

"He always talks like that," I reminded her.

"Not howling like a dog with the other dogs."

"People do that all the time in the Park."

"Not on all fours,"

"Joining his best friends."

"What can we do?" she pleaded.

"Do you think he's dangerous?"

She shook her head. "He's always acted outrageous but I don't think he can hurt anyone."

"Himself?"

"Not with all the dogs he needs to save and all the people he need to repent."

"So we're not going to call the Police to break down his door and take him to the Hospital?"

"No!" She recoiled.

"We need something to lure him out," I offered, "Someone to lure him out.

"I guess that's me," she conceded. "And the something?"

"Molly."

"It's a dirty trick," she mumbled, rising up to focus on her scattered dogs. They rushed back like torpedoes, tumbling over one another to be first to be lifted, clambering to her lap.

I watched her, petting each dog in turn, considering my idea. "Do you have an alternative?" I asked quietly.

She made a gloomy face. "No."

We sat for a while. Blondie came over, nuzzled and got a rubdown. Dori was, as usual, busy with her tangle of leashes and modifying the yapping of her dogs with hushing sounds.

Dori pumped her right arm. "Let's do it!" she said resolutely, addressing her dogs, who looked back at her with gravity, as if they were partners in this cockamamie scheme.

In the spirit of her decisiveness, Dori quickly leashed her dogs, jumped to her feet and broke for home. She suddenly stopped and called out: "What do we do when we get him outside?"

I didn't know yet. "We have to guide him somewhere."

She tapped her finger to her forehead, pointed it at me, in encouragement and resumed her trip home, almost tripping over four, floppy eared, nubby-legged creatures, each vying to lead the pack.

The onus was on me to come up with a plan. I looked to Blondie for inspiration. She looked back at me in puzzlement. A puzzle? Could I create a puzzle that would be irresistible to Roman and snap him out of his demoralized mania and lethargy? I remember Roman telling me that a person who harms a dog is soul-sick.

Dori went into the Church. She had called ahead to say she was coming. I waited outside.

Roman came out blinking into daylight he had not seen for a while. He has lost some weight, a little less oblate, pale and bearded and perfumed, courtesy of Dori. His force was still strong:

"I dove into the healing waters of the Old Testament!" He cried. "I gorged on the greatness of God's guidance. I went to the Beginning to Begin." He paused, staring at something over my shoulder. I turned around. All I could see was a large Laundromat. Did he see his clean soul in the future?

He continued, his eyes luminescent. "Beamer," he confided, "I've been dirty and damaged."

"How so?" I inquired reluctantly. I wanted to skip around his self-appraisal and get him moving to the Park where we had something planned for him.

Dori had a soft hand on his shoulder shoving him into motion. People walking down the street had to detour around him; even though he lost weight his swaying body took up a lot of space.

"I feel able to do miracles," He boasted, grandiloquently, raising his hands to the blue sky, but speaking quietly. No sense letting the world know that he can fix horse races. "The World will flock to my door!" He pronounced loudly, to the passing pedestrians.

It sounded majestic. Beautiful. Hopeful. But as I looked around at the caked pigeon droppings, Homeless camping against a wall, a trash bin spilled on the sidewalk, the muck of the night before revelry, a massive new condominium rising down the street, with astronomically inflated prices, his words belied his surroundings. It wouldn't be long before he got an offer for his Church.

It also struck me that his sudden craving for fame came from his past life as a smut writer of the famous. He envied them. A lowly seminary student turned dirt-digger. Speculation?

"I am imbued with the Spirit!" He rattled on to a young couple who paused to watch his odd gyrations, his sweeping gestures and his glittering eyes. They when off chastened or amused.

I glanced at my watch. I was fuming with impatience. Get we get this guy moving straight ahead. Dori and I had arranged to have DogPeople assembled in the Park to give Roman a boost out of his sad state. Although, the sad state had turned into a sky-high euphoria.

"Okay, Okay," I said to him. "Let's cut the blabber and get to the Park. "We have a surprise for you."

"A surprise?" He smiled benevolently, gripping his own forearms, as if to steady himself and feel his solidity. I cupped my arm into his on one side. Dori did the same with the other. Roman was between us as if in custody, we were off. Or, at least one of us was.

At first, Roman walked with a shambling gait, wearing an overcoat under ratty pajamas catching curious looks from passersby, which he returned with solemn nods, as if they were recognizing his importance in their lives. At times it was hard to tell if he was shaming or really believe he was a Big Deal.

We walked passed Safeway, which brought a sense of the familiar to Roman and as we approached the Park, his intense expression softened and his body slumped a bit in relaxation.

From across Steiner I gave a signal wave and those gathered there sprung into a series of maneuvers with dogs, making a wide semi-circle.

In the Park we unhooked Roman and was confronted, faced struck and agape (not in the religious sense) of a Happy Face painted on the side of a Noah's Ark drawn on a big canvas. And from behind the big canvas came a gaggling rush of waving arms, wagging tails barks and shouts.

"It's for you," Dori told him.

Roman's face became a happy face, after being overwhelmed by the reception and reeling back in surprise and shyness. Now he was touched. The dogs ran to him while he moved to them. I was a stupendous reunion. A joyous moment that Dori and I felt warm inside.

Roman couldn't help blessing them all and they licked him until his head was out of the Clouds. The licking certainly softened his face and the love of the above surrendered to the love of dogs." He was returning to Earth. It was a Grand moment. And, if I permit myself some levity, it was also a glandular moment for some Creatures.

DogParkers wriggled their way through the dogs to share a word with Roman. He happily let the good feeling fall over him. It was overflowing into the grass, possibly helping its growth.

The dogs were finally pulled away. Roman to them as they departed' he looked wistful. Whether this Theater cured him, we'll never know. He is normally Crazy.

We walked him back to his Church. He invited us inside. We sat. His face was blissful and he smiled at us, but didn't say a word. His injuries were healing. His voice worked. He spits out some secret thoughts, when he burst back into the World that had gathered in Solitude.

I gave my idea to Dori. "Who knows?" she shrugged. I felt she had not taken it all in. She had ideas of her own which she didn't tell.

"Get back to work," she said to Roman, who seemed to be realigning his thoughts. "You do that naturally." He listened to her.

"I think I can function around people again," he said skeptically.

"You sound better."

"I'll start contacting my Churchgoers again."

"It all started with Molly. Molly's okay."

He nodded.

"If you're going to be fixated," she said sternly, "Take care of the dogs that still need your help."

He nodded, with some guilt smeared over his face. He needed help but there was something of the actor in him. He goes into the room as a mild-mannered Dog Minister, and then open a robe to colorful flannels and imposing powers, like a comic book character.

"Don't be isolated," admonished Dori, as we headed out of the Church.

"Is he a prophet or a crazed dog liver?" I quizzed Dori as we sat in a nearby Cafe with our coffee and pastry.

"Crazed dog lover," she answered without hesitation.

"You don't mean that," I said in his defense. "He may be odd, but he's not crazy."

"He's bonkers," she returned, flippantly.

We smiled at each other. The smiles lingered.

With the abruptness of fate, they dissolved into the muddiness of speech.

"So how's your new job?"

"Good. Good," I said, stirring back to life. "Getting used to the torrent of tourists."

"I don't understand baseball."

"It's a job. Ring up merchandise, trade baseball with customers. It's Ok. Not a moral enterprise."

"So what?"

"As craftily nutty as Roman may act," I reproached myself, "At least he's got the gumption to try and make things better."

"You'd like something with a moral kick to it?" She poked, jovially.

"Sure."

"But he's loaded."

"True," I appeased her, but without conviction.

"Don't be so hard on yourself," she commiserated.

I lazily picked at my pastry. I had a thought.

"Do you think baseball can teach morality? I engaged Dori, warming to the idea. "You know abide by the code, play by the rules, learn to win or lose without killing the other guy?"

"Or girl," Dori pitched in, "I guess."

"Well, let's go to a baseball game, and I'll do something moral by teaching you the game."

Instead of saying, "It's boring or I hate sports," she said "I'd like that."

My confidence got a little upkick, but there was a small catch

"The baseball season hasn't started yet."

"That's okay." She was in a rosy mood.

It prompted me to ask: "Is your life flowering?"

"It's better," she said simply. She never talked much of her private life.

She was quiet. It seemed her thoughts meandered through different subjects. Her features made subtle changes as I watched her face.

There were few touches of make-up, she had no flaws to cover-up, no garish ornaments, they distracted. She had no need of enhancements. Your eyes settled naturally and affectionately on her comeliness.

Either I was being precociously romantic or some of Roman's inclinations were rubbing off on me. Dori dispelled the haze.

"I never know what you're thinking," She complained, addressing the floor.

"My thoughts run by me so fast, "I joked, evasively. "I have trouble keeping up."

"Right," she said, sourly, and slumped back against her chair.

"I'm basically a clerk," I caviled. The main qualifications for the job Not to steal anything and show up on time.

"Even you can do that," she mocked.

"I'd rather be a baseball player than a purveyor of baseballs," I said edgily, yet slipping in a bit of playfulness.

"How quaint."

"My dream as a kid."

"I think Beamer is a Dreamer," she lilted girlishly

"And Dori is what?"

"Dori is an allegory with a trembling heart," she mused, theatrically, flicking an invisible tear from the corner of her eye.

I let this facet or faucet of Dori soak in.

"Nothing like French pastry to bring out the Poetess, and you only ate half."

She quickie stuffed the rest of the pastry in her mouth, chewed it thoroughly and finished with a glint in her eye.

"Is that the half with the Ham in it?" I didn't mean to discourage her, but the light went out, and she made some funny sucking noises with her tongue and teeth.

I get a kick out of gently jousting with Dori. But in return I'm subject to a not so friendly kick of my shin under the table. I never remember to pull back my chair fast enough."

"You're going to keep in touch with Roman." I asked her.

"He promised to keep his cellphone and open his Church again." She stuck her elbow on the table and cupped her jaw in her hand. "Maybe," she hinted coyly, "I'll visit you at your store. It's just down the Embarcadero from my job." She gave me big-time smile.

"That's great," I smiled back. "Maybe I could interest you in some cleats."

"Cleats?"

"Classic metal spiked shoes baseball players wear to grip the ground."

"Just what I need."

"It has multiple uses," I pointed out to her. "They can crack nuts, pick up stray paper, open beer cans...."

"Quite the thing for the harried housewife," She considered.

"Quite."

"Do you tell this to your customers?" she asked merrily.

"Sometimes," I replied, looking away from her baby-blues. "It breaks the monotony and makes a rapport." I wiped my nose. "They may not buy the Classic Cleats, but they'll hang around and buy something else, probably. Tourists plan to spend money."

"Is that Salesmanship?"

"I guess. I'm just trying to enjoy myself."

"You deal mostly with men and deal mostly with women," she observed, unhooking her chin and straightening up. "My stuff smells better than your stuff."

"Not if you're a kid and you have a brand-new baseball glove."

"Flowers sell themselves," she boasted, ecstatically sniffing the air. No contradiction there. "The colors are amazing."

"They are beautiful!"

"And short-lived," I put in, dampening the moment.

"Fragility. The sadness of a withered flower. Drooping its delicate head in silent acquiescence of its ultimate fate."

"Whew! Where did you pick that up?"

"I just thought of it!" She said proudly.

"Beautiful," I complimented, with a touch of awe in my voice.

She didn't blush. I've never seen her blush. Instead, she pulled out a pad and wrote down what she said.

"In my place, leather cracks, wood splinters, baseball's scuff, jackets tear, nothing ethereal there." A thought hit me, "Woodsworth, I think said. 'There are thoughts that lie too deep for words' to me, it's I just can' think of the right word."

"Think it's time to go," Dori said, gathering her things.

"Hmm," I murmured," To use a sneaker phrase: "We are 'conversed' out."

"Me too," She spoke quietly, with a soft hissing sound. She squeezed me. "I'm sure there's a special place in Hell for punners. All you punners will have to listen to each other's puns. Awful puns forever." She had a malevolent grin on her face and she jabbed a couple of fingers into my side.

"I think of it as a high call of Creation," I winced and blocked her fingers as she was going in for another shot. We were a chasm apart.

Dori had an appointment at work and I accompanied her to the Ferry building. We walked with matching steps and lightly bumping shoulders.. Her good mood lightened mine.

We passed the refurbishing of Upper Market, staring up the new looming housing structures, impassively ugly for such a cool City.

The Powell and Market Center a focus of activity. Amplified Sinners, Religious Hawkers, Steel Drummers, Clanging Cable Cars, Euphonious Laughter, Stoic Homeless Beggars cross-legged on the pavement Radiant Tourists, Happy, Chummy, Buffooning Teenagers, Studious Shoppers, Pounding Construction or Destruction, a Gangling, Dancing Trumpet Player, Floating Sounds of Gibberish: A small piece of the Human juggernaut. And further the earnest busyness of the Financial District. The Embarcadero.

Dori entered The Ferry Building, and walked back and down into a MUNI station and took the Ocean Beach train to my stop a block from Duboce Park, where the Train went from below to above ground.

From there to the Beach was a nice sight-seeing ride, just a block or two from the long Golden Gate Park.

Back home, Blondie waggedly led me to the Park where we stayed and socialized for nearly two hours. When we were back inside, there was an Email message from Arcadia, inviting me to a rehearsal of her play. It was for 10am tomorrow. I didn't have be at work until One. I accepted with pleasure.

She was a fish.

"You look like a Tuna Fish," was the first thing that came out of my mouth.

"I am a Tuna Fish," she said, elated. "I'm the 'Star.' She did a wiggle.

"You know...."

"Don't say it!"

"Don't say what?" I gave her a puzzled look.

"Star Kist?" She grimaced.

"Is this an indictment of Star Kist?"

"No!"

"Why are you just a chicken of the sea?"

"I am not a brand name," she stamped and gave me her version of a supercilious fish. "Look at my costume, isn't it elegant!?" I nodded respectfully. "Shining silver scales!" She ran her hands caressingly down her body. "It's the Dior of fish costumes." I can't argue that. "And my gills, aren't they shapely?!" A knockout.

"May I ask what the point of the Play is?"

"Well, sit and watch and you'll see." She pointed to an overused sofa that had probably gone through the Big Earthquake.

"What's it about?" I insisted politely.

"I'm not sure," she said defensively. It's a farce pretending to be ultra-realism or the other way around."

"Enlightening."

"Hey," she said, tired of me. Talk to Jonathan over there he wrote it and he's directing it."

I looked to where she looked and saw a man half-hidden in a musty old armchair that looked very comfortable. He seemed to be swallowed in a colorful array of fresh pillows. He was writing in a black, hardbound notebook.

He was a clean-cut guy, no more than forty, He wore a well-cut suit and a solid red tie. He had no ponytail, his pants weren't shredded, there was no ashtray filled with cigarette butts. He didn't come across as very Artsy.

"What does he do otherwise?" I asked Arcadia. Obviously the Writer/Director wasn't a big living in the Playhouse.

"He's an analyst,"

"What does he analyze?"

She shrugged, as well as one can shrug in a costume that has no shoulders. "He doesn't say. We don't ask." she did a half-shrug, almost falling over. "But it must be something good. He's paying for this whole production." She slapped a fin.

"A good guess." She looked ridiculous in her fish suit but I said nothing. I asked the inevitable. "Do you have any lines?"

"I glub a lot," She explained rationally. "It starts underwater where I meet two divers."

"Yes."

"I read their air bubbles and I know I'm in trouble."

"Yes. Yes."

"I have to go practice my glubbing," She moved away. "Talk to Jonathan. He's a subdued dude, he'll fill you in. See ya."

"Good luck."

I introduced myself to Jonathan, and after he graciously put away his notebook and invited me to sit down, I asked about the Play.

"A fish is kidnapped by divers," he explained, in measured and calm voice, "Put in a large jar of water, the cap punched with air holes." He was expansive. "The bad guys have to get secret information that the Fish will not reveal."

"Fish can't talk."

"We can be persuasive," he slyly grinned.

"But physically......?"

"Well." he said darkly, "No one has ever used our methods before. We interpret the glubs," he pointed out with satisfaction.

"You're kidding?"

"It's kind of Morse Code for fishes."

"How do you pry information out of a fish?"

"It's a secret." He admonished.

"Well," I contradicted, It's no secret if the audience is watching."

"We do it behind a curtain," He trumped. We play loud music."

"Sounds cruel."

"It's not painful," he assured me. "But it's humiliating."

"How do you humiliate a fish?"

"Ah," he tapped his heart reverently, almost teary, "It's not s sight for the soft-hearted."

"Do they recover," I asked, wackily.

"Their egos suffer."

"Fish don't have egos," I said, maddingly.

"It's the fishy equivalent of an ego."

"This is the craziest conversation I ever had."

"Fun, isn't it?" He cracked a wicked smile.

"Aren't you trying to make a point?"

"Of course," he answered casually.

"What is it!?"

"That's why we have an audience."

I emitted a low growl. "I can't pin you down."

"Maybe, that's the point." He leaned back comfortably, and folded his arms.

"What?" I conjectured, "Ambiguity?"

"Maybe."

"Well, it's been very instructive, in an uninstructive way."

"A good summation." He leaned forward to grab his notebook, as I stood up to leave. "I hope you'll be there for the initial performance. I'd enjoy your interpretation."

"What's the title," I added needlessly'

"Very Fishy."

No words necessary.

Arcadia reappeared. "Interesting, isn't he?"

"Very."

"We're still trying to find a name for me, the Fish, the Heroine."

"What's been suggested?" I was amusingly intrigued.

"I go for alliteration." She proposed: 'Fiona the Fish.' "Francine Fish.' something like that."

"The others?"

"They want something less pedestrian," she sneered: 'Fluorescent Fish,' 'Saint Fish,' 'Whale of a Fish,' pretty silly."

"Lots of possibilities." I stayed uncommitted.

She was defiant.

"I am going to demand the right to name myself. I am the Star Fish!"

"That sounds fair."

"Yes. We fish have been taken for granted for too long," She pronounced with tempered boldness.

I had to put it to her. "Do you realize your lines are a series of glubs?"

"Unfortunately." She faltered, then stirred. "My glubs will be impassioned. It's a challenge. The greatest glubs ever heard on stage."

"Bravo," I clapped. "You'll be Fish with cheek."

"For sure. But you'd better leave now. Jonathan only wants the cast to know the ending, okay"

"I'm going." She gave me the address of Jonathan's home in the Avenues, where they were staging the debut performance before friends and hopefully some local critics they invited,

It will be a small intimate gathering and there will be some nice, tasty treats to go along with the mad action. I left the loft without meeting the rest of the cast, but I was sure they were all crazy.

A cornucopia of tourists, arriving in the form of credit cards, floated through the Magical Wharf. Their credit cards, heavy with money, clattered on a trove of merchandise counters. And inside the endless "cute" shops, awaiting the carefree, convivial commotion of covetous tourists were the chipper, conscientious, customer savvy and from my new perspective, RoboClones, behind the counters.

In Las Vegas, the Elvis impersonators vied to be the one who looked most like Elvis. In Bethlehem, the Jesus impersonators, competed to be the most authentic. In China, the Mao impersonators raced to see who could get imprisoned first. In SF pretension is obsolete.

Customers bustled resolutely through my workplace, appraising the merchandise, pulsating with an urge to buy, passing items, one to another, conferring, contemplating, deciding. Major league jackets are expensive, so are uniform tops. Lots of Giants' stuff for local fans. Pennants, flags, posters, dolls, trading cards: Stuff. Stuff. Stuff. There was almost a satiety, being around these Goods, half the day. Especially having to come face to face with the Yankee logo each time. Ugh.

The holidays were closing in. I shook hands with my new co-worker. He was a tall, spare, leathery looking guy, middle-aged with coarse black hair. He called himself Howard. He looked at me with a bull-terrier sort of face. Hard to read.

"I'll tell you right off. I'm an ex-con." He waited patiently for my response.

"Are you on Parole?" It was all I could think to say at the moment.

"No. All done." His eyes made a slow tour of the merchandise.

"You a Sports fan?"

"Absolutely."

"Baseball?"

"Grew up with it."

"So did I." Tension eased. "Who did you root for"

"Tigers."

"That's a relief. Glad it's not the Yanks."

"Hated the Yankees."

"We're on common ground. I'm Beamer."

"Okay."

"Take a leisurely tour. Get to know the stuff."

"Okay, Beamer."

He went off to study the merchandise.

"Let's see. An ex-con can be anyone from a murderer or a rapist to someone who wrote bad checks to someone with a habit of shoplifting expensive sunglasses and lots of bad things in between.

He was back after a cursory tour. He knew I was weighing the ex-con thing. "I don't hide it," he avowed, "But I don't broadcast it." He gave me a square look. "Your Boss gave me a chance. I appreciate it."

"This job is mostly cashiering," I advised him. "You don't have to be an encyclopedia."

Even His smile was laconic.

"Are you located?" I asked perfunctory, although he was clearly presentable and not living on the streets.

"I have a small room in a flat," he said with some pride. "I keep to myself."

"It's a Palace compared to jail. It's like living in a bathroom with bars," He said with disgust, rubbing a set of flattened ears, as if wiping something away. I didn't see any tattoos or major scars, nothing to show he'd been in rough crime.

He tried to stand perfectly erect, but he slumped when he drifted off. He seemed to have a detached acquiescence to life. "Throw it at me, I can take it."

I showed him how to operate the everyday devices and machines. He was sharp and determined and picked up technology faster than I could. He could have had some training in prison.

After he was satisfied he could do the cashiering, he painstakingly went around the store, learning the merchandise and where it was so he could point it out to customers. He wanted to do the job without asking my help every few minutes. A capable guy. What did he do?

After opening, the day went well but for a few minor new employee sscres-ups. He knew his stuff. He was polite and efficient with customers, saying: "Thank you, Maam" and "Thank you, Sir."

He located things in a jiffy, as if he had a photographic memory, though he did need my help.

"When I was kid," he reminisced, at the end of the day, "I worked at a five and dime store and had to remember a million things."

"I was amazed," I said admiringly.

"Yeah, but a good memory has a bad downside," he thought back, dejectedly.

"Of course," I agreed, "But better to keep a good memory than an unreliable one." He looked at me expectantly. "Bad thoughts may sting less in time."

He gave me a fist bump. "Yes, it is better," he agreed, some pleasure shining in his pale eyes.

Outrageous Halloween. Not participating, but observing. Costume mania. Not just small kids. It's a show. Though real kids are still Trick or Treating.

I walk around with Blondie, trying to convince kids she is my cousin wearing a dog costume. Always good for a double-take or 'I'm not that dumb' look. And askance looks as if I were disconnected from reality, which is, as we know, the purchased wish of many people.

The rainy days are coming. The Park muddy. And in a non-mysterious way, the mud will leave the ground, attach itself to a canine, who will then transport and inevitably deliver it the surface of the nearest pristine article of human clothing. It is a ritual of the Park, "Paws of Mud."

Blondie had thick fur. Unless there was a deluge, her priority was staying outside until she got heavily soaked. It took a while. Of course, whenever the world seems dry and promising, as soon as you step out and walked a few paces rain will fall. We say: "As soon as I go out it rains." Which leads me to the logical conclusion, if everyone stayed indoors, it would never rain.

Howard hadn't revealed was he was in for. After getting his first paycheck, he sauntered into the Store sporting a spanking new, tan Cowboy hat and a broad smile. He seemed comfortable in his new City.

"I've been walking around the City," he boasted, "and I like it."

"It's a great walking city."

"Getting used to the hills. The views are stunning."

"Yes," I offered. "There have been visitors so stunned by the magnificent views, they froze into statues and had to be carted off to some remote desert town, where they can recover. It's a great expense to the City." He stared at me with fathomless eyes." It's always a risk. You did well to survive."

Howard turned away, cogitating my words, then looked back doubtfully. As if he had spoken prematurely about liking the City and its weird inhabitants. He scratched his head and asked innocently: "What town?"

"What's the difference?" I deflected the question, not being quick enough to mention an Imaginary town.

"I've spent time in the desert," he claimed, "I've seen these people."

I searched his face. Not a clue. It was as blank as my bank account. Was he prolonging the joke, taking it seriously or nothing.

"You lived in the desert?"

"I traveled through."

"I meant it as a joke."

"I did see a lot of odd people there, I figured they were transported from SF."

Not a smile.

It was time to open. The gist of it was that I didn't expect the word 'Stunning' to come out of this guy's mouth. I figure he picked it up from a SF Guidebook.

The doors were opened. We arranged and manned our posts. We stood ready for the incoming tourists and assorted natives. Tourists are okay to deal with. They don't gripe or complain or steal. They are polite and are in a good or even happy mood. Eyebrows are raised at some outlandish prices. Tourists have money to spend. That and ubiquitous shoplifting lead to higher prices.

Celebrities show up and try to be the least conspicuous. Sunglasses and hats yanked down low and expressionless faces also draw attention.

Maybe, they are posers. Who knows. People are too busy touristing to notice one another.

Not much talking to customers, they are in a hurry a schedule of things to do and see. Plenty of attractions in SF. Lots to see in a short time. The word I attach to them is Etceteras.

Howard rarely brought home made food. He preferred the fast food joints. After his time in his joint it was a special treat to dine there. He always came back with a smile, relishing his freedom to make real TV appetite stirrers.

One time, after work, we went for Pizza and we talked about each other's lives. He talked about inmates he knew. "There was one guy," he remembered, 'Who had deserted the Army from a Commie country in Europe. He made it to the US. He was convicted of a felony here and was going to be sent back to his Country. I course, he would be executed there. Another country could take him, but that was long shot." He paused, recollecting. "He left, I never found out what happened to him. A Caseworker in the Prison wrote to the ACLU and told them his situation.

He blew money on that Pizza. It was stacked with extras. It was bountiful. He devoured it, slice by big slive with gustatory elan. He settled back in his chair with stomach-patting contentment."

"You left a piece of crust." He peered at the spot.

"I don't want to be a pig," he said solemnly. He took a slug of beer, wiped his mouth and added: There was an Orthodox Jewish guy, a few cells away. He ate only kosher food. On Fridays his family sent him a big Kosher Salami to help him through the weekend." Howard smiled. "One Friday his Salami got stolen. It was a hungry weekend. It's funny now, but everybody felt for the guy. Only Kosher."

Howard started fidgeting and glanced behind him. We were seated next to the window. There was a lot of foot traffic. He calmed himself and finished the story.

"The Jew was a funny. guy. He was friendly with guards and vive-versa and always asked them how they were doing. Their answer was "I can't complain." Then the Kid would answer, "You can't complain? I'm

Jewish, I'll teach you. I can give you lessons. That always broke them up. He was a funny guy."

He finished his second beer, I glugged my half-full bottle down. "Time to go," I said.

"Yep." He stood up and stretched his long frame. He twisted a veiny neck and it crackled. "Next year I'll be a fat man," he predicted and puffed out his cheeks.

I nodded.

"Well," he smiled mechanically, "I've been dreaming about food for a long time." His pale eyes narrowed, getting a little moist at the edges.

We headed our separate ways, My destination and duty always the same. Take Blondie to the Park. As I was coming in Dori and her troupe were on their way out.

"Hi, Beamer," she said with some urgency. "I was going to text you. Let's sit down."

We sat down. Blondie was unleashed and sniffing. Dori kept her dogs close.

"What about?"

"I'm excited."

"Okay."

"I've decided to have Thanksgiving Dinner at my place."

"Hostess Dori."

"You'll come?"

"Absolutely."

"I already invited The General and his truth-seeking girlfriend, I hope she can find some answers in the Turkey, Roman is thinking it over, A Doctor gave him some pills to calm him."

"Anyone you want to invite?" She asked, tentatively.

"Nice of you to ask." I thought about it. "How about Howard?" She had finally come on a short visit to my work. She was filled on Howard's background. He was friendly and polite; she was circumspectly cordial.

"Okay," she said, tepidly. "Mr. Comedian, do you have his number?"

"I think so."

"Call him and invite him." I rummaged through all my pockets and found nothing.

"Maybe, I have the number at home."

She pulled out a pad and started making notes

"Do you have enough space?"

"Not that many people, and you can help me."

"So," I looked her in the forehead, the invite carries obligations."

"Yes," she said distinctly, despite concentrating on the Pad, "I wouldn't let you near the Turkey," she glanced up at me. "But you can slice and dice and setup, 'She advised me, merrily."

"Does that mean I get first crack at the Turkey?"

"No," she said sternly, "that's for the guests."

"What, I'm not a guest?"

"You're a friend," she said, politically, suddenly bouncing forward and planted a kiss on my cheek.

A friendly kiss. I passed my hand over it and said nothing. She smiled happily and went back to her notes.

A few minutes went by.

"Can we add another person?"

"Who?" She didn't look up.

"I'm going to a performance of a Play with a quirky actress I met at lunch at my old job downtown. I'd like to ask her to come." Dori was now looking at me. Seriously. "She makes up her own countries. She'll sparkle up the conversation."

My bright idea was dimmed by a sharp, questioning look on Dori's attentive face. My smile was fading fast. "She probably has plans with her theater crowd, nut it's worth a try."

Dori deliberated. The pathway her thoughts traveled through her brain eluded me, but I knew her refusal would not go against her open nature.

"Okay," she sighed, lazily gazing past me and then consulting her watch. She lifted her head and stared at me. She said briskly: "But that's the limit.

"I'm going to take Blondie for a walk," I said casually to her back. She was fussing with her scrambling, noisy dogs. She didn't answer, but tossed off a feeble wave.

Silence can also make a big noise.

I was strolling by Safeway with Blondie nosing around for discarded scraps when I had an idea. Why not invite Dori to the Play. It might quell her sudden displeasure. I went back to the Park. She was gone.

She buzzed me into her building. She opened her door and silently waved me into her studio. "Sit down if you want." There was a studied weariness in her voice.

She went to her small kitchen area and proceeded to fling open the cabinets and with much clattering of plates and glasses, brought them to rest on the table, still shivering. She seemed on the verge of slamming the cabinet doors closed, but then eased her grip and closed them with exaggerated delicacy.

"Why are you acting so crabby?"

She looked at me narrowly. "I'm not crabby."

"Well," I smiled, "You're not acting like a Tuna."

"A Tuna," She smirked.

"The girl I mentioned is acting like a Tuna."

She squelched a laugh.

"Seriously." It's some kind of avant-garde Play.

She said to herself as much as to me. "I only get these things from Beamer.

"Wanna come?"

"Does she come out of a can?"

"She goes into a can."

"Sounds silly," she chuckled, lightening up. "Going to the Movies with friend's tomorrow night," she excused herself. "Maybe, there's a good Sardine film in the City."

After a week of stultifying work, I was glad to be at Arcadia's fishy performance. It was a quaint house in the Avenues. There as an elongated living room, half taking up with seating and the other half cut off by a make-shift yellow curtain draped across a series of unlit stand up lamps. It didn't hide very much until you sat down. Despite all the rattling's and dropping of thing behind the curtain, a convivial gathering of invitees stood around a small table nourishing on coffee, Oreos, Safeway cheddar and red house wine.

There were some twenty guests at Jonathan's mother's home in the Avenues. It was an old Victorian, with a big open space to host a Play.

There was no sense of excited anticipation. Rather, people seemed to be bemused. The seating was comfortable, lounge chairs, sofas, large plush pillows, all facing the stage. I took a seat on one of the sofas after mingling with some guests (I can't believe anyone was paying for this). The gathering were friends, neighbors and a couple of Critics who looked like Critics.

There was one from a small Bay Area newspaper I had never heard of and who was unknown to everyone else. He came in Sports Jacket and jeans, wearing an enigmatic smile and stubbled cheeks. He was young.

The other guy, who got some notice from the crowd was from a local daily. He was older, with steel wool hair and funereal shackled features. I hoped he carried a key with him to unlock his face, if he had the urge to laugh or smile during the performance.

I was seated like everyone else, very comfortably. The lush comfort would either put people to sleep during the Play or incline them to be merciful when reviewing it.

There was also a table on the side with Oreos, crackers, a block of Safeway Cheddar and Red and White wines of modest cost. No one's paying.

In front of me and to the right, was a big batch of glaring red hair with a purple ribbon crowning its peak. The hair was bobbing up and down and side to side and I suspected beneath the tufts over her ears there was an earbud embedded.

Sprawling across a chair beside me was a swarthy, brawny guy who looked like he should be perched on a wrestling match instead of sipping wine and playing Oreos.

The capper was an older man sitting stiffly at the other end of my sofa. He wore a battered fedora over a battered face. His left fist was cocked by his side as if ready to throw a jab, while his right hand relentlessly snapped his fingers. An ex-pug in reverie?

Our attention sprang to a young man standing in front of the audience. He held a guitar, strummed a few introductory chords. The place quieted down. He started singing in a soft, melancholy voice:

"If I had a wish, I'd save the Tuna Fish
I don't really like to see them getting squished
Why break up a family
Pull them cruelly from the Sea
What have they ever done to us?

He bravely sang the Chorus:

"Save the Tuna Fish, save the Tuna Fish
That's what Khrisna would have said
Save the Tuna Fish, save the Tuna Fish
Eat a potato knish instead.

Melancholy:

"Why send out a fleet
To hunt for Tuna meat

Or would you rather let them be
Jam them in a can
Would do it to the common man
And they are as common as you can get.

He sang another brave chorus, and then abruptly and deeply serious, walked off, most everyone applauded respectfully.

The only man wearing a tie found it maudlin, a few tears leaked from his eyes. A thin young woman with long colorful nails, clutched at her heart. A few yawns completed the response.

The Actors of which there were seven, strode in with intention, in their various costumes and stood in front of the audience in silence. I recognized the one with the harpoon. He was wearing an ill-fitting grey grizzled beard and bristly grey eyebrows that met in the middle. It was Charles the Comedian,

The Actors dispersed behind the curtain, which was then pulled away and the standing lamps, holding the curtain, dragged out of the room. It left a series of large cardboard sets, one in back of the other. All standards of stage propriety seemed to have been thrown out the window. Maybe it was a statement. You can be cheap, but still be profound.

Arcadia came wriggling onstage with her baubles-up, shimmering fish suit to the eager delight of the audience. She glubbed a few times, did a fishy Hula as bubbles coming from offstage floated past her. The audience applauded with glee.

She was startled by the sudden appearance of several men phony scuba gear. They grabbed her and stuffed her into a large opened mouth jar imagined to be filled with water.

"Talk! Talk!" They screamed at her in unison. But all she could do was to glub in panic. Charles came over and menacingly pointed his harpoon at her. "Talk! Talk!" They continued, shouting, circling the jar and taunting her. This went on for fifteen minutes as Arcadia the Tuna, grew limp in the Jar.

At first, the playgoers were mystified, then fidgety and gritting their teeth. They stayed in their seats. If they were good money for this travesty, they might have rushed the stage, pummeling the Actors with the cardboard fish strewn around the stage and then gleefully demolished the cheap set.

But since it was free and they felt a sort of congregational respect for the author, whoever the idiot might be, they behaved. But impatience was building. An edginess was squeezing out tolerance. The audience was deserting.

Then, suddenly, there was a heavy rapping on the front door. It broke up the monotony and knowing the dramatic perversion of the

Director, people returned to their seats. Assuming the outburst was part of the Play.

No one went to open the door. The knob jiggled, the door flew open and two masked men burst into the room, wielding big, black guns.

"Don't move!" ordered the shorter of the two. "Stay where you are!" No one flinched. They welcomed the diversion. The Actors on the stage were frozen.

"We want the big fish," sputtered the tall one, also slurring his words. "Drop your harpoon," he demanded of Charles. Charles dropped it and it fell apart on the stage.

"Move away from the Jar!" They moved.

The small audience was enthralled with the dangerous twist and the realistic acting, some were even made nervous by the scene, some jabbed ribs, mouthing, 'good acting.'

The masked figures trained their guns on the Jar. "Okay, strip!" Arcadia clutched her fish suit and glubbed back in frantic defiance. The audience was eating it up. Arcadia played the damsel Tunafish in distress to perfection. (though there were no precedents to compare it to}.

"Take it off!" said the men. The audience joined in:

"Take it off, take it off, take it off", they clamored.

Arcadia sobbed piteously and peeled off her fishsuit, leaving her in tight jeans and an untucked-in shirt. She came out of the downturned jar at the behest of a pointed gun. They motioned her toward the front door, which was still ajar.

She meekly stood between the two men. They marched her away, and at the door she conveyed her alarm to the watching crowd. "I'm innocent!" she cried and struggled to be free, but the men forcibly nudged her through the door.

The door shut with a sinister click. A car engine coughed, caught and squealed off into a rumble and then there was silence. The Actors, coming to their senses, rushed outside and stared long and hard into the darkness. Then they moped back inside.

People were on their feet, moving around in confusion. They approached the Actors. The Actors shrugged their shoulders in troubled bewilderment. One had picked up an envelope, tossed inside as the men were exiting with Arcadia. He pulled out a yellow paper read it and handed it around to his colleagues. They were in dismay.

"She's gone!" one of the divers cried, casting off his mock scuba gear. "Ransom!" he announced to the crowd.

"Perfidy!" A diver sang out in anguish.

"Fish napped," added Charles, now brandishing a large piece of his fallen harpoon at the open door.

Consternation swept through the room. No one was sure the end was acting.

"It's part of the Play," the younger critic bellowed. The crowd felt more reassured. He was a man who probably saw hundreds of Plays and he would know good acting. But the Actors were too consumed with real or pretended grief and anger to answer. "Is this a ploy?" he said the backs of the cast and they exited to another room and locked the door.

The Playgoers that were left, half had quietly slipped out, were back with the cheese the wine and the Oreos, perplexed, but munching away and chatting about the surprising and violent denouement. Will a review be in the papers? Did we misread the works of a new and great Writer and Director? Or was it a wasted evening. The wine and cheese makes up for some of that. And best of all, no one had ever seen a Drama starring a Tuna fish.

"A joke," The serious critic said, saying nothing.
"A monstrous joke," the younger critic chimed in.
"I thought it was fun," contributed the thin young lady.
"I was jolted out of my seat!"
"What trash!"
"Revolting!" said a heavy-set, balding man.
"Revolutionary!" said a stocky, intense youth.

I waited for Charles. He came out before the others.
"There was massive imbroglio in there" he related, almost dropping his Comedian facade.
"Imbroglio?"

"Nobody knew anything about the abduction," he said pensively. "All I told by the Director, and I quote, 'Wave your harpoon menacingly.' Not something that gets noticed by critics." He smiled derisively: 'Charles was magnificent as Captain Ahab, artfully waving his harpoon, as if he were born with a harpoon in his crib'"

"Well," I consoled him, Now, you have on your acting resume that you played Captain Ahab, one of the great literary characters in American fiction. The details are fallow."

"You'll back me up?"

"Absolutely."

I invited him to Thanksgiving dinner. The actors had invited him to theirs, but he really didn't know them and he would be happy to see Dori. I asked him to ask Arcadia to come, if he ever saw her again. He wrote down the detail in his 'remember the joke pad.'

He began scratching his chin and picking at pieces of glue that was still sticking to him from his precocious great beard. He had forgotten the eyebrows. He resembled a Wolfman.

He sniffed something unpleasant behind him. It was a wet underarm thrown over his shoulder by a departing actor saying 'Ciao.' His comedian parts coming back in place, he explained why it was easy to decide accept Dori's invite.

"I was imagining invitations flying in from everywhere. My mailbox was stuffed with air mail. Lots of air."

"You're back!"

"A lot of years piled up for forty minutes," he mumbled drearily.

"Buck up."

"That too."

Charles rubbed a rumbling stomach nervously. "My anger has congealed into a handball that ricochets off the walls of my stomach."

"Very descriptive."

"You like it?"

"It's gutsy."

"Good. Good." His spirits rose. "Maybe I'll use it in my self-deprecating routine."

"You are resourceful," I praised, as he put on determined face.

"Yes! The world will laugh at me!" he said with a sudden cockiness. He went off to fill up his stomach and his Ego.

People can jump from despair to elation in a thought. Our minds can plumb the wonder and mystery of the Universe yet be devastated by a split fingernail.

It's true that s fingernail is more personal than a Galaxy a million light years away. But consider that Galaxy with its billions and billions of planets, can be home to billions and billions of beings who are also at the mercy of split fingernails. Whose thirty-six or twelve or three hour days may be ruined by cracked or split fingernails. We see the vastness of Space, but lose sight of our mutual peeves.

With Charles rolling off to be reunited with his lovely dog Guinevere, the room was emptied. I looked around. No one. Silence. After being the scene of all that wild activity the room was blank. Like space unfilled. Like thins not clear. The murky goings-on had infiltrated my brain and left sticky blobs of doubt.

Then there was a sound from the kitchen. In the quiet that were riveting. Water splashing, plates and glassware clinking; like a storm after the Eye passed through. In the midst of the noise there were two female voices murmuring.

An older woman, with grey-flecked hair and hawk-like eyes, wearing a wet flowered apron and a cross expression entered the room. She was carrying a large, circular metal tray which she clanged onto the refreshment table and began cleaning up. She didn't see me.

"Hello." I let my presence be known as I walked casually over and saved one of the last two Oreos sitting primly on a cushion.

"Hello," she answered, irritably, bending to pick up napkins and crumbs and assorted cups. "Slobs," she muttered. I stepped in and picked up most of it.

"Thanks," she said, slowly straightening up with a hand bracing her lower back. She gave me a pleasant smile.

"Do you live here?" 'I wondered, smiling pleasantly back.

"It's my house," she declared, picking up the tray with still-filled cups and chipped saucers rattling perilously, as she hurriedly shuffled into the kitchen.

She was back in a flash with a dustpan, a broom and an attitude. "Pigs!" She grunted, as she swept up the smaller crumbs around the area. She finished with a huff and plopped down on a hard chair.

Unfortunately, she also sat down on pieces of Oreo cookies which crunched under her backside. She jumped up. I expected another lambasting of the 'Pigs'. Instead of hitting the ceiling, she got down on her knees and petitioned the floor. "The next time someone drops crumbs on you, give-em a splinter."

"Nice of you to host the Play," I said, temporarily, when she stood up achingly and rubbed her knees.

"The so-called 'Director' is my son," she said scornfully.

"You didn't like the Play?"

She looked at me as if I was from a planet far, far away.

"He has a good job, why is he dabbling in his illusions?"

Well said, thought to myself, but to her: "To relieve stress?"

"Ha!"

"Is he here?"

"Naw. He's gone back to his Condo," she said, with feisty disgust. She looked discouragingly at the Stage. "I'll dismantle that joke tomorrow."

"What about Arcadia?"

"What about her?"

"Is she safe?"

"Why not?"

"The guys with the guns were very convincing around a bunch of amateurs."

"They scared me," she admitted.

If it wasn't part of the, wouldn't the Actors be alarmed. But, Mr. Director tricked us all. He likes an enigma. For some reason, it reminded me of Roman vs the Actor about a dog named Molly. Bur, 'Tut, Tut' as the old Egyptians would say. It was time to walk Blondie.

As I was leaving, I thought it might be the House itself that put the idea of sinister crime in my head. It was turn of the century or so, with randomly mutilated redwood wall panels, decorative ceiling, fading with age, dim hooded lamps, dead chandeliers and cracks in the ornamental archway that led to the dining room. There was a sense of heaviness and decay. How did it square with the Director's Mother's fastidiousness? It's funny how Edgar Allan Poe sneaks in your brain on these occasions. I bowed to the clinging atmosphere and dismissed my suspicions. For now

Blondie was not decrepit like the House. She was bursting with healthiness and intent on busting loose in the Park. She dashed to her favorite sniff spots, did an ecstatic roll around in the grass and searched for playmates. It was dark and dogs were few, there was no late evening rendezvous. Instead, we circled the Park twice and head home.

Once inside there was the click of the bolt, locking the door. There was the snap and the click of the breaking granola bar I shared with Blondie. There was the click of the microwave opening for the popped popcorn. There was the click of the TV going on and then the clicking of the Porpoises on the Nature show. Blondie nails made a clicking sound on the tile. The possible click with someone on Facebook, If I ever bothered to use it. Doing a crossword puzzle, my brain clicks on a solution. Clicking on and off the hand radio, when I went to bed.

Dale, from the Football Section occasionally drifted in when Howard was on break. Their breaks coincided. He was uncomfortable round Howard, learning of his 'criminal past', as he put it. Howard never revealed what put him inside, so who knows what Dale imagined.

Dale was 'seeing the Country', taking a hiatus from his self-proclaimed status as a professional student. He was twenty-eight, a professed Cheesehead, die-hard Packer fan.

"I idolized Brett Favre," he swore, "Even had fantasies of playing for the Packers."

He had a limp, and when you looked down at his left leg you could see his left shoe bottom was much thicker than his right. He had an old fashioned, blonde crew-cut which he brushed through when he paused to find the right word. His cheeks were sprinkled with blonde specks resembling a beard. His eyes wide and blue. From his neck up he could be Scandinavian, below he was chunky with thick legs. A Man of disparate parts.

He was nice, with the easy manner of an adept, but honest Salesman. He was a stubborn Republican.

"Not many people admit it in SF."

He laughed with good humor. "Some people think I'm an ogre."

"To some you are," I educated him.

"Maybe, I'll let my hair grow and have a grizzled beard," he chuckled.

"Well, you know the old line about Berkeley.

He shook his head, interested.

"It's so far left, it's almost on the right."

"The Republicans are broken up into a bunch of rights," he said ruefully.

"If they could only get together."

I considered it. "You know, in Politics, two rights don't make a right," I said impressively.

"I disagree," he replied, an irritable edge in his voice, as if he were trying to be a nice guy, while someone was stepping on his toes.

Nice Guys?

Don't they worry about things all the time, like me? If I wasn't worried, I'd be worried. Contentment is not one of my accomplishments. Dale looked content, unruffled, hardy. When you're freezing up in the cold of Northern Wisconsin everything makes sense. The world is clear and upfront.

I launched an idea at him.

"Do Republicans exist to keep things from changing too fast? Change is inevitable, but we don't want to be overwhelmed.

It landed with a splat!

He said profoundly: I think people in general don't want sudden changes, but catastrophes force us to change." He smiles affably.

"Do you think Conservatives are more religious? I pondered.

He brushed through his crew-cut. "God doesn't discriminate," he answered or didn't answer. He looked at me squarely, "You are brimming with questions," he pursued with gracious condescension, as if I was a lost soul.

"Questions generally produce answers," I told him, with a somber prickliness.

"There are always more questions than answers," he said, rhetorically.

"You can always guess," I proposed, in sloppy retort.

"But the question of the moment," he beamed, "Is whether the Packers will get to the Super Bowl."

"Likewise the Forty Niners."

Being the same Conference our teams could not meet in the SuperBowl.

We shook hands amicably and Dale hurried back to his place as soon as he saw Howard coming through the door.

"I saw him gallop off when he saw me," Howard grumbled and squeezed his lips together. "No need for that." He stood there shaking his head. He's made things worse by owning up and telling people what he did. People tended to believe the worst. I did not see any Evil in him, if that's the term.

I didn't like hinting at it or do it point blank. There must be an in between that is both tactful and direct. Maybe he likes the apprehensiveness created around him. Or, he feels too degraded by what he's done. Just speculation. Our sovereign perceptions of others can be totally unreliable.

I'm not uneasy around him, but I understand, with his stony face and taciturn manner, he does not draw people to him and they knew he had a record, he'd be approached by only the curious.

The late morning surge came to the Football and Basketball areas and left us Baseball folk with a gloomy sprinkle of dejected Baseball fans who had to endure four months of cold neglect. A pity.

A nobility of Baseball past, whose pictures hung framed and arrayed on the walls above us with an easy but formidable confidence: The

'Babe'. 'Ted 'the Kid' Williams. Willie 'Say Hey Kid' Mays. DiMaggio 'The Yankee Clipper.' Sandy Koufax, Jackie Robinson, Hank Aaron, Stan 'the Man' Musial. Mickey Mantle, and soon to be Legends.

In the trading card bins a fusillade of Shooting Stars. The great, colorful characters who played the game to resounding cheers and then vanished from the Heavens.

On rainy days, Tourists plowed by, heads bent, umbrellas pushing against the cold, hard wind-blown rain that bounced and percolated on the ground and spanked drippingly against the store windows.

The rain is a blessed mess for the dogged, soggy, disenchanted, perambulating and often kid-towing visitors.

Rain in a DogPark has consequences. For the Dog it turns into a Spa where mud meets body. For people a place to stand around and get wet. Shelter was a couple of already sodden trees and various sized umbrellas.

I wore a rain proof jacket with a hood. I didn't like the unwieldy encumbrance of an umbrella, I liked to keep my hands free for my rambunctious dog and shenanigans, which included breaking up dog fights and dashing after skateboarders.

Blondie and I sought partial cover under a tree with dripping limbs parallel to the ground. Blondie stretched out on the grass and I looked out into the heavy drops.

There was something contemplative about watching the rain fall in the quietude of the Park {excluding the usual barks}. The sheer spectacle of water falling from the sky bestowing life, was almost mesmerizing, and in a sense, poetic. Conversely, rain can also take life in its pouring excess.

A black and white puppy entered the Park and scooted with adorable clumsiness to and around dogs as she looked for attention and a playmate. No luck. Then, she spotted Blondie lying behind the bench and zeroed in on her.

She jumped on and around Blondie with ardent puppy love. After a brief moment of tolerance Blondie shook out with a snappy rebuff and the Pup for a brief moment in retreat looked surprised and offended.

But, with floppy persistence, she was back, nose to nose on the ground, yapping in Blondie's face. Blondie stared mildly ahead as if there was nothing there.

The non-action flustered the Pup and she upped the volume. When that didn't move Blondie's glance, she began to bath Blondie's face with her flickering tongue, which had black spots on it, making her part Chow.

Puppies are protected by Blondie, but not encouraged to be equals in the dog hierarchy. She dismissed the panting Pup with an imperative voice which the Pup sort of recognized as 'Go away, you bother me, Kid.' She was undiscouraged, and resumed her loquacious quest to be welcomed, not just sniffed at.

I followed the antics of the expeditionary puppy as she tumbled and bumbled and bumbled away across he no longer rained on, but wet grass.

A tall, thin, slightly stooped woman with scraggly gray hair. A worried look and mincing steps was in neglectful pursuit, calling out: 'To-ny, To-ny' in a fluttery, plaintive voice. Luckily, others in the Park were keeping a watch on Tony and made sure he stayed inside the grass boundaries. But he wasn't going too far. He was busy getting petted.

As the woman, in a long, open coat, plodded and puffed her way up the hill, Tony ran joyous laps around the Park. She must be thinking to herself: "What was I thinking!?"

There was a soft jab into my left side. I spun around and there was Dori, a big smile on her beautiful face.

"Just been shopping," she said exuberantly, which was quickly confirmed by two voluminous bags put down on either side of her.

"You cleaned out the Store!"

"No," she smiled with delight, "Just cleaned out a tag sale." She saw my puzzled look. "Quality stuff. My size. Can't have too many warm clothes in SF," she added, excusing her spree. He pulled out a coat, then a dress, held them in front of her. "What do you think?"

"Very nice," I answered, without reservation, particularly since I was not up on Fashion. "Anything would look good on you." stumbled unbidden from my mouth. I watched her appreciative look and a bit of a blush come my way.

She stuffed the coat and the dress, after carefully folding them, into the roomy bag and asked. "What style do you like to wear?"

A tough question. Function over style is my style.

"My preference for clothing," I told her nonchalantly, "Is clothing you can crumple up and not get creased."

"Wow!" she feigned, staring at me with her eyes high in their sockets for a few seconds, and then said, "But you dress nice."

"I do have some taste,"

"Yes, you do."

Why am I having this conversation?

"Do you have a wardrobe?"

"A wardrobe?" I pondered.

"You know," she explained, "Clothes for different occasions."

"Corduroys for Coronations," I assured her. I have that.

"Don't get cranky."

"Sorry. I just don't have many occasions."

"Well, you should."

"Is Thanksgiving dinner an Occasion?"

"Yes! I'm the Hostess." She pointed to one of her bags. "In there is a new dress. So get with it."

"I'll put on my good clothes. Clothes I've had an occasion to put on before."

"I'd like to see it."

"To change the subject {thankfully}." I said, fixing my eyes on the brown back at her side. "Remember the Guy I work with."

She looked at me blankly. "Refresh my memory."

Did she forget on purpose or just had too many things running around in her brain?

"The guy I work with is a stranger to the City. His name is Howard. I thought it would be nice to invite him to the Dinner." I met her eyes, they had a curious and apprehensive look, as if by not speaking directly to her gave something away.

"And..."

"He's been in prison."

"In prison?" She made a glum face. "For what?" she piped.

"He won't say,"

"He won't say?"

She stared at me, digesting the information or lack of it.

"Violence?" she said with a wince.

"He seems easy going."

"Why won't he tell you?"

"Dunno. Maybe you could charm it out of him."

"I don't think so, Beamer," she replied in a soft crooning voice, which creepily belied the smoldering look in her eyes.

"He hasn't decided yet. I can tell him it's off."

She held out her arms with her palms up and moved them up and down as if weighing something. "What you say next can decide it."

"Giants three, Braves two," I broadcast.

"Huh?"

"What could be more innocent and assuring as Baseball score?"

She looked seriously at me and decided. "I guess anyone who works with you, and you practically vouch for and who has that redeeming feature of loving Baseball, should be given a chance."

"Well said, Senator," I complimented. "Skip the speech and get to the peroration."

"The what?"

"The best part.

Dori was satisfied and picked up her bags. "Gotta walk the monsters," she said, flippantly, just around the block, she amended.

"Still, four, lively dogs are a project."

"It can be," she agreed, especially when a comeback tired and they're jumping all over me saying hello and expecting to go out." I detected a soupcon of discouragement in her voice.

"It has to be frustrating untangling their leashes all the time."

"It gets easier," she brightened. "Gotta go," she moved on, raising her bags in a substitute wave. "Bye."

"Bye," I cried out, with a sticky throat.

The Park lights were coming on. A cold wind swept in with its usual suddenness and caught me without a heavy jacket. Blondie with her thick, curly fur had no idea of cold. She settled in the grass. She was in her natural habitat. She closed her eyes restfully as the wind swirling ruffled her fur while it screwed my eyes into slits and froze my skin

Though I hated to disturb Blondie in her blissful commune with nature, it was time to go back to my Studio where the heat would be on, the tile floor hard and there was no grass.

She didn't move, except to lift her lids and look at me innocently. She was testing. Did I really mean it? Now that she was comfortable and in her element. She gazed into my eyes. Can I change his mind? Is my sadness working? Can he be persuaded?

That's why it's fair warning. I allow for this interlude and make it feel it's a definite request and not an urgent order. That's for emergencies. She knows the difference. Sometimes, I stay longer. It's too cold.

"C'mon, Blondie, we must go."

No influence, this time. She slowly got up, trotted up to me and we went home.

The next day at work there was an incident.

It was slow during the afternoon and then a group of customers had drifted in from the Football and Basketball areas. Howard and I both attended to them. Howard turned his head and saw a youngster stuffing packets of Baseball cards into his backpack and headed for the door.

Howard took the initiative, went after the Kid, grabbed his arm and stopped him from running. Then were ten feet outside the door and were visible through the large plate glass window of the store.

I heard Howard's voice letting loose an angry assault on the scared Kid, though I didn't get all the words. The Kid tore into his backpack and produced all the packets and handed them over to Howard. The Kid was on the verge of crying, for real or for sympathy. Howard gave him some final words, patted him on the back and let him loose and the id took off running.

Howard back in grumpy dismay. Distress cracked his usual stoic, stiff manners and stony face. "That's how I started," he flushed, maybe betraying what got him into prison.

The recent customers had already moved back to Football. Howard carefully put the card packs back in their proper slots and turned to me.

"I hope I put some scare into him," Howard mulled, calmer. "When I did my Dad gave me praise." He wanted to spit but thought better of it.

"I stole things when I was a kid,' I said, not in defense of the thief, but with the fact that it's the rare kid who never stole anything.

Howard strode his regular counter, pulled a tissue out of a drawer and wiped off his face and the back of his neck.

"It's one thing to filch some change from your Mother's purse," he asserted, tossing the tissue with finesse into a trash bin a few feet away, "But this was in a store where getting caught can get you messed up." He was growing agitated. He blew out some air to cleanse himself, rubbed his palms together vigorously and stabilized back into the customer friendly employee.

The day went smoothly after that. No bumps or ruts to relieve the sameness of the job. Occasionally we'll have an interesting customer. Last week an ex ballplayer came in while touring the City. He was surprised and happy to find he was on one of our Baseball cards.

He had been a Shortstop with several teams and was more known for his slick fielding and base stealing than for a booming bat. Now he had a paunch and a slight pause in his step. He introduced his wife to us and reminisced about his time in the Majors.

It was before the monster salaries. He missed out on becoming a millionaire. Instead, he opened a Bar/Restaurant in his Hometown and was a storied citizen there.

His eyes lit up like a kid, when he saw his card with his younger self smiling back at him. "Keep it," Howard and I said in unison.

"Who was the toughest pitcher you ever face," I asked him.

He laughed. "They were all tough," he answered modestly.

"I'm amazed," I told him at batters facing 100 mph fast balls. When I stood in the coin operated batting cages, when I was young, the fastest pitch was 70 mph and I could barely get around on that.

Instead of him telling me I slow at bat, he told me, with a twinkle in his eye: "As Duke Snider once said, "Swing hard in case the ball hits the bat."

He had to go. We shook hands. It's nice to be remembered."

It was a refreshing interlude to meet an ex ballplayer. They were my idols when I was a Kid. My younger brother and I going down to the nearby Field, before and after games, to collect autographs.

A mob of kids would swarm around players entering the Park after parking their cars. Others would arrive by Taxi, and the kids, like locusts, would rush to the opening door, pen and pads in hand. Thrust out and ready to jab at the player. Instead, some unknown guy steps out and stands there dumbly alone, as a pack of frothing kids rushes wildly at him, then sudden realize in grousing disappointment: "Aw, it's nobody."

They quickly abandon the fellow who is branded a 'Nobody!' Kids can make your day.

As the kids walked away, they spoke of their faultless disappointment

"He looked like a player," said a little guy the others called a 'pip-squeak.

"Naw," said an older kid, disparagingly, "He was too old."

"And too fat," added his buddy.

Another guy, who used a fountain pen and had ink stains on his shirt, had his own idea. "He wore a suit. Baseball players don't wear suits," he declared, for all time. It was a fact not to be disputed. The other boys nodded solemnly in agreement.

Over fifty pairs of eyes scanned the area in front of the main entrance, for real players, who had to plow their way through the horde with head bowed, surrounded by a beseeching, pleading, pushing, elbowing pen and pad or notebook waving gang: "Please." "Please. "You're my favorite PlayerAn older Lady wedged into the crowd, called out: "My Mother is sick. Your autograph will help her get better. The player recognized her, nodded and quickened his pace, broke free and entered his place of business.

They were gracious players and to some kids' miserable species of humanity. One of the ways to get autographs without a siege, was to

self-address a blank postal card and hand it to a player as he whizzed
his way away from the kids when leaving. Chances are you got it back
with a signature.

One time I planted a card into the pocket of a visiting player's Sport
jacket as he was angrily pushing through the kids. He was not a talented
player, but gritty, hardnosed, but at times dirty. Hated by opposing
teams. He snatched out my card without stopping, tore it up and threw
it away. Was he trying to enhance his tough reputation or was he just a
callous jerk? For kids it was no contest.

Back in the Park seeing new and old faces. Blondie's nose in the
grass. Many ongoing conversations. But coming down the path from
the top of the Park, the Actor sauntered into view. He was wearing a
gaudy, reflecting red jacket and his favorite smug smile.

Arcadia was walking tight beside him, trying to wriggle free his
short arms encircling her narrow waist. Her eyes, when she came closer
seemed poignant and pleading. Behind them was 'Fingers,' tugging a
stop and sniff Molly.

The Actor bathed in the stormy sea of Boos that rained down on him.

Was that fake abduction arranged by him and carried out by
'henchmen' he hired. Was he now parading his captive, like a Caesar in
the Streets of Rome. Although Caesar had a much more partial crowd.

My initial shining urge was to rush over and pull Arcadia to safety.
But she had wriggled away from the Actor and didn't make a run for it.
She grabbed the leash away from 'Fingers'. Molly looked happier.

The ludicrous procession wormed coarsely through the grassy Park.
defiling it {the Dog and Woman excluded}. Before oozing its way up
Steiner and out of sight. Don't expect Arcadia for Thanksgiving Dinner.

Various thoughts filtered through my brain. Some obvious, some
strange, as to why Arcadia would be hooked up with the eerie Actor
and the violent 'Fingers?'

She must be in awe of him. He's a well-known Movie Actor. She
is an impressionable, fledgling Actress. The clincher: She looked up to
Mr. Debacle, the Director who made her a Tuna Fish.

Beside me, stood a gangly older man, wearing a loosely buckled trench coat and a pair of woolen gloves. He was cradling an Italian Greyhound in his arms. He turned to me with a bemused smile on his blotchy face.

"Does that happen often?" he asked, bending his toward Steiner.

"Once in a while," I answered, through gritted teeth.

"They aren't very popular," he observed profoundly.

"You guessed it," I said with a hard sarcasm that breezily passed his left ear, joined the ether and rose up to the Stars.

His dog was squirming to get to the ground and do dog things, but the man held it firm.

"It's too dangerous,' he cooed into his dog's ear. Those big dogs will stomp all over you."

I shuddered. Small dogs have always thrived in the Park. This poor guy, so eager to join the cavorting band of small dogs was frustrated by the fears of his owner.

"Has he played with others dogs," I inquired politely.

"Oh, no, not my Georgie," woozed the man, resting his glove on Georgie's back. "He'd be traumatized."

I wanted to say he was not letting his down in a den of lions. Italian Greyhounds are also for their evasive skills and the DogPeople will jump in if there was any risky stuff going on. But it would be useless against a brain of hardened cement.

A high-pitched grating, vibrating noise arose from a huddle of people in the center of the dog area. I drew everyone's attention and I immediately thought there was fracas among the dogs and one was frightened or in pain.

It was a dispute between two grownups, each of whom coveted a dog ball that came bounding out of nowhere and no one claimed it. Dogs, we guess, are the mental equivalent of two or three year olds, reaching their peak. But people can revert to that state in split seconds.

No one intervened to prevent punches being thrown. The pettiness turned into a lot of huffing and puffing and finally into some stupid laughter when a dog slipped in to grab the ball and make it his.

Some dogs are more materialistic than others, just like Humans. Some are more Spiritual. When you have something material to offer them, mainly, a treat. They will only come to you for that only. If you don't carry, they know and won't bother you. Others, the more Spiritual, will be content to have a good petting, even if they are initially disappointed at not getting a treat.

I came by early for Thanksgiving Dinner to help Dori prepare. She and a new neighbor, Carol, were already filling the room with wonderful smells. The Turkey was nestled in the oven. Sweet potatoes and other dishes were in various stages of readiness. Things needed chopping. That was my job, my direct contribution to the Meal. That, and two bottles of drinkable red wine with corks.

Carol, who I never met, was close to Dori's age, but blond and blue-eyed, with summery feature, as if she'd be home on any beach. She gave off happy vibes.

"Nice to meet you," she smiled and offered her hand, which kinda surprised me. I delicately folded my hand around hers for a moment released it stiffly, flustered always around a pretty woman who was friendly to me.

"I've got to see our Turkey." She excused herself for my benefit, noticing my hard to hide, dazzled reticence. I watched her bending to the oven and spreading some gravy around.

Dori was busily moving side to side in the kitchen area and back and forth to the table. She didn't see the stuff with Carol if there was anything there. It was strictly pleasantries. Whether she liked me enough to be jealous, was hard to tell, for she kept those feeling under wraps, in the sense that you could sometimes read her emotions in the clothing she was wearing.

Carol shorts and an orange blouse. Dori, who was doing the intense work, wore splattered jeans and a well-worn, slightly dripping, Wisconsin sweatshirt with a big, smiling Bucky Badger, in mid-strut, on it'

When Carol moved, she jingled. She wore a charm bracelet with small letters of the alphabet. Was she a Teacher? She had an emerald ring on her middle finger of her left hand and a ruby ring on the middle finger of her right. Was that for the Dinner? Not flashy, not subdued, just right.

Dori rarely wore jewelry. There's a simple necklace she favored. An old-fashioned white Cameo of a young woman's profile, set against a deep blue background.

Carol and I began setting the table. "Mixed dishes," she smiled, "Some of Dori's, some of mine." Dori came by, wiping her hands on a towel and gave us a fatigued look. She placed a CD into the Computer. Bill Evans Jazz Piano, relaxing and contemplative music. I sent an OK sign to Dori and she reciprocated with a wink.

"I'm going to change into a Hostess outfit," she announced, and went back into a bedroom nook and stretched out a colorful Japanese partition for privacy.

"Napkins," Carol cries jubilantly, waving a wad of decorate cloth napkins in front of me, as if they were instruments for keeping the uncouth civilized. She artfully folded them at each place, her charms tinkling merrily.

"Classy."

Blondie was with me and after sniffing out the delicious odors and being seriously and warningly eyed by the Dachshunds, sat down next to a wall with a view, and waited. She was glad be here, not waiting at home.

While Dori was changing and becoming immaculate, Carol checked the Turkey and pronounced it "Ready to be Devoured." She lifted it out and laid it meticulously among the colorful mosaic plates of fruits and vegetables. The was gravy, sweet potatoes, cranberries for the rugged, fancy labeled wine, snazzy wine glasses and stuff still covered. Stomachs rumbled approvingly.

The bell rang. Roman was buzzed in

He rushed through the door with his usual anguish. "Someone's following me!" he blurted out breathlessly and dropped down on the nearest chair. Dori and I glanced at each other in familiar exasperation.

"Who's following you," I asked calmly.

"Some tall guy was walking behind me for blocks," he bumbled. "He looked mean."

The buzzer rang. Thirty seconds later Howard walked in.

"That's him. That's the guy." Roman jumped out of his chair, aiming a finger at Howard, who stood motionless at the door.

"It's Howard, he works with me,' I shouted, "He just took the same route."

Roman's features scrunched as he peered at Howard and sat down a bit pacified, but still twitchy and on his guard. Howard's expression was blank, except for his eyebrows clutched and his self, vigilant.

The Dachshunds yapped wildly at this scene. Blondie didn't move, but made a low growl. Roman stared at Howard for a sign. A slight pretense of a smile might have helped, but he remained stone-faced.

Dori was back, ignoring the commotion, and presenting herself in a beautiful and unsurprisingly flowery dress. Compliments were thrown out with gusto. She cheerfully welcomed Howard, who succumbed and smiled. She threw a kiss to Roman, who eagerly grabbed it out of the air.

Howard took a seat, The HotDogs ceased howling, while Blondie wandered over to him to get some pets., which be obliged, relieved to be occupied and befriended. The Chocolates he brought were still on his lap. He handed them to Carol who had been standing on the outskirts, new to our dramas and trying to puzzle it all out. She laid them on the sideboard, away from the heat, where a huge cake box Roman had lugged in.

We were ready to eat, but no Charles.

"I'll phone him," I said to the impatient Dori, who was wanting to show off her cooking prowess.

I reached him. "He's searching for a [parking space."

"In that case," Dori said wryly, "he won't be here 'til dessert."

No one said anything. They toyed with the silverware, refolded napkins, made faces back and forth, stared ravenously at the aging Turkey and helplessly at the banquet of food within arm's reach.

Howard peered out the window, taking in the neighborhood, Carol realigning the refolded napkins, Roman breathing deeply and sneaking wary looks at a disinterested Howard, Dori and I tummy rubbing our dogs and dog.

My phone rang. "Charles finally found a spot. It's five blocks away. He's running."

Everyone perked up. The gastric juices were flowing. Ten minutes later the buzzer sang "Whoopee."

"Sorry I'm late," he apologized briskly, wiping his brow with a creased, wet handkerchief. He was hurriedly introduced around. On his way to the bathroom he dropped a bunch of Tillamook cheese on the table.

"Let's eat!" commanded Chef Dori, ready to slice the Turkey. Carol had brought side dishes and trimmings. The Men offered to do the cutting. But Dori was adamant. It was her show. We assumed eating positions and grabbed our implements of hunger.

Dori proved adept at carving up the Bird they couldn't fly. We gorged, some more than others. It was a Big Bird. Foods. orphaned and lonely at the table only moments before, were adopted in our warm bellies and taste buds and welcomed home.

The wine was working and chatting began.

Carol bubbled up to Howard, who shyly warmed up to her relentless friendliness. While Roman, who was closet in friendship to Dori, was giving her a running account of additions to his Dog Church and crating more incentives to have more people and their dogs to attend Services.

His closing of the Church and recent reclusiveness had upset and even alienated many regulars; some had lost faith in him. He was so necessary.

It didn't help that those at his reopening had to listen to fire and brimstone oratories inflamed by his hatred of the wicked Actor, who still held Molly.

He had to stabilize. He was jeopardizing his calling.

Charles postponed his Turkey jokes. He was sated with a bountiful Dinner. He leaned back in his chair and considered the redness of his Wine.

He had not seen Arcadia and couldn't invite her. Almost in a whisper, trying to be out of earshot of Roman, I filmed him on her unseeming infatuation with the Actor. Roman's head jerked to the side, as if he picked up an unpleasant smell.

"With the Actor?" Chares blurted out, sending Roman into paroxysm of rage, quickly stifled by Dori's steely look and a firm cautionary hand on his shoulder.

"Drop it," she urged, consolingly. He controlled himself with tight fists and quieted down. Poor Roman. The beating he got from 'Fingers,' {If you excuse the Thanksgiving analogy] knocked the stuffing out of him.

Dori had filled in Carol on Roman's fragility and, I likewise, prepared Howard not to be surprised if Roman 'lost it.'

The surprise was to see Howard smiling. Carol was facing him and I watched the back of her blonde head shaking in excited talk, her charms coordinating to the musical charms on her wrist.

Whatever she was saying, it was probably the jolly way she said it that brightened Howard. Yes, the world can still be a happy place, she insisted. Howard's full frame melted from the spray of sunshine into his gray life. It lost its rigidness. He slid down, slumping in his chair. If anyone could pry his crimes out of him, Carol had the inside track.

Charles was rattling off a bunch of untried mordant jokes. They did not go over. It felt like a smudge on the evening. He needed a very tipsy, very edgy, very black-humored crowd.

Roman had settled in safe self-absorption, distractingly playing with the Dachshunds who had gathered around him. They vied for his uplifting touch.

Coffee was poured and a two-tiered cake with icing in the shape of a Great Dame was unveiled. It was huge. Two or three slices each would not diminish its stature. Applause for Roman. Generous portions from a generous man.

Indulgence was the keyword. The chocolatey and creamy cake swelled many a belly, temptation at its most fulfilling. Roman came out of his reverie, ate cake, sipped coffee and even smiled in the comfort of his surroundings; his fear of Howard mitigated, as Howard pleasantly thanked him for the delicious dessert.

Charles and I planted our behinds and protruding stomachs on the couch, heavily sinking in with a relaxing groan. Carol resumed reciting her autobiography to Howard who was content to patiently listen. Roman snoozed in a Lounger and Dori and the Gang of Four surveyed the scene with a satisfied smile.

Clean-up. Disrupting the tranquility. Half-hour of communal business. We contemplate dirty pots and dishes. But we expose them to hot water and soap and pads, leaving our minds clearer.

Back on the job.

I tried to talk Howard into adopting a dog. He was not against it, but not for it.

"Maybe later," he said as an afterthought.

I nudged him into paying a visit to the Park. He'd see the fun being around dogs, lightening your being. It would give some sense of Community. Though, he never brought up what he did on his own time. He could be part of a Church, a Fellowship, a local bar/pub. He kept things to himself, but I guess he couldn't keep it in when he confided his 'fondness' for Carol. A neutral word of the heart. That was the last I heard of it. Maybe he wanted me to pass it on to Carol through Dori.

Two weeks later he showed up in the Park on a shivery Saturday morning. The dogs were playing like rascals and a pale sun did little to soften the cold blasts of wind that buffeted our bundled up bodies.

Howard seemed ennured to the icy wind. He wore a light windbreaker over a woodsman flannel shirt.

"The cells were rarely heated," he explained, with mirthless nostalgia.

He enjoyed meeting and playing with all the dogs. They saw him as a newcomer with possible treats. I thought of the walks Dori and I went on without the dogs. Dori wasn't so wisecracking and I wasn't so ironic. It wasn't quite intimate but certainly more cozy and relaxing.

My thoughts suddenly veered from dreamy to wide awake. The Actor, with his flunky, "Fingers," walking behind him with Molly on a taut leash was heading straight at us with provocative, jaunty steps.

The Actor liked to command attention with his villainous sneer. It always worked. He got his needed Boos and Hisses and Hissed back in competition.

They passed within ten feet of us. Howard and 'Fingers,' traded venomous looks of contempt. Howard's fists clenched, 'Fingers' made claws of his unholy, long fingers and lethal nails. He pointed and thrust them at Howard. If 'Fingers' hadn't kept moving, Howard would have lunged at him. Hatred seared 'Fingers' cold face. Out of range, he put fingers to his lips and sent Howard a taunting smile.

Inmates together.

The Actor and his flunky, with Molly in tow turned up Steiner and out of sight. Howard dropped his anger. I hesitated to fuel it by asking his connection to 'Fingers.'

He sat down on the bench and applied his lingering tension to giving Blondie a vigorous body rub with lit up her eyes with pleasure Dogs and people who had drifted away drifted back. 'Fingers' was reviled. Sympathy was with Howard.

No one approached him even as people were happy to see him face down 'Fingers.' They saw him as a man who spoke deliberately, without ornament or obscurantism, very disciplined in his manner. They read him as an ex-Military man.

My concern turned to Arcadia. Where was she? On stage? In a Movie? Was she OK? The only connection I had was through the Tuna Fish director at the House in the Avenues. Thinking of her with the vain Actor and the vile 'Fingers,' made my thoughts black.

"Hey, Beamer, a familiar voice called out. It was the General, coming to me in a rush. He wore a bulky coat, supposedly covering his bemedaled uniform, to keep people from being awed. I had the urge to peek under the coverings that went down to his ankles.

"I saw what happened," he said, breathlessly and hot, though not about to open his coat. "Nasty," he wheezed, with the authority of someone who has seen many nasty things. He looked down at Howard for acknowledgement but he got none. Howard was in his solitude, continuing to rub Blondie as if the rest of us had vanished, and this was his task for eternity, like an ancient Greek Myth come to life.

When we were back at work, Howard said nothing about it. He had buried it in his underground vault which seemed crammed with secrets.

The days were slow and we spent time keeping the Store spotless and all merchandise in order. We challenged each other with Baseball trivia and guessing the approximate lifetime averages of players randomly pulled up from the card racks. We even bantered about Politics and cheap Philosophy. When it came to Politics, Howard blistered.

"They are Salesmen who should be selling from inside a cell."

"Some must be trying to do good."

"Not the ones I met," he added, caustically.

"You were involved in Politics?" I asked, keeping the surprise to myself.

"A man with the sun shining in his face, should not go into it blind," he winked with flip sagacity.

"Our discussion closed as customers came worshipfully into the Store. We both smiled our conscientious, open, knowledgeable, trusting smiles and sold some stuff.

The gift season was upon us and the lukewarm business embers need some stoking. The Owner advertised in newspapers and magazines. No lavish spreads, just reminders of the Season.

The Theme was that Sports Gear made an ideal gift. The store was pulsating with deals. Bobble heads were bobbling. Cleats were tapping, baseball were bounding, bats were clacking and Salesmen were touting. It only lacked customers. Baseball was in limbo. But we were still ready for the big Xmas rush. We installed rolls and rolls of cheery Xmas wrap, edges to be sealed with embossed stickers, bearing the Store name.

We stood ready.

While Howard and I were lazily toying with the merchandise, and idly joking with browsing customers, Dori was swamped by the invasion of flower buyers. It happened that an icon of Taste proclaimed a house was not truly a Home, without a profusion of pricey flowers.

I learned this when Dori came to the Park in a state of rumpled fatigue, never letting the dogs off leash, worried she wouldn't have the energy to run after them. She did her stumbling best to take care of their outdoor needs. She fial came to a crashing rest where Blondie and I were having a mute conversation with our eyes.

"Phew," her tired, pebbly voice squirted.

"I can see."

"Not a flower left," she panted. "It was a whirlwind." Her four dogs' eager to play sat down reluctantly next to her. They nipped at each other. Blondie, off-leash, her tail wagging in friendship was accustomed to their brazenness and settled next to them fur to fur. Licks were exchanged.

It was contagious. I patted Dori's knee to soothe her and since her hands were occupied with leashes, she put her head on my shoulder for a moment until she was tugged away.

We got to chatting flowers, neighbors, dogs and then out of the blue:

"I don't know what you see in her?" she said, snappishly.

My thoughts were still gliding along on her blithe, color descriptions of her favorite flowers when suddenly skidded into a mud hole.

"Huh! What! Who! Me?' I croaked.

"Did I ambush you?" she fretted, without a hint of meaning it.

I rolled out of the mud stained by a substance I knew nothing about.

"Arcadia." She plunked down the name like a trump card. "Do you dream of her?"

"I was worried about her in the hands of the Actor and "Fingers.'

She said nothing. She read the expression on my face.

"You've never met her."

"Are you and Howard overwhelmed with customers like I am?" she said plainly.

I shook the mud off, at least most of it.

"Depends on the size of the occasional straggler who sidles in from the Football department."

Dori's eyes flickered warningly, "One day your facetiousness will get you a punch in the nose."

"You are a sharp cookie," I said admiringly.

"You're even sharper, she returned, "You're full of Walnuts."

"Those flowers you hang out with give you a scents of humor."

She looked straight into my eyes. "I can sure smell a bad joke."

"Shall we cut the palaver," I conceded. "You win."

"As I should," she said, jauntily. "You're only interested in dumb Baseball."

A brush back pitch. "I hope you put a capital letter at the front of that word."

"Gotta feed the dogs," she said, scrupulously. "Then get some rest. I'm bushed."

I said nothing about Bush Leagues. I watched Dori unwind her intertwined leashes with a patient dexterity I could never match.

"See ya," she smiled, reining in her boisterous buddies.

"See ya," I smiled, a little sadly.

I bought Blondie back home, put out her food, watched her eat it and when she was done, washed the dish, left her with an 'I'll be back later chew bone and pet, boarded the "N" to the Outer Sunset and the House where the Tuna Fish, aka Arcadia, last performed.

I rapped with the ancient brass knocker and waited. Lights were shining dully from the ground floor window, through a smudgy coat of cleaning solution, I guessed.

I waited some more. I moved away from the front door and tried to peek into the room. But the window was too high. The door creaked open. "Who's there?' a harsh voice sounded. I stepped back into her sight. It was the Director's Mother. I hastily said: "It's Beamer. I met you at the Fish Play. I helped you clean up."

Her color returned as she scrutinized me, head to toe and screwed up her mobile features to help her memory.

"You do look familiar," she decided, and made a small contrite smile.

"I've come to speak to your son, is he here?"

"He's here. He's eating." She was ready to shut the door.

"I'm sorry to interrupt," I said to her, despite a vague appeal in my eyes. I made a movement to leave.

"No. No," she protested. "It's not very lively here. Come in. Come in," now insisting, her smile brightening. "Have some Home Cooking."

I accepted with a dignified bow. "That's very generous."

She waved me through the door and told me to pull up a chair, which I did, which I did, opposite the ravenously eating Director.

"Dig in," she said with great encouragement as she put down a wide plate, with some rustic silverware, filling my plate with pot roast and browned potatoes. No niceties needed here.

The Director looked up at me with a mouthful of food, nodded at me, chewing vigorously, swallowing and then stuffing in another mouthful.

"He loves your cooking," I said, making conversation, starting on my own portion. Inhaling it.

"He'd better," she said, with Motherly approbation, watching him gobble it up while pushing my plate closer to my mouth. I suspect the gobbler was a spiller. "Don't forget the vegetables," she sweetly scolded. She even put them on my plate, even though I was a guest.

The Director responded to his dear Mother's injunction with a guttural son-like sound that pleased her. She apologized to me for his terrible eating habits but didn't deplore them. He was home. The Original Stomach never forgets.

I ate with gusto. Between mouthfuls, his and mine, I tried to speak to the Director. No luck. It wasn't until he gnawed down his last bone, wiped off hi last food stain, belched his last salutary belch, hid his last vegetable in the paper napkin, that I could finally engage his jittering attention.

He was no longer the upbeat, witty man I met at rehearsal. His production was a wreck, but he seemed more confused than devastated. The Wall Street mentality did not change.

"The Critics were very unkind," he informed me with placid conviction. I stared at him in disbelief. He was an intelligent man with terrific blind-spot

"It was a failure," he contradicted himself. "But I've got an original idea for a new play."

"I lost track of Arcadia," I cut in, "Do you know what she's up to?"

"Arcadia?" He broke off his meandering, lifted his eyes to the sky blue ceiling and shut them in thought.

"Yes." Yes," the pretty girl who played the Tuna Fish." He opened his eyes and furrowed his brow.

"Have you seen her?"

"I can't find the fish suit,' He complained in a grating voice.

"If you find it, add electric seels, it'll galvanize interest in your Play."

The sarcasm bounced off.

"Interesting."

"So?" I pressed amiably, "What about Arcadia?"

The Mom of us all had departed to watch TV.

"To be honest," he pretended to cringe, "I was knocked out by the ridicule of the Play." He jumped out of his chair. "I spent a lot of time and money and it never even got to the end."

"You didn't know what was coming!?"

"The abduction of Arcadia wasn't part of the script," he said bluntly.

"I know now. But nobody knew at the time.

"It was that Actor guy who arranged it." He said with bitter anger.

"Speaking of Arcadia," I tried for a final time, "Have you heard from her? Do you know where she is?"

"I have no idea."

I was ready to leave when his Mom returned and placed a glistening homemade apple pie in front of us. I thanked her for the delicious roast, as the Director and I gave the pie a warm welcome to our stomachs.

After some strong coffee, I took one more shot.

"Do you have a network with other playwrights you can contact?"

"I'm independent."

My frustrations were rising to belligerence. "So how do you get Actors?!"

"Through my assistant," he answered calmly, barely aware of the original question. So much for fine-tuning my interview.

He sat impassive. I sat explosive.

"What's your name again?" he asked in a friendly. yet formal way.

"Beamer."

"Bea...mer," he cogitated on the name, and pronounced it painstakingly as if it was from some unknown language. "Beamer," he addressed me, "I think you were immoderate."

I overlooked what I felt was an insult and reminded him, "I'm just worried about Arcadia."

I told him the story of the parades through the Park. Being in the same house as 'Fingers. I should have mentioned it earlier.

Strain crumpled the Director's smooth features. "I didn't know," he said, disconcerted, rubbing fingers back and forth across his forehead. "I'm sorry for being callous."

"Okay."

"What can I do."

While I was thinking how he could help, he gave me a look that from anyone else would be a smirk. From him it came off like a delicate inquiry.

"Are you in love with her?"

"That's not the reason," I answered coolly

"You deflected the question," he said shrewdly.

"Let's call it affection and concern."

"I'll but that for now," he said, amused.

"The abduction was not part of the play."

"Certainly not."

"It boils down to the performance. Was the abduction real or was it faked? If it was faked, then Arcadia isn't so innocent. If it was real, why would the Actor jeopardize his fame and career to pull a stunt like that? "I'm sure he has a fair measure of sanity and can't imagine his flunky talking him into it."

"She was absorbed in being the best Tuna Fish she could be."

"I wonder if she knew the Actor before then?" I suggested.

The Director shrugged his shoulders. "If you ask me," he denounced firmly, "It was a dastardly prank." Of course, a term from the old villain movies. The guy had a sense of humor. "Why would a well-known Actor commit an overtly criminal act in front of an audience."

"It's implausible," I said. "Maybe he was trying to undermine your Play. Could he have lost money in your Company, built up a grudge and gone after you?"

"Ridiculous." he snapped, "You're grasping at air."

"Just covering all the angles."

"You have more angles than a Stealth Jet."

An apt word, I thought.

"If you will excuse me," he announced cordially, standing up. "I have to do some financial work."

We exchanged cards and he told me encouragingly, that he would try to seek information from his sources and get back to me if he had any news to tell.

He had his hand on the front doorknob, when I said: "One more thing." His business wavered a bit in impatience, "Sure."

"Did Arcadia have any resentment towards you as Director and Writer?"

"You are kidding," he laughed. "All I told her was to put on the Fish suit, wriggle around and act scared." He opened the door. "A prank. Definitely."

His reassurance drifted off into the cool, dark evening. The door closed behind me and I walked into the dimly lit streets.

I called Charles.

"I need your talents."

"Yes. Tell me."

I put it succinctly. "Is Arcadia in the Actor's House."

I could almost hear his sharp, devious mind clicking away.

"Hmm.... What if I was from rag and asked him if he was shacking up with a broad named Arcadia?"

"As long as I don't have to pay to fix your nose."

"Not subtle," he muttered. "What if I showed up as President of his fan club and wanted to do an interview?"

"Who'd believe it?"

"Not me," he admitted, "But I'm just fooling around. "Now," he said expansively, "I'm inspired!"

"Keep going."

"What if I," he said sedately, "In the disguise of a distinguished business man pretended to represent a Billionaire who wanted to buy his House for ten million bucks?"

"Who'd swallow that?"

He hesitated for emphasis and added. "His family once lived in the House and for nostalgic reasons, cost no object."

I was not convinced.

"The hook is...." Charles crept up to it.... "Is... that he needs to know the interior is unchanged. I have to show them photographs." He paused. "Am I sizzling!?"

"Clever. It seems reasonable. But still...."

"Reason has nothing to do with it," he shot back, "Easy greed trumps feeble reason. He may be immune. He may be a sucker." He turned practical. "Any money in it," he asked, dubiously.

"Doubt it."

"Oh, well. Good for my resume."

"Don't forget to list con-man as one of your attributes."

"Thanks for the praise. Remember, I was the Mayor."

Charles was tall, had a believable face, a disarming manner and a sincere voice. If he offered someone the Brooklyn Bridge, they'd consider it. He was quick. I watched him perform a few times and once when a joke went flat, he went silent. His nose started twitching madly as if the joke gave off a bad odor and he disciplined it with a few soft whacks, which got laughs.

"Despite my masterful impersonations and inimitable charm," Charles. Observed. "We are dealing with another Actor, recognizing another Actor." He abandoned his braggadocio: "I may not be able to pull it off. Like you said, he'd be pretty dumb to swallow it."

I felt let down. His confidence buoyed me. But the idea did seem stupid, especially with the crazy 'Fingers' hanging around. I had forgotten about that danger.

"If you think it's too risky or ridiculous, don't do it."

Charles was deflated. The obstacles got the better of him. The mention of 'Fingers' and the beating he inflicted on Roman carried weight.

"Okay," answered me without a qualm.

"The Director said he'd try, with his limited contacts, to locate her somewhere in the City or beyond."

"Good," His cheerfulness returned. "Gotta walk the dog,"

"Don't do it," I cautioned him.

"Ciao."

Blondie and I walked through the Panhandle and into Golden Gate Park. I was troubled by my rashness in asking Charles to go on a foolish mission where he could get hurt. He tacitly declined, but he was a guy who liked a challenge and was doing a good deed. He was not predictable.

A long walk would help my worry and also stimulate the brain juices. Good exercise for Blondie, eagerly pulling toward endless gopher holes. The road was closed to auto traffic. The Skaters and the Runners and the bicyclists went by in their voiceless solitude. There was a certain relaxed quietude and enjoyment that followed the crowd. In San Francisco terms: People in their own space, doing their own thing. Which reminded me of Charles who did his own thing, but was not usually reckless. Was he thinking: 'I can outwit the Actor and his flunky.'

Comedians have no sense, except non-sense.

We walked along, passing people in the good mood atmosphere. It happened that a very good looking woman glided by and gave me a warm smile, which I returned on cue. It gave me a boost.

Twenty paces later another beauty approached and emboldened me to give her my cheeriest smile. She returned it with an acid stare that dissolved my smile and my self-confidence. Such is the world. Kismet to Bubkes in Twenty paces.

We kept walking, but I was more circumspect about throwing my smile around. Our destination was Stowe Lake, a favorite spot.

If you were the size of an Ant, you might legitimately call it a Lake. If you were a Giant you'd call it a small pond. Lake sounds more impressive. Unless it was discovered by an extremely small Explorer.

We walked leisurely around the Lake. Blondies barking scattered the Ducks who lolled at the water's edge, but she drew back as the fly less, fat Geese, with their long, twisty necks and serrated bills, advanced toward her with belligerent honks.

'We headed back home and bumped into a parade in single file carrying signs saying "BEWARE!" We stopped, along with others, to watch them pass. They chanted "BEWARE" in chilly unison, synchronized with a drum beat.

"Beware of what," I asked a very tall, angular guy who was straddling his bicycle.

"No one knows," he cracked with a dismissive shrug of his narrow shoulders. "There are several groups of them going around the City."

Even though this was SF, a city of nuttiness, people were befuddled and speculation flew around.

"Maybe some Company is pushing a product," said an older woman pulling a shopping cart filled with laundry. "Like a roach killer."

"An advertising gimmick," another lady agreed.

"Maybe a new dance," quipped a teenage girl wearing headphones.

"It's just a hoax," a shout carried over. "To whip-up hysteria. Frighten us."

"Or they want to annihilate humanity," a kid on a scooter festooned with skeleton heads, sniveled morbidly.

In the meantime, we were walking along with the marchers. They moved unbudging and in formation to the watchers' consternation at not getting any responses to the comments and questions hurled in their direction.

"They're brainwashed!" someone yelled out and were nods of agreement.

Blondie had her say. She growled and barked at the eerie spectacle. Her salvo did little to discourage them. Instead she started a frenzied digging after a gopher.

"Stop digging!" I said in a commanding voice. It not penetrates her obsession. I finally had to yank her and her snout out from the hole. How many times have you told a dog not to do something? It's wasted breath. You tell them a thousand times, hoping they'll get it on the thousandth and first time.

We followed behind the Marchers at a safe woofing distance, until Stanyon, where they turned right, next to turn left onto Haight, where they, in their protest, would get a rousing reception, though the reason for their protest would remain unknown.

Blondie and I went straight into the Panhandle, the narrow strip of grass and trees with paths on either side. Another Gopher Paradise. She was unleashed and darted right to the upturned clods of dirt and began her furious and lawless digging.

Blondies snout in the hole obstinacy set against my floundering patience made going through the Panhandle a slow, ragged, stop and go, leashed and unleashed trip I always vowed not to do again, but always gave in to her excitement coming here.

We made it through. Blondie with a dirt smeared snout and me with relief.

Back in my Park, I discovered that the "BEWARE!" procession was a stunt contrived by a movie studio to promote an upcoming film titled: "BEWARE.

The Actor had a featured role playing an out-of-character soft-hearted, bumling crook who mistakenly double-crosses the Mob. Itis to be filmed in San Francisco with the hometown Actor known to the City as "a beloved citizen and benefactor of Sf who unstintingly donated his precious time to worthy causes, such as encouraging budding young actors and actresses and his loving commitment to all Animal shelters." Ahem.

"BEWARE! meant to beware of your stomach hurting from laughing at the Actor's comedic antics." Ick.

As word spread that the film was set in SF, we wondered if a scene or two would be set in Duboce Park, since the Actor lived nearby and occasionally brought his stolen dog and his obnoxious personality here. No inside dope on that.

In the meantime, Baseball season was creeping up as the year turned. Next month was spring training. Howard and I were getting prepared.

"How was your Christmas."

"Spiritual," he replied, in his laconic manner.

"Get a visit from Santa?"

"Not since I was a kid." He shrugged off the memory. Then he added cheerily: "I bought myself a gift."

"What did you get?"

"I haven't opened it yet," he said brightly.

"But you know what it is."

"I don't know 'til I open it New Year's Eve." He looked at me with a confounding grin.

My brain wobbled. He basked in my puzzlement.

"I went to an Electronics store: I like gadgets and asked a female clerk to pick out a gift for Fifty bucks. I won't look. Wrap it up in fancy paper. "I'll buy it and put it away."

I watched him keenly, then with frowning appreciation. It seemed sad, yet lofty. "Did you write a nice card to yourself?"

"The usual platitudes."

"Will there be a ceremonial opening of the present?"

"Coinciding with the opening of several Belgian beers."

"That's part of the fun."

"It's a heightened experience," He mocked, with a dampened voice. "I'll let you know what I got."

"Can't wait."

The bouncy bantering dribbled away as w retired to our allotted tasks in the Store called, "Batter Up." which sounds like a bakery.

The night always arrived punctually at five pm, carrying a tome that he plunked down on the counter with a thud as if reclaiming his territory.

He's a skinny guy, maybe thirty, with the trademark black horn-rimmed glasses, dark shaggy hair flopping over his forehead. He's always freshly shaven with incongruous hairy hands. He clomped around on shoes that made him sound like a horse.

The tome was a very used Baseball Encyclopedia, which skims at quiet times and has made him a fount of Baseball trivia. He's an avid fan, but his sometimes severe expression, his neat but drab monotone clothing, his hauling around the large book and an upward looking philosophical air, one might take him for a religious scholar.

He supplies Howard and me with baseball minutia, which is too obscure for the most fanatical Baseball nut. Who led the league in triples in 1922? He'd spout statistics at us at he came into the door and throw out batting averages as we exited for the day.

He was from the Midwest. He never got more exact. He grew up with Bibles in every room. You never knew when sin might hit you. He occasionally flicked his fingers at an invisible something. A tic? An imaginary Satan hovering? He kept quiet about it, no sends advertising incipient insanity.

But his intensity and ardor for Baseball and its merchandise made up for his oddness. According to the Boss, who benefited from fans' obsessions, Ezekiel was "Eccentric."

We called him "Zeke" to his minor displeasure. He liked to be formal. Customers were "Sir" and "Madam," and he gracefully bowed to the Japanese who came into the Store to peruse the goods.

If the homilies he grew up with, passed on gratuitously to us, were transferred to Baseball, he'd preach:

"Keep your bats clean, don't spit in your glove, be respectful Umpires don't kick the dirt, always blow kisses to the other teams' fans and especially, be careful of bad language.

This would only work in Fantasy Baseball.

Zeke moved through the Store from half-asleep to a sudden, darting jerky quickness and then within a minute he was back in his snooze mode. It was as if he were plugged into an energy machine that alternately fizzled and exploded. It might have unnerved the customers, but it was just him, just being, a colorful San Francisco character who was performing for the tourists. His diligence, honesty and Baseball acumen made up for his weirdness.

Across the street in front of Aquatic Park, where local craft artists are lined up to sell their products, other interesting personalities have passed through.

A hatless, hairless thick-chested man with a wild expression and wilder gestures, broadcast impromptu tirades of the American monetary system, complete with ripping off his shirt and showing a large green '$' tattooed on his chest and trying to push it into the faces of people passing him.

He was finally chase off by the street merchants only to end up in front of our Store, where he then displayed his butt, with pennies scotched-taped to it and a tattoo: "I am incensed."

A Cop was approaching from down the block. He flew a few packets of phony bills in the air, declared himself a litterbug, hauled himself off, gripping his own collar, never to be seen again.

Then was the short, hen-pecked sort of guy who set up a poster board of famous people he would impersonate, for a buck.

As George Washington, clacking his ivory teeth, he proclaimed it was an honor to have a Bridge named after him.

As Noah, he stood on the deck of the Ark holding his nose, and imploring God: "Shovels!" "Shovels!"

He never impersonated anyone who was alive after 1800.

Most recently, a Ventriloquist showed up a vulgar mouthed Dummy who made offensive remarks to passing women, under the pretense of Double-Entendres and laughed when they slapped the ventriloquist. The Ventriloquist then slapped the Dummy for laughing him and they exchanged filthy smears which the Dummy returned to the Women. It was crude, circuitous attempt at humor, which eventually got the Ventriloquist a needed hard slap in the face. It was his debut and final performance across the street.

Then, more sanely was an older man who opened his folding chair and started blowing into a silvery Harmonica, a tin cup in front of him and to his side a neatly tied up bedroll and a lumpy orange small backpack.

He wore the same red ball cap over the same narrowed circumspect eyes and a mouth pinking out from coils of a gray beard. I'd pass him when I brought my bag lunch to eat in the Park. His mournful songs were a poignant contrast to the frivolous, bustling activity of the street.

When I stuffed a dollar into his cup, he quickly snatched it up and gave me a plangent smile. Then, a cunning grin, a twitching eye and stomping boot, the Harmonica burst into a riotous jig, beckoning others to drop in coins, before relapsing into another sad melody. A bill made him go cuckoo and cents restored him to apathy. He stuck around.

Work calls, but it is a grumpy voice! It is not the shrill, mechanical alarm, that you can easily heave across the room. This voice comes from inside your head and will not shut up. It finds allies in the blankness of the eyes, the posture of the nose, the buzzing of the ears and the slippery hands. As much as I like Baseball, I prefer it to be fun, not work.

Jobs can have a sequence. You learn the Job. You master the Job. You are bored with the Job. How long you stay on the job depends on how long each sequel lasts. Also, job calls to mind "Job" in the Old Testament, who suffered mightily.

"I'm tired of my job," I complained to Dori as we sat together watching a half-Sun dip behind Buena Vista Hill.

"I thought you loved your job!" Her hands were fumbling with her jacket zipper as the temperature dipped with the disappearing Sun.

"It's boring." I slickly zipped up my own jacket.

She stared at me as if I was speaking 'Goose.'

"Do you like yours?"

"I do."

"Don't you get tired of selling the same old flowers every day?"

"Flowers are beautiful."

"But you sell them."

"It is hard to part with them," she said sadly.

"Do you think they'll find a nice home?" I said ruthlessly. I never get emotional over a Baseball card, unless, of course it was worth a lot of money.

"Do you speak to them?"

"They are not plants," she clued me in, sharply.

"So flowers are dumb?"

"In the sense they don't speak, they are dumb," she retorted.

"They smell good."

"Perfume."

"You smell good."

"Hanging around flowers."

Dori was leaning slightly forward, watching her fingers fidgeting with the tasseled ends on her red and white scarf, a wistful smile appeared on her lovely face, the sudden sense of her vulnerability roused a tenderness in me.

I put my hand on the back of her hand. She turned her slightly and yawned. I took that to be a good sign. Her other hand came over onto mine. Then lifting it and then the rest of her body, she departed with a snappy wave.

A dog name Sarah, a tan Pug jumped into my lap. I started petting her while watching Dori leave the Park. If nothing is jangling, you don't hear them coming. They plop down on me as if I were a reserved seat. Poundage is a factor.

When I'm sitting on a bench, and a large dog with a madly waving tail and open mouth comes bounding towards me at too many miles per hour, intending to nestle itself on less than beefy legs, I deflect its course in midair, with a deft, stiff push and direct it back to the concrete with accompanying strong words of discouragement which rarely last for long in floppy or stuck-up ears.

A fellow of grimy girth lay down on the bench next to me and conked out. A pungent odor wafted over me. He stunk'

Not having a wind shifting machine handy, but having the option of moving, I moved to a bench at the top of the dog area, next to the one where the General sat.

He stood at my approach and offered his hand. He was wearing his Great Coat that covered his never seen General's uniform and medals. He hid it, as he often said, not to awe or embarrass the rest of us. His dog obediently at his side. Blondie went behind the bench and lay on the small patch of grass before the fence.

"You always have such good manners," I smiled back at his smile.

"Where I grew up," he said with a short laugh, "It was too dangerous not to be courteous."

I didn't ask him where he grew up. He didn't answer questions. To him they were only euphonious sounds in the air. How he had congruent conversations with Lannie, baffled me.

He spoke while he bent down to make sure the length of his coat reached to his socks. "I hear there is going to be Movie made in the Park?"

"A scene, anyway."

"With that Actor guy?" He glanced back toward Buena Vista with a scowl.

"Yep."

"He's no picnic, but that buddy of his is very spooky." He rubbed his hand briskly across his still dark stubble. "I do not spook easily." The

General looked straight into my eyes. "I have known to be obdurate in that direction."

His black shoes had their usual lustrous shine and his short-cut hair stood at rigid attention above dark, examining eyes which contrasted sharply with an abundance of impeccably white teeth. I assumed he kept his medals as shiny as his teeth. One moment, he seemed to be on the verge of tearing open his long coat and revealing his Super identity. Instead, he paused, standing erect and glaring past the Park at the misty Oakland hills across the Bay.

On the odd occasion when a poorly buttoned coat flipped open from a gust of wind or he accidently opened a flap when he dug into his pants pocket, it revealed not a uniform, but an ordinary shirt and green slacks. His quick comment was: "I didn't wear my uniform today." He said it with a combination of decorative smile and plain declaration that both mocked and ennobled the illusion.

We stopped talking to watch a trio of small boys with oversized helmets racing their scooters down the path bordering the grass and dog area. Their jubilant voices clashed with the shrill shouts of their anxious Mothers: "Not so fast!" "Not so fast!"

We watched the kids rushing toward the street, the mothers running after in growing panic. The boys abruptly stopped six feet from the curb. They look back, wondering what the commotion was all about.

On the heels of this excitement, the General's features and voice took on a rare unease.

"A strange...thing happened to me...yesterday," he said, tussling with the words.

"What?"

He cocked his head to one side, his eyes without focus

"I was knotting my tie in front of the mirror," he said, as if talking to himself, "and...my reflection...smiled...back at me." He looked at me implacably.

"What's so unusual about that," I looked back at him with an incongruous smile.

"I wasn't smiling...."

My only answer to his confused anguish was to wipe the smile off my face.

"Am I crazy?"

"Imagination can play tricks on you."

He looked at me with a strained grin. "I guess that's what it is."

The General plucked aimlessly at loose threads on his jacket, showing me he was not convinced.

"Have you looked in the mirror since?"

"I'm too nervous."

"You gotta shave."

"Which one of me is gonna bleed," he said, with risible doubt.

I skipped through his hemorrhaging black humor and put it to him:

"Your smiley side got out." It sounded insipid, but for someone who was scrambling for an explanation, it was a motive.

The General was both receptive and resentful. He was aware, Yet the immensity and vain gloriousness of what had happened made him stiffen. He projected a cold, piercing stare.

"That would not become a General," he proclaimed. He could not tolerate dissonance in his personality. "Fiendish," he muttered. He barked orders to his dog Angel. Off they went in step, a wave dragging behind them.

A series of sneezes sounded as a plump middle-aged woman, parked herself on the bench next to mine. Her conspicuous feature was a mound of purplish red hair, tousled by our ubiquitous friend. the Wind. Blondie barked at the sneezes.

"Allergies," she apologized.

"Me too."

"If you're allergic to something," she explained, "They inject you with a bit of the stuff to make you more tolerant." She paused her miniature Poodle, "His name is Shelby." Blondie had no interest as long as I was not petting him. She was calm, but watching.

"I seem to be allergic to money."

"You're allergic to money?" she laughed.

"Or money is allergic to me."

"I doubt it."

"So, if I'm allergic to money," I reasoned, "I should be treated with an injection of money."

"Don't bank on it," she wisecracked, with a gooney grimace, appreciating her own wit. She lifted Shelby on her lap and rolled her hand along his back. "I'm so excited," she burst out vivaciously, now stroking Shelby under the chin, "We are going to have Hollywood in the Park." Blondie's head jerked up in curiosity, then laid back, comfortable on the grass

"The Movie scene," I answered dully, owing to my antipathy for the Actor.

"A whole scene," she marveled. Her body rocked with anticipation, startling Shelby. "With a famous Actor!"

"Semi-famous," I corrected.

"Isn't he the Actor who is always the tough guy?"

"Yep."

"Do you know his name?"

"Nope."

My disdain was lost on her. She plowed away digging up endless Hollywood movie memories.

"He lived in the Area," I interjected.

"He does?!"

"He brings his dog to the Park."

"You're kidding!?"

"I wish I was."

She was busy musing. "I always go to Alamo Park."

"Well, you'll see him soon," I commiserated, coldly.

"I can't wait!" Her voice and body rose exuberant, a big smile on her fleshy face and a big hug for Shelby. Who accepted it basely. "Bye," she fluttered and skipping headed down the path.

Howard was in the crowd and we waved to one another. He was more interested in a face-off with 'Fingers.' Suddenly, with equal recognition, the tension heightened as they glared at each other over the heads of the small, antsy group between them.

The filming began at the corner of Waller and Pierce, when a car driven by the Actor was rammed by a dark ominous, tinted windowed sedan. Shots were fired into the Actor's car. He was hit. The word was out that he had offended the "Boss."

The black car gunned its engine and screeched off with smoking tires. The Actor lay slumped and bleeding in his seat. The shriek of multiple sirens was heard. Police cars and ambulances braked sharply and rescuers piled out. Two police veered off in pursuit of the shooters.

Quickly, the Actor was gently hoisted onto a rolling stretcher and rushed into the Park. One of the nurses running alongside the stretcher was Arcadia, making her motion picture debut.

A Helicopter had magically appeared on the grassy slope, midpark. It had been ferried to the Park earlier on a large flatbed truck. It had no rotors and could only be filmed from the roof down. A man at the back was heavily pumping its rear end to simulate motion, while a giant fan in front created a turbulent wind. A loudspeaker blasted engine and rotor noise to give the Copter dramatic life and urgency. The angle of the filming was to keep an actual Hospital across the street, out of the picture.

The spectators were huddled on the outskirts of the Park and quiet was requested of onlookers mesmerized by the fakery of the scene.

After the Actor was safely bundled aboard, the roar got louder, the shaking and vibrations increased, the wind became a small gale and then the camera averted its eyes as the Copter lifted off in our imaginations, and, I am sure, headed to the well-known trauma center at SF general Hospital. Where the next scene probably takes place.

The machines went dead. There was a roll of applause, followed by a strange numbness. Reality returned, but briefly. The Actor emerged from the Copter, tearing off his blood-soaked outer garment and saluting the crowd. There was sporadic applause for his moving, yet unmoving portrayal of a critically hurt man, wrongly wounded.

He signaled Arcadia. She rushed over and they exchange hugs. "Fingers" stepped in to a few autograph seekers on their best behavior. The Actor modestly signed the requests and the trio walked to their car.

The dogs had been on their best behavior since the start of the action. Now that the event was over and we all returned to our spots in the lower Park, their backed-up yapping and jumping and carrying-ons, while others ardently or disparagingly discussed the scene. WE all agreed, however, that we couldn't wait to see the finished film, highlighting Duboce Park.

After the dogs had their time, people slowly left the Park. I watched the film crew gathering up the props and equipment, and the dismantled Helicopter loaded on the flatbed. It seemed so short a time for the Park to be returned to normal. The only track left was the dark green color sprayed on the browner parts of the grass. Blondie and I took a desultory walk around the neighborhood before going in.

The mail was an impersonal batch of ads and requests for money and news and history magazines I subscribed to because the offers were so good. They are piling up, flipped through.

I put on a favorite CD of Grover Washington Jr. playing sax renditions of famous opera arias, then checked by Email. The one from Roman stood out: "I took Molly back."

The odds that the Actor, through the intervention of angry God, deposited Molly on Roman's doorstep, was infinity to one. He broke in when the Actor and 'Fingers' were filming. That's Big Time for Roman. My thoughts naturally zeroed in on Charles as the mastermind.

In Roman' mind, it was a charitable rescue, only the higher law applies: Save Molly from the influence of Sinfulness. Did I read him right? I sent him a small 'c' congratulations. He answered: "She's back in God's hands."

It's been a week since I left Roman's Email hanging, waiting for explosive news. But it never came. Roman was back in the Park with the giddiness of a kid, as if God descended from Heaven to him a 'Well-Done' pat on the back.

Molly was getting an extra warm reception and was lapping it up, her tail blur. It was good to see Roman finally out of his schizoid lethargy. It was like a Party. I'm surprised Roman didn't bring a two-foot-tall chocolate cake.

The sun made a special appearance, breaking through tight clouds and shiny on the happy reunion. Was it a coincidence, or, as Roman would say later, a sign that God was smiling on his endeavors. Roman was not someone you could dispute; he had God on his side. Or, do you really want to send him off on a religious ramble. He was a likable, generous guy with Prophetic motives. An Evangelist going to the Dogs. He would agree with both descriptions.

"Jumpstart your brain!"

This picturesque demand came rolling out to us from beneath the large Ash tree lined up on the Steiner side of the Park. We could see a lot of blonde hair flowing down the shoulders of a kneeling young woman. Her exhortations were aimed at a young man splayed out on the leafy ground, not moving. Impervious to a barrage of snippy insults.

He made a slight tilt of his head towards the woman, a rapid flicking of his fingers followed by more immobility. The young lady grabbed a canteen and dumped its contents on the guy's head. His body twisted and jerked and he stood up. He reached out and shoved the girl backwards. She lost her footing and slipped to the ground. She kicked out feebly at him as he danced mockingly out of the way.

She then picked up some feathery thing lying at her side and threw it at him. It never arrived. He reached down and pulled up a handful of grass, sprinkled over her hard, frowning face and shouted a jumble of confused words, including "your brain."

A few of us inched closer to the skirmish. The man, in overalls too big for his skinny frame, turned to us with a menacing stare.

"Mind your business!" he bellowed, readjusting a strap that was falling off his shoulder. He picked up a stranded towel, mopped off his dripping head, flung it at us, setting off more frenzied response from the already barking and agitated dog. They were held tightly on leash. We were concerned about the girl, so stood our ground, making sure we and the dogs were conspicuous.

"Stupid dogs," he muttered, as he waved his arms at them and then turned back to the girl. In unrequited retaliation, he picked up a cartoon decorated backpack, unzipped it, hurled its contents in the air with a whooping "Whee!" Splattered jeans, a scarlet sweatshirt and various underthings flew out. He turned it upside down and dumped the remains [Mostly gadgety things and toothbrushes} in a pile at the woman's still recumbent, shoeless feet. Her hands were fists as she rose up, grabbed the backpack, pushed him aside and started retrieving her stuff. Then they were back screaming at each other.

A quiet guy in our group, Malcolm, asked a buddy to hold his dog, Joker, a frisky old Corgi, who was adding his deep voice to the chorus of ruffled dogs.

Malcolm walked slowly and peacefully over to the trees and spoke to the young folks. No one could hear him over the pair's stormy vocals. He raised his voice. No difference. The man and the woman stood a few feet apart, beyond swinging range. As Malcolm's voice to an almost threatening shout, they toned down into a strained peace, unrelated to the outside intrusions.

It looked like they had taken familiar positions during their tirades; that they had played these scenes before, the lines pouring out in a kind of snarling harmony. Hard words slammed across an invisible net. A spontaneous, well-rehearsed for their play and benefit or ours?

In a moment, they collapsed to the ground next to each other, settled down snuggled together. The End.

There can be havoc in the Park. Petty arguments can grow into big bangs as the parties become more obstreperous and belligerent owing to Dogs' behaviors, magnified by the owners.

A man's dog made a deposit. He didn't pick it up. A woman walking by with her toddler, asked him to clean it up. She didn't want her child stepping in the stuff. He refused, stating defiantly that in his Country the city picked it up. It was not his obligation. The woman, disgusted, fired back that in this city it was the Law. He would have none of it. He turned back and started walking away. The woman yelled at him. He turned back and told her to pick it up herself. He stood there looking at her with contemptuous equanimity. It made us more furious, her face contorting, her eyes murderous, ready to knock his unbudging form back over the waters.

Imagine one country's President's dog wandering over the border and pooping in another President's country, and the first President retaliating by bringing his dog to the border and encouraging it to go over and even things up. One recrimination after another was leading to the brink of war. The dogs of war were national heroes, their butts enshrined.

The presidents sent threatening letters to each other, cheered on by the populaces, truly insulted. It was a matter of national honor. Each asked the other to clean up after their dog, each adamantly refused. It was a very nervous time.

Duke's people carried his likeness on flags and posters across the country. Sir Thomas' fans walked on four legs in homage to his bravery. They were the most poop-ular dogs in the two realms.

Each country's citizens held up plaster models of the enemy dogs and ridiculed them in public forums. They were demonized in the media. The high religious courts chimed in and revoked the belief that all dogs go to Heaven. The areas of the original poop were declared unholy ground. The UN tried to intervene but were rebuffed. This was personal.

Huge fences went up along the borders, Dog trespassing signs proliferated, was there a peaceful solution to this escalating conflict. One enterprising person offered a solution. John, a local farmer, always envisioned a world without uncrossable borders.

The Presidents, not wanting war; the lack of trading ruining both countries, making them desperate for reconciliation without degradation. Listened to him. His long-winded proposal turned out to be a confounding and brain-reeling idea of concentric circles of land.

Hailed as revolutionary by the Artistic community and crackpot by The Real Estate Alliance, it made the rounds. Politicians demolished it and Politicians extolled it.

"It's an insult to the rights of private property," decried one newspaper. "It's as innovative as Democracy," lauded its rival. "It can only lead to blood-letting," "It will put the World on a new path to equality," others ramped up the discussion.

The debate raged. It was too late for implementation. The Presidents were still at odds. If the Presidents themselves could agree to "surmount the hostility," there was hope for rapprochement "Let them rise above resentment," "Truncate their truculence." 'Doggedly pursue a truce."

There was also advice from everyday people. "Go toe to toe, not ass to ass." "Stuff your pride." and foremost: "Let's make a deal." Both populations now vehemently encouraged both Presidents to meet and resolve the problem.

The Presidents belatedly realizing they were losing the confidence of the people. Their approval ratings once soaring were now plummeting, their political futures in jeopardy, first blamed the other as the culprit, then, overlooking the other's moral deficiencies and with deep, genuine big-heartedness agreed to meet and repair relations in the interest of their beloved constituencies.

The peoples of both countries let out loud guffaw and rejoiced. Instead of being tired and stressed out, people criss-crossed each other's borders to celebrate together in anticipation of going back to the ancient friendship of the two land. There was reveling in the streets and patriotic music blaring from the windows.

The Presidents, alternatively grave and beaming, sat down with each other informally on leather lounge chairs with their dogs Duke and Sir Thomas on their laps, hopefully dispelling the gravity of the situation. Their meeting was televised and broadcast in prime time across both nations. People, of course, were practically hugging their TVs and radios, awaiting for the good news.

At a signal, the Presidents offered sincere, smiling faces as the camera rolled over them and the antsy dogs on their laps. They spoke their short, condescending speeches, and praise the agreement that would soon set things straight, they shook hands and even hugged. "Hurrahs" rang out in the audience and joy suffused their respective lands.

At their feet the two dogs sniffed each other and rollicked on the floor. Then there was a moment when everybody looked down. Sir Thomas was humping Duke. Dukes, President was outraged. Uhuh.

The wind punched its way through the Park, leading with a few cuffing lefts that rustled the trees and set the branches crackling. It heaved some body blows, toppling an almost empty garbage bin, knocking off hats, dusting eyes and with cool caresses ruffled the dense fur of the dawdling dogs, who lifted their twitching noses to the menu of airborne smells, while people pinched noses to keep things out.

"Been lookin' for you," the Actor said, with his trademark tight, sardonic smile. "Came for a dog and reimbursement for a broken window," he added, with a suggestive nod at 'Fingers.'

'Fingers' sized us up as if we were bowling pins waiting to be knocked down.

"Well." said Roman obligingly, "I want to make sure she has her toys. I need to call someone to bring them."

The Actor scrutinized Roman's blank face. "Okay," he finally said, "But make it snappy."

What? Capitulation? No fight?

Roman pulled out his dog decorated cellphone from his jacket, tapped in some numbers, waited for the connection and spoke a few words. He replaced the phone with a flourish. His nerves, usually jangling with the Actor around, didn't have one jangle. Did he have a mental breakdown?

He sat down on the grass and raise his eyes to the Actor who was standing ten feet away. "In the meantime he intoned importunely, "Let me say a goodbye prayer for Molly." The Actor's reaction was to kick at some sticks on the ground, while 'Fingers' crunched is knuckles and flexed a muscle or two for effect.

Roman began to loudly sing-song a prayer in what sounded like Latin and throwing in harsh asides that sounded like curses in gibberish.

The Actor was increasingly impatient. Fifteen minutes had passed and Roman was still mumbling a stream of sly holiness.

"We're gonna take the dog and then turn you two into mush," The Actor pronounced, with great resonance, taking a tentative step forward. Roman stayed calm. Instead of defiance, he reached out to reassure Molly, who looked warily at the Actor and gave me a sidewise wink.

The Actor glowered, while 'Fingers' was as expressionless as a shark: A gray flatness pervaded his features. Colorless predatory eyes were sunk like dull marbles in a ball of clay, impersonally searching.

Roman's phone rang with the first notes of Beethoven's Fifth and startled both me and the Actor. "Okay," was all Roman said and turned toward the Steiner entrance to see an erect, fast moving figure striding into the Park. I strained my near-sighted eyes. As the long body moved closer, there was no doubt it was Howard.

He was making a determined bee-line for us, virtual smoke pouring out of his ears. I looked at 'Fingers,' he didn't act surprised. A small smile cracked across his cement face. He was ready for a face-off with Howard. His only movement was to scratch his chin and brush his rude fingers against his rough cheek whiskers. His version of a contemplative exercise. Clumped his spread fingers together at his sides and squeezed them into fists.

Howard moved quickly, a fleeting nod to us as he pressed his body inches from 'Fingers.' Their eyes were level, probing into one another like fatal lasers. Howard stole quick glance at the Actor, who could not control a shaking hand. He was no threat. Howard and 'Fingers' traded no words but an infelicitous communication was taking place.

They stood toe to toe and jowl to jowl, arms swaying at their sides. Activity in the Park came to a stop. Tension hung like a vial of nitro hanging on an unraveling cord.

We waited. We waited.

The Actor shouted "Get him!"

Fingers shot him an ugly look and said, "Shut up!"

A brief commiserating look passed between him and Howard. They were fierce antagonists a second later. But it seemed neither wanted to brawl. It was understood that Howard was the protector of Roman and Molly and 'Fingers' was merely the Actor's stooge.

They moved apart, backing up slowly, exchanging sharp words in low tones we could not understand. An instant later they were flailing at each other, throwing wild, windmill punches without steam. They grappled and wrestled on the ground, where the pummeling and gouging were almost friendly. They rolled around grunting and oofing.

After at least ten minutes of middle-aged combat they were exhausted and flopped over on their backs next to each other, breathing heavily, barely able to lift tier limbs and feeling for blood.

It was kind of a letdown. That these two tough guys were flat on their backs gazing dazedly at the sky, too tired to wipe the sweat off their faces. Though we also realized they could make mincemeat of anyone of us. No bravado there.

When they regained normal breathing, the pair arduously lifted themselves to their unsteady feet and not saying a word, parted ways.

I guess there was some temporary satisfaction in having finally fought came to a draw, disposed of some bad feelings so they could renounce their hatred, though allowing a simmering dislike to keep them on their toes.

Howard sat down by us and attended to his bruised. He grinned up over a bloody mouth, a wrenched back, an out of socket finger which he deftly realigned with a wince. Neither I nor Roman intruded on his pain; he was not a guy who needed consolation.

We watched 'Fingers' limping off, wiping blood from his cheek with a swollen hand. His other hand was attached to an arm laying numbly at his side. He teetered a bit.

The Actor, not venturing to follow 'Fingers' too closely, called to us: "Who's gonna pay for my broken window?" He wheedled. No one answered. He walked off in a huff.

Roman explained that he overcame his fear of Howard when he saw that Howard was a great dog lover like himself and how the dogs were drawn to him. He invited Howard to help in his mission to protect Molly, and offered him a stipend, which he turned down, but Roman jammed it into Howard's shirt pocket. The collaboration burgeoned into a friendship and Howard was wanting to help Roman Recover Molly.

Looking beyond Charles, my money was now on Howard for the actual rescue. Risky. Never asked.

But Roman was happy. The Dog World was under his benevolent protection. That's all that mattered at the moment.

"He's driving me crazy!"

Dori and I were sitting together on a bench, her four Dachshunds lazing on the ground between us, while Blondie was off, scrounging for treats.

She was complaining again about her upstairs neighbor; a heavy walker who paced endlessly back and forth on a rugless floor. It sounded that thunder over her head. He had been there a week and it was getting worse. It sounded like he wearing boots. Despite a bevy of entreating notes and several knocks on his door she got no response and no relief. She was polite and begged him to wear slippers at least. He was disturbing his neighbor. There was not a flicker of interest.

The dogs got more and more upset as Dori got more and more upset, resorting to banging up at the ceiling, which changed nothing and only aggravated her ripening anger.

The Management did not consider it to be a problem. "He has a right to walk around in his own place," said a message slipped anonymously under her door. Her placid existence was being shattered into tortured bits. Though there were periods of mercy that sometimes stretched for hours, the mechanical thumping resumed like a restless robot programmed to irritate.

Dori tried a musical attack. She turned up the music on her stereo put earplugs in, tilted her speakers up to the ceiling and hoped to get his attention with the sudden burst of a soprano in ear-splitting teary agony, followed by the tortured screams of a chorus condemned to Hell. The only ones who were bothered were Dori's other neighbors.

She toned it down. It was still loud, but not deafening. Whatever dreadful and horrible music she could lay her hands was diverted upstairs, putting speakers on top of furniture. The guy would actually stop pacing for a minute or two. Otherwise, he stood it without a whisper of complaint. It dawned on her that he may be hard of hearing or even deaf. She didn't know if that was a welcoming or depressing possibility.

She was finally describing her deteriorating situation to me. "Earplug in my own place all day?' Headphones all day? In my own place?" My suggestions galled her. His heavy sounds were a persistent nuisance in her head.

"I have to go to the Park to get some peace or stay in the bathroom with four dogs crying to come in." She couldn't help laughing at her predicament. She turned hopeless again, a discouraged frown douring her beautiful face.

"What can I do to get that guy out of there that isn't criminal?" She looked at me severely. "You have a healthy mean streak, help me!"

It was a proposition I hadn't considered. She was suffering. Like me, she loved being transported and absorbed in a good book. A non-stop stomp of a boot mess with your concentration, it can penetrate your brain to distraction.

I figured the guy who spent most of the day walking back and forth was either a shoe tester, a floor tester, a microbe killer, a lousy dancer, a sadist, a jobless Philosopher or most likely, mentally ill. He needed a more socially conducive environment. We would do him a service to get him there.

."I'll be free!" Dori spun around jubilantly and gave a big hug, which I reciprocated with pleasure. There was a renewed sparkle in her eyes. Now, all we have to do, is to figure out what to do.

"Well, I'm thinking," Dori said pensively. "Remember that scary note about my dogs I got under my dog?"

"Sure do."

"Do you think it's the same guy," she asked with a little shudder.

"Do you mean that somehow he finagled the upstairs studio to harass you?"

"It's wild speculation, I guess."

"It's pretty convenient to move right above you?" I questioned. "Why would he have it in for you?"

"I have no idea."

"You've never seen him?"

"I meet lots of people," said the peripatetic Dori. "No one stands out."

"A big, weighty guy?"

She thought a moment, looking straight down at the brown and black hounds at her feet. She lifted her head and squinted in the direction of her building, while making a clicking recognition sound.

"There is someone," her eyes focused back on me, I used to see around." she laughed lightly to herself. "It's funny when I say that. This guy was really big around." She spread her hands wide beside her hips and puffed out her cheeks. "He was short. I thought of as Mr. Squat. It was hard to get by him in the narrow hall."

"Did he hit on you?"

"It was the opposite." She smiled with satisfaction. "He was very respectful. Called me Miss Dori." She clasped her hands together. "At the time I was impressed by his manners, but now, when I look back it's odd behavior." She reinforced her fingers into a clutch. "I shouldn't be saying that."

"I know. It seems so old-fashioned. Especially in SF."

"Not used to gentlemanly behavior."

She could not come up with anyone else that fit the description of the man upstairs. Her dogs meanwhile were whimpering for attention, trying to climb her legs. She gave them distracted, cursory pets.

The sun poked through the thinning clouds. It got warmer. A thicker, longer cloud crossed the Sun. It got cooler. Off with the jacket, on with the jacket, in the time it takes the second hand to go around the watch.

"What do you think?" I asked her, shaking any unpleasant thoughts.

"No. I don't think it's him." She was firm. "I was amused by his delicacy." She hoisted a wide, American flag smile to her face. "It didn't match his squatness, if you know what I mean. He looked like a bad gut wrestler, dark hair sprouting out everywhere and a fuzzy look in his eyes. I had some fondness for him."

"Whew!" I commented. "What a memory."

"Do you study the customers who buy your flowers?"

"The regulars," she admitted. "It's like habit or," she grinned mischievously. "A condition."

"That's a handy alibi."

"Do you mean ability?"

"If you were a Cop."

The sun poked its eye through the clouds again. Out came the sunglasses, like a reflex.

Dori lifted a Dachshund to her lap, Calliope I think, gave her a good rub-down, as the other three clamored and fought to be next, getting into position to not forfeit their prized spot of first paws on the edge of the bench.

"Now that you mention it, I haven't seen the guy around," she mused. "Mr. Squat would be hard to miss." She chewed lightly on her lower lip as if she could scrape off a revelation.

"Aha!"

"Do you think?" She pondered the possibility of him being upstairs.

"When I discriminate, I think."

"Huh?" Her friendly tone dissolved. She continued with the vexation she reserved for my piquant expressions. "What does that mean?"

"It sounds smart."

"Well, keep your merry propositions on perpetual hold."

It is inevitable some tension flares up when Dori and I consider things. Nerves fray, jokes grate. It happens.

"What's with your classy vocabulary?"

"I've been reading," she said stiffly, readingly for another Beamer observation hurled at her.

"Despite Mr. Squat?"

"I escape to the bathroom."

"That's awful.

"I can roll a chair in there."

"Still."

"It's temporary," she assured me. She made a comic grimace and asked: "Is Mr. Squat really up there?" There was slight quaver in her voice.

"Unlikely," I answered obliquely, resolving nothing.

She brightened up. "Maybe he'll open the door for you?"

"Me?"

"You can pretend to be some official person," she conjured, "and when he comes to the door you can get a glimpse of him."

"Official person?"

"Well," maybe someone giving away free stuff."

"Hmm," I uttered. I wish Charles was around.

"You can do it," she coaxed, laying an encouraging hand on my shoulder and a dazzling smile across my retina.

"I'll think it over."

A few days went by and no sensible ideas popped up. Dori was gritting her teeth. Then we met Elliot.

We were sitting in the Park, mulling over banging on doors to get people out when Elliot and his Boston Terrier, Benny, sat down on the next bench.

He was a newcomer and the first thing he said was: "Do you know how my dog talks?"

"How?" We bit.

'Bawk.' 'Bawk.'

Boston's you know. Sounded like a funny guy. This time his mood was grayer. We didn't ask why. He claimed to be an aspiring writer. So that could explain all forms of moodiness. He released Benny who cozied over to the Dachshunds and Blondie, who in turn rose to appraise him and the sniffing commenced.

Elliot had an unusual approach to writing. He believed it was a mistake to read Great writers. Too discouraging. Better to read crap so that his writing will look better in comparison. Except, it was hard to find crap in the Library and who wants to pay money for crap.

Dori and I struggled to digest his strange scheme to put words on paper.

"What are you writing?" I asked, pivoting, because Dori was between us. He ignored me and spoke to the prettier Dori.

"I'm plotting a SciFi novel," he quietly confided to the perky and always interested Dori. He made claws of his hands. "A monster machine devouring planets!" His hands closed around some nearby air.

"Burp!"

"Machines don't belch," he told her gravely. Very touchy.

"Just a joke," I butted in. "Haven't planets been eaten before?"

"Stop!" he sputtered. "It's a standard idea," he acknowledged condescendingly, "but with a big twist, which is a secret."

Don't argue with an Author.

"Does it involve dogs?" A light needling from Dori.

He stared at her. Did she by chance penetrate his mystery or had she nefariously insulted him?

Don't joke with an Author.

"Have you read the classic SciFi writers?" I blundered to ask.

"No!" he yapped testily, "It's against my philosophical principles."

Don't try to give advice to an Author.

If his ideas were odd, his face was even odder.

Dark thatched brows loomed over bulging gray eyeballs, appearing ready to jump out of their sockets on a whim. His rapidly blinking lids were out of sync as if he were stuck with cheap wiper blades.

He was utilitarian. His pink lips often clammed together and his chin had long ago lost its battle for prominence. He was topped off with incongruously slicked-back shiny black hair on a stork-like skull.

"How long have you had Benny?" Dori asked, trying to reintroduce pleasantness into the conversation.

He swayed in his seat, twisted to the sound, folded a corner of his writing pad, looked long in her direction and answered listlessly and perplexed.

"Months," he finally said.

Your dog and my dogs get on very well, "she chatted. "You must be a nice person."

What did glean from this striking woman's velvety voice and friendly smile?

He looked bewildered and fell off his grouch and landed with lascivious eyeballs on an imaginary chunk of deserted tropical island with the imaginary flirtatious Dori. She had breached his stoniness.

Alas, is was not to be. Her soft surface turned suddenly harsh to chasten her dogs as they ganged up to bark at Benny's klutzy intrusions.

"I think your principles are pretty flabby," I confronted him, with a pinch of jealously. He turned to me with a malevolent frog's eyes. "First of all," he said coldly, "Pretty and flabby cancel each other out." He paused. "Secondly, are you insulting me?"

"It's a valid observation," I told him, coolly.

Dori watched him with curious interest. She narrower eyes, which appealed to me. They seemed to filter out and discriminate more than those wide open, round eyes, where the whole blasted outside spectacle comes rushing in with one big gulp.

Elliot had a highly developed imagination. I thought Dori should explain her situation and see what he could come up with. She asked and to please her, he pondered:

"Invisible aliens are watching you. We know where you live. We are going to beam you up and do experiments are you. You cannot escape us"

Dori smiled.

"You like it," He asked her, bashfully.

"Leave a note."

"How can an alien leave a note?"

"Surely they've mastered the art of teleportation."

"Wow."

"He's already paranoid, right?"

"Probably," she agreed.

"Maybe he'll move."

"I like it."

"Sinister and cruel," I stepped in.

"You're not the one being stomped on," she curtly reminded me. "It's worth a try." My thoughts became crowded with visions of mayhem. If Elliot was killing aliens in Space, what would he do to them in our world? Neighborhood.

"Think of it as a prank," Elliot chipped in, enjoying his moment.

"Who would swallow this nonsense?"

Dori said; "Got any ideas, Beamer."

"Not at the moment," I answered weakly

"OK."

"Go ahead." I shrugged off my involvement.

She didn't hear me. She and Elliot were in huddle, secretly conferring on the detail of this crazy plan.

I rounded up Blondie and walked to the Panhandle, leaving the two conspirators oblivious of my departure.

When we came back to the Park, Dori and Elliot were gone. There were plenty of DogPeople still around. Blondie went on her treat hunt while I parked myself and watched the action.

Blondie was proficient moocher, one of a battalion of dogs besieging the treat givers; jockeying, jostling and straining to nearest to the giving hands. There was the occasional doggie contretemps, some traded snappiness and low warning growls, but otherwise attention rarely strayed from the treats.

Dogs had different approach techniques: The standup twirl, the sitting up on butt with paws presented, single paw lifted and poised, impressive waging of the tail, simpering, pitiful cries, importuning 'Woof,' jumping and leaping with paws high, tongue hanging, climbing up legs. The bigger dogs had the height and weight advantage, so the smaller dogs had to be more creative.

Wait your turn. The suspense. No finger biting. Spring like a Cobra at the extended savory treat. Be gentle. Good eye-mouth coordination. Timing crucial. A balancing act. Second? Good luck. No disguises. Stuck with nakedness. Not a mobile face. Look starving. No dog gets left out. Need to be noticed. Protest your exclusion. Mimic your ancestors. Get barky.

After a few days of not sein Dori or Elliot at the Park, or noticing any vacancy signs at her building and not seeing Police cars with flashing lights in front of it, I finally phoned Dori.

I waited ten rings, before she answered, out of breath.

"How are you," I said brightly, covering any hint of worry.

"Busy!" "Busy!" she answered in a breaking voice, as if she were turning away.

"What happened?"

"What didn't happen!"

"What happened?" I repeated with more urgency.

"Tell you when I see you," she replied, hurriedly.

"Are you flummoxed?"

"I gotta go...."

"Are things intact?"

"Mostly....Bye." I LOOKED UP

I had a notion to go over to her place, but within a block I dropped it. My momentum was carrying me in the opposite direction and I read it as my instinct doing its job. I looked up into sky and didn't see any aliens. Maybe they were hiding, massed behind marshmallow clouds against a spotty background of friendly blue or has Elliot had predicted they were invisible to Earthling eyes.

While I was staring upward, I banged into a tree. "Sorry." I apologized automatically, though it turned into a tree. The tree did not take offense. Growing up concrete, nature and I were never formally introduced. Going to Camp in the summer stirred up my allergies, especially breathing. Plants were my enemy.

My job had become boring and tedious. I only needed to use ten percent of my brain. It would be good to see what was going on with the other ninety percent.

Howard had left. He was becoming more short-tempered and gruff with the more obnoxious customers. His early patience and tact was eroding; he wasn't to be obsequious. He wanted, without an endless stream of strangers to deal with and be pleasant to.

Just like me.

The new guy wasn't a guy. Madeleine was a stout, near middle aged woman. She had played baseball, mostly as a catcher and had an upfront insight into the game. She learned sports from three brothers and a father who were passionate fans. She did not want to be left out. They attended hundreds of games in person and many more on TV. She learned from the conversations of her male family. And read fascinating books on the history of baseball. She was diehard. She knew the statistics.

She was enthusiastic. She sparkled as if she had just burst out of a soda bottle, bubbling her way around the store, with bright green eyes and contagious smiles, lighting on receptive customers, who couldn't help but smile back. The opposite of Howard,

She wore a Giant sweatshirt and even her perspective was different; Howard and I admired players, she 'loved' them.

When business was slower, she kept busy with small chores. Straightening, dusting, refolding. All things Howard and I did, but not with as much diligence. While we were both laid-back with customers, she approached them with vigorous friendliness, as she was an excited hostess welcoming special guests to a grand event.

Royals might act blase with such effusive attention, but the walking credit cards, also known as Tourists, were pleased with the human touch, however overboard it was.

She was generous with her opinions, too. As her drive gradually moved to overdrive, she made pertinent suggestions, with a kindly dictatorial smile; "Don't you think that would look better over there?" "We need more color on that rack." "I bet it would boost business if we put posters front and center in the window?"

I missed Howard.

Everything needed attention. She was fidgety, often rolling her fingers around her curly red hair. Anxious energy needing an outlet. She'd pick up different baseball books, leaf through them serendipitously, adding to her store of baseball lore and always willing to trade anecdotes with savvy customers. Locals liked to drop in and chat Baseball. They always bought something. Sales were up. I was worried about my job.

On the other hand, maybe it made me look. My influence and advice, though negligible, were invaluable. My mentorship was motivating/ maybe, I deserved a raise. That she compensated for my laziness was a plus. But I was stuck with all the paperwork. Did she want to help? I broached the subject as if it were a restful thing to do.

"My head's in the clouds," she reflected as if it were a philosophical issue. I drudged on. Everything around looked good. Why spoil it.

That evening Dori came to the Park wearing splattered overalls and a very glum expression. Her dogs were let loose and charged into the usual pile of excited canines. They acted if they had been cooped up for a long time.

I waited until she dragged herself to a bench and dropped tiredly onto it. She made a point to roll up each individual leash to keep them from their often Gordian entanglement.

"There are holes in my ceiling," she said with snarky solemnness.

My necessary reply was: "How big?"

She spread her hands apart. At least no one could fall through. There was brief silence as we both contemplated the disaster.

"Elliot is an imbecile," she mugged. There was no malice in it, but I'm sure, plenty of justification. "I was ready to listen to anybody," she said, obstinately.

"Where's Elliot?"

"I hope," she snipped, with expletives dangling, "his imaginary aliens have carried him off to very, very faraway planet."

"What happened to the guy upstairs?"

"He got kicked out."

"What!"

"He knocked holes in his floor, which is my ceiling." She sulked.

I stared at her. "Why are you so upset? You got him out."

"There are holes in my ceiling," she protested.

"They fix it."

"They're mad at me, too, Beamer." She sounded wounded.

"For banging up?"

"For that aloin stuff." She gave me sly look. "We went up to the roof above his place, stomping around, making weird noises, hanging alien dolls over his windows, talking angry gibberish. We were scary." She bragged, modestly.

"He got wise."

"I'll bet those notes Elliot left for him, freaked him out, and then the alien attack made it seem, pardon the word, incredulously real. If he had any thoughts in that direction."

"You could embark on a new career. It would pay well. Considering the housing shortage."

"Ha, Ha."

"Were the notes threatening?"

"I don't know." She paused. Do you think? She paused again. "No. No way." Her dark expression belied her words.

She was alarmed about what she did, her ceiling is in ruins, Elliot bugged off, her landlord could kick her out. Not counting the misdemeanors.

"And where's Elliot?" I presumed to ask.

"He went home," she said flatly.

"Where's home?"

"He didn't tell me."

"He has big responsibility for this mess," and I added, reproaching her and forgiving her, "You were the willing subject."

"Baa," she emitted. A smile widened on her gloomy face. "Despite the holes in my ceiling and the holes in my head, I will be rid of my nemesis, like you said." She offered me a high-five which I accepted. "That was the whole point." She wrapped her arms around herself, congratulating herself. "Elliot is my hero," she decided, with misgivings, "For a few minutes."

"Now, if you can convince your neighbors that Aliens inhabit the Earth, you and Elliot are off the hook. You can get all the groups who already believe to back you up in Court. You're safe.

Blondie had done her cavorting and was resting behind the bench. Dori's Four Dogs of the Apocalypse were folded, one into the other, seeking each other's comfort.

"Your dogs must have been very upset by all the racket and craziness."

"Upset?!" Dori snapped into angry mode. "They were traumatized. They stayed in the bathroom." She had to feel guilty. "I had to coax them out with extra special treats, when there was only a few flaked drifting down. They had white spots all over them."

"They survived."

"They were used to a peaceful and sober existence and the next thing you know they're plastered!" I don't know if she meant it to be funny, but it was.

"You cracked the code."

"Well, Beamer," she laughed, seeing the joke, "I've endured your cracks, give me some kudos."

"You got it!"

"How did they get the guy out of there so fast?" The questions kept coming.

"Mental illness, destruction to property, danger to others."

"Too bad."

"Now, I feel sorry for him."

"He needed help."

"I suppose."

"Maybe, you did a favor?"

"I wouldn't say that." She objected, rubbing an eye and looking at her dogs. "Elliot and I did was stupid and vengeful."

"He was driving you nuts, making you sick!"

"It's a blot."

"You can ruminate on it forever, it'll never come out pure."

"Okay," she determined, "Let's stamp the matter closed, with TOP SECRET on the top, feel that the guy is in better hands."

"Done!"

But as we know, memory's stinger does on rest on crumbly soil.

"Do you remember when we were first talking with Elliot?" I asked Dori, "Did he reveal the plot of his novel?"

She frowned. "When it comes to Elliot, I have a lapse of memory."

"So do I," I realized, "why is that?"

"It's a bad memory."

"I just thought of something funny," I said brightly.

She gave me the withering eye. "Don't!"

"When two people have the same lapse of memory," I struck, "what is it called?"

I heard the scraping of teeth.

"What!?"

"A Collapse!"

She staggered back, ever so slightly. "People have been killed for less," she warned, brandishing an invisible sword.

"Will you mourn me?"

"Bad jokes never die," she jigged,

I scratched a sudden itch. Dori deftly unfolded each leash and attached it to a dog. She gathered the leashes into both hands, stood up, tugged at the dogs to move, and was soon heading home.

"See you," she said with a satisfied smile. I waved back. All was cost again.

The Power of the Pun.

What instant misery it can inflict upon the unwary. Why drop bombs when you can drop reams and reams and reams on paper, stacking up on the ground like evil snowflakes, that never melt, intrusively cluttering up the streets and countryside, causing people to curiously read them, leading to soul-wracking groans, loss of appetite and falling morale.

I turned to the right and saw Elliot wandering towards me, he looked dejected.

"I didn't want her to see me." He had a cramp in his voice. "She's mad."

"She is."

"I bungled it," he owned up. His disparate features coalesced into a penitent whole. "We got rid of him," he spurted. "I'm sorry there were holes in her ceiling and got in trouble," he added, miserably.

"Non-sentient collateral damage."

"Exactly. I mean she doesn't live in a cradle."

"Of course not."

"If she followed my precise plan we would have had a total victory."

"Deliberately agreeing with Elliot gave him a head of steam to keep on his querulous buffoonery. I wanted to learn something.

"You should make it up with her," I proposed.

"She gave me hell," he said, now diffident.

"She's formidable"

He nodded. "I'll wait until the holes are filled in."

"Good decision."

"Women cringe when they see me," he said with resigned bitterness. I said nothing.

He contorted his face and aimed his bulbous orbs on me for emphasis. I fumbled with what to say as he dared me to say something. I've seen uglier men able to charm pretty women. It's not only the face but the naked brain. I mean the prettiest object in the Universe, but it can conjure up magic. So what to say?

He saved me. His clenched face muscles suddenly relaxed and a dreamy, faraway looked sprouted in his eyes. "I make myself the Hero when I write. My fantasy self is a Greek God, he smiled, with happy defiance, raising friendly squiggles around his mouth. If he could only decorate his stand-out eyes.

"You know," I pronounced, "the face of compassion is always beautiful. Don't be so peevish."

"Peevish?" he muttered. "I'm looking for compassion, not giving it," he added, peevishly. "You have a penchant for nosiness."

"Proclivity."

He roughly petted his restless dog. The dog put its paws on Elliot's knees and licked his human face with no discrimination. Elliot brought out his note and began scribbling furiously with a ballpoint pen that dug into the paper with enough pressure to leave an imprint on the next page.

His dog whimpered for a walk, but Elliot had jinned into his alter ego world and was disporting around the shrunken and unpaved Universe in a Hot Rod Spaceship.

He looked up impassively. "No humming."

"I'm not humming."

He was in a daze. "Nobility," he murmured, still writing, "is the essence of an impromptu Universe."

Leaning over, I could see penmanship that swept vowels and consonants crashing into each other. Only he could decipher the words.

I left Elliot in his trance, his aggravated pulpy body pitched forward over his pad. He was lost in space, his dog making sad noises, sitting at his feet. Other dogs would breeze by, lingering by him to check out treats, sniffing at his pockets, he oblivious to their snouty intrusions

We walked to the Panhandle, Blondie excited. Gophers galore await her. She went right to work, sniffing them out and digging deeper into the holes, plugging in her snout then standing at rigid attention should the gopher peek outside.

She'd stand for an hour, if I didn't intrude, pull her away and fill up the hole. Her fixation just moved to another hole. She had no success rousing one. Why should a poor-sighted sighted gopher want to show its face when there is a big dog hungrily hovering over its den, puncturing its presence with sharp claws and killer teeth.

Maybe, I could give her a disguise. A gopher mask? But I've never seen a famous animated gopher popular enough to have its own mask. How about a toupee and dark glasses/ But teeth give her away? Perhaps a clip-on mustache would curtain off those predator choppers.

On the other hand, pity the poor gopher, living underground in the dark with the possibility of being a snack for a fast digging dog. For the less fast Blondie, the Gopher would have to come out of its hole and do a dance if she ever had a chance of catching it.

We exited the Panhandle at Stanyan, where it meets GGP proper and turned off in Haight for a walk back.

Haight Street.

The damaged and the defiant, the compliant courteous tourists, the voices of cheerful lunacy, the vandal and the voluptuous, the tangible and indecorous street people, the Sixties quaintness, the clumsy crowdedness of things for sale and things to be free, the revolving outsized love revolution. The fashionable drop-ins, the gentrified rebellious, the cranked up and doped down, a salmagundi of people shops tastes and grumbles.

Part of the United States of America.

We passed Buena Vista. I glanced up the hill to the Actor's House. Was he going to revise his tough guy image after his humiliation at the 'Fingers'/ Howard battle?

Probably not. In front of the camera, there was no danger, except a bad review or tripping over some equipment. And Arcadia? Was she in his shadow? Would I see her in bigger parts on the Big Screen?

Back in Dog Spoiled Park. Elliot had left his jacket draped over the back of the bench. He was so full of his story he neglected. I put it back. It won't tempt anyone but the desperate.

I did see and hear a pink, spongy mutt named Norton whose bark sounded a gurgle from an old washing machine. I thought of the myriad sounds heard in the Park:

The clomping feet of runners and joggers wending their athletic way along the narrow path lined with obstacles like dogs, baby carriages, kids own scooter, strollers, skateboarders, toddlers and bicycles.

The small pockets of conversation: serious dog talk, eruptive laughter, disruptive arguments, cell phone chatter.

The deep droning of planes and air-whacking Copters, swing around the sky, obliterating other noises.

The delicate, delicious sounds of treats breaking in two.

The importuning cawing of cows and the happy chirping of smaller birds.

The rough play, bickering entanglement of dogs loose with one another.

Big and small dogs alike howling in their piping and wolfish voices at the Fire Engines.

The regular visits of the vehicular, multi-bladed grass cutters hacking away with their long blades, their racket and threat discombobulating various critters.

The wind rushing through the trees, crackling thin branches and rustling the leaves, whooshing it way through the Park, tumbling small objects.

The noises of construction. The grinding power saw, pounding hammers, clanking, bumping metal plates. Ubiquitous neighborhood sounds of repair and improvement.

Rumble of the MUNI trains alongside the Park. The huge, deafening blast of their horns and the corresponding pleasant sound of their clearing bells.

Jarring, grating sounds of skateboards tearing brazenly down the path, barking dogs in pursuit. People screaming at both dogs and skateboarders to "Stop!" "Stop!"

The raucous caucus of the squawking flocks of parrots tumulting their way over the Park in excited conversation

The squeaky-wheel rolling shopping carts, pushed bedraggled homeless, who dig in trash bins to recover empty bottles and cans for redemption.

Jingling, tingling, clinking of dog tags in motion.

The occasional musician. A czar on guitar, an astute flute, lord on keyboard, chums on drums, relaxed sax. Mojo on a banjo & duke on a uke.

The sky thundered, rare jagged yellow lightning stabbed at the earth, jarring the inhabitants, paling some aweing others. The immensity of nature's forces drilled into people's brains with sudden indifference.

Seek shelter. I did, with the urgent tugging from a nervous Blondie seconded my decision. We raced under heavy drops and the flashing electric sky to nearby home.

I dried off Blondie, turned on the TV to the plangent evening news. which played havoc with digestions and tear ducts, laid out kibble for Blondie. Fixed myself a TV nosh of chips dipped in hummus.

TV'd 'til eight. Checked out the computer, read 'til eleven and so to Bedlam: Into the crazy-quilted phantasmagoria of dreams, embroidered with the humdrum thread of the wacky familiar: Where dogs watch the collapse of the edible Universe and feast on the scraps.

Where I play Ping-Pong with Babe Ruth. He dazzling me with the ease of his whizzing strokes, while eating a monstrous hotdog, brimming with mustard and relish and me slamming back his casual rockets with uncanny accuracy, while talking on cellphone and no one in the Store even paying attention.

Where a beautiful raven-haired woman beckons me into a chandelier casino and then vanishes into a deck of cards, where every card turned over has her face coyly smiling at me, as I float over the tables. I yelled in jealous rage at the players handling her face, but no one paid attention to me.

Met Dori in the Park. There was atremble in her voice.

"Do you remember the guy in the elevator, the one I thought wouldn't send a scary note."

My memory flashed back to the shabby guy. Non-threatening. Off the beaten track.

"I do."

"I met him again in the elevator and he asked me if 'I loved my dogs?'"

"And?"

"He was kinda mopey, but the sly way he said it made me queasy."

"Probably no malice intended," I offered reasonably.

"Maybe," she said weakly.

"Is that all he had to say?"

"He left."

"Did he want to pet your dogs?" I gambled.

She didn't hesitate. "Never!"

"Were they uncomfortable around him?"

"They are not jolly around anyone," she said, voice rising. "You know that!"

"So, no marks against him." I replied. "Except weirdness."

"But my intuition," she countered.

"Can't discount the Animal," I granted.

"Nope."

"Maybe, he just likes you, you know," I said to her languidly, "Trying to get your attention."

"That is crazy!" She squirmed, as if a horrible substance was clinging to her and she couldn't couldn't wipe it off."

"Not boyfriend material?" I joshed, mistakenly

Her narrowed eyes sent out lethal beams meant to redistribute my teeth.

"You know Beamer, you'd make a lousy Philanthropist."

She's right. I barely had income. It's good to shut-up.

Dori was bordering on the morose. Her dogs looked bewildered. She stooped down to pet and reassure them as she straightened up she let out a hard sneeze. She pulled out a wad of tissue from her pocket, wiping her teary eyes and blowing her nose, Allergies trumping passions.

"My nose gets so clogged."

"Mine, too," sniffing for effect.

"You're making fun of me." She decided, shielding her eyes from the 'now' of the now and then Sun.

"I never know what you're thinking!"

"Neither do I."

She turned toward me with her familiar look of lingering displeasure. "I never get a straight answer either."

"Well, you know," I answered in liquid tones, "Love must have no angles, only curves are sensuous."

"What!?" She strained to hear me. A moving band of small dogs were milling around us making a barking ruckus. They blanketed my words. I said instead: "It's the Yappy Hour."

"The Yappy Hour," she laughed. "Good one."

I decided to leave on this happy note.

Blondie had made herself comfortable in the grass next to the bench and was reluctant to leave.

"C'mon girl," I called to her, "time to go."

She stared at me, not moving. Did he really mean it? Can I change his mind?

"Let's go."

She made an effort to get up, then plopped down again. I decided to invoke the magical word:

"Food!"

She concentrated on the word. It made an impression. She staggered upwards, as if it was an ordeal to get up. She slowly came to me. I gave her a "Good Dog" pet, hitched her to the leash. Off we went, she, picking up the pace as we closed toward home.

New job?

Many would like my job. Working with Baseball stuff. Talking sports with customers. Working down on the Wharf. The Wharf. Constant stream of strangers. Constant busyness. Think I'd like a quieter environment. Too much babbling. Too much merchandising. The sameness. More autonomy to be creative.

Downtown?

In an Office? Boring. No selling. No paperwork. No kowtowing. Enough money to live in SF. Friendly coworkers. Short commute. Clean air. Health coverage. Great view.

Chances are, I may have to lower my standards and expectations. Especially since my Tech knowledge can barely slop over the rim of a thimble. Yes, definitely my skills are not in demand and my assets do not include youthful enthusiasm.

The Wind was fierce as I trudged into the Park from the Wharf. I walked the entire way, trying to shake the accumulated detritus, eight brain pillaging hours and vandalized emotions, my uber-zealous coworker and wave after wave crashing wave of polyglotted, kaleidoscopic, terra cotta tourists, bulging with amplitude.

But, then, I should give Tourists some slack. They pump up the Economy. They are the backbone. My back softened, leaning over the counter too many times, fingering too many credit cards, wrapping and also being polite, despite snatches of importuning rudeness, imprecating crudeness and other deprecating things to smile through as I go slanting obsequiously through the day.

A tiring tirade tilting at commerce gone berserk.

"Hi Rafe, how you doin'?"

"Not too bad," he said with a little ginger.

"Are you implying that things are basically bad?"

"What?"

"You didn't say it was good, just not so bad."

"He looked me square in the eye. "Music has power to drive people crazy."

I drew a blank. "What does that have to do with it? I asked warily.

"Well," he propounded testily, "What does what you say have to do with anything?"

"Just an observation," I obliged.

"A flimsy philosophy," he imposed, cuttingly.

"Keen mindedness," I rebutted.

"Disagreements vivify the Mind," he declared, pompously.

"It adds growth," I added, amiably.

"Pistachios!" he voiced vehemently.

"Naturally."

"Quotients matter," he insisted, batting the air.

"Indeed they do."

He stared fervently into the distance. "Truth is all around us, its forms are endless," he spoke with feeling. "People are always searching for the Truth Formula." His eyes tried to penetrate mine. Then they strayed back to a distant point and he spoke to it:

"Is truth a gigantic thing or something small?" Does Truth have meant shining facets like a Diamond or is it dull and grungy like a slab of wet concrete? Does it anoint you or crush you, or is it the God beyond Understanding? He paused to loaded up on breath. "A reflex or a ponderable? A word or a measure? Something that lasts until the end of a page and runs out of space so it prints lasting conjecture?"

"Absolutely."

The Park was a gallery of goofiness, with dogs setting the standard. Rafe casually walked through the every few weeks, doing a bit of panhandling. Heid zero in on Blondie and they'd commune, wrapped up in each other.

He was a sketchy character. He politely squelched my nosing into his life, comically twisting his lips into a half-smile and uttering a series of perambulating grunts.

His average looks made him anonymous. His eyes, like Elliot's were odd. They didn't work together, moving on two different tracks, I like the way his mind worked. He'd be absorbed with one thought while communicating with another. His step was loosey-goosey, which he called "ambling" and he found the World "humorously dire."

He claimed he wasn't 'Homeless', but he had the restless air of a Hobo, and the unconcern for the proprieties of the social ramble. He was clean-shaven, clean-clothed and well-nourished: maybe the eccentric scion of wealth, innocently masquerading as a 'hand-to mouth' philosophic wanderer.

What didn't jibe were his luxury backpacks. A different pristine, different one each time he showed up. Since I didn't know his true name, the gold laid initials were open to interpretation. "A.I.R." could be: "Ain't I Ridiculous."

Such ostentation was always welcomed in the Park. Where DogPeople generally dressed down in deference to the hang drool, kicked up dirt, lap jumpers, slimy tennis balls, muddy paws and the old reliable: Stepping in it.

His attention was diverted to a woman diligently pushing a two-tiered baby/toddle carriage.

"They're getting a free ride," he mused grumpily.

I looked around. Nothing. "Who's getting a free ride?"

He pointed to the carriage. "Kids."

"They're kids," I shrugged.

"They don't appreciate all the free chauffeuring," he insisted.

"They won't remember."

"That's too bad," he drawled, his eyeballs minutely drifting.

"You are a lunatic," I told him, using the word in the kindest possible sense.

He ignored me.

"Meters," he announced speculative, rumpling his neat, parted hair.

"Meters?"

"Meters." he repeated with confidence, patting down his mussed hair and fingering a comb in his shirt pocket. He looked off yonder as the idea brewed. "Parents should install meters to tote-up or tot-up the accumulated miles." He gathered steam. When the kids grow up they should get a bill for their transportation costs."

I got into the swing. "But they didn't use gas."

"Muscle power. Extra food intake."

"Who sets the charges?" I barged into his flippant certainty. "Twenty years from now money will have different value."

"Hmmm," he intoned, his eyeballs rolling around trying to agree. "An 'Economic Quandary', another question of need and greed, worth pondering......"

He abruptly walked away, calling out: "Parents, meter your children!"

The words 'subjective coherence' come to mind.

He ambled to the corner, swaying with his thoughts, side-stepping incoming dogs, crossing Steiner merging unsteadily with a rush of bicycles rolling up the street.

"Beamer," Dori said delicately, as we strolled to the Park. "Why aren't you more ambitious?"

I felt a tingling resentment. "Why should I be?"

She looked up at me with implacable blue eyes that half-melted my stiff expression. She knew it.

"You know nothing," I blustered.

"You're so touchy," She worked on her leashes, catching a small smile on her face. She was surprisingly tolerant of my silly outburst. I almost wanted to test her, see that sappiness come back. I Took another tact

"I wrote some really good dog songs," I bragged.

"I know."

"There's ambition in that."

"Some."

"What's your ambition?"

"That's nobody's business," she snapped, tossing her loose hair with a theatrical shake of her head.

"Sounds criminal."

"You're scratching the surface," she said, darkly.

"Is it anything to do with taking over the World?"

"Possibly."

"Very mysterious," I smiled devilishly.

"Now you're smoking."

"You're in league with Satan."

"Could be," she answered grimly.

"You're very recalcitrant about this."

"Oh, big words, heh," she sneered, "trying to confuse me." She made an erasing motion in front of me as if to negate my words.

"You're acting very strange," I confronted her, suddenly worried.

"You're the Stranger." She made some Priest-like signs in the air. She stomped her right foot three times on the ground and tapped each dog three times on the head.

"Are you expanding your repertoire?"

"Don't try it?"

"Are your horns retracted?"

"Don't joke." She glared at me. "It's dangerous."

I figured once she recognized my puzzled face, she'd break out laughing. A feigned menace? An act? Has she lost her marbles?

She reached into her jacket pocket and pulled out a pair of sunglasses from its pouch and put them on. She turned to me and bared her teeth. Which were very white and even with no hint of dried blood on them.

Her eyes were unreadable but their pearls of sweat perched on her forehead. She wiped them off with a violent twist of the wrist.

"Whew," she uttered, as if relieved of a burden.

"Quite a Performance," I offered, magnanimously. "Are you rehearsing A role?

"Yep," she snorted. "Believe that."

"I know you don't do drugs."

"Don't need'em."

"Is this your natural self?"

"Sometimes."

It's the Park effect I reasoned. Dogs know there are Ghosts here. "Maybe the fog has some strange element in it.

"Dream on."

Dori and I are in this bizarre bubble, detached from the ordinary goings-on in the Dog Park. Dogs frolicking, People socializing, grass growing.

We are having an allusive conversation about the Devil, with Dori's scary predilection for the Dark Side and I am wondering, who has she been hanging with. What's going on?

Dori spoke up. "The space you are used to has become warped, bent into terrifying shapes." She had a glazed, triumphant look.

"I know what it is," I told her, confidently. "You Just Watched thirty episodes in a row of a weird TV horror series."

"Bingo!"

"At least you didn't murder anyone."

"I hope not."

"You haven't stepped over any bodies your way out."

"My dogs would know.'

I did a quick search. "No blood on their paws, you're cleared."

"I could have washed it off."

"Basta!"

"How dare you!" she cried in shock.

"Italian for 'Enough.'

"Arrivederci." Off she went, her dogs kicking up beside her as she tussled on the run with the intertwined leashes on her way home.

The World flattened out.

It all started when she asked me about my ambition. She mentions Philanthropist. I would like to be one, what would be greater. But I don't have the means. What would be a greater ambition than to end suffering?

If you are just thinking about and talking about, you are not doing anything about it. Does it have to do with your disposition with the World, toward Life. What can I do? Is it a question? Or is it an assertion.

At times, life is like a blank wall, where a thousand clichés are scrawled and you are looking for the one that might sum everything up. But, it is never there.

Sometimes, you mistakenly think it's there and you are frustrated. So you bang your head against the wall, leaving drops of blood dripping down. And there you are! Life is summed up in Blood.

So, I, Beamer, stare at the blank wall in my studio. I study it for a long time. An experimental meditation, broken up by the occasional cockroach passing by and distracting me.

Spring. Things were humming along with Dori. Although we were not always humming similar tunes, even though our musical tastes were fairly compatible. She was still tending and selling her flowers and I was still pretending to be a diligent employee at the Baseball store.

The birds were tweeting their tunes and allergens were in the air. The Park was inviting and filled with veteran fur and adorable puppies bouncing around and bringing their joyful yaps and yips into the world. I prefer the cool San Francisco. The cold is more hermetic.

Blondie and I were sitting in the Park. A pair of gray corduroy pants stopped in front of us. Without raising my head from my crossword puzzle, I knew who it was. The pants had a sharp crease in them. The only corduroy pants I ever remember seeing with a crease. It was one of his signature looks. He figured if people didn't remember him for his jokes maybe they would remember him for his outfit. Not the attitude of a confident comedian.

"Hi, Beamer," He spoke, looking down at me.

"Huh?" I blurted out, looking up at his newly bearded face and scanning for his dog. "Anything wrong?" I asked anxiously, thinking she was ill or even worse.

"She's all right,"

I pointed to his beard.

"Wisdom is sought," he mused, lovingly stroking his wispiness. "Thought I'd do something new for my act, he confided, with a self-conscious hint that things could be better.

"Has it helped?" I inquired dubiously.

"Bearded jokes have a limited engagement." He wiped his sun-unseen forehead and clicked his off-white teeth.

What was the portentous news? Was he setting me up for a joke?

He looked me straight in the eye.

"I did a fill-in gig for a buddy the other night. A classy joint, downtown, with an older, richer crowd. It was a good payday." He shrugged. "I'm surprised they even paid me. My routine clanked like I was wearing chains. The two people listening gave me false hope." He made an ironic laugh. "I ad-libbed some mildly ribald material to some mild applause and ushered myself off the stage to thinner applause."

If anyone could be glum and smiling at the same time, it was him.

He sat down next to me, folded slightly tremulous into half-fists and watched the dogs happily playing on the grass. Something that helps improve your mood.

"When I was done with my act," he said pointedly, "I sat down at an empty back table and had myself a thick ham sandwich and a Belgian beer on the House." He gave some scratches to Blondie, got a lick, and continued. "I got to listening to the boisterous conversation of some rich guys around a table near me." He bent down, retied a shoelace, aligned his pants cuffs and looked at me warily. He resumed his story. "The talked abruptly stopped when a man came hobbling to their table. 'What's with the limp?' a table guy asked. "Some punk surprised me', he sniffed, as he sat down. 'I'll get back at him.' he swore, 'He's on my hit list.'

I jumped in crisply, "Must have meant 'shit list.'"

"No," the Comedian insisted.

I looked at him with impish skepticism. "You recognize this guy?"

"Of course, you told me the whole story of kicking him in the knee." I didn't remember telling him. He must have heard it from someone else. "He told them your name was 'Beamer', Streamer or something and they all laughed. Confirmed!"

I squinted at the low sun. An image of a granite head with cold, corrupt eyes and a homicidal grin snapped like a grainy photograph before my eyes.

Dori and I were back together again. I sought her cutting advice. Clued her in on all the recent developments.

"He deserved what you gave him," she divined. "He's louse."

"A louse, but not a mouse. I need a gun."

"A gun?" she ridiculed. "You're going to walk around with a gun!"

I stood my ground. "To protect myself." I gave her a hard look. "In some States you can carry a gun."

"And the state you're in, is the state of craziness."

There was a period of quiet.

"Why don't you challenge him to a duel?" she chirped.

"Not a bad idea."

"Oh."

"AK-47's at twenty paces."

There was a pause.

"Why don't you run him over with a car?"

"Don't have one."

"Rent one."

"No credit card."

"Hit man?"

"Very expensive."

I had a sudden thought. "Since I was a great stickball player, I'll get a bat, and if he shoots bullets at me, I'll bat them right back at him with my classic swing."

"I understand irony can stop a bullet."

Maybe, I'll carry a Bible. The New Testament. The Old Testament is thicker but it's too heavy to lug around.

"You are being ridiculous," she said flatly. "Charles was trying to provoke you."

"Seriously?"

"That stuff about 'hit' and 'shit', so pat," she delivered. "I'm sure he wasn't performing in some ritzy club."

"He's a friend. Why would he do this?"

"I don't know. Maybe he thought it was funny. He's a Comedian."

"So, I'm safe."

"As safe as a Snicker bar in my fridge."

THE EGGMAN

I was at the front window, wiping the dust from the "Giants" beer tankards and watching the street, when a King-Sized Mercedes pulled up in front of the store and who pops out but Hayward. Not my idea of a beautiful genie. More like an ogre. Maybe I have a defective tankard.

He comes in the door, goes directly to my co-worker, not glancing in my direction. I can't say he looked intimidating. He was bent forward, a slight tremor on his left hand and a gimp in his step. He was fatter.

He spoke with an accommodating voice, almost placating. Maybe his head hitting the hard floor and our fuss in the Park rerouted the pathways to his brain.

He quietly paid cash for two Giants' jackets with lining, putting one on. He headed for the door and looked at me. I stared straight at him. No belligerence in his eyes, just a quizzical head tilt.

He angled into the passenger seat of the Mercedes and it went regally into traffic, like a thick steak between two slices of white bread. Why did Charles give me all that malarky?

I was sitting in the grass at the hilly upper end of the Park, across from the children's' playground; a cool wind carrying the happy shouts of kids drifting over me and over my thoughts, which were drifting stickedly over my finding a job. It was a leashed area so Blondie lolled near me.

Dori came charging up the hill, strenuously pulling her dachshunds, who were churning their little legs and bumping into one another to be the first up. They were competitive rascals.

"I'm...so...excited..." she cried, between breaths. She plunked herself down next to me and corralled her snappy dogs around her and told them to take a break. They obeyed and settled down, each trying to edge closest to her.

"Guess what!"

"What?" I asked, needlessly.

"I'm a press secretary!" she beamed. "Part time."

"Wonderful."

"'Case you haven't noticed; Roman has become a minor celebrity."

"I haven't noticed."

"Mrs. Hayward has been throwing his name around and the Mayor dropped in with his dogs. How's that!"

"The Mayor?"

"Yep," she continued excitedly. "People from TV and radio are calling for interviews. But," she said coolly, "He refused. Now he has this mystique."

"What mystique?"

As Dori and I both know, he is a little crazy. In a good way, of course.

"He asked me to deal with the media and his coming and going mail," she said proudly.

"Glamorous," I said teasingly, giving her a big hug of congratulations.

"He doesn't want notoriety," she said, seriously, "He's afraid he'll be branded as a sleaze biographer and drudge up his years in the seminary. It'll intrude on his work."

She went on: He doesn't ask people for money. It's out of his own pocket. He's scared he'll be called a quack.

"I'll be his public face. Part-time."

And a nice face it is, I thought. But I didn't want to toss the flattery out too often and too lightly. She will soon be getting it in bunches.

"I didn't realize he was so popular."

She was surprised.

"He has a spiritual Church for animals," she said brightly "Kinda unique, huh?"

"True."

"It's legitimate. He's got a famous writer praising him."

"True."

"I refer you to his write up in the "Only in S.F. column in the Chronicle."

"I'm sure out of touch."

"Well, he's not on TV or the radio."

"You're much closer to him than I am. He trusts you." She nodded.

"How is he going to deal with media people coming to the Church to get him on their TV or radio shows?"

"That's my job," she bubbled. Then, a little more subdued, she vexed: "It's created quite a pile of mail to wade through. I dread it."

"If there's a fireplace in the Church you could save some wood."

"Ha. Ha."

"Aren't you excited by the job, anymore?"

"Not at the moment," she shivered comically. "Yet, there was a package in the mail that struck me."

"How come?"

"It was a gift box," she frowned, and "I had to open it."

"Even though it was addressed to Roman," I tickled.

"Even though." She avoided looking at me and went on: There was a hard-boiled egg with "Fat Man" written on it. She turned her eyes on me. "I was bemused."

"Making fun of him because he has a little paunch?"

"Very little."

"Enough, to make a crack?"

"If you're really skinny." she snorted. In a very feminine way. I was thinking: An Egg!?"

"You know," I opined, with brows creased, "I had a thought."

"Good for you."

"No, seriously Remember the note you got threatening your dogs."

"Sure do," She said, perplexed.

"Do you still have it?"

"Absolutely. It's evidence."

"Well," I pondered, "What if the sender of the gift wasn't referring to Roman being fat."

"What else could it be?" she shrugged.

"I think the person who sent this package was threatening a bomb."

She looked at me in stark bewilderment.

"A bomb! That's nuts! You are crazy!"

"Fatman was the name of the first atomic bomb."

"No way."

"Did you notice that the hard-boiled egg is in the shape of a bomb?"

She gave me a wry look.

"Okay, I fell for your stupid joke," she said with a twisted smile, "but you had me scared. Not a good joke."

I ignored it.

"I was thinking that it was the same person who sent you that note about yours, both deadly."

"Whew, you're blowing me away."

"It's pathological humor."

"It is weird."

"There may be fingerprints on the box."

"I'll save it." She studied me with a look of wonder. "You are clinging to your fantasy?"

"I am."

"Either it's a stroke of genius, or you're as daffy as Roman."

I enlightened her.

"It's my private detective instinct."

"Beamer, you're not a detective," she razzed.

I stared up into the sky, avoiding her insult.

"I'm detecting some disbelief from you."

"You're right," she smiled.

"That proves it."

"I think that's a sophism," she threw at me.

I brushed it off, not sure what it meant.

"Is it curable?" I asked amusingly.

"It's be around for thousands of years," she answered somberly.

Time to move on.

"Should we tell Roman?

She plucked a few blades of grass, wiggled her nose, pulled on her right ear lobe, gave each dog a head pat and said nothing.

"Sounds like a no."

She nodded and spoke:

"Maybe, it's just some goofy guy who admires him or a woman who's stuck on him."

"No name."

"Anonymous love."

"Do women leave bombs?"

We left the Park. The day turned gloomy. Long, dark clouds like smudges in the sky sailed indifferently overhead, as if they had a more important destination.

"It's going to be tough for my dogs working for Roman and selling flowers." she looked up at me innocently, with the merest hint of supplication.

I met her eyes and said nothing.

She brought a little more sadness to the table.

I stayed quiet. On alert.

She gave up. "Maybe I can hire a cheap dog walker."

"You'll have to find one under the age of ten."

"Can I take them to the Church with me? She appealed, blinkingly.

An abstract of the four dachshunds racing around the Church would make Picasso blush.

"Does the Church have a backyard?"

She cheered up. "There's something back there."

She gave me an adios smile and hurried off and I, eager to see the latest incarnation of Roman, walked with Blondie to the Church.

It could be closed in mid-afternoon so I texted ahead and after knocking the new dog tail knocker, Roman briskly opened the door and proudly usher me inside.

He was wearing a green, well-fitting sports jacket, with, what else, a mutt looking emblem on the pocket. Next to it was pinned a shiny gold medal (military?).

"You were in the service," I dared to ask.

After a beatific smile came: "I am in the service of God and his animals."

He was bursting with good intentions and intonation. He invited me to sit down on a rich smelling leather lounger. He sat back in its mate.

"People are giving me donations," he crowed merrily. Knowing that I know he does not ask for them.

"I take them and make a more comfortable Church."

The visitors' chairs were now well padded.

"Isn't it easier to fall asleep during services?"

He winked. "My preaching voice blasts them awake."

"Are you going to have some entertainment," I ventured, making a veiled pitch for my dog songs.

He studied the question. He pulled a pad and a silver pen from inside his jacket pocket and wrote a short note. Then he turned back to with interest.

"Some people's dogs do tricks."

Was I barking up the wrong tree?

"The mayor came in and sat down with his dogs."

"I didn't notice."

"How 'bout TV and radio. They want to interview you."

He said nothing, checking his watch against the big electric one on the wall. I was surprised it did not have paws marking the hours and the minutes.

His indifference was bugging me.

"From what Dori told me, you're a local folk hero."

I was trying to lead him to the idea that he had over-admirers and others who had a beef with him, or dogs or the Church. Was he close to certain people? To infringe on his personal life.

Move on.

"Dori is now working for you."

His attention to me came alive.

"She's my buffer."

"She's very excited."

"Get lots of mail. Lots of phone calls."

"Gifts."

"A few," he winced.

"Did you get something with an egg in it?"

He was staring up at the unpainted ceiling, hardly distracted by my friendly grilling. I'm sure he was thinking it would be great for his Church if Michelangelo could come back to life. He turned to me.

"She showed me a box with an egg in it."

He paused to glance up at the potential canvas of a ceiling.

"I didn't know if it was a gag or an admonition," he snickered in a biblical manner.

For a guy who did not care if his clothes were a little rumpled, his shoes a little scuffed and his hair hurriedly combed, he was now smartly dressed, new shoes shined, hair nested and arranged. Despite his disinterest in being a local celeb, he was certainly warming to it and glamming up to the attention. I bet Moses cleaned himself up and put on something to catch God's eye when he went up to receive the Ten Commandments.

Roman once told me that in his "sleaze biography" days he had asked a popular actor how fame had changed him. The actor told him, "He didn't change. Everybody else did."

I went back to walk Blondie through the Park, ate a simple supper, watched some news and went back to the Church to check out the crowd. I brought Blondie.

I rambled around as another visitor with his dog, mixing and trying to match a personality or an attitude or a belief to the Egg. Roman would be surprised to see me, but pleased with my interest. If he only knew whose interest, I was there for.

And I expected to see Dori. I took a seat on the side, where the extra chairs were placed and looked toward the office to see Dori coming out. There was no Dori.

Roman was roaming through the half-filled Church, shaking hands and offering personal salutations. He went down on his haunches to greet the dogs, who responded with licks and wags. First-timers, I was sure, were overwhelmed by his attentions. Kudos to Roman.

In his sermon, he gave his usual blistering indictment of people who were cruel to animals and blessed the dogs who were brought for spiritual and physical nourishment. (when leaving, people left with bagsful of dog food and treats). He also blessed the people.

I watched the crowd. It was a humble bunch. I thought to myself, 'what could I do here?' My job at the wharf was monotonous. I loved baseball. But to be saturated with streams of goggling strangers with hardly a ripple of personality, of human intercourse, was soulless without solace.

I was fixed on moving on and if my observations were acute, by working in the Church I'd be in a position to discover the chicken who laid the egg on a cushion in the box.

One of the guests was a wispy-haired, thin as a rail older gentleman who rocked himself mesmerized by the soaring falling cadences of Roman's sermon. Several chairs to his right was an artistically shabbily dressed young woman with a weak smile, fondling a squirming black kitten. In another row, a very erect, suitably dressed lady was murmuring to her small, bejeweled poodle as she clasped it tightly to her bosom. In front of her, a broad construction worker with a red face dozed, emitting short, percolating sounds through a bandaged nose.

Another man who caught my eye was a younger chap with a shaved head who was hastily writing in a notebook, maybe jotting down highlights from Roman's speeches. Or maybe not. Except for three youngsters, sprawled out on benches in the back, snickering and imitating Roman's zealous arm waving, the others were quiet and attentive. No problem.

No one looked crazed. Blissful expressions were on many faces: Possibly picturing heaven on Earth or maybe picturing the destruction of the world.

My thoughts drifted back to the Egg. Was it a real threat or a prank? Or just a weird gift, with my imagination spiraling out of control? Why then, was the message so esoteric?

It was early evening, a friendly, light mist was refreshing the Park and Blondie and I took some loops around the block chatting and sniffing with the usual dog people and the usual dogs.

My cell phone, jammed into my back pocket, made a muffled ring. It was Dori. She had found another stranger letter. I was planning to go home and make some fried spaghetti. I invited Dori to dine with me, and bring along the letter. She agreed happily, recalling with relish my memorable dish. A gourmet she wasn't.

I was standing over the stove, urging the water to boil faster, and thinking back on last night's visit to the Church. Roman amazed me with his generosity and concern. So good.

He gave homeless men and women clean-up jobs around the Church, paid the standard wage and gave out countless dog and people food parcels. Very catholic (in the universal sense). Then another thought butted in. Good deeds and lots of money can be a formidable and friable mix.

Dori came in with a big smile, a tote bag, a big hug and a brief kiss. Wonderful. She draped her coat around the nearest chair and showed-off an "I love Roman" sweatshirt.

"Roman never mentions Jesus," were her opening words.

I was dumping the cooked spaghetti into a large, nonstick fry pan and proceeded to smother it with ketchup.

Dori sniffed the aromatic aroma. "I'm hungry."

"Soon, soon," I assured her while cavalierly mushing things around in the pan. My food vocabulary was lacking, as was my technique. If had set this dish before a king, I would have been hanged.

The spaghetti was finally done and I heaped it on to cover our two plates. There was a canister of parmesan cheese and an uncorked bottle of red wine, which I liberally poured into stemmed wine glasses. Classy.

"It has this year's date on it so I know it has to be fresh."

Dori sipped some without comment. She was in a good mood.

"Yes," I added slogan I once saw on a storefront. It impressed me. It said: "We will sell no wine before it is bottled." With that generous thought we dug in our spaghetti.

"Yum," she smiled sweetly, "You are a whizz." She put down her fork. This fabulous repast has made me forget the letter."

"The letter?"

"It may be important. We can always warm up my spaghetti and finish it later or I can take it home with me."

Dori opened drawers until she found a plastic sailing bag and put her spaghetti and stuck it in the frig for when she leaves. We cleaned the dishes and sat down with our glasses of wine at hand.

Dori withdrew the letter from her bag with her fingertips and gently set it down on a small table pulled over in front of us. It had a cancelled stamp.

Delicately, as if she were taking a small, shy flower from a thick bunch, she then pulled a paper from the envelope, open it up by the edges, placed it on the table, where we hunched forward and read it.

It read:

"God says to Jesus

Stop sitting on your ass

People believe the tabloids

And there's so little ready cash

Where the heck is Jesus? They say

When things are so egregious

Well, he's sitting on his hemorrhoids

Watching things go past."

"Roman never mentions Jesus," she briefed me, "I mean, what peanuts means to Snickers, Jesus means to religion."

"You're overboard on Snickers."

"Well," she edified me, "You know what a great German philosopher said."

"What?"

Her eyes burrowed into mine, finding a passage to my uninitiated brain.

"He said," 'Without Snickers life would be a mistake. You mentioned him once."

"I thought he said that about baseball."

"He was very well-rounded."

"Nietsche?"

"Yes, I looked him up and read his aphorisms."

"Were they compelling?"

"One stuck with me," she said provocatively with a twinkle in her eye. "Now, people will think he went mad because he ate too many Snickers Bars."

"There were no Snickers Bars then," I said reprovingly. "Then it doesn't make sense."

"Ah," she enlightened, "He was prescient."

We went back to the letter. It was pristine. No obvious marks or fingerprints. Not typewriter oddities. The return address looks like it was written in Latin.

Doris cellphone pulsated a synthetic beat, she dug it out of her tote bag and put it to her ear. She said "Yes?" and then listened intently with a widening smile. "Yes, I'd love to do it." Five seconds later the call was done.

"Guess what!?"

I nodded vigorously. "What?"

"An early morning radio show wants me to come on and talk about the Church tomorrow morning," she breathed out in wide eyed wonder.

"Calling so late."

"A cancellation."

She punched the radio station's address and phone number into her phone.

"Glad they picked you."

"Thanks, Beamer," she said, barely looking at me, fumbling with her tote bag and jumping up. "Need to go. Take the dogs out and get enough sleep. If I can sleep." The words tumbled out. "Coat? Coat?"

"On the chair."

"First time on air," she babbled, "Nervous."

"You know your subject."

"Yes! Yes! Yes!" Gotta prepare!"

"Luck!" I gave her a hug."

She put an arm in the wrong jacket arm and swept through the door with a parting wave of the empty jacket sleeve. A consummate touch.

Dori was rising in the world. Tomorrow she'll be even rising earlier in the world. Blondie needed a walk. She was quietly resting on her favorite rug, I had put her bowl out after she and Dori had their usual petting session. It was filled up with food and love. She was content.

It was dark outside, but some Park benches were lighted by turn of the century Central Park, New York City lampposts, which were funded by the residents.

Jonsy, an outgoing guy in his thirties, known, like many other denizens, for his tech wizardry, was busily dishing out treats to a bunch of besieging dogs, all eyes lifted in perfect begging mode. (I think they learn in the womb).

As it always happens, treats run out. Jonsy splayed his empty hands to the unbelieving dogs, saying: "No more." He was speaking in a language dogs refused to understand. Even if they understood it. They wouldn't understand.

He had an idea: Teach the dogs to read and when people are out of treats they could hang a sign around their necks clearing saying: "I have no more treats." So simple, but there were skeptics. Some dog people worried that it would lead dogs to read trashy novels and comic books. The idea was kept on leash, but not taken away.

I was at the Church. Roman was studying the letter Dori had left on my table when she rushed out to debut on the airwaves.

"I heard this reference about Jesus before," he stated blandly.

"In the Church?" I quizzed him discreetly.

"Yes."

"Do you discuss that subject with visitors?"

"No," he said, flatly disinterested.

He read through the letter again.

"This person," he spoke formally, "This person should look elsewhere for his spiritual salvation.

The firmness of his calling reminded me of the time when he was bonked on the head and off singing grandiose notions of himself. Is Jesus in the way?

To think people might be plotting against him does not coincide with his sense of fate. I had the dope, he had the dough. It made him immune.

Just then, Dori sallied out of the Office and pushed some letters into Roman's reluctant hands. She nodded at me and gave a hard look at him:

"Read them!"

He jerked out of his contemplations and scanned the letters as if he was a kid being reprimanded.

"Okay, thanks," he smiled back at her.

"See to it!"

"I will. I will," he complied, trying his darndest to be emphatic. He raised his arms appeasingly.

Roman headed toward the Office quietly, abashed by the only person who could abash him.

"You've got Roman on the run," I said admiringly to Dori's stern countenance following Roman until he disappeared into the Office and the door was closed.

"He puts things off," she said captiously, "Or forgets."

"How did it go at the radio station." She was on very, very early. I slept.

Her expression changed from wanting to give Roman a kick in the rear to a reflective consideration of my eager question.

"Crazy callers," she grumbled. "How can people have so much vitriol so early in the morning."

"Big word."

"Reading," she explained. "Anyhow," she went on, leaning towards me at the edge of her chair, her tone now lilting, "There were callers who loved the Church and Roman. They referred to him as Reverend Roman." Her expression changed quickly back to disgust. "People said the most awful things. Ugly!" She adjusted her position, sitting back up in the chair, as if to give more breath to her vinegar. "The last call was from a woman who nicely asked: 'Where's Jesus?' I couldn't answer her and she got hopping mad and vowed never to bring her animals to that unholy Church!"

She looked over at the Office with a grimace.

"I mentioned this to Roman," she said, turning back to me. "He wasn't interested."

"Jesus is tough competition," I insinuated cheerily. It brought a passing smile to Dori's face.

"Being on the radio wasn't as much fun as I thought," she moped, and then gave me a sideways, cheeky look: "At least no one can throw anything at you."

She weighed that remark and looked out the window.

"Would you do it again?"

"Not at that hour," she said gloomily. "Maybe, people aren't as mean later in the day."

The idea brightened her outlook.

Or even meaner, I thought. But I didn't want to derail her.

I softened it. "Maybe, you'd do better on TV. Where people could see how lovely and sweet you are."

"Cut it out!" she laughed and blushed a bit.

I took a deep breath. The words had just spilled out.

Never looking at me, she fooled with her hair, straightened her body, stood up and moved off with a slow gracefulness, saying to the air in front of her: "Back to work."

I sat for a while, meditating on the stuff happening. I was ready to leave when Dori came out of the Office carrying a batch of letters in each hand.

"Wanna come," she said in stride, "Gonna mail these."

"Sure." I hustled over to get in step.

We stepped out the door, carefully closing it and turned down Market. The mailbox was a few blocks away.

"Does he live in the Office?" I asked Dori's jutting profile.

"It's a studio."

"Spartan," I guessed.

"No way!" He's got all the good stuff. "She tightened her grips on the Letters as a bandit wind sideswiped us. "But," she sidetracked with disapproval, "No decorations."

"No religious ornaments at all?"

She hemmed: "Well, not entirely. There's a small wooden sculpture of St Francis of Assisi."

An illuminating moment. Of course! St Francis!

"God, have I got a slow brain!"

"Well, it's better than nothing," Dori piped in.

"Does he talk to it?" I wondered.

"Never heard him. But he pats it on the head."

"In reverence?"

"Sometimes it topples over."

Dori slipped the envelopes, one by one, into the mail slot, until, finally, they were all gone. She whisked her hands together to heightened the good job done, and boasted: "I wrote all those letters."

"Your job."

"Answering all those letters he gets. He gets a lot."

We started walking back up the hill, the wind invisible, but visible in the dirt swirling at the curbs.

"I tried to answer each letter with a personal touch," she told me with professional pride. "But it was too hard, time wise, and I had to resort to a sort of formula." She smiled vaguely. "At least, they don't come off a copy machine."

"That many letters."

"A horde!"

"He needs more help."

"If it gets worse, I'll beckon."

"He won't get anyone more scrupulous than you."

"He did recognize that I was handling tons more work and he upped my pay."

"That's consolation."

"He'll pay to avoid doing these down to earth things," she defended him, But, he knows they're necessary and have to be done."

She felt appreciated. "That's where I come in. I'm integral to the Church."

"He's developed a genius for drawing people to him."

"At least, a genius with taste," Dori augmented, with a twinkle in her eye.

"Fastidious?"

"After 8pm, I know nothing of the man.

"And you know him best."

Dori went back to work and I went back to the Park with Blondie. While she cavorted with her doggie pals, I thought Eggman. I reckoned that he or she was older, being intimate with the ABomb and probably showed up at the Church and knew of Roman's fondness for food and the result of that fondness. He wasn't thin as a rail but neither did he span the track.

Blondie and I were sitting together on the grass after she finished her play, and who strolls into the picture, but Charles the Comedian and his dog Guinevere.

His shaggy, unkempt hair brushed his shoulders, his beard showed 'shaving interruptis' and his features, once sharp and canny, were forlorn. The picture became dismal.

"I'm sorry," he mumbled, staring down at my startled face. He bent down and petted Guinevere to give him some succor. "It was a lousy thing to do."

"You bet." He was pathetic. I let my anger rest. "You're a mess."

"I was hopped up then," he wheedled. "My mind was jacked up. It seemed funny."

"You have a macabre sense of humor."

"Yes, isn't it great." he said caustically.

"If it wasn't for Dori, I'd be trying to find a gun."

"Gee."

"Gotta go, buddy," he saluted limply, barely focusing on me, and launching his body southward, he left with the ominous words:

"Got an appointment."

Depressed and hopped up he couldn't help me track down Eggman. I was hoping he had an appointment with someone to get clean. But his condition and his eyes said: "I'm on my way to get a fix, not to get fixed up."

Our interpretations would be different. Right now, I see the denigration of a good guy. Guinevere seemed OK. A good sign.

The sun was doing its job. The day was too hot and when sitting under the big, old tree that shaded the bench. There was no more big, old tree.

The tree had been creaking, decrepit and in danger of crashing down. It was sawed down by ParkRec and lumbered away. It was a sad event for everyone. I posted a memorial to our favorite Park tree:

The Tree is gone, no more shade
Hope it's not too centigrade
We've gained a vista and a stump
But, lost a place to cool our rump.

I was sitting on the shadeless bench, Blondie couched under it, working crosswords to keep my mind alive, when I raised my head to find two strange women, wearing bright smiles, standing in front of me. One was young, the other older.

"Remember me?" the younger one said.

She had me.

"Don't you like tuna fish?" she asked familiarly.

I stared at her. It was disorienting. I looked her all over, it was rude, But I must know her. I thought back. Then it struck me. 'The Actress!' I had seen her in so many guises, to see her in ordinary dress was new.

"You look pretty normal."

She was wearing a dark sweater and blue jeans, not the elaborate get-ups she wore inventing countries or playing a fish.

"I look normal?" She sniffled.

"The emphasis is on the pretty," I amended, quickly.

"Quite the tongue."

"It surprises me sometimes."

She introduced her Mother, who said 'Hello' and then excused herself to go to the dogs. She brought treats and was soon surrounded.

"I brought her to the Park where I had my movie debut." She gazed reflectively back to the hill side.

"A happy coincidence," I assured her. "Are you in the movies?"

"That was it." She waved it away. "I'm a stage person."

"Are you in a play now?"

"Don't you know?" She looked at me as if I had just taken a trip around the Solar System.

"Know what?

"We've reprised the Tuna play."

Oh, God!

"It's a small hit." She said joyfully.

You could have knocked me over with an empty tuna fish can.

"What!" It wasn't a miracle. A miracle is a good thing.

"We added the kidnap scene and a ransom scene and an exciting denouement.

"It was awful!"

"I know," she moaned. "But," her joy kicked in again. "We tried again with an expanded version and better props and found a decent space in a warehouse." Her sense of reality was encouraging. But I was still mystified, but rooting for her.

"We treated some local critics to expensive meals and asked them to come and see it," she enthused.

"They must have been derisive?"

"One paper's review, I quote:" 'It takes a special talent to write something this bad.' She laughed.

"So that ended it?"

"No."

"But it was fried."

"True. It was meant to be serious, avant garde or something."

"Something."

"But," she laughed genially, "That horrible review and the cheap admission, lured some people in. And they couldn't stop laughing."

"I see."

"People recommended it to their friends, etc."

"Wow."

"New critics called it "hilarious," she said proudly. "They singled me out. I am famous for my glubs." She was lit up.

"What a distinction."

"I'm the Glub Girl," she went on gleefully, "No one has ever been a Glub Girl before."

"Aren't you Lucky."

What could I say. I was baffled by the whole incredulous phenomenon.

"People were leaving the theater exchanging glubs."

Does it never end.

"I got an offer from a Japanese Company to be their spokes fish., she continued, unmercifully. But, she was puzzled. "I don't know how to glub in Japanese."

"I think it's a universal sound."

"And a company in the City, wants to create a line of Tuna Dresses."

"Will it have the tuna smell?"

"You're making fun," she chided.

"I'm flabbergasted." I glanced over at her mother playing with the dogs. "What does your mother say about all this?"

"She said:" 'They should give you better lines.' "She misses the concept."

In my ignorance of the theater I asked her: "Do you smell like a fish on stage?"

She was aghast.

"Of course! Before every performance I rub my body over with some canned tuna, so the audience gets my essence."

"Do they get hungry?"

"We have tuna sandwiches for sale."

"I can see a new perfume."

She looked at me approvingly.

"Essence of Tuna Fish," she said dreamily, "I'll be on every bottle!"

"Every girl's secret dream, to smell like a tuna fish."

"On the other hand," she realized, "I don't think we are going to have a long, long run. No movie producers or Broadway people have shown up." She managed to be cheerful. "It's camp. It's fun now."

"By the way."

"What?"

"What is your name now?"

"Charlene."

"Charlene,"

"Yes, Charlene," she sang it. "Don't you think it has a musical sound."

"It does."

"I like to sing."

"You sounded sweet."

"I tried to Glub into song but it didn't work."

"There's an idea! Why not turn the play into a musical?"

She grasped it as if someone was handing her a beautifully wrapped present from Tiffany.

Whether she thought it was a marvelous idea or turn out to be a dumb idea, she kept silent.

"Do you think this play will lead to other roles?"

"Well, I hope I can hook up to something when this ends," she said, snappily, her present tucked away.

"No one has played a Rhino," I suggested.

She nodded. "There was a play years ago called Rhinoceros."

"How about a boa constrictor?"

She considered it. "Maybe. Something to wrap my talent around." She threw her arms around herself and jutted her tongue in and out." I love to hiss."

"You deserve it, A witty snake."

"A parrot," she said happily. "At least you get to speak some words."

"Gotta go. Here's a ticket if you want to see the new version. I'll gather up my mother and take off." She gave me a solid wink. "Good seeing you."

"You, too,"

She took a few flying steps away from me, turned and said: "Glub, Glub. That means 'Love' in Tuna Fish."

"Glub, Glub", I returned. I guess it's all in the tonality.

I checked the ticket. The name of the new play was "Very Fishy." Not a surprise. It was complimentary and had an address that left me with no idea of the neighborhood. I had the idea of asking what happened to her after she was 'kidnapped' in the first show and what happened with the Actor. Maybe, someday, Maybe, never.

In the Park with Blondie. I marveled at the variety of dogs and their personalities:

There was 'Quick Rick,' ten-year-old Chihuahua, the most accomplished treated getter in the Park. The beautiful, all white, fluffy and friendly Phoebe, a Japanese spitz whom the kids adored.

So many. Lots of Labs and Doodles, the current popular King Charles Spaniel and the ubiquitous Chihuahuas and Terrier mutts. Pickles the Greyhound, smooth as silk, an awesome sprinter and so easy to pet. So many twisting, leaping, graceful ball catchers. Great eye- mouth coordination.

Blondie and I are heading down Market, off to the Main Library at Civic Center. As we approach the Church, I notice several people in fold-up chairs sitting back by the curb outside the big front door.

They were holding up homemade placards and as I pass, I read them: "Where is Jesus?" is written in black letters. The folks holding them up are older and silent. They don't watch me staring. They are somber, serious and peaceful. They are not blocking the sidewalk, making vocal demands or chanting.

I was impressed by their standards and courtesy. However, as we continued walking I felt a distress for Roman. His Church was an irritant to believers. But, it was never espoused as being attached to a

Religion. Although, St. Francis was a Catholic, it was for his love of animals for which Roman revered him.

Maybe, the Eggman was one of these people. And, as we know from History, violence can be provoked by a misspelled word. So, with my investigating juices at a simmer, I decided to pull-up a folding chair and join this group (no placard) get involved in their circle and snoop. Not detective parlance, but it will have to do.

On the way back from the Library, we passed them again. The dozen or so men and women were still sitting in formation and this time, moving their eyes side to side.

Now, a young woman, at least a generation younger, but with the same lofty expression of purpose as the others, sat with them. She bought out sandwiches, a thermos with paper cups and a bag for garbage.

The siege begins.

There was no sign of Roman. We went straight to the Park. Blondie roamed and I phoned Roman. My name popped up on his phone and he answered. He did not like answering it. Dori's job. He was surely getting surly calls from those believers who learned of the "Where's Jesus?" protests.

"What?" he spat, with biblical forbearance.

"You are pissed."

"Of course, I'm pissed. This is a stupid distraction."

"I just saw the protesters outside."

"It's ridiculous," he exclaimed, "My Church is for Cats and Dogs."

"The people feel, if you have a Church, how can you ignore Jesus?"

"There are a thousand Churches for Jesus," he argued sincerely, "Why bug me?"

"They are harmless. Why not make a simple concession? Put up a modern picture of Jesus as a regular guy."

"This is my Church!"

He was quiet for a short minute. Then, in a temperate and almost solicitous voice, he asked: "Why don't they pray to St. Francis, he is the savior of animals? San Francisco is named after him."

"I know."

"Right!"

"It's hard to fight devotion," I offered discreetly.

His tone changed when he described what happened earlier in the day. He spoke matter-of-factly: "About a dozen young guys came in, all in ties and sports jackets. They were from some small religious school in the Midwest. They had heard about the protests while visiting S.F." Roman was praiseful: They were well-mannered and were visiting S.F." He said they wanted to donate a picture of Jesus, painted by one of the fellows, that was reminiscent of their visit. They brought out a painting from protective sheets and presented as a gift. "To me!" he exhilarated, "and of course the Church. He accepted it with great fanfare, shook all their hands and blessed them fervently. They left in high spirits.

The painting was leaning against the nearest wall, still shrouded.

"You haven't looked at it."

"No."

I gave him an ingenuous stare. "Why not Roman? "It's perfect. You can pacify the believers."

"It's not appropriate," he said stuffily. "St. Francis would be appropriate."

"You can hang it in a little visited corner," I tempted him it would still be on display."

"No."

"Okay," I thought to myself, no use dragging this on. But I was intrigued that it was reminiscent of S.F. My curiosity was stoked.

I pushed him: "Does it bother you to see a portrait of Jesus?"

My edginess sharpened:

"Well! Unveil!!" It was definitely a demand. I had him in a corner. He was acting like an idiot and he knew it.

"Okay," he agreed, without a fuss.

"Thank you!" I said a bit harshly.

"A caveat," he deployed, reverentially.

"What!"

"I'm not hanging it up here." His words came out distinctly.

"Your choice," I conceded, I had no say in the Church.

A few minutes later.

"Where is Jesus?" he asked mysteriously.

"Describe it."

"Come and look."

"It's a guy sitting at a computer with red, white and blue hair and a ponytail."

Roman gasped.

"There's a red scarf around his neck and he's wearing jeans." Stylish."

Out of the blue, he stammered, "Is there a brand name?"

"His eyes have a strange orange glow."

"And dark stubble," he burst out, "He looks like my nephew."

"There's also a big, black Bible on his table and he has a "MOM", tattoo on the side of his neck.

"Do you know who this is?" I said to a gaping Roman.

"No."

"It's all about the contemporary Jesus."

"Huh?"

"Yep," I filled him in. "There are groups, mostly young, trying to bring Jesus up to date."

His eyes swung away from the portrait and riveted on me. He was shocked. "Jesus?"

"Exactly."

"Is this some cult?" he asked sensibly.

"Same old." I assured him. "New perspective." I enlightened him: in the Midwest, He's wearing overalls and milking cows."

"In the painting he looks pretty grubby," Roman derided.

"They were taking a whack at S.F."

"Not nice."

"It's respectful in its way." I said, sounding a little uncomfortable. "Patriot hair, not smoking, no marijuana butts, smile, Holy Bible at hand, Apple computer, referencing Adam and Eve."

"I'm vanquished," Roman chuckled, with good spirit.

"It's an end to your problem," I pitched in.

He gave a serious and unmuddled look. "An end? "How so? He did want to resolve the protest situation.

"If you hang it up, not too conspicuously, it could satisfy them."

He countered without a blink: "Don't want to hang it up. Gotta go."

I stood in his way. We had to resolve this. "Hear me out." He wanted to pass. "Two minutes," he relented.

What I had to offer him was definitely weird, but it was a twist he might be able to live with, considering other complications. First the Church.

I hurried my words: "Pretend it's a portrait of your nephew."

"Won't people think it's blasphemous? He said, cozying to the idea.

"It's contemporary," I gushed, It's San Francisco seeing Jesus in a new way, painted with true religious spirit, but uniquely modern. I didn't have to fool Roman, he had a sharp, obviously independent mind.

"It's a bargain I can live with." He gave me a pat on the shoulder. He looked at the picture without confusion and disgust. "It's quaint," he decided. "My nephew never looked so alert."

I went back to my place, gave Blondi a chew bone to gnaw on, pulled a folding chair from the closet and walked back to the Church to mingle with the "Where's Jesus" people and try to get a lead on the Eggman.

When I arrived, the WJP had gained mass. It had almost doubled; single filed along the sidewalk, careful not to block the walkway. Suddenly, the big Church door creaked open and Roman came out.

He was booed and chastised.

He carried two signs which he meticulously and unhurriedly nails to the wooden door, getting some frustration and anger out with pounding the nails even when they didn't need more pounding. He never looked at the crowd.

He heavily wiped his hands together, to finish and celebrate the job, opened the door with commanding flair, slammed it shut. The crowd ended up gawking. The dramatic and choreographing banging and posturing briefly mesmerized the audience. They watched the door slammed shut with a thrust and the lock click in place with a hard sharp rebuke.

The top sign read in big caps: "DON'T YOU KNOW?"

The smaller sign: "Closed for Redecoration.".

A few in the crowd were furious. A frail man shook his fist at the departed Roman. But many, being good Christians, meekly picked up their stuff and trundled off in a slow moving but unbroken line. Darkness was setting in.

I saw Roman peeking down from a narrow upstairs window. My phone sang. "Had to close the Church for services," he said with penitent bitterness. "I didn't feel safe," he roiled, they would take this place apart."

I doubted it, and finally so did he. "I don't trust religious nuts."

"They aren't nuts."

"Well", 'devotion leads to emotion which leads to explosion', "as a seminary friend told me."

"Okay."

Roman responded to the WJP with: 'Don't you know,' the idea that God is everywhere. Why are they picking on him? Has he deliberately offended anyone. Is it personal? It's hailing question marks.

I expect the protesters to come back, but more sparsely. Roman's bold message may have led believers to more conciliary thoughts. My mission is to probe their ranks for a suspect who neither Dori or Roman believes exists. A lonely job. Just need a scrap of convincing evidence that the Eggman or Eggwoman or Eggkid is real and bent on harm. My critical sense, however, tells me it is a man. A bombs are more a male's bailiwick.

When my workday was over, I took Blondie a few times around the block, left her something to chew on and went to the Church. I maneuvered my fold-up chair into a narrowed space, just before the curb behind and behind dedicated protesters with placards resting on their laps. I had seen them before. This time, chatting amiably with curious passers-by.

It was a grey day, with on and off rain which opened and closed the umbrellas of those who brought them. My rain slicker with hood was adequate. The plopping rain was light but gathering. The people in front of me held their umbrellas at the ready.

The umbrellas sprang to life, to their function, as a downpour sloshed the crowd. There was no shelter but the Church was locked. Some were immersed in prayer, heads bent, holding Bibles protected by plastic.

Most of the protesters were heading home, in a tumble to keep dry They traded articles of clothing each lacked and alternating umbrella use.

I heard amens from the prayers. There were wet smiles exchanged and a clasping of hands. It was a warm scene despite the chill and soggy weather.

Fat drops danced on the sidewalk. I wanted to engage someone in conversation but the pelting rain made it impossible to stop and talk. I jumped ahead and walked next to the fast walking man guiding the group out of the tempest. At least it wasn't raining frogs.

He was well bundled up, tightly gripping a swerving umbrella as the wind in its restless and reckless way, blew. I shouted to his ear: "I want to join your community." He hardly looked at me, he freed one hand from the umbrella. It dove down into his coat and he came out with a bent card. I took it and quickly stuffed it into my pocket. I gave him a signal with my hands, which I meant to be a benediction. He gazed at me, mystified.

I took Blondie around the block. Came back, toweled her off, hung up my slicker in the bathroom, placed my wet shoes by the wall heater, sat down on the futon, put my feet up, felt in my shirt pocket, pulled out the card. It read: 'Charles Renfield' and a phone number.

That's it!

I expected the name of a church or an arcane religious society or something with the name Jesus in it. It seemed so ordinary, considering all the aggravation they were causing for Roman. The man had no hesitancy handing out his telephone number. Maybe, I had a narrow notion of things. To find out was to call. In a day or two.

The cell rang. It was the message ring. I felt no obligation to answer. I was ensconced in my chair and the cell was too far away to reach. I could not disestablish myself from a lounging position. Terrible form.

Blondie was good company and she wasn't going to burden me with human dilemmas which I could hardly fix. Right now, I need a truce with the world; I won't disrupt it, if it does not disrupt me. Sometimes, it can last a whole five seconds.

There was a knocking at my door, rapid and firm. It jolted me as I was dozing off. There was a bell. It was "Whapp, Whapp, Whapp." Rhythm unchanging.

I had it figured out. It was Caesar, the shepherd of my neighbor across the hall. He was frantically wagging his tail; I was afraid he was going to break the thing. I opened the door and pushed him out of range. My neighbor came out with collar and leash and a reluctance to go out in the downpour. I closed the door. "Whapp, Whapp, Whapp."

I phoned Charles Renfield the next evening, after a predictable day of work, dog, Dori, Park and a bunch of etceteras. It was a brief and easy-going conversation. He saw that I was a dedicated Giants fan; he spotted my Giants cap under my hood and my lined Giants jacket under my see-thru slicker.

He was surprised to see me out there in such miserable weather and figured I must be a trustworthy man. He invited me to watch the game with him tomorrow evening. I accepted with pleasure and asked to bring Blondie. He liked dogs, but his daughter was nervous around them.

I passed through the usual activities the next day, obliterating everything from my thoughts that did not verge on my meeting with Renfield: How not to gum things up by being too nosy, yet trying to pin things down. Subtlety was my mantra. Good luck.

He met me at the door of his house, across from the Panhandle. It was a sturdy, solid house. It was the same impression I got from Renfield when he ushered me in with a big smile and a 'Welcome to my shack.'

He told me to 'Call me Charlie' and led me straight into a den with filled bookcases and a tapestry of baseball memorabilia stretching across two walls and notably, a giant screen TV.

He looked proudly around and bid me sit in one of the leather loungers. Between the two was a small table, crowded with beer, chips, onion dip and peanuts with raisins in a bowl. A dictatorial remote waited.

"You sure love the game," I said admiringly, as we contoured our bodies into the soft leather. He picked up the magic remote and clicked on the TV. I crunched a dipped chip and sipped a beer.

"You have a lot of mementos,"

"I played."

"You played?"

"Major Leagues." He watched my eyes widen.

"No kidding!"

"No kidding."

"Wow!" I searched my memory for the name, it was new to me. He saw that. He broke it down.

"I was mostly a utility player." he knew that I knew what that meant. But still.

"Bounced around: Twins, KC, Angels, Cards." Always a spot with a contending team. Good defense, step in for injured players, experience, pinch-hit. I had skills." He gave me a confident smile. "Lasted twelve years. Left no mark," he confessed with a wistful look in his eyes. "But it was fun. Playing baseball. Great pay. Good pension." He made an affectedly sorrowful face. "My nemesis though: The high fastball. The pitchers knew it and threw it. I was a sucker." He tried to outwit the pitchers by changing his stance to a crouch. The high fastball would be easier to lay off. "Would get on base with walks. Being on base is the main thing." I heard a sigh. "It worked for a while, but the pitchers being pitchers caught on to my scheme and they, of course, adapted. Hard to outwit a major League pitcher. They found another way to strike me out. Never had the average, but it was fun."

I didn't know if I wanted to look him up on the internet, not only to confirm he played, but also not to be embarrassed by his stats. He spent a lot of time on the bench, but was an essential ball player. He had to be good to play that long.

We watched the game, me enjoying Charlie's analyses and reminiscing about great players he played with. It's a tough game. I was also racking my beery brain for something to lead into the religious stuff.

It came. An opening. He pointed out an older player he once played with. "He's a hard-boiled guy. Not to mess with."

"Like a hard-boiled egg? I joked.

"Egg?" he gave me a weird look.

"Yes."

"Hard boiled eggs are actual," he educated me and shrugged off the oddball question.

"He's not soft."

He was leaning forward intently. A bases loaded, two out situations. Giants one run ahead. Relief pitcher marching in from the bullpen.

"I guess I was thinking of the decorated Easter eggs," I said, "That's when Jesus arises."

"He does," he said, his eyes not straying from the screen, as the batter dumbly swung at the first pitch and flied to center for the third out. He turned to me with a smile on a ruddy face with a slightly bashed up nose. He sat back relaxed. "It reminds me of my tuna salad, I use three hard-boiled eggs."

"I only use two."

"I know I'm not a cook," he laughed, "I want the water to boil faster."

"I know the frustration. Need patience."

"Amen."

"You seemed very serious about Jesus, sitting there in the rain."

"Oh," he said, "I'm just filling in for my daughter. She had tons of homework." He turned, palms up, "Jesus is her new idol."

"I see."

"She picked it up from a guy she's friendly with at school. He got off drugs, she said, when he asked Jesus to help him."

"I see."

He received a phone call, excused himself, and went into another room for privacy. I walked over to the bulging bookcases and found shelves crammed with books of WW11. I casually thumbed through the volumes until Charlie returned.

I was impressed that he was a consummate history buff.

"Well," he said, dismissing the accolade with a short sweep of his right hand, which had a few bent fingers from his years filling in for catchers. "They were my father's, who gave them to me when he moved to retirement home."

I mused on that one.

"Is he far to visit," I asked delicately.

"It's in SF."

"Good."

"He was a History professor," Charlie continued with pride and respect. "Served in the war and memorized it.

I threw in, interestedly, "Is he a religious man?"

"Staunch."

"What do you think of Roman?" I asked him in a casual and friendly way.

"He seems screwy," he half-joked and half-smiled.

"He means well," I assured Charlie, "But he can be a bit jarring at times."

"Why so many questions," he asked with a quizzical frown.

I tempered my approach: "I don't mean to pepper you," I apologized, "I just wanted to know why your community resents him?"

"That's ridiculous." He took a long swallow of beer. "There is no community. It's just individuals." He belched for emphasis.

"I didn't know."

He was irritated. To keep the friendship intact, I decided it was a good time to leave. He saw that I was feeling lousy about it and raised his palm. "Gimme five!" We slapped hands. A good guy.

"It's time for me to go."

"Oh?"

"Gotta get back to my dog, Blondie. She's used to being alone at night." It was a reasonable excuse, with a little fudge.

"Okay, no explanation needed. I miss having a dog."

I stood up. "I can watch the rest of the game at home," I said to his sprawling form.

"Good." He pumped his fist. "Go Giants!"

"I'll let myself out," I called to him heading to the door. "Enjoy the game!"

"Regards to Blondie!" he yelled. Suddenly, as I was opening the front door I felt a strong clap on the back and in a mildly inebriated way he proclaimed, as only he could: "Baseball is a glorious game."

I was out the door and walking home. "Wow!" I said out loud. "A Major Leaguer!"

At home with adorable Dori. She was fixing me an exquisite meal of meat and potatoes.

Could it get any better?

"So, you had a conversation with a baseball player."

"We watched a game together," I said, with the inference: 'How could you not be impressed.'

"How exciting," she muttered unexcitedly, over the frying potatoes.

Cruel. Cruel.

"Did he look like......?" she asked, resisting any more unholy jabs at my friend the Major Leaguer......"What do you call him?......the Eggman?"

I pounced. "A real baseball player would never do anything like that," I reminded her, with sacred conviction.

"Like what?"

"Threaten Roman."

She gazed at me with a questioning sympathy, put down her cooking tools, took my hand and felt my pulse, pressed her palms against my forehead, shook her head in hopelessness and went back to the stove. "Demented," she said to the cooking meat.

"But," I offered an appraisal, "I now have a roster of new suspects."

"You pumped him?"

"I did. In a nice way."

"Shame."

Dori was getting her kicks out of this. I couldn't blame her.

"Remember," Dori said, enigmatically, putting a beautiful plate of food in front of me, "Geese can fly at 30,000 feet."

"And I love at zero feet."

Quiet.

I'm waiting for another zinger.

"How's it going with Roman and the Church," I inquired with carefree interest.

"Same."

"Lots of calls and letters to answer?"

"It's tailed off."

She sat down with her full dish. I dug in and ate heartily.

"It's delicious."

"Thanks," she smiled, her eyes averted.

She pushed her meat and potatoes into a pile and toyed with it, like she was at the beach. "Sorry I jerked you around," she said, with a soupcon of remorse.

"It's okay," I said cheerfully, "I look forward to your jabs and barbs."

"My jabs and barbs!"

Oops.

"Your gentle kidding?"

It was too late.

She finished off her meal swiftly, swiftly and noisily removed our places, set them down noisily in the sink and turned on the water full blast.

She came back with dessert bowls. She set one down quietly at her spot and slid an empty bowl roughly in my direction. She sat down very properly and daintily spooned a little ice cream into her mouth with meticulous concentration as if it was the only thing in the world that interested her. She stopped spooning, went off and came back with the ice cream carton (Cherry Vanilla) and a scooper. She moved to the side of me and plopped two scoops spattering into my bowl from a great height. Then with elaborate grace and precision laid a single scoop perfectly on top of her original scoop.

"Chocolate syrup?" I asked, cautiously.

A squeeze bottle of chocolate syrup appeared next to my right ear, moving down to my bowl. The squeezing began before it hit my ice cream and unfortunately spread over my pants.

Must be bad aim.

Was I chastened? I guess so.

"I must get back to my dogs," she remarked, with disdainful aplomb, tidily gathering her things together. She left with a cool smile, filled with teeth.

"Whew!" What could I say." My vocabulary was too limited. I'll watch baseball instead, where I can do my best meditation. Bad things happen Sometimes, the Universe is generous and tries to balance things out. Or else, life would even have fewer letters.

The next day when I arrived at work, the owner and his son were there to greet me. He looked somber. I tried to look somber. He noticed that I was 'fatigued' with my job. His son was going to work in the store and learn the business. I was expendable. His words were kinder. The lady who replaced the ex-con was doing a bang-up job. He pinpointed my 'fatigue.' I put up no fuss.

I was expendable. Great. I was happy to be expendable. Unemployment benefits. Getting laid off. I'm glad I stuck around. The Boss gave me my current check with a whopping month's pay added.

We shook hands and I tried to look downcast as I was leaving. But once outside, the Sun and I were partners: We were both warming up the World. "Yippee!"

I called Dori to tell her the good news that I lost my job.

She gave me a restrained "I'm so happy for you."

Now that I had the time, maybe she could convince Roman to give me some work during services so I could carefully check everyone out without acting suspicious.

"I'll think about it."

'Will she be in the Park this evening?' It sounded like 'Possibly'. I heard her four dogs barking angrily at the door and there was a furious, staccato buzzing of her bell.

"Gotta go,"

She called me a minute later.

"There was nobody there," she said, uneasily.

"Has it happened before?"

"Yes," she said warily, "At the same time."

I thought: Next time I'll be on guard. Then I reasoned: "probably some kids riling up the dogs."

"There are always kids running through the halls." She sounded relieved.

"Maybe, a joker has just been added to the bunch. "Scared me for a moment, though," I confessed.

"Scared me too."

"I can't think of a silly, funny thing to say."

"That's encouraging. Bye."

Time is a dimension. Time can bend. Time can compress and expand. It takes up a lot of space. We're surrounded by it. Time has an invisible weight. We can't see it, hear it, feel it or smell it. But it's always right there. Not hopping a train to Milwaukee.

Time reminds me of dogs. Dogs are enfolded in Time.

Blondie and I took long, leisurely walks around the City, in no hurry to be anywhere. The Wharf, Golden Gate Park, the Beach (Blondie preferred the grass to the sand), the Haight. Places I had been to many times before, but they now seemed to be lighter, airier and more interesting.

During our last sightseeing walk of the day, through Chinatown, Dori phoned me to tell me that the Church had received an identical to the Egg box. She didn't think it was dangerous.

"Don't open up!" I screamed into my cellphone, causing some consternation in the people around me. I shook my hands in the air, indicating things were OK and smiled. They moved on.

"Okay!" Dori snapped, distressed from my screaming, "I won't open it!"

"I'm coming over. Keep your distance from it."

"Okay." The word had a little chill in it.

Blondie and I strode down to Market, then fast-clipped it to Van Ness, constantly serving around walkers, then up a few blocks to level ground and the Church, I was sweating and Blondie panting. First thing, water for the dog.

Dori immediately brought a bowl of fresh water up to Blondie. She drank and lay down. Dori brought the package over, looking at me warily, since she didn't believe there was anything sinister in the gifts. Was I cuckoo?

Just an hour ago the Church was home to a congregation enraptured with Roman swelling the atmosphere with Biblical phrases and high thoughts, singing ecstatically of human goodness ahead and whatever else Roman threw at them. It was deserted now, Roman invited to a dinner in his honor by a generous donor.

The box sat on a table, in pretty wrapping, on the other side of the Church. Even though Dori thought I was loony, I bet she carried around a doubt, tucked away, that she may be wrong. She brought that doubt with her as we both walked across the Church to the box, she standing slightly behind and to the side of me, she didn't refuse to move when I asked her too. Close to the box again she acted more on my side.

I gently untied a wide, red ribbon, tore off the flowery wrapping paper and there it stood: A replica of the original box. Dori looked on, eyes wide, body motionless as I deftly pulled out the gift with unbearable slowness and very carefully laid it down on the table, trying not to jar the insides.

Brave Dori edged closer to me as my fingers moved to the lid opening. She flinched, as I jerked it open, while taking a step back. "Why couldn't you open it slower?" Dori railed at me.

No doomsday. We looked inside. Dori and I both nervously idling. On the usual soft carpeting, sat a miniature, chocolate football. On top of the football were sprinkles, spelling out: 49ers. We both felt very relieved.

"It's very sweet," she gushed, smiling at my confused expression. "See, nothing nasty," Dori," assured me," He knows Roman is a football fan."

"I'm touched."

In her triumph, lately, of always trying to see the good in people, she lifted a small manila envelope from the bottom of the box, undid the clips and with two fingers, slowly pulled out a sheet of expensive looking paper. There was a sketch, beautifully colored with an array of inks'

"Talented," flew off Dori's lips. "What is it?"

"Football field."

"Ah, I see it now," she said, changing her focus. "I was impressed by the design."

The players were slashes in red and blue. Except for two. One was the red quarterback standing tall, his right arm extended forward as a brown football sailed in the air toward a red receiver who was running at the other end of the field, looking back and up at the football, with his arms outstretched close to the goal line.

Like the first gift, it seemed clear and unmysterious. All my hazy skepticisms of intrigue and foul play were massacred by good angels. Dori was here to see me fall on my face. She didn't give me a blunt:' 'Told you so.' But a shiny smile that read" 'All is well.' I smiled back and theatrically swept the back of my hand across my forehead, clearing off the sweaty thoughts.

Dori tried to rewrap the gifts. The red ribbon was still intact. There was still no return address: the postmark was SF No accompanying note. Maybe, Roman knew the sender.

Dori locked things up and we walked together to her building. She was going to take her dogs to the Park and I, to take Blondie on a stroll around a few blocks. She rumpled my misbuttoned jacket jokingly, kissed me partly on the cheek, hurried up the few outside stairs, sought the keyhole of the outer door, found it quickly on the inner door and scampered up the stairs to her digs; to be welcomed by four adoring, loving creatures.

Did Blondie duty. Had baked beans. A big bowl of popcorn flavored and made healthier with a covering of nutritional yeast which, believe it or not, has a cheesy taste.

Turned on a baseball game. I desultorily followed the game, my thoughts distracted as I remembered my reaction to the first gift. It was an instant reaction. There was something creepily strange about this brotherly gift. All through this affair I was certain something was wrong. And, now, suddenly, all apprehensions are dismissed. Just like that!

I recalled the box. Chocolate. Poison? That would be sacrilegious. Dori had praised the drawing and looked for a hidden signature or hidden initials. Nothing. But she billed him as a 'very good artist.' No question. The artwork stood out. It was simple: The Art of the Pass. I repeated it, saying it out loud.

I juggled it around in my brain. Why this particular play? The quarterback throwing a long to a receiver at the other end of the field? No one else is involved. It's an exciting play, often when the team is in jeopardy. Then it hit me! a BOMB!

Blondie, well-acquainted with my thoughtful preoccupations, roused herself from her personal throw rug and put her paw on my knee.

"You are right, Blondie," We need to convince Dori that there was a plot afoot.

What impressed me about the Eggman was how he could do something so terrifying, appear so ordinary and innocuous. Of course, I'm banking on my own fallible instincts and inner detective to see through this devious charade.

Took long walks with Blondie through the quietude of Golden Gate Park cogitating on the case. Hiking steep hills to reach clear vantage points and look down at the city in miniature. How would I get Dori on my side? We saw the same gifts. What I saw as 'demonic', she saw as 'cute.' It behooved me not to horse around. To pin her down to realizing that 'Mr. Cute,' was a very crafty person, intent on doing harm.

She was regularly in the Church with Roman. Did he have some special buds or budettes in the congregation? Does he ever mention other people to her? She may have noticed something in casual observation. Make her think she was protecting Roman, not spying on him. She knows I'm not crazy or befuddled. It's just a long jump of reasoning. That is was worth being circumspect, since we both had high regard for Roman, even if he was a maniac.

I thought, then I unthought, trying big, high-sounding words to buttress my case. But I discovered she could 'out big-word' me. She keeps it simple. "Please," might work.

I laid out the whole thing for her as we sat on our usual bench, flanked by the friendliest dogs in dogdom. Following my explication, she finally saw a bomb motif in each gift.

She gazed at me with a bit more respect and a little less credulity. What helped to clinch it was the new questioning expression in her eyes and a gravity in her voice, when she said: "I didn't see that,"

"It's not a joke, is it?"

"Nope."

She looked at me with grave benevolence. "If I can't believe Beamer, who can I believe?" She reflected with a musical riff in her voice.

"Brilliantly stated."

"It's still a stretch." she enunciated with retroactive firmness, "You're reading too much into it."

"My senses tingled."

She looked at me quaintly. "If you were a dog, I might believe you more.

"I can be very frisky."

She smiled brightly and we got off the subject. We devoted ourselves to our furry beasts, who were impatiently pawing us to provide them with some mischief.

Our talk of the Eggman continued at Dori's place. Her dogs wolfed down various treats dropped into their bowls and settled down to dognap. Blondie was also treated and she nestled between us on the sofa. Refreshments were a walk to the frig.

Dori made a piquant observation: "if he's trying to be a sadist, he's not trying very hard. People have a genuine fondness for Roman."

"You make sense, but he doesn't."

"Your detective imagination went berserk," she chided, teasing with a protruding bottom lip. "Poor Beamer."

"Berserk is not a nice work," I kicked back. "It's childish."

"I am stretching my imagination where no one has stretched it before."

I stared into space. She tapped me provokingly on the shoulder. "Let's hear it."

"First of all," I pushed an idea I was mulling over. "Roman is not fat."

Dori was indifferent and settled back in oblivious mode. She took in a big gulp of air and let it out in little puffs, like a little train puffing its way to its destination.

"Pudgy," she allowed, "but certainly not fat."

"Yet," trying to recatch her serious interest, "There was 'Fat Man' on the Egg, not 'Pudgy Man.'"

"Couldn't," she finally said, after looking hopelessly distracted.

Did she want to be swayed? She was acting deliberately indifferent. After all, she was the one handling packages. Was that fair?

"We have clues!" I argued, stepping on the gas and bumping into her resistance.

"Yes," she answered promptly. "He's an artist. A football fan. Very religious. A cohort of Roman. A visitor to the Church."

"But why no return address?"

"That does put a crimp," she conceded, "But. Big deal."

"For a person so meticulous with detail, leaving off the return address is not neglect." Dori's head bobbled cutely to this consideration. "It shows he is hiding something."

Maybe, I'm mistaken that these gifts are the work of an evil-mastermind. It sounds far-fetched. So, I offered this deal to Dori:

"I hope nothing bad happens in the meantime, but if he sends another gift and there is no bomb motif, I will drop the matter." She listened patiently. "But," I emphasized to her with a shrewd, dark look, "if there is another obvious bomb motif, will it convince you to help me track him down?"

Dori listened keenly as I summed up my spiel.

"A deal?" I formally asked, putting out my hand to shake on it.

Her arm did not move.

"Well," she said, jauntily, "I hope, meantime will not be mean, she poked, with witty, black humor. "If you are right." She straightened up, scrunched her back, got up, went to the frig and came back with some beers, with names I couldn't pronounce, but with a word I could pronounce: Good.

Dori made her decision: "Based on what we know now," she said austerely, "I accept. But who knows what contingencies might pop-up."

"Let's seal the deal with scotch tape."

"Done!" We shook hands and exchanged a few tricky slaps.

I couldn't help laughing at her bargaining.

"Dori," I said, with praise, "You are equivalent."

"I certainly am equal," she replied, forcefully, and waved her fists, very ladylike, in my direction.

"Don't worry about bobbing my facade," I told her, "It might improve my looks."

She brought her arms back to her sides and stared at me disagreeably, "I like the way it is."

The days zipped by. The mail rolled in. But no gift boxes.

Dori actually approached Roman about my working there during services. He didn't say anything, but at least it put the idea in his head. Contingencies might show up, as Dori foresaw, due to the Eggman. That would help me get in with Roman.

I came up with an idea that would be irresistible to the Church.

"Plants?" Dori assumed.

"No way!"

I would stand outside like a barker, enticing people into the Church to see naked canines dancing in the aisles with the Holy Spirit to witness the stripping of the Bible to its ethical core. See pictures of St. Francis of Assisi in loving intimacy with God's innocent creatures and Roman baring his beautiful soul to the congregation.

A new box came, sooner than the second came after the first. He's speeding up. Dori brought it to my place as soon as she finished her duties. She arrived forty-five minutes later.

She excitedly, but carefully, eased it out of her backpack and placed it solemnly on the table, like a relic that has been buried for five thousand years.

I took a deep breath and unwrapped it with clumsy fingers. I inched it open and when nothing happened, I swung it completely open, with incaution and a still curious dread.

As usual: Two articles.

Aluminum foil around and around a sweet potato and another fine drawing, this one a rendering of a 1950's Edsel, orange colored. The color of the sweet potato matched the color of the car. Next to the car were the words 'Sweet Potato,' like someone's pet name for their car.

Dori scanned the picture, picked it up, shook it, turned it over and rubbed it. "It's only a car," she smiled, happily. She picked up the sweet potato, squeezed and sniffed it. "It's a real sweet potato."

She didn't say she was right and I was wrong, but her expression couldn't help broadcasting it. She did a quick short jig around the table, not directed at me, but to celebrate an end to worry. No bomb motif here.

I wasn't wrong. She finished her little dance and saw that I wasn't smiling over the good news.

"Aren't you happy that it's over?" she beamed.

"I wasn't wrong."

She drew back in sudden confusion. "What!?" She flinched, the sun in her eyes vanished.

"I wasn't wrong," I repeated in the same tone.

She was trying to digest my words.

"Do you know the Edsel?"

"Never heard of it," she said with dismay, trying to shrug off a bad answer.

"I was a 50's car that didn't sell." I filled her in. It wasn't a lemon, but it was a flop. There was no niche for it.

"So what! So what!?" She shot back, getting more irritated.

"Do you know another word for a flop?"

Her eyes were darting, her mind racing to get it. She made fists and concentrated. It came. A minute later, her fingers spread open and she mouthed the words: "A bomb." Her figure sank. "Oh, no."

"Oh, yes," I told her. "Look at the shape of the Sweet Potato."

She came out of her disappointment and nodded. "I didn't pay attention." She assumed an innocence: "It's a sweet potato."

I added an ingredient: "Look closely at the bumper on the car," I motioned her to the drawing. "There are dark, red splatters." She peered at the artist's work. "Looks like blood."

"Sure does."

"Blood on the Bumper," she gee-whizzed, "Sounds like a British mystery.

"Artistic blood."

She came out of her indifference. She felt the full impact of the Eggman.

"Running over someone." She was uncomfortable with her stubborn view of his goodness. There was something to be afraid of. No more cute. Only ugly.

"It could be a decoration to cheer up the dowdy Edsel." I considered off-handedly, to let her make her own conclusion.

"It's blood," she said, overcoming her artistic impulses. "Definitely

"He's speeding it up." Dori gulped, like her stomach slumped. "We have another clue," I said to her, acknowledging her joining me. "He's probably fairly old and even owns an Edsel, stored away in a garage. The car is priceless now."

"Roman sometimes goes into raptures about owning a Lambergetti."

"He and Roman have the same interests. It should make it easier to locate the guy, yet...."

"Yet?...... Yet?......" she primed.

"Yet," I've gotten nowhere.

"You decoded the mystery!" She said with wonderment.

"I uncovered a danger and a crazy guy," I said, deflecting the premature compliment. "Who is this guy?

No hesitation.

"Even though you are the smartest person in the world," Dori smacked her lips softly and Sherlock Holmes would be ready to wash your sneakers, you don't have crime fighting equipment, no legal credentials, you can't go around busting people on your own."

"You make an outstanding point, Dori," I said with no mocking attitude. "But, do you have an idea?"

"I do."

"Tell me."

"Cops."

"Based on what?"

"The gifts."

"You are welcome to bring the Gifts to any police station and explain to them that you deduced from these gifts he was plotting to blow people up."

"Foolish?"

"At best you're acting quirky. At worst, you're insane."

"Maybe," she reasoned, "But a check of fingerprints, DNA test, Edsel buyers, 49er ticket holders could find him."

"They'll tolerate you "cause you're pretty, but they will think you're a nut. This is SF."

She bowed out. Too risky and stupid.

"But you gave me an idea."

"What is it?" she asked, smiling at me, pleased she was contributing.

"Do off-duty cops show-up with their dogs?"

Her eyebrows went up a notch, then scrunched down hard, while her eyes threw out laser rays. Her mouth puttered out sounds from untuned wind instruments. It was like she was composing a wild symphony in her head. But Mozart did it with a lot less effort. But, then, he was never asked to flirt with a cop.

"Yes," she said quietly smoldering, "Cops come with dogs."

"If you could get him to do you a favor."

"Fingerprints, DNA, etc.," she said, super sweetly with a touch of murder in her eyes.

"That would be big."

I was momentarily, for the last few minutes, distracted by my idea and didn't realize I was stoking a fire.

I rambled on. "It would be easier for a fellow officer to ask a buddy to do a check, than for a nut off the street to ask for it."

"There's logic in that," she cracked, her anger on simmer but scorching with sarcasm: "The charm, the persuasion, the helpless need, the pleading beautiful eyes, the tender touch of the skin, etcetera."

"That's your department."

I had never seen annihilation in someone's eyes before.

"Poor Beamer," she said, shaking her head in pity. "You've been there. Did she clean out your bank account?" She burst out laughing and spent a minute drying her eyes. Then she got back to the painful point. "Your crackbrained idea was not a contingency, but a humiliation for me."

"I'm sorry."

"I know he's a danger," she said considerately, "But we've just been going around in circles to protect Roman." She calculated: "Why not ask Roman if he knows this guy? He probably does."

"He prizes all the gifts."

"Exactly."

"Now you see why I wanted you on my side," I smiled at her beneficently.

I got the Dori beam.

"We still need to hurry things up." I picked up the gift and studied it again. "When you give it to Roman, Dori, find a time soon when we can talk together tete a tete a tete."

"I never studied repetitive French," she recited. "But I'll get him to agree quickly."

"Great."

She was off to church.

Two hours later, after giving Blondie some outside time, I was in the Church sitting in a soft recliner. Dori and Roman had been sitting for a time and preferred standing and moving their parts.

"Dori gave me a synopsis." He was troubled and squinting as if he wasn't sure he was seeing right. "It's unbelievable, if I believe it," he said, unmoved.

"We didn't want to shake you up."

"I'm not shook up," he protested, still uncomfortable with this daunting news. He sat back down in his recliner, put one leg over the other, leaned back into its coziness. He clasped his hands together over his stomach and gazed skyward. But he couldn't hide a flicker of worry on his face.

"Don't you take it seriously?" I implored. He was implacably unmoved by the evidence.

"Bombs?" he joked

"Isn't it possible?"

"No," he affirmed.

"Why not?" Dori pitched in, flurried.

He looked at us with a soft expression. "I know the man who sent these gifts."

"A friend?" I asked in confusion.

"A colleague."

"A colleague?"

"Reverend Larry," he smiled with pride.

"Reverend Larry?"

"He tends to speak in question marks," interjected Dori.

Roman conveniently explained. "He runs a small, storefront Church in the Mission." He dug into his obscenely expensive wallet and pulled out a card. Dori, who was nearer to him, took it and passed it on to me. Roman rubbed his chin briskly as if he were trying to remember exactly who Reverend Larry was. He did give much help to burgeoning, but poor ministries. "I gave a hefty sum lately and these gifts are thanks for it."

"He's a very good artist," Dori reminded him. He looked confused.

Roman guffawed. "His one painting he sent to me was an abstract monstrosity."

"Maybe, he was hiding his talent."

"It worked," chuckled Roman. He gallantly shrugged his shoulders.

"It must be someone in his Church," I reasoned easily.

Someone who was not there long," Dori chipped in.

"Well, what about this bomb stuff?" I said harshly to the charitable Roman. "You can see why we were worried."

"I don't doubt what you picked up," He sympathized, "You are very keen" He opened a space in front of him with his hands. "But it is so esoteric, that it would be lost to everyone except to the one who was meant to see it."

He made a neat and cogent distinction. I nodded in appreciation.

"So would the purpose be," he continued, taking a peak at his watch, "And why would anyone want to hurt me? Speaking the last words he looked distressed.

Dori came over and gave him a salutary hug. He went back to the Office and Church business. He had lives to fix and tails to set wagging. But, not to forget for a moment, Eggman was speeding up.

Roman had made a salient point. What is the point of terrorizing someone, who didn't know they were being terrorized? An audacious idea popped into my head. But the only one that made any sense. Was Roman sending these gifts to himself? Could he be depending on Dori and me to unravel the mystery of these oddball gifts? For publicity?

Dori and I both witnessed his bouts of monomania in his calling, maybe fostered by his years in the seminary. It was crazy, but something to explore. Did he have a classic case of split-personality? Two Romans inhabiting the same pudgy body? Jealous of one another. Not beyond the realm of detecting imagination. Dori spends the most time with him. She may accidentally know something of his intimate hours beyond the Church.

Dori and I met outside Reverend Larry's storefront.

The store was crammed with men and women of a mostly riper age. They were enjoying themselves with camaraderie, loud laughter, loud talk and frequent slapping of palms. They acted like they hadn't been together for a long while.

The store was next to a taqueria and some youngsters were sitting in unfolded chairs on the side eating choice Mexican food with enthusiasm. There were already some empty food containers stacked and scattered on several small tables.

We had no description of RevLarry from Roman. They had never met. We figured we could pick out a man of cloth with ease. We made a bet on who could pick him out first. Loser would pay for our Mexican lunch to be.

We separated and ambled around the group. The pretty Dori was soon welcomed into small herd of lively gentlemen. She moved away to sit on an ancient sofa, in between the lumps. Probably donated. A guy quickly sat down next to her on a lump and made some remarks. She signaled me to join her. A move that dispersed her admirer. Her eyes diligently swept the room, searching for the mysterious RevLarry. She didn't want to pay for my meal. She knew I would order something expensive.

I glanced from face to face, clothes to clothes, voice to voice for the elusive Rev. People weren't clustering around any particular person as it would be with Roman in his Church. Dori stood by me and together we passed around the huddles of people until they stared us away. We were a nuisance.

"We could ask someone?" Dori concluded.

"There are no dogs?"

"I guess it's just for needy humans."

"I suppose." None of the crowd seemed to be in any financial, moral, criminal, drug or bodily jeopardy. Despite the crummy furniture the only things that could conjure up a religious image in this place were the stains on the walls. It was cheap and rundown, stale and dingy and had no pretension to be a sacred place of worship and healing. Roman had got it wrong. Unless, the party atmosphere was the initiation of a plan to fancy-up the space.

I was not inclined to eyeball anyone, so my interest turned to a nicked-up wooden podium at the front of the room piled with notebooks and next to them a glass of water and a pair of sunglasses left unfolded.

Finally, with frustrated and betrayed senses we butted into conversations to locate RevLarry. We explained we worked with Roman who had donated a lot of money to the Reverend. People turned affable and courteous, but told us nothing.

We noticed a guy sitting lonely on the lumpy sofa, who had bowed out of the noisy, bustling familiarities and seemed dazed by it all.

I modulated my voice to go under the racket, Dori sat next to him, to translate, if necessary.

"Which one is Reverend Larry?"

"What?" He bent his ear forward.

I repeated the question in a low growl.

"Reverend Larry?"

"Do you know where he is?"

"Yes, I do."

"Where?" I growled, without mercy.

"In the bathroom."

Did that sound right!

"In... the...bath.... room?" I spaced out the words dryly.

He stared at me as if I were crazy. Dori was enjoying the whole spectacle. When I turned to show her my hanging-out tongue, she already had a big smile on her beautiful face. Oh, well.

The guy stood up, and seeing that my revving engine was back to neutral, he added that Larry often retreats to the bathroom for a break. Then he moved hastily away from the weirdo.

"Is he coming out?" I yelled after him. The guy checked his watch and yelled back: "Anytime now." He headed for the outside door.

Can the line of sense be anymore jagged?

Dori was having fun and what she was saying was cut short by a sudden double-loud uproarious cheer and mad applause. The event was a man coming out of the bathroom, from a door behind the podium, vigorously wiping his hands on a paper towel. He rolled it up, stood over a trash basket, threw it into the air and watched it land into the basket. His eyes never moved. There was another, quieter cheer. Maybe, he was demonstrating basic gravity. Bewildering.

He was a regular looking guy with big ears, out of an average looking guy catalogue. If he sold you something on TV, you'd buy it.

No Reverend aura about him. No halo, either. He exuded nothing religious. No fervor. He just stood there, very plainly, facing the gallery. There was one thing that stood out. He was blind.

He felt along the top of the podium, picked up and put on the dark sunglasses as the crowd scurried around grabbing folding chairs set on the side walls and opening and arranging them orderly, sitting down and priming their expectations. There was buzzing and then a silence as Reverend Larry stepped out in front of the small podium and opened his arms wide in what looked like an embracing of the worshippers. For he certainly seemed to be worshipped by them.

Dori, rising to the occasion, squealed like a teenager over an idol, as the group was enraptured. A ````` blessed moment. The man had hardly said a word or exercised a muscle.

"My sight failed me," he spoke waveringly and humbly. Or do I exaggerate. Maybe Dori's squeal wasn't a squeal but a lament on his blindness and maybe the crowd wasn't as enraptured as tired. A few heads drooped.

"But," the man's voice, valiant and steady, spoke the words: "There is hope." A heartfelt cheer rang out from the audience and a gratifying smile rose on the man's somber face.

"I'll not go into details," he apologized, as he could pick up the restlessness of his listeners. "Some of my sight may be restored." People clapped resoundingly and cried: "Great! Wonderful!"

"How?" A well-dressed man asked, and the group. became silent for the answer.

"Surgery."

"Where?" asked an older woman avidly, with a cellphone nestled in her hands.

"UCSF," came the not unexpected reply. Heads nodded. One of top hospitals in the USA. "Don't need to add," said the Reverend decisively,

"But I will," the levity eased things up, "That it is a daring procedure, with no guarantees," he cautioned. "But my insight tells me to believe."

The room erupted into more cheers as Reverend Larry waded into the crowd with abandon, as the crowd abandoned their seats to surround him: Hugs and handshakes and pats on the back smothered him and he soon disappeared from view.

Dori cried, but I kept my composure, but felt warm inside, rooting for Larry and his friends. They were not churchgoers but friends. There was nothing 'Churchy' about the place. Roman heard the name and thought he was in the religious business. It must have something to do with dogs. But, what? As Dori once observed: "If you ever leave your mark on the world, it will be a question mark." Mr. Interrogative.

The suffocated with love Reverend eased his way out of the mass of bodies, gained his balance, sucked in some fresh air, waved and went back into the door behind the podium. People spread out around the rooms in small cliques. Dori went over to one and asked what this was all about. I was wondering where the dogs fitted in.

We canvassed the room and from snatches of conversation and questions, we gleaned the story. A young woman, still blissful from meeting Reverend Larry told us in an excited rush of words: "If this operation works, He can bring back RangerDog."

Before I came to SF there was a comic strip in the Chronicle called: "Canine City," with none other than RangerDog as the hero. There were coy resemblances to big-shots and the bevy of odd folks in the City. SF in furry disguise.

There were dogs and other animals in supporting roles. There was Reverend Rabbit and his long ears. That's how Larry got the Reverend tag. Kids loved the rascally characters and the adults the bite, the reflective mischief and antics portraying the City.

When he lost his sight, the comedy and crusade ended. He was a good talker, and made a modest living doing radio. But Canine City and RangerDog was his baby. He created it, wrote it, drew it. No one else. No RangerDog to fight corruption. No Reverend Rabbit to threaten the miscreants with loss of the heavenly DogHouse.

We left the storefront without speaking to Larry. Did he have any notion of Roman? An anonymous someone plopped down a hunk of money in his lap and that was it. It did have something to do with dogs. His dogs already had spiritual and also tactical guidance. Both Dori and I wished Larry well and hoped RangerDog would wag his tail once more.

We were walking back to the Church to expose Reverend Larry to Roman, when I made an blunder. To lighten the outing, I told Dori that sometimes I felt like a Dragon. Strange clicking sounds came out of her mouth in an effort to distract her ears.

"You mean one of those creatures that coughs fire?" she said helplessly.

"No," I corrected.

Her eyes narrowed as if not to see the punchline.

"My life is dragging on."

We walked on in double silence.

"There's a word I discovered, you might be interested in," she spoke civilly. It has to do with punning.

"Yes," I acknowledged, interested and suspicious.

"Paronomasia." She pronounced it quickly. "It means the Art of Punning."

"Wow," I said proudly, "There's a word for it. I never thought of it as Art. Unless, groaning back is an Art, too."

"Well," Dori stopped, stood still and said majestically: I can't discourage, or demean or dismiss with annoyance to my person such an elegant creation that can grind peoples' teeth and cause fingers to turn into claws." She paused, with an icky smile. "But I can try."

"Quite a profound statement," I complimented her. "A punch on the arm would have been more Dori-like."

"I am trying to be more Lady-like."

"You wasted a whole spiel on a real cellar pun," I admonished her cordially, "It didn't even deserve to be called punishment."

"A pun is a pun," says the dictionary, it doesn't describe the amplitude or the attitude."

"Gosh, such language!" I watched her give me two V signs with her fingers. "Nevertheless, Princess Dori, it was bad. Your diatribe loses some it's sting." I finished with a flourish and a bow.

"Well, I'll be," she punned, sort of.

"He's a Rogue Reverend," roared Roman, enraged that he had handed out money on false pretenses.

"You've never met him."

"On faith."

"Did he ask for it?"

"No," he slurred.

"He didn't send any gifts!" I harangued Roman. "He didn't know who sent the money. Anonymous. Remember?"

Roman fell silent.

"It was a good deed," I commended him and tried to cheer him up. "It will help him return to drawing dogs and other lovable animals. If he regains some of his sight."

"He draws dogs?"

I clued Roman in on Larry's comic strip. "In that case," Roman spoke regally, I was mistaken. It was a mix-up. He's a dog lover. That makes it good. I was fooled by his title."

"It came from Reverend Rabbit." Roman didn't even twitch. A man who could adapt to the ridiculous with no fuss.

"The Rabbit in Canine City."

"Peacock the Pastor!" Roman wondered aloud as he tried a few hops on his way to the office.

"Looks like we hit another dead-end." I needlessly pointed out to Dori. It needed to be said. "But at least I got to associate with Princess Dori and King Roman." Instead of blushing, she was pensive. What was brewing in that fertile feminine brain?

"What's up?"

"I'm trying not to believe what I am thinking," she said, forlornly, looking almost ghostly.

"What is it?" I showed her my concern.

"There is something else," She pointed to herself.

"What!?" I steamed."

"I received the packages first," she panted.

"You mean......."

"Yes," She stared at my knees. "They were meant for me."

"That's crazy!" I bludgeoned her with my words. "They all related to Roman. You know that!"

"Who else could it be?" she softened, less frightened.

"It still boils down to Roman," I assured her, "You are way off the track."

"Like a runaway train?" She pushed out a tenuous smile.

"Exactly."

She stoked the flickering fire. "What about the scary guy in my building?" She scraped nervously at a fingernail.

"He doesn't know Roman," I said convincingly, without any evidence, trying to get her off the topic.

"Maybe he did some research?"

I had never seen Dori in this state before. She is usually self-assured and practically fearless.

"No. No. No." I spoke stiffly, "You are stretching it."

"Am I?" She said, partly relieved.

"Yes." No need to say more.

She put her hand in mine and squeezed. Whatever had stirred her so violently and fearfully can be traced back. If she ever wants to tell me.

Her confidence snapped right back into place. "It has to be someone who knows Roman really well," she speculated, reasonably.

"That includes a lot of people."

"I know."

"From his past?"

"Good point."

"I asked you before, if you remember, to ask Roman if I could help him out at Services. With pay, of course." We both smiled in recognition of the Holy Dollar. "Unless he has ancient friends turned enemies, these gifts must come from a pal nearby. Postmarks.

"I'll make sure to ask," she definitely assured me. She wants to clear herself. She can't totally shake the lingering feeling she's a target.

"To make it worse," I announced to a suddenly worried Dori, "I just had a very riveting thought."

She watched my brow furrow in consternation. "What is it?" Her voice had a tiny bit of shakiness in it, which she could hide from others, but not from me.

"Remember, Roman was a fairly well-known writer." Dori nodded eagerly. "He probably was interviewed in various magazines or on the radio, or even TV, promoting his books and surely he wrote some pieces about himself." She caught my drift and the gleam in his eyes faded.

"That's thousands of people!" she burst out.

"Lots."

"It's like going from Supersonic to WarpDrive." Dori was a devoted fan of StarTrek, just like me."

"It sure feels that way." I agreed.

"It's like the Universe expanded." She was getting locked into Space.

"Beam me back to Earth, Dori."

"Zap!"

"Good job," I saluted, though the ground didn't feel as firm as before.

"We will find our footing again," she consoled me. "I'm holding a glass of Zarconian Rum in my hand to toast the success of our upcoming Mission."

"I hold a fluted glass of Sarusiam brandy to also toast our Mission."

"Let's toast!"

"Clink."

"Clink."

"We had to ditch the overwhelmingly futility of our goal and heal ourselves with fantastic possibilities that was Star Trek was all about. Go into the unknown with a new spirit of discovery to what now looks in the distance to be empty Space. If Star Trek did it in an Einsteinian hour, we can do it in a hundred years. Rah!. Rah!. But lurking around the corner, the Eggman smiles, but not at our playfulness. Boo!. Boo!

Dig into the gifts again.

The Edsel is the oddest one. Do we scour the streets to find an Edsel. It a collectors' car. I've never seen it on the streets of SF. There must be Edsel clubs. Check the internet. In the meantime, Dori went off to see her dogs. I was stranded in the Church on the island of old-fashioned inertia. Time to see Blondie.

Roman was the key. We never thought of him with a private life. He was in demand. Think of all the people outside the Church, and because of the Church who knew him. Usually, well-established and wealthier. No reason for petty malice from that direction. It just made things seem impossible without the tools of the trade and stymied for clues. The great detectives of fiction were backed by first-rate writers. My bad luck.

Edsels. Narrow it down. Dori now knew what one looked like. I asked her to keep an eye out for one on the streets. I'm sure she didn't take me seriously. But it would stand out among all the sleek new breed of cars. It was rare to see two American cars in a row in our neighborhood. Poor Dori. It's like checking for a Dinosaur around the corner.

It's time to stop the search. We gave Roman the heads up and let him figure it out.

I confessed to her that II had egg on my face. I was stumped and frustrated and decided to drop the whole thing and consider myself mistaken and acting ridiculous.

She understood "My thoughts get too scrambled to make sense."

"I'm not the hard-boiled detective I thought I was.

"Compared to Sherlock Holmes you're barely a yokel."

"Despite all the clues I came with?" I was hurt.

"You're right," she quickly pardoned, "I upgrade you to soft-boiled detective."

"It's true. I'm not poaching on Sherlock's territory."

"Whoever is writing this is punch-drunk or brain-fried," Dori screamed, "I can't take it anymore!"

"Don't egg him on," I warned.

"STOP! It's not our fault that the writer is an idiot!"

"Can't figure it out. THINK! THINK!"

"We are not quitters!"

"We are leaving! No more punishment!"

"Yeah! We're leaving! Gonna binge on Baseball."

"Screw you writer!" Lashed Dori.

"I'm going to visit a cousin in L.A. who I don't even like."

A BLANK

We were back at my place. Dori was resting on the futon sofa. I was sitting almost in good posture in a chair near her, ready to make my pitch:

"I came up with an idea during the lapses in my beer-sotted, brain-fogged, Baseball and other sports binge."

Dori still wore the grimace she picked up at her older sister's house. "Don't sit there! Use the fork! Don't read so much! TV off at nine! Etcetera. The exclamation point came back to haunt her.

She raked her sister. "Strangulation would not be satisfying enough" She glared at me as if I was a continuation of her misery. "Now," she added methodically, "I come back to a drunk, whose bumbling brain managed to percolate an idea that will bring me to a writhing state of aggravation."

"I hope not," I replied pleasantly, not following her line of reasoning, by skimming over her familiar and in a way, "touching" tumble of words. I'm always impressed by how she can be furious and articulate in the same passionate breath.

"Let's hear it and get it over with," she said with reluctant resolve, damping her anger from boiling to simmering, seeing that I didn't fall for that 'drunken' bit.

"Okay." I smiled at her hands folded demurely on her lap while her features see-sawed between anticipation and apathy. "No one believes me about the Eggman, right!" She nodded, making bored, puffing sounds. "In short," I said confidently, hoping to gain some attention, "Put his gifts on display at the Church, since they are so eccentric." Her expression changed to slight interest. "He'd want people to come to see them, show them off. It could coincide with a benefit or special occasion." I wanted to give a flourish to my vaunted idea. But my listener remained stone cold.

Dori finally made a movement. She stretched her neck backward and stared at the ceiling. I could see that my idea was peppering through her brain. Her head slowly came down, with some neck twists thrown in, her eyelids raised.

"Not as grotesque as I expected," she obliged, with the faintest sympathy. Her hands rose and made short, softs clap together. "It has merits," she proclaimed, with sententious approval.

"Gadzooks" I trembled, Is Dori morphing into an English Professor. Who knows what lurks in the hearts of beautiful women with brains.

"If enough people studied the gifts, meaning the perspicacious media invited, some might see what I saw. Take pictures to keep and analyze."

"Smart."

"Roman would be pleased with the attention and we could raise some bucks for charity."

"As long as they didn't have horns." Was the Original Dori back?

She peered in my direction and shook her head with 'tut tut, tut' and tried to look astonished. She said nothing. I said nothing. Nothing could be more compelling.

Dori had to get back to her dogs, Four of them. They had their own group, but they surely missed her. Just as I did when we went on strike. We weren't paid when we went on strike. The dogs stayed with two of her friends. Two each. Very good friends.

We did the whole smear. Roman loved to show off his gifts. The benefit was to raise money to help people supplement the sometimes extravagant Vet bills that could always pop-up. Basically, help the Church goers. People who could be generous, were generous. And lots of small sums led to another generous sum. A good word, generous.

Dori's contacts with the few media people, could not resist her honeyed pleas to play up the event and use their cameras, especially on the unique gifts.

It didn't make the ten o'clock news, but that did not matter. There were scores of men and women strolling about with their dogs, trading dog stories and recalling the friendly, quaint, quirky and heartfelt gifts given to Roman.

I kept my attention focused on people milling around or stopping to inspect or take a photo of the 'bomb motif' laid out, I hoped, for their critical eyes. Their artistry or eccentricity were striking. They had no relation to religion, the City or the Church or the Dogs. Roman?

Dori's role was to buddy-up, in a charming, provocative and whimsical way to men with cameras and deftly steer them to the Three Gifts, praise the artist, expound on their uniqueness and present to them the rare opportunity to photograph them for hidden meanings.

Dori had spent the evening before memorizing and perfecting her spiel and her persistence paid off. The Three Gifts were the most photographed items in the Church. Excluding Dori.

There was a quiet swarm around Roman, including many regulars who were surprised by the catered event, with delicious snacks and pastries spread out on two long tables. We all indulged tastefully.

The good will of Roman poured out. A man true to his preaching. He had no idea, yet, that we suggested this event to weed out the Eggman. We hoped he had a sweet tooth and a loose mouth. Roman almost blushed when he was face to face with so many people who appreciated him. We know of his over the top, inexhaustible willingness to welcome recognition. But, for him it was okay.

Dori, in her selected wisdom, handed out her representative cards to the picture takers, asking that they call her if they discover erudite meanings in their deciphering of the Three Gifts. It could add valuable depth to the Holy Animal Church's mission. Thank you.

Would anyone take up this lofty challenge? Digging up mysterious clues? Can anyone really get hooked, realizing that this was not a 9th century artifact? It was more facile than frustrating. Are we awaiting something or just waiting?

If it doesn't work, at least I have Dori on my side. Her consolation and gumption. She is the ineffable female, an allusive version of the girls' game of hopscotch. She can't be pinned down. She hops to her own tune.

Back out with faithful Blondie.

Does the Eggman have a strong egg-like smell? Blondie and are scaling the steeper hills to Buena Vista Park, keeping her on leash since Coyotes have made it their home. They venture onto the streets at night. They have a penchant for small tasty creatures. Warnings are out.

Would the Eggman have a crayon-like smell? A criminal smell a dog could detect like a disease. If she could smell the gifts in the Church, could she pick up the scent of the Eggman? And would that lead her to sniff for him in the pews. Outlandish? Dogs do amazing things: Keep us healthy, sane and safe, not to mention laughing.

Coming back down to Duboce Park, with its romping dogs and patient owners, petting and patting and petting and petting, as Blondie and I walk through the grass, I spy Dori urgently waving at me from the benches. I went straight in that direction, unfastening Blondie. She walked by my side, knowing something was up.

Dori patted the bench for me to sit down. As soon as my bottom hit the wood, she was off. She intriguingly told me what happened at her outside flower boutique at the tail end of her shift.

"I was putting a corsage together, for a woman who would soon be back to pick it up, when this weird guy was suddenly standing right in front of me, staring."

She scowled. "His nose and mouth was covered by a hospital mask and he had a beat-up sombrero practically sliding off his head."

She stopped and looked at me as if I could visualize this crazy scene. I said nothing and moved she moved on.

"He saw that I was startled and was eyeing his mask. He said he had a cold and didn't want to spread germs." She rubbed her nose with the back of her hand. "It still didn't make me feel comfortable, even though there were plenty of people around."

"Good, they were there."

"Then," her face contorted into a mixture of smile and disbelief, "He started cooing about how much he liked flowers and the people who sell them."

"It made you nervous again."

"Of course."

"Then what"?

"Then I noticed," she said, reliving a bit of panic, "That his eyes kept zeroing in on mine, like he knew me."

"Did you call for someone?"

"I turned back to my flowers and got busy so he'd leave," she reasoned. "Then," she said, her hands jumping up to her face, he moved closer and I felt a cold hand on my hand. I yelped. He drew back and gave a look as cold as the feeling in his hands. He snarled like an animal. She shivered. I grabbed her hand.

"I'm not kidding," she fumed.

"You were in danger," I pleaded, "why didn't you call out for help."

"I thought I could handle it."

"What! It sounded scary as hell!"

"He was no ordinary jerk," she said comparatively. She dealt with and handled a lot of obnoxious, cruel and volatile men in her career. I listened. She had a history of sizing up men.

"What happened?"

"I grabbed some roses and mashed them into his face," she said gleefully with a snarl of her own.

"It must have left a mark."

"Thorns!"

"An identifying mark."

"Let's hope it's permanent," she said with relish.

"Do you think?"

"Yes, I think."

"The Eggman?"

"Or a good imposter," she managed a joke.

Detective talk: "What was he wearing?"

"Aside from the crazy sombrero, it was the usual ensemble for bad men, bad taste." Her crude descriptions were conquering her edginess. "He was tall, like I said." She had been engrossed in remembering. She suddenly lifted her head towards mine. "Aren't most of these evil men short?" she said puckishly.

"An exception," I volunteered. "But why would he make such an obvious appearance and so frightening impression?"

"Scare me?"

"It worked," I said uncomfortably. "My idea of him is that he is a rat and afraid to come out of his rat hole. Besides, his whole approach has been subtle.

"You're being very generous," Dori added scornfully. "I get the chills thinking of him. Brr. Brr Brr."

"Yes."

"So cold."

"You've made your point."

"Ice cold."

She was getting playful. Good. I wrapped my arms around her and she sank into my warm body. The dogs were very pleased.

We decided to eliminate Mr. Crooked Sombrero as the Eggman. He was too crude and stupid.

"I'm glad I put that hard-boiled egg in the freezer," Dori reminded me. "When you talked fingerprints I had to preserve it."

"Good thinking, Dort!"

We looked at each other and laughed, aware that we really didn't know what we were doing."

"Maybe it stopped smelling."

"Maybe."

"And maybe, it's a woman," Dori suddenly declared, in defense of women criminal genius.

"A very crafty woman."

"I could be as smart as the Eggman," Dori proclaimed. "You always think of mad scientists as men, never women." She gave me a stern and stormy look.

"You're defending crazy women?"

"Well," she said, more peeved than angry, "If men want to blow up the world, why can't women blow up the world?"

"Hmm," I scratched a bit of beard in conscientious thought. "It is unfair." She gave a rocking nod. "Equality."

"Absolutely. Why not," she posed, with a twinkle in her eye, as she herself felt capable of dastardly demonic deeds. "And I would not leave such a big mess to clean up. It would be neater."

"The woman's touch."

"Exactly,"

She saw my dismissive look.

"I could."

"If this turns out to be a game," I conceded. "You could be that clever. "But," I struck to her heart, you could never actually hurt someone."

"If roses aren't considered a dangerous weapon."

"I forgot."

"But I could be that clever?" She put it to me with a humorous glint in eye.

"Yes."

She got feisty and gave me a medium hard shot in the shoulder What was I doing now? Rating intelligence? It wasn't an I.Q. Test. It was an L.D. Tests. Loving Dori.

Save the mush.

Blondie and I canvassed the neighboring dog parks to find out if their dogs or themselves were being harassed or were receiving strange gifts. I got some strange, concerned looks, but no one confessed to any serious problems.

While taking a side journey to the Panhandle, one of Blondie's favorite gopher haunts, I got a call from Dori that she had heard from one of the Photographers.

"He especially wanted to speak to the instigator of the project."

"He said: 'Instigator?'"

"Yep."

Is this good or bad? It's a good thing my elation is equipped with a parachute so it can drift down without crumpling to the ground.

"Call him," Dori instructed." She gave me the number. "When will you call him?

"Around seven."

"I'll be over with the rascals and something tasty."

"I'll be ready with dog treats."

"They adore Blondie."

"I hope she can stand four helpings of adoration."

"My dogs can also be respectful guests."

"The toasts of Doghood."

"Indeed!"

"I won't badger them."

"You'd better not."

I spoke briefly to Mr. Richardson. He wanted to meet in person. I invited him over at his convenience. Two evenings later, he buzzed the outer doorbell. Dori and I, the respectful quartet of Dachshunds and the almost ever friendly Blondie welcomed him to my dog smelling abode with little fanfare.

He dressed in conservative, standard grey suit often worn by people in business or other professions. A serious, formal middle-ager with an intelligent searching face, well-shaved, a confident matter and an affable personality. He immediately, after greeting the two humans, introduced himself to the dogs, getting down to their level, and gave them some vigorous petting. They of course, after some brief sniffing, wholly accepted his attentions. He seemed like a good guy.

We sat him on the sofa-futon. He scanned the studio and accepted a soft drink. Dori graced the lounger, while I pulled up a recently rescued Rocker and seated myself, trying not to rock.

Richardson and I chatted sports and Dori got the lowdown on his family. No tension. We talked openly as we hastily got acquainted. He pulled a wallet from inside his jacket and extracted an ID and handed it to me with the familiarity of a favorite grocer or uncle.

I looked it over as I glanced back at Richardson and gave it to Dori who brought it close to her eyes and handed it back to him, Or Roger, now, as he asked us to call him.

This was not to be a grilling session, but the I.D. read Fed agent. He suspected something wasn't kosher when Dori latched onto him and with soft conversation drew him over to the Three Gifts on display. Dori looked on with chagrin. They seemed to him to have no value. What's the big deal?

He was not a handsome man. Bald, with a fringe of hair on the sides, incipient bags under both eyes, eyeglasses with wire frames that seemed glued to his head. An accountant look? But he had eyes that moved rapidly and alertly, as if he was collecting information for a photographic memory. Who knows what he picked up or wanted to pick up.

"I'm often mistaken for an Accountant." he confirmed. He spoke in Dori's direction, I was on the periphery, not exactly excluded. He jerked his head to get me fully in his sight.

"I do work at a desk and computer," he also confirmed, "But occasionally some outside stuff."

He sounded very warm and neighborly. Nothing cop-like about him.

"Do you carry a gun?" I naturally asked.

"My weapon is in my car in a secure locked box, hidden from view." He grasped my question. "It makes some people nervous to see it in their home." He took a sip of his drink. "This is a social call."

He sat up and addressed Dori and me alternately, although we weren't that far apart.

"I have dogs," he explained with a generous smile, mostly aimed at Dori. I've been to the Dog Church. I went there for the 'Cause' that Sunday." He spoke in sharp spurts with minimal words. To the point. Maybe an acquired habit of his profession. "As it happened, with Dori's help, I stumbled into taking photos of the gifts." He smiled steadily to Dori until she smiled back. Very awkward. "I am a practiced photographer and the photos were clear as a bell. They puzzled me. I examined the articles." I'm sure I'd be most interested in his observations if I wasn't drifting off to sleep from his brisk but droning monotone.

Dori threw something at me and I tried to pay attention. "In my job," Roger forswore solemnly, as if someone was questioning his rectitude, "I am entrusted to look for signs." He looked at us earnestly: "What made you realize these gifts could be dangerous?"

Roger was silent. I gathered my wits and tried to make my explanation as brief as possible. "Protesters outside the Church, the 'Where is Jesus People'

"I remember that."

"It was peaceful, but a few raged at Roman, insulted and cursed at him."

"Inflammatory."

"No return addresses."

"Suspicious."

"Listened for ticking. Then I thought: Can a package be ticking, but we can't hear it ticking?"

He blinked.

"The egg said: 'Fat Man', but it didn't jive. Roman is not fat or a hard-boiled personality. Probably a gag."

Roger, or Richardson merely nodded and waited for me to continue.

"Then it hit me!"

"It was his birthday," Roger anticipated and leaned back on the sofa.

"Fat Man," was the name of the first atomic bomb and the egg was in the shape of a bomb."

It was so outrageous that even an experienced agent like Roger was startled by the idea. The idea seemed to fly around and around in his head looking for a place to land.

While he was managing to fit that in his thoughts, I filled him in on the other gifts and how I gleaned the bomb motifs. Whether he believed these wild conjectures or not, he gazed at me impressed.

I gave Roger the inquisitive eye.

"Why am I not writing this down?"

I nodded, almost reproachfully.

"I have a complete memory of everything." He smiled. "I can bring up the pictures at will and remember any salient point you make. An asset in my profession."

"Absolutely."

He switched his attention to Dori. "It must have been a burden for you to learn this and not bring it to the Police.

"They would have taken us for kooks," she informed him, tersely.

"And that would demolish your chances right off the bat."

"Precisely." Dori was getting very tired of his oozing manners "Psst. Psst," I said to him in thought. He didn't turn around. I spoke up, a bit loudly: "It might just be one miserable crackpot trying to scare people, who didn't even know they were being scared."

"He could also be very clever."

Maybe it's a game," I offered.

"Can't chance it."

"Your Agency," I questioned, "What is it called? Part of the NSA?"

"It doesn't exist."

"But it exists."

"We don't publicize."

"Why are you telling me it exists, when no one should know it exists."

"You and Dori must sign an agreement that you will not violate security by revealing any of this."

"An anonymous package with a hard-boiled egg in it, gets this kind of attention?"

"Yes." Then he shared with me his confusion. "How did this package which arrived with the mail get through without cancelled postage?

"You mean the Post Offices are very careful about packages with no return address."

"The clever man slipped up on this one," he said sanguinely.

"I was thinking that, too.

"And?" He welcomed my input.

"After all, I was the guy who discovered it."

"He is a skilled artist," Roger noticed, 'He could have drawn a cancelled postage stamp that would get by a quick glance.

"Well done," I complimented his insight, but reminded him that none of the packages had return addresses. He couldn't slip three times."

"Likes the risk."

"Part of the game."

Shrug

Richardson rose up quickly swiftly and swiftly moved to the door. He never needed to go to the bathroom or needed a glass of water. He said he was in a hurry to get back to his Office and deal with an angle he had, concerning the Eggman.

He had tried to give Dori a hug but she resisted with cloying politeness, sarcasm oozing out of her. He took no offense, and made a slight bow. She held her hands behind her back in case he wanted to kiss one of them.

He gave me a firm, formal handshake and went out the door to his car, with his gun concealed in it. It's hard to believe that this man could kill someone. His tact with us was to kill us with kindness.

We sat back together on the sofa. Dori had resisted his advances, but I couldn't resist the unsipped beer we offered him, which was sitting so lonely on the sofa table. It was warm, but then, it was English.

"He's keen on you," I said flippantly to the unmooning Dori.

"So?"

"He was so easy going and friendly, like a Buddy," I told Dori. There was a conflict." I expected an Agent to be detached and dedicated to business. He was pretty casual.'

"He wasn't pretty," Dori hastened to tell me. "Yes, he was casual, he was not punctilious."

"There you go again!"

"Isn't that the right word?"

Did she have misgivings, or was she checking me?

"I have to look it up."

She smiled her pert smile.

"Can you believe it," I grumbled, "He knew about the bomb only if I mentioned it."

"That doesn't mean anything." Dori disagreed, sliding into other thoughts beside the Eggman.

"And the questions about our lives and our jobs. Where we grew up."

"His job," Dori assured me, "He had to know something about citizens playing Bomb Detective. Huh." She watched my changing expression. "He just did it in an 'Oh, shucks' way."

"If there was ever a perfect Eggman, he's it!"

"C'mon, be serious."

"Got carried away. It's so bizarre."

"Relax." she whispered, pressing her back against the sofa-futon, putting her chin on her chest, which was enfolded by her worked over hands.

'I have to admit, my ideas about Agents come from TV and movies.'

"Relax," she repeated with a yawn. "You should be glad we handed it over to a cop with resources to track him down." She made a circle with her forefinger and thumb and held it out to me. "Your idea of the photos bagged it. You did it."

Praise from Dori, its Premium.

"He'll still want our help."

"It's possible."

Can I let go completely? I couldn't quite grasp it. The burden was off me. Do I keep hunting? Here we were discussing a bomb suspect and the code words we were to use with him were: 'Daisy Duck.' I yawned noisily.

"Daisy Duck," I said to Dori. We both laughed.

The tension was slowly draining out of us. I was slumping and Dori was nodding off. I dragged myself to the lounger, fell in, stretched out and fell asleep.

Of course, the next morning Dori phoned me, earlier than usual. I was scanning job ads. Another package, another gift box.

"It's light as a feather!" She chanced to open it. "It's empty."

"No note?"

"No note."

"Anything?"

"Nothing I can see."

"Save the box."

"Planning to."

"Did he quit?" I wondered dubiously.

"Maybe, he got the message."

"What message?"

"That the Fed were involved."

"How would he know that?"

"Maybe, he has long range sensors protruding from his head," Dori speculated inconsistently. He would be instantly recognizable in the Church.

"At least you have an answer, I have none."

"Maybe," she said, Roger did quick work."

"Overnight!"

"Maybe, he got the guy because he was already known and sent us the empty box to show they got him."

"You have a lot of long-winded maybes, 'Miss Maybe'" I joked.

"Maybe, we should keep it as a souvenir," her voice was jolly.

"I think Hollywood would want you as their chief writer."

"Truth is stranger than fiction," she grunted. A very feminine grunt.

Does she really believe all this stuff? I pondered, but not for long. Lately, she's been showing off her smarts; inherited from someone in her family tree, without regard from what kind of tree it came from and what grows on it. Does the tree have nuts? Coconuts? Lemons?

She eventually tamped down her wild credulity. I'm sure she got shook-up when she saw the package and the relief when it turned out harmless. At least, this was the insight of Beamer Todd, Truth Detective. Unfortunately, I was not elastic enough to pat my own back.

Later that day walking with Blondie around the neighborhood, picturing cracking open the Eggman, frying him in butter and feeding him to the pigeons.

As I turned the corner at Church and 14th street, heading home, was a familiar dog. It was Guinevere, excited to see Blondie. Charles the Comedian tugged up next to me.

He looked better. A no drug look. Sunshine in his eyes. Deviltry in his heart. Wit in his words. "I like that description,' he said. "Did you just make it up?"

"No," I returned, humbly, "I was quoting what prominent citizens said about VLad the Impaler."

"As you can see," he smiled, a front tooth missing. "I've been out in the sun much more. I'm not so pale."

"Vlad should have gotten out of Transylvania more often and gone to the Riviera," I considered.

"Don't steal my thunder," he threatened, "Guinevere eats comic impersonators."

"And it's good to see you back in form."

"It's all about material," he said seriously. "You to dive in and you often miscalculate the depth of the pool, not that it's shallow, but that its depthless and you're desperately splashing around."

"A scary picture," I commiserated. "We are talking about jokes here."

"Funny is not always fun."

"You make us laugh."

"I'm obsessed with succeeding," he confided.

"Don't punish yourself," I reminded him that many great men were obsessed, it seems to go with the territory. Whether always true or not, it got him temporarily out of the dumps.

"I'm certainly not cured."

"You've got an object. You have talent and you know it."

"A joke is like a yoke."

With a charged up motion, ready to fight off the admirers he'll have some day and with Guinevere in eager tow he strode down the street.

It was good to have that link in the chain of friendships soldered. If this thing with Eggman drags on, despite Dori's upbeat certainty that it's done. Charles' many talents would be invaluable.

Dori came to the Park with her dog quartet. They were barking out together, but if I thought they could displace Mozart, they were barking up the wrong treble.

I was sitting on a far bench stroking Blondie. She caught sight of me and walked quickly across the Park and stopped abruptly in front of me. Her dogs in their mischievous hurry piled on top of each other. She dropped the leashes, the dogs untangled, sixteen short legs got their balance and scampered away, snapping playfully at each other, and then became ardent referees of the scruffy to scruffy wrestling matches. She watched with her usual 'What will be will be,' then smiled at me and said: "Guess what?"

I had no idea of what? "Your dogs are writing a memoir and describing all your faults."

The smile descended into impatient popping sounds. Then, unruffled, she had the equanimity and quickness to put me in the corner.

"Four dogs can contradict one another and never pin anything on me," she challenged, "But you have one dog and her account stands."

"As the song goes," I marveled, 'You make me feel so dumb.'"

"Not really," she said gracefully, while her eyes shone together like a winning combination on a slot machine: "CHING!"

She swung her nicely formed form sideways and searched the play field for her dogs. She ticked them off with four quick nods.

"Guess what," she smiled, satisfied.

"Santa knows," came into my head unbidden, but I said nothing.

"I got a call from Roger," she chirped, "He wants to come over and pick up my statement."

"What about mine?" She shrugged. "Can't you send it Email?"

She made a sharp tilt of her head, like a pretty robot.

"Security."

"Regular mail is very safe."

"Security," was her stiff response. "He wants to do it at your place so it won't look so suspicious.

"Suspicious? We are the good guys." I pretended not to be sarcastic. "I thought he solved the problem."

"No. Not quite," she said, dove like. "I was premature when......."

"Okay," I stepped in. She did a great rendition of how to top off a victory! She 'whooped' a few 'whoops'. It sounded idiotic, but was appreciated. "We will save it for the real McCoy."

She was stumped. With a vaguely interested look in her slightly slanted eyes, she muttered: "What?"

"The true downfall of the Eggman.

She brightened. "Like Humpty Dumpty?"

"A bad analogy, but a good result." It was supercilious, but in small letters. She called my bluff.

"Should I just call you 'Mr. Truth,' Beamer?"

"If I was the truth, people would stay away from me."

"You'd still have dogs," she sympathized.

"No one would rent to me. I'd be a pariah."

She thought about it. "There must be someplace where truth is welcomed and even revered."

"The Dentist chair is very close to the truth."

"It does rhyme with Truth."

"See."

"He'll be over at seven, please be there."

"Sure. I'll have my statement all ready to go."

Dori stepped through some doggie mayhem and corralled her squirming girls, one, by slippery, one. She leashed them with extraordinary dexterity into one zippy mob. A blur of sixteen rushing feet went out of the Park, yapping about something they all seemed to agree to yap about.

He didn't come a seven. He came fifteen minutes before seven. We shook hands. He presented Dori with a small vase of yellow flowers. "Flowers for the flowery," he quietly gushed. Not, obviously, hiding his attraction for Dori. She accepted them with undisguised indifference.

"They are beautiful," she said remotely, put them down on the nearest flat surface, as we moved to the sofa-futon, the lounger, a standard chair and the rescued old rocker.

Roger watched her movements meticulously, as a cop might watch a suspect, but with a dumb smile on his freshly shaved and slightly pockmarked face. His eyeglasses, though not heavy, kept sliding down the bridge of his nose. Perspiration? Dori told him sit on the sofa. She sat comfortably in the lounger.

"So," I said to him, breaking his trance. "How's the investigation?" My voice, traveling light years through Space, finally reached him.

"Investigation, you said?"

"Yes."

He did not wrestle with the question. He quickly put it to rest. "Coming along."

He was strictly engaged with Dori. She was telling him about the empty box.

"Empty box?"

Dori was glum. She dismissed him as an unwanted suitor but recognized him, respectfully, as a Federal Agent. A bit of a dilemma.

Since he told us he had a photographic memory, I tried something. "Are you a football fan?

"Big fan," he shook a fist in emphasis.

"I know this is no big deal," I smiled at him naively. "But remember in the second gift there was a quarterback throwing a football. He bent his head to consult his perfect memory. "He had the number fifty, right?"

"Yes," he answered confidently.

"Isn't it odd for a Quarterback to wear that number," I queried, innocently. "Fifties are reserved for linebackers."

He faltered. "You know, he recovered authoritatively, "I missed it. Thanks for pointing it out."

"No problem, the guy drawing sure doesn't know his football."

"No way," he agreed strongly and swung back to Dori.

Dori brought out her statement. I brought out mine. Hers was neatly printed on white letter paper. Mine was hastily scrawled on lined, notebook paper. The sloppiness must have made clear, as he scanned it, that these doings were not serious and maybe caught on that I knew he was a jerk.

He folded it clumsily, with no technique and along with the neatly folded Dori statement, missed the inside pocket twice, before he finally jammed it in. This jacket had a little more dash, then the last one. It was more' NOW.' Or maybe, it was sitting in the closet for a long time.

"Irrelevant," the pretty robot was probably thinking, as she, with sudden and jerky movements, was trying to get around the obstacle, Roger Richardson. She finally succeeded. They sat on opposite sides of the sofa-futon and had a long fifteen minute and distant conversation, that she would later relay to me. As if any of this mattered.

The departing ceremony was brief, as Dori excused herself to go to the bathroom. Roger was crestfallen, which was appropriate since had no hair on the top of his head. He left in a sour mood. Good.

I shut the door and noisily rattled the security chain. Dori tentatively poked her nose out of the bathroom. I pointed outside. Her tongue hung out to get some fresh air.

During their conversation, I ducked into the kitchen nook and puttered around. I was not a devoted cleaning agent. Messes and I can coexist. I did a lot of rearranging of things to clear some space. Finding things behind other things, that I could get rid of. Scouring areas that had become visible with this shuffling around.

As Dori once advised with a steady, meaningful look: "You need a housekeeper." I didn't think it was that bad and how could I afford a housekeeper. Neatness was never my forte. My strength was in creative disarray and a bit of abstract materialism, to give it an artistic name, which people may criticize. But I say it is "Art.".

What she got from the interview with Roger was 'nothing.' He was prying into her life in the guise of learning the authenticity of a witness. He was gentlemanly about it, but it was futile. He didn't brush her questions aside with a sincere and certain, 'don't worry,' but mowed them down with 'secret' and severe expressions.

Dori shook her head. "He wanted a date," she said miserably.

"Okay, Dori, listen to this, tell me what you think, I buzzed. Credentials? Hah!" She looked at me hard. "Remember the picture with the Quarterback throwing the football?"

"Yes."

"He claimed to be a big fan, right?"

She backed into her memory for a moment. "Right."

"Football player's numbers show their position."

"I didn't know that."

"True fans know that."

"I guess."

"I asked him why the Quarterback's number was fifty."

"Okay," she sort of mumbled.

"He said," I zinged, "he noticed it and he wasn't surprised to see it on a quarterback."

"He said he was surprised?" Dori, bored by football, was trying to catch on. Good for her. She waited blankly for the next confusion.

"He had a photographic memory. Right!"

"Right," she echoed, annoyed, probably thinking, "Get to the point already. This football stuff gives me a headache."

"Well," I stated dramatically, "The quarterback had no number on his jersey."

"Wow!" She cried, thrilled with the insight or out of relief that it was over.

"So," I concluded, "Scratch out photographic memory, strike out die-hard football fan and scratch out Roger Richardson, Federal Agent.

Dori was stunned.

"He wasn't after the Eggman, he was after you."

"I got that."

"He never studied the photographs."

"My faith in the secret service has collapsed," she rebuked the stinker. "At least for the moment."

"Contemptible."

"You know," Dori enlightened me. "I wonder if he was only playing a part."

"You mean he was faking?"

"Men will do the craziest things to attract a woman?"

"But to pretend to be a federal agent?"

"Now, he would deny it."

I only glanced at his credentials, but you looked at them closely. "What did you see."

"I saw a face and a complicated government insignia. It was a little faded.

"That alone should have triggered doubt."

"Yes, but remember, we were so happy to have someone on our side who believed us and he was a real nice guy at the beginning."

"You are right."

She suddenly stared at me with menace in her eyes. "Don't say it!" She watched a thin smile desert my face. "Do not say it!"

I didn't say it. "Well, I couldn't blame Roger," she gave me a grim going-over. "You're a dish."

Her features deliberated to find an apt expression. She gave me a big smackeroo on my nervous lips. I told her it was tasty.

"I want to celebrate the empty box," she burst out with joy. Come to my place and I'll cook up a sumptuous something. There's wine to make some toasts."

"I'm all appetite. Let's go, poor, lonely, hungry Blondie. You're in on the feast.

I was first out to the Park, next morning. It was wet from mist, not from needed rain. Blondie and I walked around meeting, greeting, petting and sniffing, chatting and playing.

I heard Dori arrive in the cool, wet air which collided with the superheated, cracking chorus of sentry barks and piercing yips. A cacophony of doggy opinions.

We met at the bench. Dori brought dry things to sit on. Blondie wandered and four maniacs drifted, only sporadically annoying.

"I had a thought last night," I said avidly to the back of her head which was revolving to keep track of her dogs.

"You did?" she bickered. She was in a crappy mood.

"You have a nice nape," I complimented, to raise her spirits.

"Thank you," she said with mechanical and begrudging politeness, as if it had already been said to her numerous times on her walk to the Park.

"You need a nice tattoo on it," I said in fun. I couldn't see her reaction. "Do you like goats? She kept staring ahead. "Octopi, they are very smart. You can have tentacles reaching down your back and curling around your shoulders. Very smart these days.

"Too expensive."

"You can one in prayer?"

"Too religious."

"You can have a tattoo of an Octopus on a plate in a restaurant."

"Too cruel."

"How about a baby Octopus sucking on all its thumbs at once?"

"Very cute."

"Maybe, I can do an outline sketch, to be filled in later."

"She acted alarmed. "With what implement?"

"A crayon?"

"Something I can wash off."

She finally turned around. I had another pretty view.: She said with pride: "I bet Da Vinci never did a nape."

"Getting back to the idea I had."

"Oh, that," she stifled a real yawn. "Oh, well, shoot."

"If the Eggman actually sent a bomb," I told her Cheshire Grin, "The Police and FBI would be over it in an instant. They'd track him down."

She got serious. "Yes. As long as he fakes it he's safe."

"Right."

"Right."

"Also," I went on, He tries to scare people who don't even realize they're being scared."

"Yes, you said that before."

"Is he calling it off with the empty box, even though no one knows what it's all about."

"Except you."

"And you, I think."

"Is he nuts?"

"Beats me. Is this Act One?" Does he mean to hurt someone?"

"There is something theatrical about it." Dori brought a new focus to it. "I did some acting in a local theater when I was younger and dreamier."

"You've done some very convincing acting in our adventures."

"Thanks."

"It boils down to the Church."

"The Phantom of the Church," said Dori eerily.

"Who knows?"

"Is he sane enough to be done?" she asked me.

"I could only answer: "If we don't get another gift box, he's either over it, or on to Act Two, where he will act."

"Scary."

"We've got box seats."

"Got to get to work soon."

"So early?

"It's not that early." I pulled out my smartphone to check the time. It was dead. Needed recharging. Dori looked confused. "What is it?"

She twisted her head around as if it was stuck. "Since this whole thing began." she reflected philosophically, I have lost my feeling for time." She went on, bending her neck sideways until it touched her right shoulder, "Strange," she said, swerving her head to me, "I had regular jobs, a regular schedule, yet, nothing seems definite, no resolutions, just burps." Her eyes beckoned an explanation from me.

"Did Einstein ever consider burps in time?" I comforted her, you may have experienced an unknown phenomenon." She barely smiled.

"I. right now have a very definite sense of time. My rent is due next month and no job."

Dori tapped two palms to the side of her head. "Darn it! She chewed her bottom lip and faced up to it with a guilt soaked smile: "I forgot to ask Roman about a job there. You asked me twice already."

"I can ask myself."

Dori went off after offering to help me with rent. I thought: "No way!"

My pride. A job became more urgent. I should have been more enterprising, so I shouldn't get in this predicament. But, it's so nice to be free of time.

I went searching. Left my name, left resumes, my phone number, my self-respect. Didn't hear anything from Roman. Dori advocated for me with him. It was harder to refuse her than me.

Dori worked at her jobs and spent some evenings with her friends, going to movies and going shopping. I read and watched sports and practiced my dog songs, just in case.

I was with Blondie, sitting on the usual bench, when Dori came over straight from her job. She was excited with news:

"Guess what?"

"Catapults will make bridges obsolete?"

"What!?"

"A good time to invest in mattresses." She ignored my tip.

"Charlie was at the Embarcadero and passed by my flowers!" She pushed her head into mine to make sure I was listening, and not dreaming up ways to avoid traffic jams. "He was swaying a little too much. I called to him. He squinted and recognized me. I told him to sit down in the customer's chair." She turned sad. "He was hiding a bottle behind his back so I figured he was drunk. "But he was in a buoyant mood, if you'll excuse the expression." She gave me a coy wink and went on with her narration.

"He started telling me about a new cereal, sold and sponsored by the Vatican called, 'Christ Crispies.' He looked for my reaction and I said: "New material?" He didn't say." She paused. "I had a customer and couldn't follow right away... He was in a little fog but very keen on this new stuff."

"It sounds offensive."

"When have comics not been offensive, when it comes to laughs," she remarked, incisively.

"Good point."

"He made it sound like a business opportunity."

"What else?" I was intrigued. A business opportunity?

"Like legitimate news. The Church was running out of money and they needed a quick way to make some bucks."

"Like a gambler: "Pope needs a new pair of shoes.""

She laughed. Charles told me the Pope endorsed it and made it ritual that he has a bowl of 'Christ Crispies for breakfast and as a late night snack."

She said that Charles, who is an unhappy Catholic, liked the idea. Not only could you ingest the body of Christ on Sundays in Church, but can have a helping every day of the week."

"This could only be some new desperate material he's trying out. By the way," I asked curiously, if you were waiting on a customer, how were you able to listen to his whole spiel."

"The customer fled," she laughed. "He told me not to knock it, it would increase converts. He even had a jingle: "It takes good, like a savior should.""

"That repels people!"

"Everyone in the Vatican was ordered to eat it. And they did."

"Yum. Yum."

"The Church sanctions it." Dori went on with her fantastic memory. "If you can't trust the Church, who can you trust?"

"He's got quite an imagination."

"He's ludicrous," she said, not mockingly, "He wants to be their spokesperson in America."

"From ludicrous to ludicrous."

I had to ask her. "Do you think he's delusional or was he acting?"

She kept in step.: Sometimes it's hard to tell with comedians."

"You've had dealings?"

"Yes. He even said through his ramblings, and I did miss some of it, that from a religious perspective it was repellent and sacrilegious but from a business standpoint it was sure-fire."

"Lots of reality in that statement,"

"Yes."

"By the way," I said to her with amazement, "How did you remember all those things he said?"

"How could I not?" she answered, breezily.

"You could do his routine?"

"I asked him if he wanted to go to the Park and join us for a meal. He jumped up from the chair and left."

"Wrapped up in imagination. It warms him up. It's a cold world."

"There are flowers and dogs," Dori mused. "Darn!" she said abruptly. "I didn't ask him about Guinevere," she grieved, "I wonder if he was looking for her."

I didn't realize Guinevere wasn't with him.

"Was he panicky?"

"Not like people would usually be if they lost their dog."

"Just the usual crazy intensity."

"Yep."

"Let's assume he left her with someone."

"Lets. He's not that scatterbrained."

"I'm thinking........"

"That's progress."

"I'm thinking that since the Church's respectability has been sinking, his stuff may go over with some people."

"Maybe," Dori observed sharply, "He's not delusional, but up to date."

"Well said."

She loved it.

She reminded me, before leaving to bring out her dogs "People think you are crazy, too."

Dori had two jobs. I felt like a schmuck not even having a part-time one and in jeopardy of not making the rent. You'd think, having this detective experience behind me, it would be a cinch to find one, without even totally relying on that expertise, and though I have scores of rebuttals clogging my path, I landed a job as a Security Person in a bookshop. Minimum wage and minimum prestige.

I watched cameras in an up, upstairs office trying to catch customers stuffing unpaid for books into backpacks, jackets, briefcases, in their pants and other cunning methods I missed. It wasn't in color. At least there were no commercials.

After a few days of infinite length, I wished there were commercials. Monotony to the third degree. I did shift with another fellow up there who took naps on his off time.

I could shift the cameras around some and focus on pretty females. I soon got the feeling that the thieves were too deft for me to catch them, especially with my wandering interests. Books did disappear from the store, mostly on my watch.

When store became crowded, I was to put on my store I.D. and amble around on the pretense of keeping books neat and in place, When I was really a spy. The regular clerks were too busy ringing up sales and answering questions to deal with all the sneakiness. I hated it. I wasn't fooling anyone. I got dirty looks when I watched different folks secretly as I tried to be occupied handling the books, but they felt the eyes.

Some people had guilty looks, someone deliberately stepped hard on my foot, without apology. I had to squeeze between bodies, jostling arms and breathing into unfriendly faces. Nobody asked me for information or recommendations. I gave the impression that I was in a Den of Thieves. I suppose with experience one could spot a clever shoplifter and give him or her the heave-ho.

I wanted to quit. I couldn't quit, I needed the bucks. I didn't quit. I was fired. I was too sympathetic, they told me. I caught no one on camera or in person in two weeks. 0 for Ten. I was surprised about how honest book reading people are. But, I was outfoxed.

I collected two weeks' pay, which I didn't earn, but it gave me a breather. I deposited the check in my dwindling bank account and the two sums together mostly paid my rent.

I was glad to be back with poor Blondie who spent more time alone, while I was at work. We hastened to the Park, my step a lot quicker, at least for a day. I enjoyed the wind. The moving cool air. Away from the crowdedness of downtown. In younger days, crowds were exciting. Now they are just crowds.

It turned out to be a good day. Dori phoned me. She had been pestering Roman to give me some work and finally relented to give it a shot.

"Great." Roman paid well. Could spend more time with Blondie. I told Dori that I'd be coming down to Church to set things up with Roman. Was he very busy?

"I'll tell him you're coming."

A Boss could make a job miserable. Roman was a good guy who allowed goof-ups and paid well for good work. Could I tell him what I could do to enhance the Churchgoing?

We talked it over. I could get cozy with his flock, take donations personally, pet their dogs, add friendliness and ease to Roman's often rigorous pronouncements and high-intensity preaching which had people in tears with jubilating cries of 'Amen, Amen.'" It was a spectacle I would watch over and over working for him.

Roman splashed his creed over the people like a cleansing wave and they felt it. They felt faith. Part of my job was to help the unfaithful to be cool. Some people dropping in could be deliberately obnoxious with objections to everything or could be looking for a place to sleep. Myriad possibilities for interruption in an open Church. For my part, I wanted to play my dog songs, for all the people with dogs. It seemed a good fit. We'd establish that later.

A good deal. Still tentative. But I hoped that with my exertions with the flock, I would come face to face with the Eggman. Also, Dori could be around, adding a pleasantness to the job.

I was creating my job. No manual. No overseer. Roman trusted me. Just do it. See how it works. Try things. Do good. It was all about goodness. Be polite and respectful. Watch the puns. Not everyone is immune. They haven't gotten their pun shots yet. They didn't come to be punished but to be relieved of their sins. I love dogs. Remember this pep-talk to myself.

I was nervous when people began coming through the door, spreading out and mingling, walking their dogs over to Roman for a blessing. They were animated, yet humble. Fastidious in a churchy way. The roaring will come later.

Dori was going in and out of the office with papers and packages. She stopped at table where people were pouring house coffee into hot proof cups, stacked up like white towers.

She signaled to me to meet her. I went over to her. She had a tomelike book in one hand and the other hand tapped lightly at her forehead as if she was trying to solve a problem.

"I am miffed," she complained, while exchanging the tapping for some serious rubbing while the other hand tightly clutched her book. "You know; I'm always trying to improve my vocabulary."

"Indubitably."

She ignored me. "Lugubrious."

"What? Do I have something crawling on my face?"

"Lugubrious, the word." She finally rested her heavy book on the table. "I came across it and I can't figure it out."

"What does it mean?" I asked, interested.

"I always forget." She looked at me in surprise. "It just sounds lugubrious." I could only nod. "I can't picture someone being Lugubrious." Her hands came together in friendship. "I'm pixelated."

"In a nice way I hope," I smiled, reentering the one-way conversation.

"Oh, Beamer," she scolded me in frustration. "You just don't get it."

"Now, when I think of that word, Dori, which I didn't till now," I mugged, "I think that if I threw that word at someone, they'd be a mess, wet and sticky."

"Oh, Beamer," she laughed, springing happily from her fixation. "People can't be lugubrious around you."

Her compliments are rare. I let it linger in the air.

The nimble, carnival tilt with Dori, got me in a good mood to mix with the folk before Roman took the stage. I cruised around the congregation, formally introducing myself to those not busy chatting and made an impression. I was wearing a tie. I thought it distinguished me and made me readily believable as a part of the business of the Church.

Roman liked to wear a tie, which he abandoned and flung into the crowd with an Oscar sweeping gesture. No one returned them. He had a flair, a non-religious acumen to give fun with the seriousness of his preaching.

Dori walked happily with me into the mostly standing and socializing crowd. There was a staple mixture of breeds: Mini and terriers and Labs. Basic hounds. The more costly French bulldogs the ubiquitous Doodles and a rare Churchgoer, the King Charles spaniel.

All dogs are entitled to spiritual redemption and awakening, the cornerstone of Roman's message, even if they had no idea of what was going on, or seemed to thrive more with religious osmosis. Did Roman ever consider the dog's point of view? Did they grasp his yearnings for them? Even if it eluded them, it was still a firm relationship, based on good rubs and good treats.

I enjoyed getting acquainted with the dogs who were accustomed to sitting patiently with their people, tossing some strident, possibly pertinent barks into the general conversation, which may be reinforcing their holiness, since, according to the Gospel of Roman, dogs are our spiritual superiors.

I carried a pocketful of dog treats, and with permission, offered them up on my palms. Dogs were swiftly alerted to this action and sniffed their way to my stop, dragging people behind them. Dogs waited politely in front of me in electric posture and then cleared my palm, gobbled the treat and repostured for more. I had instantly converted a dozen dogs to friendship forever. I liked doing business with dogs.

As I made the rounds, skeptically, but with an honest smile, I made a passing study of faces and expressions and voice, and even dress. What was I looking for? Oddness? Displeasure? I was just skimming, no one stood out. No one looked like they wanted to blow up the Church.

I had plans, to off-handily, buddy to buddy, talking with men, find out if they were artists, car fanciers, football fans, anything relating to the Gifts. People without dogs.

Right now, Dori and I sat side by side on the sidelines, while Roman, without summary or preface launched us into a tour of the world from Space, landing at different societies and cultures, reminding us of the ugly and depressing fates of cats and dogs. He was inflamed by the world's indifference to their cruelty. He certainly wasn't the only one. His flame was like the eternal flame, a volcano that spews boiling lava over the land, burning peoples' conscience. But lava eventually becomes rich soil. Keep the pressure on.

His audience listened gapingly at his burning defiance of measured responses. "Now! Now!" Was his mantra. He was overwhelmed by his own urgency. Yet, he knew the bad situation was not miraculously erased in a sermon. After these explosions he was back down to Earth, calm, and making quiet and even joking conversations. Figure it out.

Dori and I watched the people during the service. I took the more crowded front rows, Dori got more rows but sparser attended rows. She suddenly gave me a memorable elbow to my side. She pointed out a man in the second to last row. He was slouched down in his chair, his legs stretched out in front of him, arms folded across his chest and looking disinterestedly before him. He must have slipped in late. I didn't see anything strange.

"He kicked the dog." She poked me in the new sore spot, while giving him a steely stare. He took no notice.

"Kicked?"

"The dog's rear end was sticking out from the chair in front of him." She tried to intensify her stare. "It wasn't in his way."

"Maybe, just a reflex."

"No!" she grimaced, "He meant it!"

There was no one in the last row, no one would see it.

"I'm glad you don't have a gun." Dori's fury slowly subsided, after a poke of my own, which spooked her.

"Keep an eye on him," I said mildly to Dori, who was holding back her impulse to reckon with the creepy guy. "We want to be invisible to him."

"Okay," she cooled, picking up my plan. "At least the dog wasn't hurt." The dog, an older Chocolate Lab, remained motionless, half-asleep.

We left our seats and Dori could not help hissing at the man, who was blandly studying the architecture of the Church. We moved around the thinning population, saying good nights, when a piercing squeal scared up our attention. A recognizable sound among dog people. A puppy got a stop bothering me nip from an older bigger he jumped at to play. The big one was saying: "Don't bother me kid." The pup was tended to and reassured. It wasn't a trauma. Puppies like babies make sure they are heard. I commented to Dori as we strolled and petted and petted, included the puppy, who was getting lots of attention:

"Some people are so lax; they never oil their dogs."

She became too distracted by the dog kicker who was stirring, sitting up and staring into the darkening street through a barred Church window.

We went to the door to say goodbyes, have nice evenings, praise Roman and the Church, pray for Goodness, thanks for coming, come back soon and Love your Dog. There was no request for donations, sometimes called money, and people felt cheered and uplifted while going back into the weird, weird world of SF.

We hurried people out and made sure we saw which way the 'dog-kicker was walking. He was heading in the direction of the corner Safeway, which was two blocks from the Park. We both inspected him closely as we blessed him on his way out the door.

I jolted out the door, pointing a shaking finger down the block, telling Dori I'm trailing this guy. She gave me an understanding wave. I couldn't wait. I had the opportunity now. He might not show up for days or weeks or never.

I was far enough behind him. Not conspicuous. I hoped he wasn't a long distance walker who lived near the Ocean. Didn't see him waiting at a bus stop or descending into a nearby Muni Station. He crossed to the Safeway side of the street and approached the store.'

"Don't go in!" "Don't go in!" I said to myself. "You don't need anything!"

"You don't need anything!"

Before my thoughts reached him, he hesitated in front of the entrance, read something plastered up on the glass, stepped back when people came out, studied the contents of full out going carts and continued walking.

"Whew!"

He turned the corner onto Church street, then one block up, a left at Duboce, crossed the street to the corner building where Dori lived, walked up the few steps and directly through the two locked doors at the entrance, not ringing a bell. I had never seen him before in the neighborhood.

He was tall with long legs and it was no surprise that he bumped into the butt of a dog. He could have moved his chair back, no one was behind him so that gave some credit to Dori's 'keen sight.'

He had a haystack of shiny black hair low on his forehead. Dori, with her excellent vision and expertise with hair declared it a toupee and a ridiculous one. It fitted in with the sharp-edge greying beard. She asked me what kind of beard it was: "It looks like an upside down triangle."

"It's a Van Dyke," I confirmed to her puzzlement.

"Who was Van Dyke?"

"Van Dyke was the first guy to sport a Van Dyke."

"Oh."

He wore a green sweatshirt with strange letters emblazoned on it, which Dori thought looked Slavic, but she couldn't read it. Baggy jeans, polka-dot socks and sneakers covered with graffiti, completed the ensemble. Maybe he was in sync. It takes a heap of imagination to really stand out in SF. He wasn't even close.

I was back in the Church. "He lives in your building."

"No," she squinted.

"I saw him go in."

"Maybe, he's just visiting," she said.

"He let himself in."

"Some gave him the key."

I had not thought of that. "You're sure you've never seen him?"

"Are you kidding," She glanced at me as if I were an idiot. "In that get-up?"

The idiot had an out. "The Eggman is very clever."

"Well," she kicked back, "Since he's done no harm, has not scared anyone but you, I have to say he's amusing." She gave me her poke of triumph in rendering the obvious.

"Speaking of amusing," I moved on, "I'd like to locate Charles, we could use a devious and evil-like mind to even the odds."

"You're devious," she challenged.

"Not constitutionally."

"What does that mean?" she said tartly.

"I can turn it on and off. He can't."

She gazed at me shrewdly. "Does that mean Eggman can't quit?"

My brain was trying to crank up an answer. I couldn't find one.

"What was his walk like?" Dori was good at noticing these things.

"His walk." I made an effort to picture it. He was far ahead of me, with walkers in between.

"Did he lean to one side?" she submitted. "Was he jaunty? Did he walk on his toes or on his heels? Did he stride? Did he mince?" Any limp?"

"Okay! Okay!" I surrendered. "He didn't walk fast, I kept up with him.

"Despite his long legs?"

"It wasn't his walk that I noticed, but what he was doing with his hands when I got closer."

"Yes?"

"It looked like he was conducting an Orchestra." I performed gestures for Dori. "I don't remember him wearing headphones."

"I've seen it before," she briefed me, unimpressed.

"Wait! Wait! Wait!" A scene clicked in my memory. "I was across the street, catching up to him as he crossed to the intersection the NTrain passes through. He pulled out what I figured was a MUNI pass to get on the N, which went to the Avenues and the Ocean. There is a traffic island to wait for the train."

"And?"

"And, a 22 bus came down Church, followed by a big trunk with pictures of vegetables on its side."

"And?"

"It hid him."

"So, did he get on the train?" she asked, wearily.

"The train came by."

"So it did!" She was acting a little punchy.

"He was still in the same spot!"

"Huh?"

"And he was jotting something down a pad." I paused. Dori was peeved at my sloppy elocution, but still very interested. "He did that for another minute, occasionally lifting his head to look at something ahead." I paused again, as the drama unfolded. "Then he tucked his stuff in his pocket, and as you said, jauntily, went into your building." I dropped my voice and put my eyes on Dori. It was a weighty moment.

"What do you think he was doing?" She was rubbing her eyebrows and finally asked, tiredly intrigued. "What did you think he was doing?"

"I think he was sketching your building." She brought her head up higher. She held my attention with an inquisitive, almost supplicating gaze" Maybe, he was just making out a shopping list." She saw my displeasure. "I'm not making fun of you," she told me with a contemplative smile, "I'm just negotiating possibilities."

"On the verge of discovering Eggman," I yelled at her, "And you become a Lawyer."

Dori flinched, dumbfounded. She sat straight up, hurt, a pitiable look on her face. I didn't feel guilty, I didn't feel cleansed and I didn't like looking into Dori's eyes. I turned abruptly and walked out the door. I felt exposed, embarrassed and bloody mad, mate. A long, directionless walk made me realize how formidable Eggman had become to me. The rest of the world would consider him a generous, harmless crank, who remained anonymous, the highest form of gift-giving. Gee Whiz, a

Saint. Saint Scrambled. There is a lot to be angry about and a lot to like in the world. You can't encompass it, no matter what direction you take.

I felt lousy and I also felt justified. If there is a threat, I'm the only one taking it on. Dori still tosses the coin. Don't know if she is tossing a coin about seeing me again. I'll do my own snooping and planning. I'll keep to myself and my buddies in the Park. Dori and I both work at the Church, but our times rarely overlap.

Two days and no sign of Dori, whether by chance or design, I can't say. Halfway through the third day I was on the verge of an apology. Then she called me. In her excited and also friendly voice she said"

"Guess what!?"

"What?"

"I know that out-of-sync guy."

"You do?" I peaked.

"Isn't that what you called him?"

"Yes! Yes! Where is he?"

"In my building."

"You said you never saw him before," I questioned her, feeling Dori made a mistake.

She caught my dejected tone, "I never did, not crazy dressed and not on two feet."

I rallied. "How many feet does he have," I joked.

"Two feet!" she trumped, ticked off.

"I don't understand." I said gloomily.

"In my building he's in a wheelchair," she said with aplomb.

At least I did not say: "In a wheelchair?" But did manage to blurt out: "What kind of wheelchair?"

"A chair with wheels," she schooled me, like a lapdog is a dog.

"I meant," I explained, not taking offense, "Was he pushing himself or was someone pushing him?"

"Himself."

"What about the hair?"

"He's bald."

"And the beard?"

"No beard."

"Sneakers?"

"Slippers."

"Blue jeans?"

"Everyone wears blue jeans."

"How did you know?"

"Tee shirt."

"Tee shirt?"

"Flag on Tee shirt. Looks Slavic."

"Great job, Dori!"

"He was agitated as usual, wheeling fast through the halls, weaving around people. A skilled driver," she approved of this skill.

"He seems to have many talents."

"Do you think he's the guy?" There tremoring hitch in her voice.

"I'm leaning on it. What about you?"

"I'm leaning on you."

"Does he live on your floor?"

"No, but we have elevators."

"Good."

"I'm sure his jaunts through the halls has made him well known."

"But, he wants to be anonymous."

Dori speculated: "By not being anonymous, but a deliberate, annoying presence, not would think he was hiding anything."

"Makes sense. Just can't pin him down, literally."

"Not friends with him,' she responded to my hint. "But I can act neighborly.

"His apartment will reveal a lot."

"I'm not going in there!"

"Understood."

"Charles. We need Charles."

"He still has Guinevere," Dori reminded me.

"Yes. He may come to the Park."

"Guinevere has friends there."

"We have to keep watch. But right now?"

Dori was silent. I heard a deafening Muni horn. I kept expecting her to hash out my behavior at the Church. Nothing. "When I first saw ro rolling down the hall my instinct was to press myself against the wall. "Next time, I'll make sure I have a lacy handkerchief smelling of perfume and drop it on the floor in front of him."

"He'll run over the handkerchief."

"That's the plan, she coaxed. "I'll make sure it's a big handkerchief."

"Think he'll buy you a new one?"

"No," she tut-tutted. "But he may slow down and apologize."

"Good strategy."

"Good tactic," she corrected, "We don't have an overall strategy."

"Does your reading," I intimated teasingly," Happen to include the 'Art of War' by the Chinese General?"

"Glanced at it."

Not surprised. I was ready to close my phone.

"You are a brooder, Beamer," I heard her say with kindly seriousness.

"Isn't everyone?"

"Too brood is rude," she quipped.

"I don't brood in public."

She dropped it. "Goodbye."

What the hell! Great artists brooded. People once admired brooding. Now it is psychologically suspect. To brood or not to brood. Something to brood over.

We think we've zeroed in on the Eggman. But the subtlety that showed up in his gifts hardly matched his outlandish personality.

He hasn't shown up at the Church again. He was wrecking all my theories. Dori worked two jobs, so I didn't expect her to hunt the Eggman. Especially alone. But there it was. She had moxie. In the meanwhile, Blondie and I kept a lookout for Charles and asked others to call me if he showed up with Guinevere.

I persuaded Roman to give me twenty minutes before a seated congregation. He agreed to hold off his sermon to let me play my dog songs for the group of dog people.

"How 'bout Friday," he suggested, "More audience." Next he said: "If they enjoy it, we'll do it on a Sunday. A packed house."

He was in a bountiful mood. I struck at the right time. In twenty minutes I can slip in four songs, with brief prefaces. My guitar has a pick-up for my compact battery or outlet amp. It's funny choosing and going over the songs. I mean dog songs. What's not to like?

I never mentioned Eggman to anyone in the Park except Dori, and she kindly never hinted to anyone that I could be a bit fanciful. It must have taken a lot of fortitude and self-control not to blab it to her girlfriends. Although, they may have gotten a fictionalized version of it.

She was part of a seductive secret. She may turn out to be a heroine. There was danger. Of course, the bomb thing may turn out to be a dud. Would she be disappointed? Would I?

Blondie and I were spending more time in the Park. Getting to know the always incoming puppies. We had located the Eggman, we believed. He lives around the corner. No more traipsing around. We got more acquainted with new people and had nice talks with the regulars about our lives and our dogs. It was normal.

Naturally, it didn't take long for a character with a load of T-shirts to pass my way. He didn't tell me his name, right off, but his dog, a Chihuahua mix was Consuela. He finally told me his name It was was Darvin," Not Darwin!" he emphasized. He shook his down jacket off his shoulders and let it soak up some morning dew.

He peeled off his top blank T-shirt and stuffed it into a large jacket pocket. As he was turning towards me I saw black letters starkly printed on his T-shirt: "I LOVE DEATH."

"Is that the name of a band?" I said, obviously.

"No, sir," he said, grimly, with a touch of pride. "I only go for the real thing. Don't want no phony Death. No pretenders. I'm talking about the real thing." He stood up straight like a private before a Drill Sergeant. Not me. He never looked at me. Not condescending.

"Most people don't like to talk about Death," I reminded him, conversationally.

He moved off to clean up after his dog.

"I do." He fumbled with his dog's leash as his pooch circled him and the leash curled around his legs.

"Do you expect to go to Heaven?"

"If there was a Heaven I'd pass." He lifted a sneer to the sky and began sniffing, searching, checking the soles of his shoes, nothing turned up. "I smelled nothing but the smell of the dog park," he reported.

"What about being reunited with God or Jesus?"

"We never even shared a beer together," he said, without bitterness.

I posed the ultimate question to his solemn face. "What happens after Death?"

He resumed sniffing, took a small spray bottle from a back pocket and sprayed his shoes. "More Death."

"Not encouraging."

He gave me a secretive wink. "Death has its pluses."

I quickly answered: "How so?"

"It looks good on your resume."

"I see."

"By dying you automatically become a Genius or a Saint."

"I hadn't thought of that."

"Just a matter of seeing things through," he revealed, thoughtfully, More jovial than solemn now.

"If you are a scoundrel or a thief, you have less chance of getting a job, "But, if you're a Genius or a Saint," he said with sunny conviction. "They are waiting for you with open arms." He spread out his arms and waved air into his chest.

I had to ask. "Isn't Death a drawback in getting a job?"

"Why should it be," he asked, casually, "Some people have more chances of getting a job when they are dead. It's logical."

"But when you are dead your body's falling apart," I answered, logically.

"It's not the body that does the work, But the soul?" He said soundly.

"Naturally."

"The soul works invisibly," he explained to my incoherent state.

"Does it get you hard cash?" I called him on practicality, for the heck of it.

"A dumb question." He scrutinized me. "Soul has no pockets."

I didn't ask if they had a Labor Union.

He started leashing up Consuela and gathering up his coat.

"Final question?"

He shook Blondie's paw goodbye. "Shoot."

"Some people are moribund," I paused as he gave me a sharp-eyed look. "Dead on their feet. Does that count?"

He was perplexed. He kneaded the idea in his brain. It was an Oddball question for an Oddball. Will he come up with something half-baked or with a tasty nugget?

"I would say," he replied, his features twisting into hard concentration. "I would say," his features relaxing, his eyes lit up, "It would get them a part time job."

It made no sense, but he had an answer, stretching reality. Who knows if the Universe is a rubber band gone haywire. Maybe, the String Theory should be upgraded to the Rubber Band Theory. It sounds much more snappy.

I can't say that it was inevitable that Charles would show up with Guinevere and his talents. But Guinevere loved this Park and he loved Guinevere.

Dori saw him first. She was the one he wanted to see first. He had a crush on her. She filled him in on the crucial details of Eggman, Guinevere and the Daschunds had a convivial reunion. Each hound vying to be the number one greeter and licker.

Charles welcomed a new adventure, meaning new material for the Open Mikes he's been frequenting to make himself known again. If he has patience to wait his turn at a crowded Open Mike and his old pugnacity to get in front of tough audiences, then he seems to be healthy and in good form. Dori brought him over to my place and we tried to make a plan.

Right off, he wanted me to hear his come-back to obnoxious people in the audience, drunk or otherwise, but sometimes nasty.

"I sluff off their stupid remarks and say to them: 'You know, there's a new element named after you.' "Even the jerk from the audience wants to be special and the audience waits for the 'Zinger.'"

"Then I repeat: 'There's a new element named after you. It's called MORON.'"

I told Charles that our objective was to find out if anything in the Eggman's apartment was criminal. Like bomb stuff. If you could recognize bomb stuff. It could be hidden. He'd have to trust you or you'd have to sneak in when he wasn't at home. That's desperate and dangerous.

He gave me a salty look as if I was adding flavor to his day. His purpose was to reprove his mettle and establish his fettle, if he could be excused from sounding like a "Beamer." No offense.

It is easy to get into the building. Pose as Dori's relative. She had located Eggman's apartment on the Fillmore side of the building. Rappelling down from the roof to look through the window was quickly rejected as was setting off alarms to empty the tenants.

He was stumped. He had used his smarts with private homes, but a large building was a formidable target. And if this guy really was a bomb maker he'd have no intruders. He might have a gun and be unhinged enough to use it. To think about this operation was grueling and too risky. Charles bowed out.

I had to confess to Charles that all my evidence was still hypothetical, but there was a lot at stake. His parting words as left with Guinevere were: "I don't want anything more to do with hypos." We hated to see him go, but Dori and I awaited the opportunity to see him perform again.

Dori and I sat together in the Park the next evening when a guy ran into the Park yelling: "Do you know what happened?!" Park people clamored to him in alarm. "What!?" What?!" What happened?!" He stopped and caught his breath. "Someone set off a bomb at the Dog Church."

Dori and I looked at each other in confused panic. There was no smoke or fire coming from the Church a few blocks away. We didn't hear any explosion. We heard sirens, Police and Fire Trucks, but we heard them regularly.

Others were also confused. They questioned the guy. "Did you see anything? Was anyone hurt?

"I got it second hand."

It had to be a harrowing false alarm. "Should we go over there?" Dori asked, nervously, but relieved.

"To see what?" Who was this guy delivering such terrifying news? He was gone. The crowd broke up, also angry at the messenger. They drifted home their separate ways. Dori decided to take her dogs home. They were anxious and agitated. They were appealing to her to go home. Blondie, too, wanted to head back to a safe place. I obliged.

Turned on the TV and caught the tail end of the local news. There was a TV newsman, microphone in hand, standing in front of the Church. People were milling around in small bunches, like Dori's Daschunds, anxious, agitated and instead of barking they were coughing heavily.

The Church was intact, no damage to be seen, except for the disgusted faces, the cameras constantly focused on. But no one looked injured, though a Med team was treating a line-up of standees, giving oxygen. Cops were questioning parishioners, taking notes, so something serious had happened.

Roman gave me a wave and attended to his outdoor flock. The Newsman confirmed that a man sitting in the back row of the Church had set off a bomb. A woman described him as being tall and wearing a 'hideous black toupee.' Another woman, younger and angrier, was waving her hand in front of her face like a fan. She was driven out of the Church by the 'Absolutely putrid smell.'

It was a Stink Bomb. I watched dumbly. A Stink Bomb!

I was thankful that it wasn't deadly. But it was a bomb. I read the script right, but I misread the man. Still, it's not a light thing to set off a stink bomb in a Church, during Services and causing panic. People in the Church not knowing if it was real or a malicious prank, caused terror.

I watched the aftermath for a few more minutes more and then called the Police. I spoke to a Sergeant. I told him I had a good idea who set off the Stink Bomb in the Church, directing them to Dori's building and the guy's apartment number. He wore a disguise at the Church. I didn't know his name.

The Sergeant thanked me and said it confirmed an address he had already been given a few calls ago. "We are checking it out. Officers are on their way."

Dori beat me to it.

Dori's name was in the newspapers, heralded as the woman whose timely call to Police, led to the quick apprehension of the suspect.

Roman gave her a lollapalooza bonus and her lovely face decorated the news article. The Chronicle sent a reporter to interview her. She gave a synopsis of our hunt for the Eggman, based on my suspicions and gave me all the credit.

No one came to see me. It was okay. I do not have a newspaper face. A radio face would be my level. The Police, it turns out, were temporarily confused by the Eggman's transformation. They found other Stink Bombs clogging up a drawer.

We hoped the Eggman had some bravado and confessed, to keep us out of Court. At least, me. Dori didn't mind the attention. I quote: "I like the attention of being a celebrated snitch." She didn't publicize it.

The Church closed to get unstunk. Roman persevered. Though his Church was desecrated, invaded by an unholy odor that bumped off the prayerful ambience. He was so busy calming and reassuring the parishioners and their dogs. We know people were disgusted and sickened by the foul smell. But the Dogs?

I can hardly remember any instance when my dogs jerked back from an object that for us was nauseating, filthy and disgusting. All smells were interesting. I wonder if they got high on the potent Stink Bomb.

So, Dori was a heroine for a day, or two, or three. The Eggman was quite a character who drew peoples' curiosity and malevolence "String him up!" He was evil twins in one body. Satan in human form.

All the stuff about the Gifts were made public. He acknowledged them with hubris. It revealed his talent and cleverness, and rose from Caveman to Misunderstood Artist. Who was in his olfactory way, fighting the system. Or something.

Some bought it. Others were violated. Roman hated the guy. In a very religious context, of course. Burn him. Set the Dogs on him. Carve an S (for Satan) on his forehead, send him to the galleys. But we are too enlightened for that, said the new school.

What options might be equivalent to that kind of torture, to make him pay for his crimes? It was a No Brainer. Before any sentence could be passed, he had to see an endless battery of Psychiatrists, Psychotherapists, Social Workers, Religious Leaders, People running for Office, etc. Take that lawbreaker. Dori and I were ignored.

Dori moved up in the Floral World. She was elevated to something called "Marigold Management" in their main downtown shop. She was second in command and learning the ropes or the "stems."

I, surprisingly, was not forgotten. There were some onlookers who actually appreciated my role, from start to finish with the Eggman. They liked my zeal and doggedness and insightful imagination in deciphering the Gifts and noted my dismal state of virtual unemployment.

I was now in Advertising. A beginning salary, but salutary. I gave Blondie some super rubs and laid back contently in my lounger It felt good to be redeemed and for Dori to be even more redolent.

The case of the Eggman pends. He has never come across with a motive. Although the word "Stink" in a Stink Bomb may give us some idea. But why target a Church, especially one for spiritual enrichment of dogs? Is it competition in the wackiness business?

Questions. Questions

Reverend Larry, the creator of Canine City Comics gained enough sight back from his delicate eye surgery that with some ingenious new devices to see through, he can bring Ranger Dog, Reverend Rabbit and his other unique characters back to life. Larry was back to giving corruption and evil doings a hard kick in the butt.

We brought our dogs to visit him back at the storefront. He was enthused and funny. He promised to give our dogs cameo appearances when he went back to his work. Dori's Daschunds alone could form a formidable posse. Blondie would be the gorgeous but tough saloon owner.

As we walked back to our neighborhood from the Mission, we talked about our new jobs. Dori was nervous about having a future "Executive" title, and bossing people, if necessary. But she would still be handling flowers. I knew she'd do well and told her so. She gave me a winsome smile.

I said I was looking forward to my advertising job THE and planned to do some "Pun-jabbing in India ink." Her eyes narrowed and her teeth clenched. It was her favorite expression when I expressed my 'Art.' With mischievous outrage she sizzled: "Have you no shame!"

Now that this adventure has ended and Eggman has been discovered and brought to Justice, Dori wanted to say some kind words to the overmatched writer:

"I want to thank you for not butting into my personal life or sticking your nose into my Past. It's none of your business!

Made in the USA
Las Vegas, NV
26 July 2023